Thanks for the support

'22

Calinthia Chronicles

Giant Wolves Of The West

Blaidd Gwyn

Blaidd Gwyn Publications

ISBN: 978-1-915707-01-7

Gloss cover edition

Map by Blaidd Gwyn

Typeset in EB Garamond Via https://Atticus.io

Blaidd Gwyn Publications

61 Bridge Street

Kington

HR5 3DJ

Book One

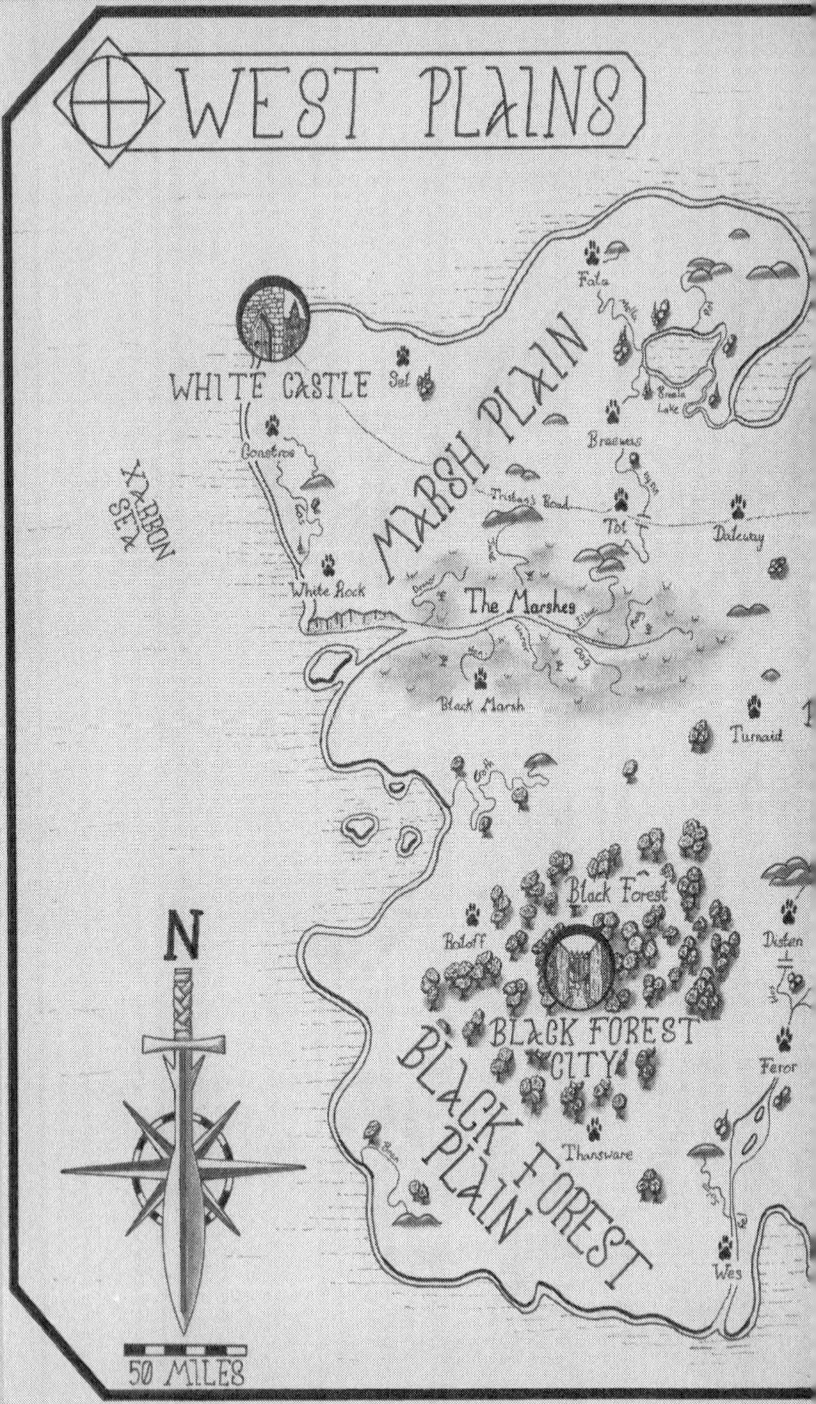

WEST PLAINS
WHITE CASTLE
MARSH PLAIN
Sal
Fala
Braewas
Tristag's Road
Tol
Daleway
XARBON SEA
White Rock
The Marshes
Black Marsh
Turnaid
Black Forest
Baloff
BLACK FOREST CITY
BLACK PLAIN
BLACK FOREST
Thansware
Distan
Feror
Wes
N
50 MILES

TOROS SEA
Leree
Great Hills
GREAT PLAIN
Beador
Trenas
Blas
Orett
Keepa
Smora
Llanor
DRYSOR GLASS
Shogun Camp
Wolf's Fang
Bedthorn
Brass
Esor
Ingrin
Gosor
Col
Pearah Fort
TOWN OF NIAMH
Shrompy
Goloth
NIAMH PLAIN
Veror
Neror
Itlas
Drotta
CALINTHIAN SEA
BLy '22

Chapter One

BIRTH OF A LEGEND

Entering into the world, the newborn was stimulated by a dry cloth. As she drew in her first breath, the cool air caused the baby to cry.

The healer tied string around the umbilical cord. "Congratulations, Isolde, it's a girl. Do you want me to fetch your mate?"

Isolde nodded, smiling at her child.

Cutting the umbilical cord, the healer laid the infant into Isolde's arms and said, "You can give the baby her first feed." Turning, she paced to the other end of the room, opening the door to the hut. "You can come in now."

Nodding at the healer, Llewellyn gingerly entered the hut. His gaze fixed on his firstborn child, nursing in Isolde's arms. Beaming with pride, her eyes met his as she spoke softly, "It's a girl."

Standing at Isolde's side, he leaned over to kiss her forehead and slowly pulled away. "I knew you could do it."

When the baby had had its fill of milk, Llewellyn cupped his arms around the infant and lifted her into his chest. Grinning, he greeted her softly, “Welcome to the world, little one.”

As Isolde began to moan in pain once more, the healer took the child from him. “She’s ready to pass the placenta, and the baby needs her rest. You can come back tomorrow.”

He looked back at Isolde, who nodded, displaying her approval for him to leave. Kissing his hand, he held it towards her with a smile.

Closing the door behind him, he turned to see his six brothers waiting outside.

“Well?” one of them asked, raising his eyebrow.

“It’s a girl,” Llewellyn replied.

The oldest brother held his arms out to the sides. “The youngest of our pack is the first to bring a new pack member. Congratulations, Llewellyn What’re you going to call her?”

Interrupted, a voice called out from behind. “Llewellyn, who’re you talking to?”

Turning around, he saw his lifelong friend. “What do you mean, Gethin?”

As he turned back, he saw no one there. Looking from left to right, the reality sank in and his smile faded, lowering his head with tears filling his eyes.

“You’re acting strange. Are you sure you’re all right?” Gethin asked.

Lifting his head up, straightening his back as he did so, Llewellyn answered, “Yeah, I’m fine. I was just thinking aloud, that’s all.”

Gethin walked over and placed his hand on Llewellyn's shoulder. "You don't look all right to me."

Looking at him with a tear rolling down his cheek, Llewellyn tapped Gethin's hand and replied, "I'm fine. It's just been an emotional day, that's all. We have a daughter now."

Gethin grinned, slapping Llewellyn's shoulder twice. "Tonight, we'll wet the baby's head by having plenty of mead. But first, we have matters to attend to. Balgair wants to see us right away."

"What does he want with us?" Llewellyn frowned.

"I don't know. Maybe it's about what happened three weeks ago. But he wants to see us both for some reason. You're a hero, after all."

Lowering his gaze to the ground again, Llewellyn's back hunched as Gethin took a step back.

"Look, we've known each other for a long time, and I know we ain't of the same pack, but you still have one brother left," Gethin stated.

Gazing at his lifelong friend, Llewellyn grinned, "Thanks. I know I can always count on you. Come on, let's go. We don't want to keep Balgair waiting."

Later that night, Llewellyn started to toss and turn in his sleep. His breathing rate rose as his body soaked his bed linen with sweat. The playback of the dream felt like reality once more from what happened three weeks earlier.

Walking through the town, Llewellyn and his brothers noticed a group of people surrounding something or someone outside the pathfinder's hut, so they picked up their pace and rushed to the scene. In the centre of the crowd lay a wounded man, his hands holding his stomach, face grimaced with pain, with the pathfinder on his knees next to him. The blood staining the man's torso began to dry as he let go of his abdomen, exposing his small intestines. Raising one bloodied hand up to hold onto the pathfinder's shoulder, he nodded as his life left his body, with his hand sliding off his shoulder before flopping to the ground. The pathfinder tapped the dead man's chest, looking up to the group of brothers.

Llewellyn started to mumble in his sleep, with tears rolling from his closed eyes.

He looked at his brothers and then down towards a small wood. Thirty bears and eight archers mounted on them broke from the treeline, advancing into the open ground. Counting their numbers as they emerged, two of the brothers removed their robes and transformed into wolf form. The alteration was rapid, taking only a split second.

"There's a lot of them, which means we're outnumbered. Even so, we ain't outmatched on open ground. When they get far enough from the treeline, we'll attack. Keep tight to the wood so the bears will be trapped in open ground. Don't let them get back amongst the trees, or we'll be slaughtered," the pathfinder ordered.

Everyone else removed their battle robes, transforming into wolves, ready to charge into battle.

Llewellyn's breathing rate increased with short, sharp breaths, unable to escape the flashbacks.

He could feel the grass under his paws with the wind pushing through his fur, as if he was physically back there. He could hear the others running, paws hitting the ground with each stride, accompanied by minor growls and heavy breaths. Extraordinarily, they equalled the bears in height with half the body mass.

The party of wolves reached the halfway point of the thicket, and they heard the snapping of twigs and branches as a large silhouette emerged from within. A loud, bass growl emitted from the shadows, followed by an almighty roar originated from a bear like no other, revealing himself from between the oak trees, being over twice the size of all the other bears. Striking the left-flanking wolf with his brute strength and oversized left paw, he made an instant corpse of one of Llewellyn's brothers. The lifeless body was thrown into the others, knocking Llewellyn over, pinning him to the ground.

The other bears remained still in the open ground, watching with the knowledge of no longer being the wolves' main target. Llewellyn could not escape, so he transformed back into human form, hoping to wriggle free. The others stopped and turned to meet their new threat head-on. Most of them with their heads down, muzzles tightened, displaying their teeth.

Llewellyn witnessed the bear standing on his hind legs, forepaws waving outwards with a burning rage in his eyes. His mouth opened wide, creating an ear-splitting roar before slamming his front paws into the ground with so much force, even the ground itself trembled. The pathfinder met his challenge by running head-on towards the giant. Shuffling his hind legs forward slightly, the bear leapt forward, swinging his right paw swiftly, hitting his target. His long claws ripped into the flesh of the pathfinder's body, with unmatched power snapping his neck, pushing another corpse out of his way in mid-air.

With a cracked voice, Llewellyn screamed out, "Dad!"

With the pathfinder's body crashing to the ground, Llewellyn saw another brother charging at him from the right. Swinging his right forepaw down to the ground, the bear opened his mouth and sunk his teeth deep into his brother's head. With the power of his jaws, he crushed the wolf's skull, lifting yet another limp body high into the air as he did so.

In disbelief of what he was witnessing, Llewellyn looked away, placed both hands on his brother's remains and pushed as hard as he could, wriggling his hips wildly to free himself while holding his breath each time. With great struggle he managed to get one leg free, with only one foot leaving him trapped, but at this point, he noticed something; silence.

Eventually freeing himself, he scrambled to his feet, spotting one of the bear's paws resting on his deceased brother.

Llewellyn looked around, seeing the massacre before him. All his brothers lay still on the ground, alongside his father—the pathfinder. Their bloodstained fur became matted as the rest of the blood from their bodies begun to congeal on the grass around their lifeless bodies.

The bear was too close to escape. With wide eyes, Llewellyn pleaded as he paced backwards. "P-please, I don't know why you're here, and I don't care. J-just let me go. My mate needs me."

The bear removed his paw from atop his brother, placing it underneath and lifting the lifeless body up, tossing it to one side as if it was a twig.

Staring intensely at Llewellyn, muzzle wrinkled, the bear boasted, "I don't care what your partner needs, boy. When I'm done, I'll smear your guts in the dirt."

"Please, I have a child on the way, just let me go."

The bear rose on his hind legs and hissed, "Your loved ones can meet you in the afterlife, boy. And they'll meet you very soon."

Llewellyn's jaw tightened; a snarl depressed his cheeks with his lips peeling back. His heart rate rose fast as the adrenaline surged through his veins, causing his body to shake. Staring at the bear while dipping his head, the saliva escaped his gritted teeth with each breath. Without another word spoken, he transformed from one step to the next, charging across the clearing. With all of his power in his rear legs, he leapt high towards his enemy's face. The bear roared as he dived forward, thrusting his left paw outward as Llewellyn opened his mouth wide.

Just before they engaged, Llewellyn's eyes shot open as he bolted upright in his bed. Looking around the room, he started to calm and his breathing eased. Dropping his gaze to the three wounds on his abdomen trailing down to his groin, he ran his fingers across the scabs and stitches. Raising his hands to cup his face, he began to sob.

Eleven years later, day had broken. The sun shone down brightly from the purple-coloured sky, with a cool breeze flowing through the Town of Niamh.

"Tabitha! It's time to get up, I won't call you again!" Isolde shouted.

Yawning and stretching, Tabitha slowly opened her eyes, mildly annoyed at one of her parents for waking her so abruptly. Looking around the room while disorientated, she stretched again. A build-up of excitement started to overwhelm her, realizing that her eleventh birthday was today. She quickly scrambled out of her bedroll, rushing to get dressed and ready for the day, before flinging her bedroom door open to enter the dining room.

The hut walls were made from brown coloured clay and wooden beams, with the ceiling formed of straw from the thatched roof. The pungent smell of burning wood, accompanied by the background sound of crackles from logs splitting under flame, made it seem cosier inside. In the centre of the room stood an old wooden table, covered with wooden plates of fruit, meat, freshly made bread and a large greyish-brown cloth, which was non-uniform in shape.

Llewellyn stood in front of the table, towering over Tabitha, like a muscular mountain. Perfectly combed hair sat upon his head like a golden crown. His emerald green eyes looked at his unkempt daughter as he greeted her. "Happy birthday, trouble."

A big smile emerged on her unwashed face, showing pearly white teeth. "Thanks, Dad. Where's Mam?"

"She's stood behind you," he replied, nodding his head towards Isolde.

Her astonishingly beautiful mother looked at her daughter with the same piercing blue eyes. Her long hair wafted around her body like metallic grey smoke, stopping just above her knees.

"Happy birthday."

"Thanks, Mam." Tabitha looked back to her father, discovering something new on the table behind him, asking, "What's that?"

"Why don't you go over and take a look?" Llewellyn replied.

Shuffling closer to the table, tilting her head slightly, Tabitha inspected the greyish-brown cloth. She saw it was folded in half with some sort of object within it, rising up off the table by an inch and a half in height. On further inspection, while getting closer, she spotted where the cloth began and ended. Reaching out and grabbing the corner of the top half, she peeled it away, revealing a sort of stick attached to a bit of string. Her eyes widened as her face beamed, throwing the top of the cloth away from her.

"A bow!" she squealed. On further inspection, she found another item. "A-a-and a knife!"

Jumping up and down with excitement, she finally had her own training bow and hunters' knife, a tradition in all the wolf clans at Tabitha's age.

"They're better than I wanted, thanks so much, I love them," Tabitha beamed.

The training bow was just over half the size of an adult bow, so the young user could grasp the skill of accuracy before power. The unstained wood of her bow was engraved around the entire circumference in a basic unspecified Celtic design, with thick plain wood for the handle. The knife was beautifully crafted; a seven-inch blade had the spine arching away from the user, with the sharp edge within the curve. The handle was made from the antler of a deer, the main source of food in the West Plains. The four-inch handle, grooved for a better grip, was attached to a flat, oval-shaped bronze guard, separating the blade and handle. Finally, a bronze wedge mounted to the butt of the handle was engraved with the letter 'T'.

"How did you get such good ones? These are the best," Tabitha enquired.

Llewellyn started giggling at his child's innocence, not realising it was a rude question to ask. "Well, it helps when you're a protector, and even more so when your dad's the lead protector's right hand," he answered, winking at Isolde.

Suddenly, a wild knock on the front door interrupted the moment.

"I know who that is," Isolde said. As she opened the door, a small boy holding a woven basket looked up at her. "Good morning, and what brings you here today?"

"Hi, Izzy. Is Tabi in?" the boy replied.

"Yes, she's right here."

Recognising her best friend's voice from outside, Tabitha ran to the front door. "Hey, Wikki."

Almost two years older than Tabitha, Wikki only lived a few huts away. They looked at each other as he stretched out his arms, presenting her with the basket. "Happy birthday, Tabi."

"Thanks." Tabitha took the basket while looking inside, and to her delight, she saw it filled to the brim with blackberries, her favourite fruit.

"Do you wanna come in and see what my mam and dad got me?" she asked.

"Sure," Wikki replied.

Tabitha turned, heading to the table, with Wikki following. His eyes widened with what he saw. "Wow, that's outstanding. I really like your hunters' knife."

Tabitha handed the knife to him, so he could inspect it more closely. Mesmerised by its craftsmanship, he could but admire it as he passed it back to her while suggesting, "Hey, now we can sneak off to the forest and do some bow training together."

"I don't think so. You're in enough trouble from last time. Why are you two always getting into trouble?" Isolde interrogated.

As both of them looked down, Llewellyn started to chuckle.

Glaring at him, Isolde spat, "And don't you encourage them either!" Llewellyn became silent as she brought her attention back to the others. "You two are not allowed in that forest on your own until you're sixteen. Do I make myself clear?"

Tabitha and Wikki both replied together, "Ok."

"Well, in that case, I'll take her today," Llewellyn said as he looked at Wikki. "Do you want to come and help with Tabitha's bow training?"

"Yeah, ok, Lew," Wikki replied.

"Well, why don't you run home and get your training bow? That way, you can join in."

Wikki nodded, dashing out of the front door, disappearing to his hut.

"Come on, let's get our things together and wait for Wikki outside."

As Tabitha gathered her things, Llewellyn picked up his bow and arrows resting by the front door and slung them over his shoulder. He looked at Isolde and smiled, "I don't know how long we're going to be."

"Make sure you're safe and that she has fun. Don't put her off, because she really wants this," Isolde replied.

With a wink, he pulled Isolde's hips into his, kissing her passionately.

Standing behind them, Tabitha exclaimed, "Eww! Do you two always have to do that?"

Isolde and Llewellyn giggled at each other, with Tabitha dragging her father out of the hut by his arm.

Wikki married up with them, breathing heavily and dropping some arrows on the ground as his quiver slid off his shoulder. After he gathered them back up, they all made their way to the forest.

The wood surrounded the east side of the town, housing very tall pine trees. Entering the training area cautiously, Tabitha saw many targets attached to the trees, with some hanging by ropes from branches.

Spotting a large target, Llewellyn suggested, "Right, you two, I think we'll start with this one. Wikki, how would you like to start? Tabitha can watch your technique to learn the basics, and I can see where your skills are."

"Ok, Lew."

Pulling an arrow from his quiver, he placed the bowstring into the groove at the rear of the arrow. Holding the bow, he positioned the arrow on top of his index finger, bringing the bow up to an aiming stance. With one eye closed and his tongue sticking out to the left, he drew the bow and released it, loosing the arrow and hitting the outer middle section of the target.

"Not bad, not bad at all. You've been keeping up with your practice. You still need to improve on your technique though, and I know your dad's teaching you correctly because he's a brilliant archer. Just take a little more time with your aim before you release," Llewellyn advised.

Observing Tabitha watching Wikki, he tilted his head slightly to the right and said, "Wikki, try that again for me."

Proceeding with the same technique as before, Wikki took a little bit longer to aim this time. Releasing the arrow, he hit an inch inward to the target's centre from his previous shot.

Llewellyn missed the arrow landing, watching Tabitha figuring something out as she walked up to the firing line with a smile.

"Tabitha, do you want any advice before you start?" Llewellyn asked.

"No, I can see what to do, and what Wikki did wrong," Tabitha replied.

Not impressed with her comment, Wikki scrunched his face while poking his tongue out.

Tabitha took an arrow out of her quiver, placing the arrow on her index finger and into the bowstring simultaneously. She took a deep breath, moving the bow into the aiming stance. Aiming with her left eye closed, she released the bowstring, and the arrow took flight, striking the target dead centre.

"Yay, I knew I could do it!" Tabitha squealed, jumping up and down.

Wikki was amazed initially, but a wave of jealousy hit him as he sneered, "I bet you can't do that again."

Placing the backs of her hands onto her hips, she closed her eyes and demanded, "Yes I can. I'll show you."

"Hey. You two stop arguing, or I'll give you both a clip around the ear," Llewellyn commanded. "Tabitha, try it again."

Turning around, she used the same technique as before, striking the target right next to the previous arrow she shot. A wave of pride encompassed Llewellyn as he folded his arms while standing tall.

"Well, Dad, what do you think?" Tabitha asked.

"I think you two need to get some more practice in," Llewellyn replied.

Now determined to do better, Wikki nodded at Llewellyn as he pulled an arrow from his quiver. Tabitha just looked up at her father and grinned.

Four months had passed since Tabitha's birthday, having not seen much of Wikki as she would have liked to. She knew why he had been occupied, as he had been through the 'change', transitioning from a boy into manhood. At the start of puberty, the children that were therianthropes transformed against their will into animal form of their respected race. The first transformation was very slow and painful, and Wikki had had his three months ago. But unlike most that could, not every person had the ability to change, and these were known throughout all races as inertias.

Late one evening, Wikki and Tabitha were sat on the ground outside her hut.

"Tabitha, it's time to come in now and have your supper before bed," Isolde called.

She looked up and replied, "Ok, Mam, I'll be there in a minute."

"Ok, don't be long. Good night, Wikki."

"Good night, Izzy, I'll see you soon," Wikki replied.

With Isolde closing the door, they continued their conversation.

"So, are you finding the training hard?" Tabitha asked.

"Sometimes. They shout at me when I mess up."

"It must be hard, but you're in training, so they gotta get that. Do you know what you wanna be after all the training's complete?"

"I really wanna be a protector when I'm older, like my dad, but I don't know if I'm gonna be good enough."

Tabitha looked up at the stars appearing in the twilight sky, with three moons above them. "You'll be a protector. I just know it."

"Thanks. I better go home now, goodnight."

"Goodnight."

Wikki stood up and wandered home as Tabitha jumped up and entered the hut, joining her mother and father at the table where they all talked about their day. A short while after they had eaten, Tabitha finished clearing the plates off the table. Isolde held Llewellyn's hand, looking at him longingly, so he responded to her obvious request. "Ok, I think it's time for bed. Do you want me to tuck you in?"

"Yes please," Tabitha replied.

As Llewellyn tucked her in, she inquired, "Dad, I was wondering, if I was to ever transform, what could I be in the clan?"

"You can be whatever you want to be, but don't forget, there's no certainty that you'll ever have the ability to transform. Why do you ask anyway?"

"Just talking to Wikki today, and it got me thinking that I want to be someone important, that's all. Like a protector, but I can't because I'm a girl."

Llewellyn smiled at her and said, "You're the best of us all, Tabitha" – he reached out and stroked her hair – "you just don't know it yet. With the talents and strengths you already possess, and as long as you keep improving them, I'm sure you can achieve anything you put your mind to. So, don't chase others' approval because you're already important, and I'm very proud of you, and so is your mam. Now get some sleep, and tomorrow, I think we can do some knife training if you want."

Kissing her forehead, he pulled her bedroll tight around her shoulders.

"Ok, that sounds fun. Goodnight."

"Sweet dreams."

Llewellyn blew out the candle on her bedside table, exiting the room and closing the door behind him.

After a few hours, Llewellyn and Isolde were snuggled into each other, when they were woken by a piercing scream. They immediately opened their eyes, looking at each other while slightly disorientated. Then, another scream echoed through the hut.

Isolde's eyes widened. "Tabitha, I think she's hurt."

"I, I think it's the change," Llewellyn replied.

"Let's go now!" Isolde demanded.

Scrambling some clothes on, with the screams getting louder, they rushed out of the bedroom. Lighting two thick candles from the dying embers of the fire in the dining room, they heard the screams change into a sound that they both recognised, a whimpering noise, high-pitched and drawn out.

Opening Tabitha's door, Isolde lit another candle next to her. With three candles slowly illuminating the room, they noticed Tabitha's nightgown torn on the bed. As the candlelight brightened, they saw Tabitha in the corner of the room on all four legs, standing over four feet tall. Dark grey in colour with light grey highlights, the fur covered her entire body. As with all female wolves, her head became glorified with a long mane, starting from behind her ears, flowing down the both sides of her head and ending one foot below her face. Her feathering, like a fluffy white cloud, covered her chest and underbelly, all propped up with long spindly legs. But one thing didn't change—the colour of her eyes.

She stared intensely at her parents while shaking violently, growling and displaying her sharp teeth. Her tail tucked between her hind legs, so far in fact, half of it lay on her abdomen.

Llewellyn gingerly entered the room, placing his candle on Tabitha's bed while trying to soothe his daughter. "Shhh, it's ok. We're here for you."

As he advanced, she snapped her jaws at him in her confusion, pain and fear, creating a high-pitched bark as she did so. He jumped backwards, dodging her attack, before continuing to press on to comfort his daughter.

"Hey, hey, it's me, it's ok. Shhh, shhh, everything's going to be ok."

Entering her personal space, he placed the back of his hand out to her nose so she could gain the new scent of her father. Still whimpering, she began to trust him, moving forward slightly. He stretched out his hand, stroking the side of her face while moving forward. "It's ok, it's ok."

Following the same pattern as Llewellyn, Isolde advanced towards them while saying softly, "It's ok, it's me."

Stroking her head and feathering, Isolde moved into her, giving Tabitha a hug to console her while gently whispering into her right ear, "Everything's going to be ok now. We're always here for you."

Isolde moved her head back so she could look directly into Tabitha's eyes. As their gaze met, the shaking stopped instantly as if she had some great calming power that only a mother commands.

They both leaned into Tabitha, hugging her tightly, calming her and helping the pain fade away. Isolde looked at him with tears in her eyes, knowing she would lose her daughter to the rituals and customs of the Grey Wolf Clan. Even though she was still a child, she knew her daughter would now be on the path to become a woman, and she did not want her growing up so fast.

Now, Tabitha would soon find out what it truly meant to be a giant wolf of the west.

Chapter Two

THE NEXT STEP

A few years had passed since Tabitha had her first transformation, with her being a day away from her sixteenth birthday. Rivalling her mother with beauty, flowing down her body like a liquid silver waterfall, her light grey hair ran past her hips.

Walking home, she saw her best friend and called, "Wikki, come here for a mo."

Turning, he saw Tabitha waving at him. Grinning, he waved back and approached her. With a lean frame, his clothes hung off his body in an awkward manner, unable to fill them out like most men. His dark brown eyes matched the colour of his untamed short hair.

"What's up?" Wikki replied.

"Your final trial's coming up, isn't it?" Wikki nodded so she continued, "Well, I know your dad won't help you with any of the trial because of his position. So I've asked my dad if he could give you some pointers and guidance, so you have an edge on it. I reckon you can become a protector without his help, but the option is there if you want it," Tabitha suggested.

Looking around to see if anyone was in earshot of them, Wikki smiled, "Why do you and your parents look after me so much?"

Tabitha looked him up and down and replied, "Well, it's because we all love you."

Staring at her feet, he sighed, "It's just a shame my actual family isn't as nice as you guys."

Tabitha held his arm. "I know your family are a bit shit to you. They don't hate you. They just expect a lot from you, that's all."

"Maybe it's, it's just...Never mind. Tell Lew I'll take him up on that offer."

"Well, if there's anything I can do to help, you know I'm here anytime you need me," Tabitha added.

"Haven't you got a trial of your own tomorrow?" Wikki asked.

"Yeah, it's my hunting trial, but I'll be fine."

"Of course you will. You've got a reputation among the clan, you know."

Tabitha's face scrunched up as she spat, "What reputation?"

Standing tall, he puffed out his chest and grinned, "You're the swiftest trainee, and no one can match your speed, accuracy or ferocity."

"Isn't Ren the best?" she frowned.

"Probably. No one has ever come close to defeating him in combat. I think the current rumour is that Lew is the only one that could beat him. Even Balgair has taken him under his guidance. So, it looks like he's expecting a challenge from Ren when he becomes older and wiser."

"My dad? He isn't the fighting type."

"I know he doesn't flaunt his strength, but your dad's a hero, you know. Some say he stopped a war with the bears by his actions."

"Well, you could be right, but I've never even seen my dad transformed. And who knows, Ren might be beaten by someone in the future."

Wikki shook his head. "That's unlikely. Look, I've gotta go now, but I'll see you tomorrow during your trial."

"Ok, I'll see you tomorrow then."

Unknown to both of them, his brother advanced from behind. Grabbing Wikki with his right arm, accompanied with a wide stance, he placed him in a headlock. Twisting his hips in a smooth motion, he threw Wikki into the air, causing him to crash to the floor with a loud thud. Even though he didn't make a sound, the impact certainly did. Peeling his lips back and tensing his jaw, his left hand swung to his hip as he gripped it tightly.

At 25 years old, Gibbi was a big lump of a man. His glossy black hair was slicked back with animal fat, and with the same brown eyes, he looked down at Wikki on the ground.

She knew he had hurt Wikki from his expression and reaction. With wide eyes, she stared hard at Gibbi. Her face turned red, and her lips tightened, partially displaying her teeth, as she fumed, "What's your fucking problem, Gibbi? You hurt Wikki!"

Gibbi looked at Tabitha and scoffed, "Shut up! You don't know what you're talking about. And, anyway, who are you to shout at a protector? You're just in training, and a girl! Keep your nose out, you stupid bitch, you know nothing of the ways of the warrior."

Hunching over with two deep breaths, she reached down and unsheathed her hunters' knife from the scabbard attached to her right thigh. "Try that shit with me, and we'll see who the girl is after we're finished, you fucking wet mutt!"

Scrunching his face while lowering his head slightly, he gave a challenging stare, clenching his left fist, with his right hand reaching down for his hunters' knife.

"Stop! You don't need to worry about it, Tabi. I'm fine, just let it go, please. Gibbi, she didn't mean what she said," Wikki pleaded.

Tabitha stood up straight while taking a slow deep breath, sheathing her knife while still holding the handle. "Ok, I'll leave it alone if he does."

Gibbi stood up straight, took a few steps back and glared at Tabitha with an ominous grin. Clenching both fists, he thundered, "See, you stupid girl, the runt is fine. But if you challenge me again, I'll kick the shit out of you. And if you ever call me a wet mutt again, I'll bite your fucking throat out. No female ever talks down to a man."

Quickly pivoting his upper body, he punched Wikki in the side of the head, drawing blood by splitting the skin over his cheekbone, and he collapsed to the ground once more. Chuckling, he spun around to instigate another challenge with Tabitha, but his laugh turned to complete silence. His smile vanished, eyes widened with his complexion turning pale, seeing his superior standing calmly with his hands behind his back.

Trembling, he proceeded to greet his superior. "H-hi, Llewellyn, h-how are you?"

"Front and centre, Protector," Llewellyn commanded.

Scrambling to Llewellyn's location and standing to attention, Gibbi held his right hand on his chest, covering his heart. This was known as the wolves' greeting, bearing the message, with respect, I honour you.

"Gibbi, I've been watching you for a little while now. Can you tell me what the main role of being a protector is?" Llewellyn asked.

"T-to p-protect the members of the c-clan," Gibbi stammered.

"That's right, and you have been nothing but a bully of late, hurting several members of the clan."

"I-I haven't, Llewellyn, i-it's a lie," Gibbi pleaded.

"You've been reported by a few people. I don't know what has happened to you over the years, but you've changed. That's your brother you just hit; don't you care?"

"I was just toughening him up, I'm only messing around."

All three of them were surprised at how calm Llewellyn was; even Tabitha thought he would have at least hit him for threatening his only daughter.

Llewellyn gave his orders. "Well, you've been summoned to the alpha's hut. So, come with me now because Balgair, Gus and Quinn are waiting to see you."

"Ok, but why? I didn't bully anyone," Gibbi implored.

"No, Gibbi, you have. Because of your actions, you're about to be the first member of your pack to be stripped of your rank. You've dishonoured yourself and the protectors with your actions over the past few months. Now, listen to me carefully, because you need to know this. I know your dad and I are like brothers, but after the recent actions that I've just witnessed, I will not hesitate to kill you if you try to resist me. And, trust me, your dad will understand. Or do you disagree with what I've just said?"

Gibbi's head lowered, shoulders bunching up as he hunched forward. His vision became blurred, with tears building in his eyes. He knew he abused his position within the clan, and he dared not even look at Llewellyn to impose any form of challenge, because Llewellyn was a man of his word, and he knew it. He immediately walked to the alpha's hut, with Llewellyn marching behind as Tabitha and Wikki watched him go for his judgement.

Wikki picked himself up off the ground, holding the wound on the side of his face.

"Are you ok?" Tabitha asked.

"I'm fine, really. I've gotta go now because this situation with Gibbi won't go down well at home. Thanks for sticking up for me, but I could have handled it," Wikki replied.

"I know you could have, but it just pissed me off that you have to handle anything without reason."

Turning around without looking at Tabitha, he held his head down as he walked away. He wasn't a gullible fool, knowing she was lying to him out of pity, and he knew he could handle nothing at the time of the assault. A shroud of shame wrapped his aura, hanging heavy on his body. He loved Tabitha, but for the first time in their friendship, he felt beneath her, with his pride truly shattered for the first time. Tabitha knew that pity was the last thing he needed, but she didn't realise her mistake. Turning swiftly, she walked home in the opposite direction.

Later that night, when Llewellyn came home, Tabitha and Isolde were already placing the food on the dining table. Tabitha had already told Isolde about the events of the day, so they all sat down and ate their food in silence. After they dined, Isolde and Tabitha were halfway through clearing the table as Llewellyn lifted his head up, breaking his long gaze at the ground. "Hey, I need to talk to you."

"Ok, Dad."

"Why didn't you come and find me? Gibbi is stronger than you, whether you like to admit it or not."

"I'm sorry, Dad, I'll make sure I will in the future," Tabitha declared as she continued to empty the table.

"That's not the reply I want. Don't lie and make empty promises. Why did you challenge Gibbi?" Llewellyn questioned again.

Tabitha dumped a wooden plate back onto the table and folded her arms. "Because he was hurting Wikki for absolutely no reason."

"He could've hurt you today, and he may try to do it in the future. It pains me to say because you know me and Gethin are close, but his eldest son is a vicious person."

Throwing her arms down to her sides with clenched fists, she protested, "I'm not afraid of him, and I'll never back down from the likes of him!"

Llewellyn leaned forward, slamming his palm onto the table. "This is not a game, Tabitha! Your first big trial is tomorrow" – taking a deep breath, he leaned back in the chair and composed himself – "and secondly, you've not even started your basic combat training. Gibbi was a fully-fledged protector that's had advanced combat training. You don't realise the danger you put yourself in."

"I don't care what he was or is. He's a fucking coward and a bully, and I'll fight anyone who hurts the people I care about!" she thundered.

"It isn't just about you; Wikki was also affected by your actions today. You claim you want to help him become a protector, but all you did was baby him and make him look like a coward and a weakling. Wikki is capable of standing up for himself, but he will do it in his own time. He's a brilliant strategist and can be calm under pressure, but your actions today might have hurt his chances. Your heart is in the right place, but your head isn't," Llewellyn explained.

Tabitha folded her arms, looking down. "I know, Dad. Look, I was foolish, but I just reacted. I didn't mean to cause Wikki any harm."

Closing his eyes for a second, he took in a long deep breath while leaning back in the chair. "Well, you did. Look, you need to look at the bigger picture before you react like you did today. The wrong actions for the right reasons can be just as destructive as doing wrong actions for the wrong reasons. Gibbi would have beaten you today, not just because of his strength over yours, but because he was thinking, and you weren't. Now, lastly, I have been told off by Balgair because of your actions as well. You are not initiated into the clan, and you have about two more years of training before that even happens. You must show respect to your superiors, even if you don't agree. If you strongly feel that you have a case against any superior member of the clan, you report it and don't try to handle it yourself. Do I make myself clear, because I won't want to talk about a matter like this again?"

She looked back up and replied, "Yes, Dad. I'm sorry for my actions today."

"It's not your actions; it's just the way you handled the situation. You have a big heart, and I'm proud of you for that. We make mistakes to learn from them. Now get to bed; you need your rest because you have a long day ahead of you tomorrow."

"Ok, Dad, goodnight. Goodnight, Mam."

"Goodnight," Isolde replied.

"Goodnight."

Tabitha shot off into her room, closing the bedroom door behind her.

"Llewellyn, is everything ok with you and Gethin?" Isolde asked.

Leaning the chair back further on its rear legs, he replied, "Things between us are fine. I don't know what I'm going to do with your daughter. She's too much like you."

"Oh, so it's like that, is it? She's my daughter when she messes up, and yours when she is doing well?"

"Well, you're trouble, and I blame your genes."

Isolde tapped the underneath of the elevated chair leg with her foot, causing Llewellyn to overbalance and fall backwards as she giggled.

"Owww. See? This is exactly what I mean, nothing but trouble you are."

Llewellyn scrambled to his feet, grabbing Isolde around the waist with both arms as she tried to retreat, letting out a mild scream as he picked her up and gently placed her on the floor. He hovered over her, and the pair of them started giggling, then the chuckles turned into a passionate kiss before they retreated hastily to their bedroom.

The next day, stood at the gathering point on top of a hill with nine others, Tabitha waited for the trial. She already knew three of them, but the other six were from nearby villages and towns of the clan. She stood tall, arms resting behind her back, with her eyes fixed on the endless field in front of her. White clouds filled the sky as a warm breeze pressed her loose clothing around her slender figure, with her long hair gracefully flowing with each gust. Moving her eyes over to the east, she noticed Wikki and her parents standing at the edge of the forest on the hill.

A few moments later, two men approached the group. They both inspected each member, with one of them making an introduction. "Hello everyone, and welcome to the hunting trial. For those who don't know us in person, I'm Gus, the pathfinder, and this is Quinn, our peacekeeper."

Quinn continued to detail the day's activities. "Today, you will be hunting deer that we have captured. We will be testing your movements, skills and the proficiency of your kills. You will go one at a time, and you will each have three deer to hunt. Does everyone understand?"

"Yes, Peacekeeper," everyone replied in unison.

"Good luck and good hunting," Gus declared.

A protector that gave them their orders of what to do in the trial pointed at the young boy who was chosen to start first. With a nod, the young boy left the group and started the trial.

Eight of the trainees completed their trial successfully, with the quickest kill time of around fifteen minutes. However, these hunts were messy affairs, as they all immobilized their prey before they made the kill.

Tabitha's time had arrived, disappearing to the private penned-off area known as the changing den. Taking off her clothes, ready to transform, she lowered herself to the ground, preparing to sprint.

As the pen gate opened, three deer fled into the open field. Eyes open wide, taking instant strides, Tabitha transformed into a wolf, growing just over six feet tall on all four legs. The deer ran in the same direction four hundred metres away, but she began closing the gap at great speed. She knew she had to be swift, or the deer would split up to survive and escape.

Choosing the centre deer, she lowered her head and picked up her speed. Getting close enough, she lunged onto its back, biting down into the nape of its neck. Her back paws pushed off the deer's body, veering right and spinning in the air. With a fluid motion, she lifted the deer from the ground, snapping its neck in the process. Flicking her head while opening her jaws, she threw her first kill into the deer on the right flank. The fresh carcass clipped its rear legs, forcing the deer to crash to the ground hard before sliding a few metres.

Tabitha cleared just over a three-hundred and sixty-degree mid-air spin before her paws hit the ground, instantly picking up her sprinting speed again to close the gap with the last deer fleeing. Some of the trainees' mouths opened wide with awe, as they had never seen anyone do that manoeuvre before, and neither had her superiors.

Turning sharp to her left, biting into the third deer's neck as it was running. Her teeth buried deep into its hide, twisting her body downwards at a right angle, separating the deer's vertebrae while slamming its body into the dirt. She spun around, coming to a halt, watching the last deer recovering from its fall. Locking her sights onto it, she ran in for the last kill.

It did not take her long to complete her trial, but all of her peers were extremely impressed at everything. Most of all, Quinn became impressed with the clean kills and her superior agility, making her top of the intake.

Still in wolf form, Tabitha stood majestic with one paw raised, looking over to the end of the hill where her parents and Wikki stood. Isolde and Wikki were jumping up and down, screaming and shouting with excitement, but Llewellyn had already began marching back into the town.

Tabitha lowered her paw to the ground, thinking, *Why is he going? Did I do it wrong? I knew I should've done better.* The pride she initially felt turned to doubt and shame, hanging her head low as she slumped back to the changing den.

Twenty minutes later, the last person had finished, concluding the trial with everyone passing. To celebrate, an open feast in the town was held, with all the kills being cooked. Almost everyone in the towns and villages of Niamh Plain was invited to the open feasts for all the trials that were held. This involved a large number of tables filled with food, multiple barrels of mead that the people had a taste for, and the musically gifted playing their instruments and singing songs of old tales and legends.

Traditionally, the ones to successfully complete the trials would eat first, but Tabitha wasn't quite feeling the celebration. Then, she felt a hand on her right shoulder. Turning, she saw it was her father.

Standing tall with his chest puffed out, Llewellyn stared at his daughter with the biggest smile she had ever seen. Mixed emotions overwhelmed her as her eyes welled up, pulling herself towards his warm embrace.

"Hey, where's my hug?" Isolde questioned.

Tabitha let go of her father and hugged her mother. Wikki, standing next to Isolde, started to feel a little out of place, but she trapped him into a big hug as well.

"Dad, why did you leave during my last kill?" Tabitha asked.

Llewellyn smiled, "Well, it's a matter you don't need to concern yourself with right now. But I'll tell you the reason when the time comes, I promise. But now is your evening, and you must enjoy yourself, because these great personal moments don't pass by very often." He turned to Wikki and asked, "Will you come to my hut in two days' time? It's the opportune moment to teach you what you need to know for the path you wish to choose."

"Yeah, ok, Lew," Wikki replied as he turned to Tabitha. "Let's go and join the celebration, shall we?"

"Ok, let's go," Tabitha replied.

"Hey, I know you can drink the mead now, but don't go over the top. We'll be watching," Isolde warned.

Tabitha rolled her eyes. "Ok, Mam."

And just like that, Wikki and Tabitha lost themselves in the dense crowd, enjoying the feast to its fullest capacity. Drunk with happiness and mead, the people sang the popular songs enriched with tales of legend. The mead and songs led most of the people to dance around fires as the night drew in, with no one going hungry or thirsty, making it a joyous time indeed.

Two days later, Wikki woke early, ensuring that he had enough time for any activities Llewellyn had planned for him. He arrived at Llewellyn's hut, knocking wildly on the front door. Waiting for a reply, his breathing rate rose, and his palms became clammy.

"Morning, Wikki. I'm guessing you're here for Llewellyn and not Tabitha today?" Isolde inquired.

"Yeah, that's right, Izzy," Wikki replied.

"He told me to invite you in. He's getting ready, and I've been instructed to give you guys some private time. I'm going into the market for the morning, so if you want to join us for dinner tonight, you're more than welcome. Though, I'd like to know if you're coming now, so I can grab some extra supplies for the meal. Just to let you know as well, Tabitha has already gone for the day to start her basic combat training, so she won't be back until this evening."

"Umm, yeah, ok, I'll come by later. Plus, I'm sure Lew will run me ragged today to get me ready for my final trial, so I'll be starving."

Isolde rolled her eyes with a smile, shaking her head. "You're always hungry, so there's no change there."

"Ha, you got me there."

"Come on in and make yourself at home. There's a jug of water on the table if you want any."

"Ok, thanks, Izzy."

Wikki entered the hut as Isolde left, closing the front door behind her. Sitting in a chair, he waited patiently for Llewellyn with his legs bobbing up and down.

"Oh, you're already here," Llewellyn said, emerging from his bedroom.

"Yeah, I wanted to get as much training in so I can be ready for my final trial. I'm ready and willing to learn anything you can teach me, so maybe I can be good enough to be a protector," he replied.

Llewellyn gave a faint smile, raising one eyebrow and mumbled, "Interesting."

Walking over to the dining table, Llewellyn held the back of a chair and said, "Well, stay where you are because I'm going to give you some home truths, which is the last part of your training."

Llewellyn rotated the chair to face Wikki. Sitting down, he leaned back, placing his left arm on the table as he gently rocked on its rear legs.

Wikki's thoughts got the best of him. *I knew it, I'm not good enough to be a protector, and I've been kidding myself this entire time.*

Looking directly at Wikki, Llewellyn began. "I'm going to speak now, and you're going to listen. I've been watching you closely over the past year, and I've been getting updates from the protectors training you. I know why your brother was pushing you around the other day. You lack confidence, and with him beating you down with every turn, he's been holding back what he fears the most...you." Wikki frowned at him for a second as he continued, "What you lack in physical strength you majorly make up for with your talents. Everyone is impressed with your strategic knowledge. You even excelled yourself with making a new battle formation, which we've tried and tested. Your physical attributes will come in time with more hard work.

But now, you must show redemption from what happened with your brother the other day, which is a path that you must take yourself. Only you can break your own barriers, which are obstructing your potential for greatness."

Wikki looked down, thinking to himself again, *I knew it, I've let myself down.*

"You'll find redemption eventually, but this matter with your brother has had people question your motives to protect the people. Now you've heard the hard truth, so I'll give you the last lesson you'll need from me or anyone else. What I'm about to tell you must stay between us, as others wouldn't agree with the knowledge I'm about to tell you. We've already decided what final trial you'll take. Your dad was not invited to this council meeting because of who he is to you, so they asked me to convene with them as I'm your dad's right-hand man. With a long talk and your actions so far" – he tapped Wikki's shoulder – "we've decided to put you through the protectors trial."

Wikki looked back up, eyes widened with a faint smile.

"Don't get excited yet. You still have to prove yourself on your final trial, and with a year's worth of protectors training after that. You have the skills and advanced knowledge to be a protector, but you'll fail if you don't show confidence. You have about a month to work on that, and no one can help you with this. If you can overcome your own self-destructive weakness, then you'll get what you desire. Do you understand?" Llewellyn concluded.

"Yes, Lew. I won't let you down, I swear on everything I hold dear."

Unknown to Wikki, the next thing Llewellyn said would stay with him forever. "I hope you're right because you'll be a vital addition to this clan. And, in the future, I have a feeling that Tabitha will be relying on you more than you realise."

"Tabi? How will she rely on someone like me?" Wikki questioned.

"I don't expect you to understand now, but you will in time. Like I said, this conversation stays between us, right?"

"What conversation?"

"All right, it's time for me to leave and for you to reflect on what I've just said. We'll see you later. Until then, think hard and figure out who you are."

Llewellyn got up, immediately leaving the hut to catch up with his beloved mate, leaving the front door open.

With a thousand thoughts racing through his head, Wikki stared at the open door for a few seconds, shaking his head slightly. With a frown, he mumbled, "What would Tabi want from me?"

Chapter Three

DAWN OF DARKNESS

Dirty grey clouds covered the sky and wind gusted through the town, causing fine droplets of rain to wisp around everything and everyone, catching every dry surface it could.

As Tabitha and Wikki walked through the town, they saw Llewellyn surrounded by strangers outside the alpha's hut. Overhearing broken conversations as random people spoke over each other, they both decided to see what was happening.

"What will happen?"

"Where's the alpha?"

"Who's going to do something about this?"

"They killed people from our village!"

In the confusion, the people seemed both scared and angry about having little protection at their village. Wolf's Fang stood on the furthest north-east point of Niamh Plain, surrounded by three bordering countries, those of the Great Plain, the Silver Kingdom and the Neutral Land.

Llewellyn stood in the wooden pavilion outside the alpha's hut, calling out to the crowd, "Everyone, everyone, please settle down so I can answer your questions. The pathfinder has taken his party out to investigate, and we're doing all we can. Please stay calm, we'll sort out this issue very soon."

A voice from the crowd asked, "What about the others?"

Llewellyn replied, "Our alpha has taken Gethin and the majority of the protectors out to aid the other towns and villages, but he should be back soon. He's leaving protectors at each location, and the others are out on patrols until this issue is dealt with. Until then, I'll be in charge of the defence of this town with the protectors I have."

Another random voice shouted from the crowd again. "There's only nine of you left here. You can't protect us from them!"

Scowling while pushing her lower jaw forward, Tabitha addressed the crowd from the rear. "Yes he can. How dare you talk down to my dad?"

Llewellyn recognised the voice that shouted and said, "Tabitha, please. I'll address the people, not you. I swear to you all, I'll protect you when you're here. You have my word."

Tabitha watched her father walk down the steps of the pavilion and join his comrades to address them with some type of instruction or order, with the crowd talking and muttering amongst themselves in disbelief.

Tabitha looked at Wikki. "Well, I don't know what's fully going on, but I don't want to get caught up in all of this. These people are pissing me off with the way they're talking to my dad. Do you wanna go to the woods and do some training?"

"Yeah, let's get out of here. Just to let you know, though, I understand your frustration because they pissed me off too, but you should have let your dad sort that out because the villagers are scared about something, and your outburst could have caused trouble."

Exhaling heavily, she replied, "Yeah, you're right. I'll apologise to my dad later for speaking out of turn."

An hour later, the rain had stopped, clearing the air of mist. As they finished off their training, three howls came from the north-west of the town beyond the forest.

"Wikki, what's that?" Tabitha asked.

"That was three howls, it means an enemy is nearby. You'll learn that on your combat training," Wikki explained.

"Let's be honest, with what the villagers have been banging on about, it's probably a training exercise to keep their mouths shut. Do you wanna go and have a look? Come on, it can be good for both of us to see what the protectors do in training," she suggested.

"Tabi, I don't think it's a drill. It's probably real because you know Lew won't let any protector howl for enemy that ain't there."

"But what if it's a drill? We could both miss out on a valuable training opportunity."

Rolling his eyes, he sighed, "Oh, come on then. But if it's not a drill, we get out of there, ok? No ifs or buts."

"Deal."

Hastily walking to the edge of the north-west side of the forest, they kept a look out for the protectors. Beyond the treeline lay a small hill, ending eighty metres away, rolling both left and right into a big field where Tabitha had completed her hunting trial.

"Wikki, look there, to the left, seven of them are running to the east!" Tabitha squealed with a big smile.

"Isn't that your dad?" Wikki inquired.

"Where?"

"There, leading the formation."

Pointing at the lead wolf, Tabitha's smile disappeared. Her heart sank, knowing her father wouldn't transform into a wolf without justification. With the people from Wolf's Fang acting the way they did and saying the things they said, it made her think. Now seeing her father to be doing what looked like charging into battle, she felt a dread like no other. Then, they heard another faint howl to the west of their location.

"That's the alpha's howl; they're about four miles away," Wikki pointed out.

"We need to go to the top of the hill in front of us," Tabitha said.

Wikki turned to face her. "Tabi, the alpha's party is getting involved. We need to get back to the town now, this is not a training exercise. You agreed to my compromise."

"I need to see what my dad's doing; I'm worried because my dad never talks of fighting," Tabitha replied, with her eyes tearing up.

Never seeing her so upset before, he shook his head. "Ok, but if there's something wrong, we go back into the forest and back to the town. Ok?"

Acknowledging his order, she nodded. The both of them ran, breaking out of the treeline, stopping on the brow of the hill. Revealing the formerly dead ground, their eyes intensely scanned the field from her father's location to the right, and then, they saw it.

Wikki's eyes opened wide. "No, this is impossible. Do they even banish their people?"

With his words falling on deaf ears, Tabitha's eyes welled up as her body began to shake. Clenching her fists tightly, her knuckles whitened as she peeled her lips back, screaming as loud as she could, "Dad!"

Only one opponent stood against the seven protectors, but this was not a cat from the south or a bear of the north. This monster came from the Eastern Wastes, giving them good reason for concern.

These dark and twisted people turned into foul creatures, and had not been seen in the West Plains for centuries. This deadly giant dwarfed all the grey wolves, being slightly over twice the size, and was unmistakably recognisable as a tenebrous, a breed of stygian.

Long, Tyrian purple fur encompassed the terrifying monster. Its humpback merged with the neck, supporting a large head with a short muzzle, emphasising its overgrown sabretooth fangs. The tenebrous opened its mouth, producing an unworldly roar, shaking Wikki and Tabitha to the core.

The tenebrous took a defensive stance, moving one of its thick legs forward and a spindly hind leg back. Its skinny tail whipped the air, displaying this creature's excitement. However, this was all they could see, being too far away to show defining features.

Llewellyn, being the first to engage this terrifying beast, broke away from the attack formation. Leaping forward, he missed its leg, disappearing behind the beast on its right flank before reappearing, rolling on the ground.

Jolting forward, the tenebrous opened its mouth, catching another protector in mid-air. Clamping its jaws together, its sabretooth incisors fully penetrated the wolf's body, killing him instantly. The wolf's corpse slid down the large sabretooth fangs as the beast flicked its head, flinging the protector's body into the air. The carcass slammed into a charging wolf, causing him to yelp in pain, lowering the offensive numbers to take on the beast. Breaking their attack formation, they surrounded the mighty tenebrous at all angles.

Wikki grabbed Tabitha by her arm and demanded, "Let's get out of here now!"

He pulled her away, and they both turned and saw a man looking directly at them from twenty metres away. Naked and covered in dirt, he tilted his head while staring at them both with silver-coloured eyes, licking his lower lip with an ominous smile. Leaning forward and opening his leg stance, Wikki knew what was to come.

"Run into the forest!" Wikki commanded.

The man took three running steps, turning into the same kind of beast they had seen on the field. His eyeballs became pure silver, adding to their terror. Wikki knew if a fully-fledged protector with advanced combat training couldn't fell the beast, then they had no chance in direct combat.

As they both ran, Wikki came up with a plan. "Don't change into a wolf. It's probably too big to fit through the trees, which can give us the advantage to manoeuvre through them."

With the tenebrous hot on their tails, they retreated into the forest. Wikki was right about the beast's size and the clearing between each tree, but he never considered its forward planning and raw power.

Bounding forward, he uprooted the first tree with his powerful front legs. The two-hundred-foot-tall tree snapped the branches of the other trees as he forced it to the ground. The impact vibrated the ground underneath their feet, forcing them to jump to the right. Leaping to its right, the tenebrous tried uprooting another tree, but the roots ran too deep. However, this did not stop the tenebrous felling the tree, snapping the trunk while forcing it to the ground, producing another earthly tremor. With the foliage blocking his newfound prey on a direct path, he charged hard and fast at his victims. The trees slowed the tenebrous down, but with raw power, it broke or pushed them off at thirty-degree angles down the narrow trail it had created.

Wikki tripped over a tree root, stumbling to the ground with a cut foot. Tabitha skidded across the damp forest floor covered in pine needles, quickly turning around and scrambling back to him. The tenebrous almost caught the pair until it wedged itself between two trees.

As Wikki recovered, the tenebrous swiped with its left paw, gouging its claws deep into his back. The torn skin caused him agonising pain, sapping his strength, as he pushed Tabitha as hard as he could from danger. Stumbling backwards, she fell onto her backside.

"Run!" Wikki screamed.

Paralysed by fear, Tabitha watched the tenebrous open its large mouth to finish him off and, for the first time in her life, she felt truly helpless.

Wikki dived forward onto the floor, forcing the tenebrous to miss its target. The beast gave an almighty roar, throwing its head into the air while arching its back, displaying some form of pain. Tumbling from under the second beast, Llewellyn appeared after biting one of its hind legs, tearing a small amount of flesh in the process. The timing was a stroke of luck, but the interaction was not. With the wolves' acute hearing, Llewellyn clearly heard Wikki shout at Tabitha to run before the second beast transformed. Without hesitation, he ran to their aid on his own after seeing the second beast transform on top of the hill, leaving the other wolves to deal with the first threat.

Tabitha's eyes caught the movement, noticing her father. Llewellyn got up from the ground, standing between Wikki and the beast. He quickly snapped and barked at Wikki, ensuring he got the message to get away from the fight, and then he gave a high-pitched yelp. Finding its mark, the tenebrous bit Llewellyn's tail. Trying to drag him back, its jaws proved too powerful, ripping three quarters of his tail off with a single bite. Turning, he squared up to the dangerous giant, standing strong like an unmoveable object with the remainder of his tail pointing into the air. Staring the beast down while growling, his muzzle wrinkled up, displaying his teeth, with the tip of his tongue sticking through the centre of them.

Through the trees' foliage obscuring the left and right jumped two other wolves flanking the beast. The wolf on the right dived onto the beast's side, biting into its hump on the nape of its neck. The other wolf used the fallen tree as a platform to jump higher, mounting the beast's back. The tenebrous roared in pain as the two wolves started tearing into its flesh with everything they had, gaining the upper hand. Making the most of this advantage, Llewellyn jumped to his left flank, using the fallen tree to lunge onto the beast, continuing the assault by biting its ribs.

Wikki scrambled to Tabitha's location, getting out of immediate danger, looking at her squarely in the eyes as he shouted, "Tabi, look at me, you need to look at me because we need to get out of here now!"

His shout sounded like muffled noise, as all she could hear in her head was her father's voice: *This is not a game, Tabitha. You don't realise the danger you put yourself in. It isn't just about you.*

Failing to take control of the situation, Wikki turned around, following Tabitha's gaze, fixed on the fight. One of the protectors slipped, trapping himself between the powerful beast and a tree. The tenebrous, becoming overwhelmed, dropped down with another almighty roar.

On the path to victory, something strange started to happen. As Wikki and Tabitha looked into the silver eyes of the tenebrous, it emitted a vision of lightning. All of a sudden, a flash covered its body, and all three wolves yelped in pain. Immediately after the flash, its fur stuck up on end.

Llewellyn, hit by the electrocuting effect of the tenebrous, propelled into a tree on the beast's right flank with so much force, he bounced off it before falling to the ground. The wolf wedged between the beast and the tree alongside the other wolf atop the tenebrous was no longer in the position of dominance, but certain death. For when the fur of a tenebrous becomes electrocuted, it stands on end while turning hard as stone for roughly ten seconds.

Both protectors aiding Llewellyn had been impaled on the fur, and their blood run down the tenebrous' body from the wolves' corpses still attached to it. As the power wore off, the fur became soft again and the wolves' lifeless bodies slid off and hit the ground.

Neither Wikki nor Tabitha could believe what they saw, but she became overwhelmed with concern for her father's wellbeing.

As the beast recovered, it focused its attention back on the pair of them, and begun moving forward. The remainder of fur that was stuck in the tree, slid out with one step. Wikki slumped over, strength depleted from the pain and loss of blood.

Tabitha's eyes widened as if a switch flicked in her head, bringing her back to reality. "Let's go, Wikki! Come on!"

She pulled at his arm, but he was too weak; his wounds were getting the better of him. He looked up at some movement behind Tabitha. Breathing heavily, he spoke: "Tabi...he's here...he's never been beaten."

Before Tabitha could turn to find out what Wikki was talking about, Ren walked past and stood between the beast and the young wolves.

Locking eyes with the tenebrous, Ren declared, "I'll rise with glory from your death by claiming your corpse for my own."

Charging at the tenebrous head-on, Ren transformed into a wolf from one step to the next, clothes tearing away from his body as he became the largest grey wolf in Niamh Plain. Leaning forward while swinging its head up to the left, the tenebrous clamped its mouth shut. Ren pounced slightly to the right, causing the monster to miss him. Meanwhile, he found his target, biting the side of the beast's neck, and with all of his might, he tore open its flesh, exposing the neck muscles, tendons and blood vessels.

This being the first time Wikki and Tabitha had seen the brute strength Ren possessed, they could not tell if it was luck, skill or both that helped him achieve such a manoeuvre. A spray of blood burst out of the beast's neck, covering the forest floor in a crimson glass puddle. As the tenebrous collapsed to the ground, Ren pushed off its chest, avoiding the beast's corpse. As Ren composed himself, he heard the snapping of twigs and branches to the west. Jumping into a defensive stance, he picked up a familiar scent. Knowing there was no immediate threat, he transformed back into a human.

This young man's bronzed complexion complemented his light blue eyes. Brown hair hung in well-groomed circlets, resting on his back and chest. His ripped, muscular frame, stained in tenebrous blood, reflected the sunlight creeping through the forest canopy. Walking back to what was left of his shirt and trousers, he picked up the tattered remains, wrapping the torn cloth around his waist, covering his manhood.

"What're you two doing here? Why aren't you in the town with the others?" Ren asked.

Wikki stood up with the aid of a tree, jaw clenching while breathing heavily. "We were training...then we...were chased...by that thing."

Tabitha stood up without acknowledging their conversation. She walked towards Llewellyn, who as still lying beneath the tree, mumbling, "D-dad? Dad?"

Observing Tabitha walking away from them, Ren realised who she was. Even though Ren and Llewellyn didn't interact often, he had the greatest respect for him, but now he had got to meet the daughter Llewellyn bragged about for the first time, albeit under terrible circumstances.

Getting closer with no response, Tabitha took a wide birth around Llewellyn's limp body. Hoping for a reply or some movement, she called out again, "Dad?"

Unresponsive to anything in his line of sight, his pupils remained dilated. Approaching her father, she stretched out her hand, aiming for the feathering on his chest. Grasping warm, damp fur in a clenched fist to pull at him, she withdrew. Immediately looking at her hand, she could see her father's blood on her palm and fingers. She started shaking, her breathing rate increasing as her vision blurred. With her lower jaw trembling and her lower lip quivering, she continued trying to get a response. Her voice grew husky from the lump in her throat, pitch changing as she spoke: "Dad, get up. Come on, Dad, get up." Tears broke away from her eyes as she continued. "Dad, I still need you, please."

Her body shook more violently, and she clenched her jaw tightly while snarling in a last-ditch effort to get any response. "Dad, get the fuck up!"

She grabbed the fur above his shoulder and placed her other hand on the top of his head, her tears of pain rolling off her cheeks, crashing into Llewellyn's muzzle. A deep breath exhaled through her gritted teeth as she nestled her face into his. In a softer tone, she started to speak again, "I still need you because I don't know what to do next. So you have to get up, you can't leave us yet. I won't let you."

Reality sank in as Tabitha buried her face into the side of his neck. As hope faded away, she started to scream with the pain and anger never felt before, with Llewellyn's neck muffling the sounds of torment she expressed.

Wikki felt powerless and fell to his knees, his eyes watering, with the realisation that he had lost a second father. He looked up with tears streaming down each side of his face, wondering what he could have done differently.

Emerging from behind Wikki at the opening of the fallen trees, the alpha and his party investigated the screaming. Balgair looked upon the fallen tenebrous, then swept the scene of devastation. When he transformed back to human, a protector threw him a battle robe from his backpack. The plain brown, hooded robe was poorly made, used for tactical reasons, such as reducing their scent, giving complex orders or reducing their size for recognisance.

Balgair donned the robe and said, "It looks like your gut feeling was right, Ren, and you got here in time before this thing gained any ground into the town."

"I know my gut feeling was right, but I wasn't quick enough. Maybe I should have come in wolf form to gain more ground. Llewellyn has fallen," Ren replied.

Balgair looked at Tabitha crying into her father's neck and noticed Wikki crying on his knees before giving his orders, "Ren, get these two back to the town now. There could be more of these beasts around here."

"That isn't very compassionate. Let the child weep for her dad," Ren replied.

"Compassion is less important than safety. Get them back now and take Wikki to the healers' hut as well. That's an order. Everyone else, come with me."

Taking his battle robe off, throwing it back to the protector mounted on a comrade, he transformed back into a wolf. The protector stuffed it back into his backpack, as Balgair led his party out of the forest to secure the area.

Ren walked over to Tabitha, holding her shoulders firmly while pulling her up from her father. "We need to go, Balgair's right. I'm sorry."

Tabitha, stained with her father's blood, nodded while wiping her eyes and nose.

"Can you help Wikki to the healers' hut? If there are more of those things, I'll need to protect you both." As she walked towards Wikki, Ren commanded, "Wikki, you need to stop crying now and use the rest of your strength to get to the healers' hut. Be strong and move forward for both of us. There'll be time to mourn, but it isn't now."

Wikki wiped the tears from his red eyes and nodded. Using a tree to get up again, Tabitha took his left arm, draping it over her shoulders to act as a makeshift crutch so all three of them could head to the town.

Chapter Four

THE AFTERMATH

Approaching the healers' hut in town, Wikki was near the verge of collapse, managing to hobble the last one hundred metres with Tabitha and Ren supporting most of his body weight. As Tabitha banged hard on the door, Wikki crumpled to the floor. Two healers answered the loud knocks, finding Tabitha and Ren stained in blood with Wikki on the floor between them.

"Please help him. He's been injured," Tabitha said, pointing at Wikki.

The healers picked him up by his arms and his legs, carrying him to an empty bed close to the entrance, with the aid of Tabitha and Ren supporting the trunk of his body. Ren moved out of the way, and with a single lifting motion, the two healers and Tabitha placed Wikki onto the bed. The healers walked off to a cupboard, collecting medical supplies to clean and dress his wounds.

"You're gonna be all right now. The healers will help you," Tabitha said softly.

With tears forming in his eyes, Wikki replied, "Tabi, I'm so sorry, it's my fault that he died."

As their eyes locked, she said, "No, I won't let you blame yourself. It really wasn't your fault."

"It is. Your dad gave me some advice two days ago, and if I'd reacted to his advice sooner, then he might still be alive. But I'll never make that mistake again."

Frowning, Tabitha asked, "What mistake?"

"I shouldn't have let you investigate what was happening, and because I showed a lack of leadership, I put us both in harm's way. From now on, I'll follow my heart and gut. I won't be swayed into foolish errands again. If I'd brought you straight back to the town, then we wouldn't have been in that situation, and Lew might still be alive now."

With a tear rolling down her cheek, Tabitha replied, "Wikki, I don't know what to say. It wasn't your fault, it was..."

Turning his head away, Wikki interrupted, "Stop. Please understand, but I need to be alone right now. Just go with Ren to your hut, your mam needs to know. I'll be fine, but I need my space right now."

Tabitha looked at the ground for a few seconds with another tear rolling down the other side of her face.

Leaning in the doorway with his arms folded, Ren said, "It's time to go to your mam's hut and explain to her what's happened. I'll tell her because this ain't a task for you to handle."

Tabitha continued to stare at the ground. "No, Ren, I think I need to tell her."

"Trust me on this. It's sometimes better to come from an outsider. Also, you've been through more than enough today, and now ain't the time to add more burden to yourself," Ren explained.

"Ok."

Under the escort of Ren, she wondered how he would start the hardest conversation anyone would ever have with her mother. With so many emotions running through her head, she just seemed to drift back to the hut.

As everyone remained sheltered in their homes, the town was lifeless. As the two of them walked past the huts, silhouettes emerged from each window, inspecting the only moving thing outside. They all wondered what had happened, guessing different scenarios as a half-naked man covered in blood accompanied a blood-stained teenager. A random voice came from a doorway, but Ren stopped and looked directly at the person trying to get their attention. The icy cold stare, followed by complete silence, commanded the person to close the door and slink away back into his hut. Not a sound came from any other onlookers as they completed their short journey.

About thirty metres away, the hut door flew open. Isolde emerged, running to Tabitha after she saw them approach.

"Tabitha, where've you been? I've been worried sick since I heard the alarm for enemy forces close by. Why're you covered in blood? Are you hurt?" Isolde asked anxiously.

"I'm fine, Mam."

"Are you cut?"

"Mam, I'm fine!" Tabitha snapped.

Isolde became surprised as her daughter had never shouted at her like that before. She looked at Tabitha's eyes and could see they were red and puffy. "What's wrong, Tabitha? Wikki was with you. Is he ok?"

"No, his back has been cut up pretty bad, but I think he'll be ok eventually. He's at the healers' hut," Tabitha replied.

"Oh, we need to go and see him now. I can see if there is anything I can do to help him."

Clearing his throat, Ren joined the conversation. "Isolde, we need to go inside. We need to talk. Wikki's in good hands, and the healers will look after him now."

Looking at the young man before her, she frowned for a second before her eyes widened. "You're Ren, right?"

"Yeah, that's right. Look, we need to go inside so I can talk to you. We can continue with the pleasantries later."

Examining Ren, she knew something had happened. From seeing his naked body and the remainder of his torn clothes, she figured out he had transformed recently. Isolde stepped to one side and stretched out her arm, directing them both into the hut. As they all entered, she closed the door.

Gazing at Isolde, Ren said softly, "I think you need to take a seat. You too, Tabitha."

Isolde proceeded with the request, moving out a dining chair to face Ren. Tabitha sat down on a chair beside her, but she did not turn her chair around, facing the table instead.

Ren looked at Isolde, awaiting the news. "There's no easy way to say this" – he drew a deep breath – "so I'll come straight out with it. Llewellyn has fallen."

Isolde's hands came up to her mouth with a tremor, her eyes squinting with a shroud of emptiness enveloping her entire body. Silence encompassed the hut before she threw down her arms, face grimacing while demanding, "No, it's not true, not my Llewellyn, he's second in command of the protectors, and known to be the strongest protector in the West Plains. No one could beat him, not even you with your reputation. You're wrong!"

"I'm sorry, Isolde, but what I've said is true. It wasn't any ordinary enemy, like another wolf or an exiled outlander; it was a tenebrous that got him."

Isolde stood up, denying the information further. "That's a lie. Even I know the stygians haven't stepped foot in the West Plains for hundreds of years." Unable to say anything, Ren stood in silence for fear of starting an argument by correcting her. "See you're lying and..."

"Mam, it's true, I saw it happen," Tabitha hastily replied, cutting off her mother's attack on him.

Turning, Isolde frowned as she watched her daughter lower her head. A tear fell from Tabitha's chin and Isolde's stomach twisted. Now, she knew it to be true.

Ren gave the wolves' greeting and said, "I'm sorry, I think that you two need to be alone. I respected Llewellyn with the highest regard, so I'll be the one to collect his body, with your permission of course."

Isolde didn't verbally reply or even look at Ren; instead, she just stared at his feet, nodding to his request. He turned around without a word, exiting the hut while closing the door quietly behind him.

Lifting Tabitha from the chair slowly, Isolde embraced her daughter in her arms. Tabitha's arms swung around her mother's body as they started to cry together. Their family was now torn and shattered, with a void that could never be filled again. Tabitha, without her role model and hero, looked up at her mother, who was confused, lost and feeling truly alone. Their household darkened with grief and sorrow, blackened by the light that had been extinguished by evil.

"I'm so sorry," Tabitha mumbled, between her tears.

"Hey, it's ok, it wasn't your fault. You still have me, and I'll always be here for you."

The night was long and painful for too many families of the Grey Wolf Clan. So much devastation caused by so few, with emotions running strong, changing lives forever.

The next morning, Tabitha and Isolde were woken by a loud knock on the door, having fallen asleep in each other's arms on the floor in front of the fireplace. Another knock on the door caused Isolde to stand up, with Tabitha sitting, still stained by her father's dried blood.

Opening the door, Isolde saw Balgair stood in the doorway. Giving the wolves' greeting, he said, "I'm sorry to disturb you, my child, but I thought I should inform you directly. Llewellyn's body has been taken to the hut of the dead. If you wish, I can escort you there personally, so you can clean Llewellyn's body yourself in preparation for the ritual."

Tears formed as, without speaking, she nodded. Looking back, she saw Tabitha's tears roll down her face.

"Tabitha will not be alone. Gethin here has volunteered to look out for her in your absence. Once you have cleaned the body, we'll send for her."

Gethin placed his hand on Isolde's shoulder and said, "I'm sorry for your loss...our loss. All I can do now is look after you both. I need to talk to Tabitha about her dad, if that's ok with you?"

With another silent nod, she walked out the front door as Balgair followed behind with two protectors. Gethin entered the hut, closing the door behind him. Pulling out a chair, he sat down, observing Tabitha still sitting on the floor.

"Why don't you sit on one of your chairs?"

Without looking at him, Tabitha replied, "I'm fine where I am. How's Wikki?"

"He's fine, the healers say that he'll make a full recovery, but he'll carry scars from yesterday," Gethin replied.

"And how is he, you know, in himself?"

"Only time will tell, but he'll get over it like a man."

Short brown and silver hair showed his age, large in build and even larger in status, which made Gethin stand tall with pride. Being a structured man with an appearance to match, he was quite different personality-wise from his late best friend.

"I know your dad's death is hitting you hard right now, but I think it's time you knew the truth about your dad. Believe it or not, he was offered the lead role of the protectors just after you were born. He is, well, was better than me, but he turned the position down for me."

Tabitha frowned. "What do you mean, for you?"

"He wasn't as wise back then, and he refused the position for two reasons. He had no desire to lead anyone because he'd lost all his brothers and parents. Your uncles and granddad were killed in battle, and your grandmother died of a broken heart, so he was dealing with grief. Secondly, he knew someone that he respected wanted the position, me."

"Yes, I kind of know about the battle of the banished bears trying to gain entry into our lands, but Dad didn't talk much about it. I understand that he loved and respected you, but I'm confused. How can he have had no desire to lead, but became second in command of the protectors?"

Gethin smiled, leaning back into the chair. "He was forced into the position."

"What? By who?"

"After he refused the position of lead protector, I was then asked to fill the position. It was Balgair who asked us both on the day you were born, but I told him I would only take the position if your dad was by my side, as second in command. Balgair agreed, and he forced your dad to take the position as my right hand. But in all honesty" – Gethin smiled as he looked past Tabitha towards the back of the room – "he's always been the true leader of the protectors, maybe the clan. But now, the both of us must stand without him. I tell you this now because I wanted you to know what type of man your dad was, a humble hero of this clan."

Tabitha looked up at Gethin. "Why're you telling me this? I might not have known this story about my dad, but I've always known how great he was."

"I'm telling you now because your dad didn't take his rightful place in the clan. You need to think long and hard about your future. This is the harsh reality of battle and war. This is why there're no female protectors. It's not the true place for any female, no matter what your dad thought."

"Don't the cat and bear races have women in their ranks?" she replied.

"We're not the cats or the bears. What works for some, fails for others. We have women in our hunter ranks that are used as a last resort. When Wikki told me what happened in the forest, you reacted as I thought any woman would have. Wikki assures me it's because of your age and inexperience, but I know it's because you're a female. Your dad told me you might be a protector one day, but you can have a much easier life that would suit any woman. You're beautiful, so you'll have many admirers to choose from when you come of age, so I think you would be more suited to be part of the clan's militia and become a hunter. Besides, the men of our race are naturally stronger, whether you accept it or not."

"Well, men might have the brute force, but us women can be more cunning. And besides, there are men who can't even transform in your ranks, so I think I would have the natural strength over them, and even you."

"That might be true to a degree, but you're the only heir that Llewellyn had after his injury from the battle with the exiled bears. I'm looking out for you now your dad's gone, so even if you pass all your trials with the best results, I'll refuse you a position among the protectors. One way or another, I'll protect you, even if my decision seems harsh. You can have an easy life with a great warrior as your mate and have a family of your own. So think about that life instead."

Tabitha stood up red-faced, clenching her fists and eyes burning with fury. "No, you can't do that. I'm not some bitch you can control."

Gethin folded his arms and replied, "My decision's final. You'll never ascend the ranks of the clan past a hunter, and that's the end of it. I promised Llewellyn years ago, if anything should happen to him, I would look after you and your mam. This is the only way I know how. You're disobedient, and you have a fire within you that needs to be dampened."

Tabitha opened her stance, shouting, "That's unfair, and you decide this a day after my dad's died!"

He took in a slow, deep breath. "It's your dad that would've shaken up the order and traditions of the clan, all for you, and the people would have followed his wishes. But he would've been protecting and guiding you all the way. I'll not make the same sacrifice. You'll know your place in the clan, so I suggest you make your peace with it and move on with your life."

Turning side on to Gethin, slowly lifting her right arm up with a clenched fist, her eyes widened, lips tightened, itching to swing a punch. Then, she heard her father's voice, *Look at the bigger picture.*

Unclenching her fists, her face relaxed, and her arms lowered back to her sides as the fight drained out from her very soul. "I understand, I'm sorry I spoke out of turn."

"I know your dad gave you false hope of ascension in the ranks, but in time you'll understand that this is for the greater good of the clan."

Tabitha, now totally broken, asked permission for the first time in her life, "Can I go and see Wikki at the healers' hut, please?"

"Yes, you can, but get cleaned up first," Gethin ordered.

"Ok."

Lifting a bowl of day-old water from a side table, she slunk away into her room to get cleaned up. As she re-emerged, Gethin looked at her and said, "The ritual will happen tomorrow. I have ceremonial grey robes here for you and Isolde."

"Ok, thank you, Gethin."

"And don't think of me as a bad guy after our conversation. You and your mam will want for nothing, I'll make sure of that."

"That's very kind of you. I'll go to the healers' hut now."

"Don't forget, only there or here. Because your presence will be requested for soon enough."

As she arrived, the door opened, and a healer greeted her, "Hello."

"Hi, is it ok if I see Wikki please?"

The healer looked her up and down. "Yes, come on in."

Tabitha walked in, and to her surprise, she saw Wikki sat up in a chair. "By the look on your face, my dad's talked to you then?" he stated.

"Yeah, he has," Tabitha replied.

Folding his arms, he leaned back in the chair slowly and fumed, "Fuck him, he talks shit anyway."

"Wikki, that's your dad. You can't say that."

"I can, and I will. He's wrong, so don't you believe everything he's told you. He's just threatened, like a lot of wet mutts around here."

"Threatened, by what?" Tabitha asked.

"You. So many of them threatened by a strong woman. Don't you let those wet mutts break you down."

"Maybe your dad's right."

"No he's not. Look, it's too much to take on now, but in time, you'll see I'm right."

"Anyway, how're you feeling? Is your back still hurting?" Tabitha inquired.

"Yeah, it still smarts, but I'll be out of here by the end of the day."

The door flung open, stopping their conversation instantly, with a protector stood in the doorway.

"Excuse me, how very rude of you, there're sick people in here. You could at least knock, protector or not," one of the healers demanded.

"Sorry about that, but we're here to get Tabitha. She's been summoned to the hut of the dead," the protector replied.

"Tabi, I'll see you later or tomorrow," Wikki said.

Tabitha stood up, leaving the hut with the protector without saying anything.

After a short walk, she entered the hut of the dead and saw her mother cleaning her father's head. Welling up with emotion and tears, she approached the lifeless body, standing at her mother's side. She held out her hand, touching her father's head before she withdrew after feeling the cold, damp fur. Tabitha wiped the tears away as she asked, "Mam, why has dad remained in his wolf form and not returned to his normal self?"

"I don't know why, but I saw this when his dad and his brothers were killed by the colossal bear," Isolde replied.

"Colossal bear?"

"Yes, your dad was a young protector then, and I was heavily pregnant with you. Your dad and his brothers were part of the pathfinder's party. They should have waited for the alpha's party to arrive, but foolishly, your granddad ordered the assault on the banished bears."

"Why were they banished from the Northern Peaks?"

Isolde scrunched up her lips, looked at the ceiling and shook her head before replying, "I don't know. All I know is their leader Andrew must have done something horrible because to be banished from the bear's country is very rare, and they probably did it because they couldn't kill him without more bloodshed. Other bears just followed him into his banishment willingly. Well, according to the rumours."

"Why? Was he powerful or something?"

"Bears, when transformed, are normally between six to seven feet tall, you know, about the same size as a wolf. Your dad told me that he was terrified when he saw him at first. He was trapped while his brothers engaged with the pathfinder. He watched them all get ripped apart by Andrew, even killing your granddad with a single strike. According to your dad, Andrew was about fourteen feet tall. That's why he is called a colossal bear. I don't know any more than that."

A familiar voice came from behind, making both Isolde and Tabitha jump. "And he was right. I saw him with my own eyes."

"Oh, you startled me," Isolde replied.

"Sorry I intervened, but I heard you talking about Llewellyn's great battle," Balgair replied.

Tabitha looked at Balgair, asking, "You saw my dad fight?"

"Yes. He was scared at first, like you were with that tenebrous, but something came over him when Andrew shouted something at him. Both your dad and Andrew engaged in single combat. Your dad fought like no other, fearless and determined. He rose up and badly injured Andrew, but with great cost. He was also injured badly, which is why you have no siblings, to put it politely. When Andrew and the bears saw my party advance to them, they retreated and fled to the Neutral Land and were never seen again."

"So my dad beat a colossal bear?"

"Yes, to a degree. But we didn't pursue them because your dad needed help. When he recovered, I asked him to be the leader of the protectors, and he refused through respect and love for the person he called his last brother."

"I didn't know my dad had that sort of strength," Tabitha replied.

"He was my greatest warrior, and that's why everyone in the clan respected your dad without question. But when my pathfinder died, I then appointed my childhood friend to become my next pathfinder. A lot of people in the clan disagreed with my decision and thought your dad better suited for the position. Maybe they were right, but as alpha, my word is final."

Isolde looked at Tabitha and spoke softly, "Your dad didn't want you to know this tale until you were older, but now I think you should know about his true strength."

Balgair took a few steps closer to both of them. "There's also something else that I have only told my pathfinder, so I want you to keep this between us. I didn't just respect your dad because of what he did. Out of the whole clan, he was the only protector under Gethin I would take council from." He turned as he continued, "I'll take my leave now, take as much time as you need, I'll instruct the protector standing guard that you and the other families are not to be disturbed. The passage to the Meadowlands ritual will begin tomorrow at noon."

Balgair left the hut of the dead, leaving all the families of the fallen to grieve privately for their loved ones.

Staring at her father for a few seconds, tears of pride started trickling down her face, and for the first time since her father's death, she gave a little smile. Isolde put her arm around her shoulders, and together, they cried.

Chapter Five

THE MEADOWLANDS RITUAL

As dawn broke, light entered Isolde's room. Rolling over, she stared at the empty space next to her, dressed in a long gown as she found the bed cold without him. Forcing herself from beneath the covers, she went into the dining room to wash her hands and face next to the fireplace. She proceeded to make breakfast for Tabitha, but not herself, as she had no appetite. Tabitha's door opened, alerting Isolde that her daughter was awake.

Looking at her mother preparing food on the table for a few seconds, Tabitha walked in. "I'm not hungry, Mam. Don't worry about making me anything."

"No, you need to eat. You'll need your strength for the day ahead. You don't have to eat it all, but please try and eat something," Isolde replied.

"Ok, Mam, I'll try."

Isolde placed some logs in the fireplace, striking straw with flint to ignite the fire. While the flames started to encompass the fresh logs, she went out to the well not far from their hut, filling a bucket with water. Returning, she poured the water into a small black cauldron containing salt and porridge oats, placing it over the fire. While the porridge cooked, she filled a larger cauldron with water. After a few minutes, she swapped the cauldrons over the fire, took a wooden bowl and spoon from a shelf and piled it to the top with porridge before placing it on the table in front of Tabitha.

Turning to the fire, she stared at the boiling water for a few minutes as she said, "Just eat as much as you can, ok? I'm going to get myself ready."

Isolde filled another bowl with the hot water, retiring to her room. Tabitha struggled to swallow each mouthful of porridge, with anxiety and grief swelling within her.

Emerging from her room in a long grey ceremonial robe, Isolde handed Tabitha a ceremonial grey robe of her own. The embroidery showed impressive craftsmanship, as not many Grey Wolf Clan members cared for fashion. The male ceremonial robes were hooded and plain, similar to the battle robes but smarter and more streamlined on the wearer, used only for mating ceremonies and funeral rituals.

"This is for you. I think Gethin has already told you about wearing it, yesterday."

"Yeah, he told me," Tabitha replied.

"Did he talk to you about anything else yesterday?"

"No, nothing that's important anyway."

"Oh, ok then. I would've thought he would've spoken to you about your dad at least," Isolde frowned.

"He said a few things about him, but not much."

Tabitha grabbed a bowl from the shelf, gathered hot water and went into her room to get ready. Isolde sat down on one of the chairs, staring at Llewellyn's bow and arrows by the front door. Tabitha returned from her room dressed in her ceremonial robe, noticing her mother's gaze fixed on the bow and arrows.

"Are you ok, Mam?" Tabitha inquired.

"I'm fine," Isolde said. "I think it's time."

Another pause in the conversation came before Tabitha asked, "What's time, Mam?"

"Yes, it's time, I know it's a little early, but it's definitely time," she said again.

Isolde walked over to the bow, picking it up. The four-and-a-half-foot longbow was commonly known as a warriors' bow. The wood, engraved with small Celtic symbols, was beautifully encrusted on the tips and handle with steel. Isolde inspected the bow as if it was the first time she had seen it.

"Mam, you're worrying me. What do you mean by it's time?" Tabitha asked again.

Placing the bow back down, she replied, "Time I became a hunter again. I was a hunter before I had you, and I gave my bow to your dad as an apology when we first started to speak. This bow is how me and your dad began courting."

Tabitha's mind eased. "Well, I didn't know that. I think I should've asked sooner, but how did you and Dad get together?"

"Don't worry about it. Not everyone asks because they just accept it like you did, or they're not interested." She smiled as she continued, "He just became a protector, and I was in training to become a hunter. He never noticed me at all, but I noticed him. He was the youngest of his brothers, and all of them could transform, which is really rare in a pack, and even more so that they were all protectors. He was the last one in his family to become one, so I guess he was under a lot of stress and pressure. Anyway, I was practising my arrow training, and I missed a moving target. I heard a wolf yelp in the forest where the arrow went astray, so I went over, and it was your dad. He pulled the arrow out of his rear leg using his mouth, then he changed back into human form, and he was naked."

Cocking her head back, Tabitha scrunched up her face and interrupted, "Mam, please don't, you can leave that type of detail out. I don't want to imagine Dad naked."

Isolde snorted. "Ok, I won't talk about that. Your dad started shouting at me, calling me stupid and telling me 'You should learn how to fire a bow before hitting moving targets'. You know, he was just in a rage. So I told him I did hit a moving target, I hit you, didn't I? Well, he went all red and got angrier, and I started laughing in his face."

"What? What did Dad do after that?"

"I can't remember exactly what he said because I was laughing. Anyway, he came up to me shouting, and I told him, 'Don't shout in my face'. He didn't listen, so with the bow, I hit him across the head, then I did a twirly thingy and hit his legs from under him with the bow. He fell to the floor, and I just panicked and ran away, but your dad didn't follow. I thought I was in so much trouble because I struck a protector. I thought my final trial would have been stopped, and I was going into the hole for what I did."

Tabitha chuckled. "Mam, Dad was right when he always called you trouble."

"Ha. Maybe he was onto something. Two weeks later, I became a hunter with a few others, so you know, a big feast and all that. Your dad was sat opposite me during the feast, so we started talking, and we just hit it off. He was still a bit pissed off at me for firing an arrow into his leg and hitting him. At the end of the night, I gave him my bow as an apology and thought nothing more of it. The next day he was outside my hut with my bow."

"What did he do?"

Isolde looked up to the ceiling. "The conversation went a bit like this..."

Loud bangs erupted from the door, as a young Isolde opened it and saw the young Llewellyn in the doorway holding the bow.

"What're you doing here?" Isolde asked.

"I'm returning the bow," Llewellyn replied.

"But I gave it to you as an apology."

"Well, it's not good enough."

Isolde's lips tightened and tucked into her teeth, face turning red as her eyes opened wide. "What! That's a fine bow, and if you return it, I'll shoot your other leg, you ungrateful git!"

Llewellyn chuckled, holding his left hand out. "Ok, ok, please calm down. I didn't mean it that way. It's a nice bow, but I want more than a bit of wood and metal."

"Yeah, you'll get my fist in your face if you're not careful. Who the fuck do you think you are?" Isolde snapped.

Staring at her with a smirk, he complimented, "Did you know you look very beautiful when you're mad?"

Starting to blush, her angry face turned into a frown. "Shut up."

"Well, look, I just thought if I give you the bow back, you must remain with the bow, and therefore me, if I don't let you keep it."

"What's your game? Are you trying to court me or something?"

"Yes, I am. I've never met a woman like you, so that makes me want you even more," Llewellyn replied.

"What? So I'm some sort of prize now, am I?" Isolde spat, folding her arms.

"Well, if that's what you think, then that's fine because you'll be my prize."

Stretching out her right arm, she snatched the bow out of his hand and said, "You'd better come back in about an hour because I'm not ready to go out yet."

Before Llewellyn had a chance to reply, she slammed the door in his face, turning around with the biggest smile and started to bounce with every step, singing in an upbeat tone before she gave a little scream of excitement.

With a grin, she looked down from the ceiling. "Your dad was always the smooth talker. He pissed my dad off to no end though."

A knock on the door disturbed the moment they were having, so Isolde got up and answered it.

Gethin stood in front of her and only spoke two words that broke their hearts again. "It's time."

Isolde's grin faded as she looked down. "Ok."

Tabitha heard what Gethin had said, so she got up, and they left the hut together.

Outside the town stood seven wooden rectangular pyres, laced with straw for the burning of the bodies. Tabitha and Isolde were escorted to the pyre at the front. From the hut of the dead, protectors carried the bodies of the fallen through the town and towards the pyres led by Balgair, Gus and Quinn. They placed the fallen on top of the pyres, with Llewellyn being the last, as priests stopped in front of each one, muttering their prayers.

Balgair addressed the people gathered to pay their respects. "We're here today to honour our fallen warriors that protected us from the evil that invaded our lands. These protectors will ascend to the Meadowlands to meet their ancestors for the great hunt. These are dark times to lose so many in a short space of time, but their sacrifices will never be forgotten."

Staring at her father's body, Tabitha mumbled, "I'm sorry for being so weak. I promise I'll never let that happen again."

Shedding a few tears, Isolde held her hand. Gus started to light the pyres with a lit torch from the rear, leaving Llewellyn until last. Balgair stood next to Llewellyn's body with a torch of his own and lit the pyre; it was deemed a high honour for any alpha to personally light one. As the straw ignited, the flames weaved between the logs, rising higher and higher. The smoke shrouded Llewellyn's body, making it hard for anyone to see him.

"Llewellyn was a great warrior, a great leader among our protectors, and he'll always be remembered. He'll be survived on this mortal realm by his mate, Isolde, and his daughter, Tabitha. He's the last of his name, being the last male of his pack. Farewell, Llewellyn Greyclaw," Balgair stated.

As was the custom, the alpha started to sing, with everyone else joining in as the bodies burned. This folk song passed down through generations would be used by all the wolf clans in times of sorrow and loss, and was named the song of the fallen.

Song of the fallen.

I

End of night,
Start of day,
We will always search for prey.

II

They will stand,
They will fight,
They will defend our lands with might.

III

The brave shall strive,
Valour runs free,
Always to be remembered in history.

IV

Some will rise,
Some shall fall,
They will always answer the call.

V

Their spirits free to join the hunt,
With the Great Wolf,
In the Meadowlands.

Smoke and fire engulfed the bodies as Tabitha and Isolde stared into the flames of Llewellyn's pyre. Suddenly, a hand appeared on Tabitha's shoulder, and she broke her gaze to see Wikki stood behind her. Without any words, she grabbed him, and they just held one another tightly in a warm embrace. The people began to return to the town while the bodies burned, as the smell of burning flesh and fur was not a pleasant one. A small feast would be held in the town centre as part of the wake, if anyone wanted to honour and share stories of the fallen. Tabitha and Wikki stuck together, with her telling him the tale of how her mother and father started courting, as Gethin and Isolde liaised with each other. "Thanks for keeping an eye on Tabitha yesterday."

"It's no problem. I had to speak with her anyway," Gethin replied.

Isolde asked, "What about? Because she said you didn't tell her anything important."

"You and your daughter will want for nothing was one of the points I made, because I know Llewellyn would have done the same for my family."

"Oh, that's very kind of you, but we'll be fine. Was there anything else you talked to her about?" Isolde inquired.

Overhearing their conversation, Tabitha intervened, "Mam, there's no need to worry. It was nothing important."

"If that's the case, why try to hide whatever it is from me?" Isolde frowned.

Tabitha looked at the ground and hunched her back.

"I know you and Llewellyn agreed that if your daughter was good enough, then she could become a protector," Gethin replied.

"We talked about it, yeah, but no decision was made final," Isolde stated.

"Years ago, Llewellyn and myself made a pact, and we vowed to protect each other's families if either of us fell."

"Yes, I'm also aware of that because you two were like brothers."

Gethin took in a sharp, deep breath. "I've made a decision to stop your daughter from ever ascending above the rank of hunter, to protect her, of course, and to keep our clan's traditions."

Without hesitation, Isolde clenched her fist and, with great speed, punched Gethin in the mouth. The force of the punch split his bottom lip open, making him lose his balance and fall backwards onto the ground, landing on his arse while holding his mouth.

"Listen here, you wet mutt. We're the Greyclaw pack. We don't need charity or protection. We can fend for ourselves. You might stop my daughter from ascending the ranks, but trust me, if she wishes to, she'll become a great warrior with or without your so-called blessing. Don't ever speak to me or my daughter again," Isolde snapped.

Tabitha and Wikki stood wide-eyed with open mouths, in disbelief of what just happened. Still on the floor, Gethin wiped the blood from his bottom lip before he got up slowly. His face flushed as he licked the returning blood off his lip. "Me and Llewellyn always saw eye to eye, but for the first time, we didn't on this matter. This is my final word as the lead protector. I'll not have any female in our ranks. If you wish to cut contact with me and fend for yourselves, then that's your choice. I'll not go against your wishes. But know this; I'm not your enemy. The matter of having a woman in our ranks causes more complications than you know."

Without waiting for a reply, he turned away and walked off, bringing his hand back up to his bleeding lip. With a grin on his face, Wikki looked at Isolde, and his face dropped, wondering if he was going to be cut off from his second family.

"Don't worry, Wikki, you'll always be like a son to me, and you're always welcome into our home," Isolde declared.

"Izzy, you can come around mine if you do that to my dad again," Wikki replied, as they began to laugh together.

As good as it was to feel normal for a brief time, the laughter died down as reality started to sink in again.

"I think that's enough for today. It's time for me to go home now before someone else gets hurt or I do something I regret. Tabitha, come home when you're ready. And don't worry about his words. He's a boar-headed fool that's trapped in the past. I'll see you soon, Wikki."

"Ok, Mam."

"Goodbye, Izzy."

So she could mourn alone, Isolde took her leave and walked off back to her hut. Tabitha watched her mother disappear into the crowd and noticed a young girl staring at Wikki. She must have been around 15 years old, because she was in the training group below her.

"Wikki?" Tabitha said inquisitively.

"What's up?"

"I think you have an admirer over there."

Tabitha nodded slightly towards the young girl's direction so she would not notice the gesture, but Wikki being as subtle as a blacksmith pounding hot steel, spun around and caught the gaze of the young girl. Noticing his movements, the girl went bright red, spun around quickly and shot into the crowd to vanish from his sight.

"Why don't you go and talk to her? I think her name's Arwyn or something like that."

He licked his bottom lip, sucked it in and held it there with his teeth, before replying, "I think it's too soon for me to be courting. I have so much to prepare for, so I definitely don't have time for any distractions. I know you mean well, and you always look out for me, but when I'm ready, I'll walk down that path alone."

Tabitha grinned, "I understand."

Wikki looked around at the crowd and asked, "Have you seen Ren? He wasn't at the ritual today."

From behind them, Gus intervened in the conversation. "He went... He went against Balgair's wishes. And, and, has gone to our home village to do his own investigations. Investigations about the tenebrous gaining entry into our lands."

From sight and smell, Tabitha noticed Gus was intoxicated, as she asked, "What? I don't get why he'd investigate when you already have."

Gus gazed past them both with one eye closed, observing the crowd behind, slightly swaying side to side, as he slurred, "If he... If he finds out. Someone... Someone will suffer the consequences. And, and, it can cause trouble."

Before Tabitha or Wikki could follow that statement, Gus stumbled between the pair of them, staggering into the crowd.

They both looked at each other for a few seconds before Tabitha stated, "He knows something, and he's not telling us."

Wikki held Tabitha by the shoulders and replied, "He probably does, but we can't just jump to conclusions."

Tabitha lifted her arms inside of his, hitting him away from her in a swift singular motion. Her eyes widened with a wild look, face reddening as her lips tightened. "My dad's dead. I want to know why if he knows." Watching him almost disappearing into the crowd, she shouted, "Gus! What do you know? Tell me!"

Wikki grabbed Tabitha from behind, lifted and swung her around so she faced the other direction. Gus, too intoxicated to notice, didn't hear her and continued on his way.

"Tabi, stop. He's the pathfinder, and you must not speak out of turn to him. Please, just leave it to Ren. If there's an answer, he'll find it."

Wikki released his arms and, without another word spoken, she walked home. As he watched her disappear into the crowd, his gut feeling told him there was something underpinning what Gus had said.

Three nights later, two protectors patrolling the town spotted something. As the shadows got closer, a protector challenged them. “Halt. Now advance to be recognised.”

As the shadows emerged, the protector asked, “Ren, is that you?”

Transforming back to a human, Ren replied, “Yes, and I’ve come back from Wolf’s Fang with a protector who’ll be held in custody until tomorrow. I suggest you get the manacles to restrain him.”

Afon transformed and protested, “There’s no need for manacles, I’ve come willingly. Unless you want to be up all night watching me, I suppose.”

“No, I won’t, pal. I’ll need my rest for your trial tomorrow at the alpha’s hut. I’ll present the evidence I gathered from your village before I was led to you. Now, cuff him.”

The manacles were a very unpleasant tool used to confine criminals. An iron ring around the neck, waist, ankles and wrists, all connected together by iron chains. Not only did they restrict the movement of the wearer, but they also had large iron spikes towards the front of the neck, smaller spikes around the circumference of the wrists and ankles with longer iron spikes at the front of the waist covering the abdomen. The manacles’ main purpose was to stop any criminals from changing into a wolf to break free, and if they tried, they would not live for long, if at all. One of the protectors put the manacles on Afon, and they escorted him to the prisoners’ hut.

“Don’t any of you tell anyone of his presence here, I’ll inform the alpha of his arrival myself. Is that understood?” Ren commanded.

"Yes, we understand. We'll get ourselves relief and guard the prisoner for you," one of the protectors replied.

Anxious, Afon demanded an explanation. "Ren, what's the meaning of this, you bastard? When my uncle releases me, I'll make sure you'll answer for this."

Ren gave a smirk and replied, "We'll see what tomorrow brings then, won't we?"

With Afon escorted away, Ren disappeared back to his hut, resting for the next day.

Morning had already broken, and the sun shone brightly in the clear purple sky. Ren realised he had slept later than intended, bolting out of bed and scrambling his clothes on. He left his hut on a direct course to the alpha's hut, but on his approach, he noticed that there was already a mass of the town's people around the alpha's pavilion. He knew the trial had already started without him, so he ran the rest of the way. Pushing his way past the crowd, he saw all the clan leaders sat in their respective seats within the pavilion, and Afon unshackled in front of the leaders of the clan. Then, he noticed just past Afon at the front of the crowd stood Isolde and Tabitha.

Gus was midsentence on Ren's arrival. "—have come to a decision with the confession you have given us here today, and we have chosen to strip you of your rank and retrain you to pass the protector's trial in the near future."

Ren broke rank of the town's people and thundered, "No! A confession! You're full of shit, Afon! I'm the one that brought him here from his village, and I've got evidence and a witness that confessed to me, he was drunk and fell asleep at his post!"

Gus stood up and shouted back, “We’ve listened to this man’s confession, and the alpha has ruled his sentencing accordingly. So stand down, Protector!”

Tabitha took two steps forward, shaking in a rage and roared, “Is this true? Is this why my dad died; because you was drunk, you wet mutt?”

Gus turned to Tabitha, demanding, “Hold your tongue, little girl!”

“No, Gus, she should know. The only reason you’re so lenient towards Afon is because you and Balgair come from Wolf’s Fang, and he’s your nephew. Isn’t he, Balgair?” Ren spat, with anger burning in his eyes.

Gus opened his mouth, but Balgair interrupted him. “Yes, he’s my dead sister’s son. But this trial has been concluded. If you were here earlier or you had someone inform me of his arrival last night, we would have considered your evidence. But you didn’t, so the judgement has now been passed. I’m the alpha of the grey wolves, so my decision is final, Protector.”

Tabitha’s eyes welled up with the injustice she witnessed before her. Ren looked across at her, seeing her devastation and stated, “I’ve been at your side for some time now, Balgair, and you think you can breathe easy with Llewellyn gone.”

Tabitha looked up with her teary eyes as Isolde looked back and forth at both of them arguing. Taken off guard by what Ren said, Balgair stood up from his chair and asked, “What’re you talking about, boy?”

“You know exactly what I’m talking about, old man. You feared Llewellyn for as long as I’ve known you, and I know why. He was stronger than you in every way, and I bet you have feared him since he fought that colossal bear about sixteen years ago. Yeah, that’s right” – taking a pace forward, he pointed his finger at him – “I know. That’s why you tried to give him the lead protector’s position, and when he refused, you palmed it off to

Gethin in the hope he would have some sort of position to keep himself occupied. But in the council meetings, it was Llewellyn that called the shots, making you look like the so-called great leader," Ren sneered.

"Listen, boy, you're walking a fine line with me, and if you wish to remain in my party, I would hold your tongue," Balgair demanded.

"Not this time. You've abused your position again and spat on the memories of our brave fallen. It's time. I challenge you for the position of alpha in front of the whole town."

Eyes widening at the shock of someone challenging the alpha, Tabitha had only heard stories, but Ren was very young to be a challenger.

Balgair smiled at the young protector and responded, "You might be right about Llewellyn, boy. But I'd think long and hard about what you just said. Because if you lose a challenge against me, you'll be stripped of your rank and position by my side. Is that what you want?"

Ren looked directly into Balgair's eyes and declared, "I offer a challenge!"

"So be it, boy. Now, I'll give you your final lesson you'll ever have off me. Humility and pain."

Chapter Six

THE GREY WOLF ALPHA

Balgair leapt forward, transforming into a wolf, leaving nothing but ripped clothes on the steps of the pavilion as he charged at Ren. As he transformed, Ren was unable to counter Balgair's charge; due to his speed, hitting him with so much force, he flew through the air before crashing into the ground with a loud thud eight metres away, facing the opposite direction. The town's people dispersed from their newfound battleground, fleeing between the huts so they could still see the fight before them.

Getting to his feet, Balgair mounted Ren's body from behind, biting down hard on the scruff of his neck. Ren's legs buckled to the ground from the weight of his adversary. Shaking his head back and forth, Balgair's teeth tore the flesh on Ren's scruff, but even with his attacker's body weight shifting side to side, Ren recovered his balance. With the strength in his legs, Ren sprung his body upward, using a little bit more power in his front legs to throw them both onto their backs. This manoeuvre caused him to land on top of Balgair, knocking the wind from the alpha's lungs and causing his bite to loosen.

"Come on, Balgair, don't let that boy make a fool of you!" Gus shouted.

Ren rolled hard to his right, forcing Balgair to release the scruff of his neck as Ren quickly recovered to his feet. Balgair quickly rolled and stood up to face off against his challenger, as Ren quickly went on the offensive, attacking low. Vaulting upward, Balgair withdrew his front legs in the air, keeping his rear paws firmly on the ground, causing Ren to miss his target. Spearing his head into Ren's scruff again, he pushed him back down to the ground, puncturing his flesh.

With Ren displaying lack of combat experience, the people assumed Balgair had the advantage, but Ren had a trump card to use against him—his youth. Superior agility, alongside abnormal strength from his intense personal training, gave him an edge. Moving forward slightly, Ren placed his head under the alpha's left leg. Pushing up with all of his might, he lifted Balgair off the ground, sacrificing the flesh of his scruff between his rival's fangs.

Thrusting upwards at an angle brought Balgair off balance. Ren used his front paws to push Balgair away from him, with the old wolf crashing to the ground, and rolling over in the process. Even though Ren's neck was wounded and bleeding, it did not slow his attacks down in any way or form as he pounced forward and bit deep into Balgair's scruff. Ren moved his body side on with his adversary, and with all of his strength and might, he twisted his head to the left, pulling Balgair off the ground.

"By the Great Wolf, that's impossible!" a voice shouted from the crowd.

With teeth tearing into Balgair's flesh as he rotated and lifted him through the air, Ren released his grip, throwing the alpha headfirst into a hut five metres away, creating a large crack vertically up the wall on impact. A small blood splatter flicked up the wall as Balgair his head, with his body slamming into the hut with a loud thud. Sliding down and crumpling onto the ground, Balgair became dazed.

"Get up, Balgair, and finish this!" Gus bellowed.

Ren stood composed, snarling and displaying his teeth with the tip of his tongue in the centre, as his opponent scrambled to his feet to face him. Balgair responded in kind, but he had lost his left canine fang and a small tooth next to it. With blood dripping from his mouth, the open air stung his gums where his teeth had been. Ren took the offensive again by attacking head-on, Balgair met the challenge. As a mild thud was heard by the town's people from the sheer force of these warriors colliding, Balgair became overpowered by Ren's strength, pushed backwards by a superior fighter, eyes widening from fear, knowing he had lost the challenge at this moment. Before landing on the ground, Ren had put his jaws around the front of his neck. This move marked the death of any wolf, being the most vulnerable point on their bodies, as they could not counter this sort of attack in any way. Gripping his throat tightly, Ren speared his body downward, smashing Balgair's head into the dirt.

Quinn ran closer to get a better view, seeing Balgair on his back with fear illuminating his eyes. With the old wolf's front legs bent over, his paws became limp, showing no signs of resistance. The peacekeeper could see that all of the fight had left his body, so he declared, "The challenge is won!"

At that very moment, Balgair's life was in Ren's hands. He released the neck and stood over his opponent, staring him down. Balgair laid his head back, exposing his neck, and turned away, displaying his submission to the grey wolves' new alpha.

"It is done! Now show respect for your new alpha, Ren Greyfang!" Quinn shouted to the town's people.

With this declaration, the crowd shouted and screamed as some of the adults who could transform turned into wolves and howled, as was tradition with the rise of a new alpha.

Without shame, Ren turned back into a human and walked to the alpha's pavilion naked, with blood trickling down his back from the wounds on the back of his neck. Lowering his head, Gus stumbled off the pavilion, almost falling down the steps before pacing backwards, unable to look his new alpha in the eyes.

Ren stared at Gus as he ascended the steps of the pavilion, walking on the torn clothes Balgair had worn before transforming. Turning his head, Ren gazed at the alpha's seat for a few seconds before Quinn came behind him, placing a battle robe over his shoulders as he said, "Here you go, Alpha. You can cover yourself with this so you can address the people if you wish. After that, I recommend you go to the healers' hut and get your neck cleaned up."

Placing his arms through the robe's sleeves, Ren overlapped each side and used the four material ties to make two knots; one around his waist and one across his chest. He turned around and took a step backwards, lowering himself into his chair, as Quinn remained on his feet next to him.

"Balgair, stand before me," Ren demanded.

Still in wolf form, Balgair had not moved, and was still wondering how the young wolf had got the best of him. Rolling over off his back, he stood up and walked towards him with his head hung in shame, presenting himself in front of his new alpha before lowering his head further.

"I'd like you to serve as my pathfinder, because you have experience of ruling this clan. Your council would be welcomed if you accept the position."

Balgair transformed back into a human and looked up. With blood trickling out of his mouth, he bowed his head and gave the wolves' greeting. As he replied, blood spat out of his mouth, landing on his chin and chest. "Alpha."

"Good. Now go to the healers' hut and get your wounds seen to."

Bowing his head again, he heeded his alpha's command, retiring to the healers' hut. The crowd gathered back around the pavilion, ready to be addressed by the new grey wolf alpha.

"Now, Afon. We come to the matter of your crime and punishment."

Afon's eyes squinted, filling with tears as he knew real punishment was to come.

"This is my judgement and sentence. Because of your incompetence and lack of responsibility, you caused many deaths, even if it was indirectly. You're stripped of your rank as protector, and you'll be shackled and placed into a hole for two months."

The holes were the worst prisons in the West Plains. Naked, shackled prisoners would be placed into a dug hole no more than four metres in diameter and three metres deep, completely lined with stone with open iron fencing above them that would be locked. The fencing over the holes left prisoners exposed to all of the elements with nothing but a thin blanket for protection. And, to top it all off, the prisoners were kept alive with nothing but dry bread and water.

"Please no, don't do this, Ren!" Afon pleaded.

"Through your incompetence, we lost great warriors and the strongest wolf of our clan. You're lucky I haven't sentenced you to death or banished you to the Eastern Wastes. But, if you like, I can change your punishment."

Two protectors stripped him naked, ready to place the manacles on him. Afon thought about it for a second and realised he had got off lightly compared to the latter of the punishments, and he did not speak out of turn or plead again.

The protectors put the manacles on him and led him away to the hole, where he would carry out his long, lonely sentence.

"Gus, stand before me," Ren commanded.

Shuffling to the front of the pavilion, Gus was unable to look at his new alpha through fear and shame.

"You've got a part in this crime as well, pal, by trying to cover up this matter. You'll retain your rank as a protector because of your bond with my pathfinder, but I think two weeks in the hole will be enough time to think about your actions."

Expecting a reply from him, one did not come, as Gus kept his eyes to the ground. Instead, he removed his own clothes, knowing that his new alpha was in the right and that he was very fortunate not being more severely punished. Two protectors placed manacles on him, and without a protector touching him, he made his own way to the hole. Walking past the crowd, he briefly stopped, looked over to Tabitha and Isolde and uttered only two words he could think of before continuing on his way. "I'm sorry."

Ren stood up from his chair to address his people. "Everyone, you've witnessed what's happened here before your own eyes. I'm your new alpha, so before I begin, I'll ask you all this one question, is there anyone who wants to challenge me right now for my position?"

Not one sound could be heard from the people of the town, only a mild breeze and the birds chirping in the distance.

"Now that's out of the way. I declare to all of you, if you stick to the old ways and conduct yourselves with honour and respect, you'll receive my respect. But if you cross me, you'll find from now on I'll come down on you hard, with harsher punishments. I've chosen my pathfinder, and in time, I'll assemble my own fighting party, with protectors that I'll choose. So, until that time, go about your daily lives."

Still sat in his chair, Gethin asked, "Ren, there's a matter that involved Llewellyn's daughter. I'm asking, is the agreement that I had with Balgair still honoured?"

Tabitha looked at Ren with intensity, hoping that he would overrule Gethin's decision stopping her from becoming more than a hunter in the future.

Ren looked at him and replied, "I know of what you speak, and I honour the old ways, so your agreement still stands with me."

Her lips tightened, eyes squinting as her head dropped. Her world had just got a little smaller, and there was nothing she could do about it, as Tabitha's soul had been crushed, finally understanding the world of the wolves was a male-dominated one.

"Quinn, before I go to the healers' hut, I recommend you get your party together and prepare for your journey to the other clans, to tell them of my uprising. You'll leave tomorrow."

Quinn bowed his head and replied, "As you wish, Alpha."

Ren descended the steps of the alpha's pavilion and made his way to the healers' hut, overhearing comments from the crowd as he walked away from them. The people were still stunned by what had happened, but he was not surprised by the way they were talking. One comment repeated over and over because of his previous exploits, giving him his new title—Ren the Unbeaten.

Because the peacekeeper had important duties to perform the next day, the celebration for the new alpha would be postponed until the peacekeeper returned from informing the other clans.

The crowd went about their daily lives but, as they dispersed, one person remained. Isolde's hands appeared on Tabitha's shoulders from behind. "Let's go home. There's something I must give you."

Back at the hut, Isolde went straight to her room and came back out after two minutes, presenting Tabitha with an item wrapped in a cloth. She opened it up and looked up at her mother with a faint smile and tears in her eyes.

"It was your dad's, and I know he would've wanted you to have it," Isolde said.

Tabitha hugged her mother tightly. "Thanks, Mam. I'll always wear it."

Inside the cloth was a strap made from a very rare material called shrompy weed. It would take a skilled person months to strip the weed and use its fibres to construct such an item. Because the fibres of the shrompy weed had elastic properties, a transformed person could keep a knife or other weapon attached to their body, unlike leather or other materials that would constrict the wearer or snap, making these the most expensive items in the West Plains.

At the healers' hut, Balgair was already having his wounds and mouth tended to. The only healer working that day had let her party have some downtime after the tenebrous attack a few days earlier. She was young, but she had made her mark on the West Plains by claiming the reputation of being the best healer of all the clans, making her the lead healer at only 26 years old. Cheekbones defined the shape of her face, complimented with beautiful blue eyes and full red lips, with a perfect glossy blonde bob atop her head.

"I'm sorry, there's no way I can repair the damage done to your teeth, Balgair, but I can burn your gums to stop the bleeding," Aelish said.

Balgair nodded slightly, opening his mouth wide with the blood dripping from where his teeth had been. Aelish placed a small leather block at the back of his mouth then took a small, red hot metal rod from the fireplace.

"Ok, are you ready? Because this will hurt, a lot," she stated, with the hot metal rod inches from his mouth.

"Uh ha," he replied, clamping his eyes shut while shaking.

"Ok, try not to bite down on the leather too hard, or you'll damage your back teeth as well."

She grabbed the back of his head firmly and moved the rod quickly onto the open wound, pushing upwards on the gums for a few seconds, which felt like an eternity to Balgair.

"Arrrggghhh!"

Pulling the bar away, the wounds blackened from the dried blood, and the gums turned bright white from burning into the healthy parts. Balgair pulled away and held his mouth, still making sounds of anguish.

"Now, you'll need to swill your mouth several times a day with salt water to prevent infection. I'll clean up your neck and dress your wounds now," Aelish told him.

Walking over to the fireplace, she poured hot salt water from a large metal pot into a bowl and placed it on the table next to Balgair. She picked up a dry, clean cloth ready to cleanse the wounds. To both their surprise, the front door swung open, and Ren entered the hut uninvited, closing the door behind him. Aelish exhaled a short, sharp breath, clenching the dry rag in her hand for a second, before throwing it into the bowl of water. Ren stopped instantly, feeling the anger from his healer.

"How dare you! You might be the new alpha of the clan, but I'm the alpha in here, so you will show some respect and knock before entering in the future. Do you understand me?" Aelish commanded.

Ren's eyes widened, and, to Balgair's surprise, he stood to attention.

"I'm waiting. Do you understand what I just said?" Aelish asked.

"Yes, I apologise for any disrespect I've caused," Ren replied, giving the wolves' greeting.

Aelish walked over to the fireplace, picked up another chair and placed it in front of Balgair. "Here, you can sit there, so I don't have to walk around the whole hut, and I can keep an eye on the both of you," she explained.

Ren sat down as Balgair dipped his head down. He looked at the top of his head, wondering what was going on inside it for a few seconds, before sitting back and folding his arms. "You're my pathfinder now, so you'll have to look and talk to me at some point. So, it might as well be now because we'll be here a short while, and I hate silence."

Balgair lifted his head and looked at Ren; his speech was impaired by his missing teeth, which caused him to have a prominent whistle that became dominant with certain words. "What is it you want to talk about, Alpha?"

Ren smirked as he looked off to the right to contain his laughter. Then, he leaned forward and looked back at him. "My name's Ren, so use it when there ain't no formal duties to comply with. Look, you were my mentor, and you still have my respect, but not as much as I had for you before this day."

"Yes, winning will make you lose respect for the loser, I suppose."

"No, Balgair. The way you tried to cover for your nephew. I lost respect for you when you were going to let him off with a slap on the wrist. You know your decision was wrong deep down."

"I guess it was. Well, I paid the price for my actions."

"Yes, you have."

Balgair turned to Aelish and asked, "Do you think you can treat the alpha first because he'll have duties to perform, and his peacekeeper will want a private word with him?"

Aelish looked at him and huffed, "Fine. Ren, head down so I can see your wounds and clean them."

From behind, she started to bundle his matted, bloodstained hair into her hands, forming a ponytail. She reached into her pocket, pulling out a small, thin piece of string and proceeded to tie up his hair. After she was done, she placed the ponytail over his right shoulder. "Move your head forward and hold that, don't let it go so I can see what I'm doing, please," Aelish ordered.

Ren dipped his head forward, holding his ponytail as he carried on talking to Balgair. "I want us to be close because I'll rely on you for advice, now Llewellyn's no longer with us."

"You admired Llewellyn then, I'm guessing?"

"Yes. He had a true leader's mind, and he was a good man."

"You say that as if you knew him well, but you hardly knew each other."

"He might not have known me, but I knew of him, thanks to Gus and his tales of that colossal bear, Andrew is it?"

Balgair swallowed hard. "Yes. He was a brave man, braver than me because I was too afraid to pursue Andrew. I used Llewellyn's injuries as an excuse to let him go."

"Anyway, did he talk to you about his daughter?" Ren inquired.

"Yes, something like she could be the first female protector, but that was just his excitement. I'm not sure if she's as good as he made out, but I'm glad Gethin has chosen to stop her."

"Hmm, so more than one defeat today."

“No, it’s more complicated than that. You know the other clans would hear about a woman in the ranks, and not only that, what if she was better than most of our brothers, or even the best. The other clans would see that as weakness and possibly attack our clan, united together for rumours of weakness and breaking our traditions.”

“I assumed that to be the reason, which is why I agreed with Gethin. But, in the future, we could look into it further, maybe?”

Balgair shook his head and replied, “No, there’s nothing to look into. Look, you were right out there.”

Ren looked up with one eyebrow raised, and then from behind him, they heard a sigh. “Head down, Ren, I’m trying to clean your wounds,” Aelish huffed.

Disgruntled, she pushed his head back down as Balgair continued with his explanation. “I was afraid of Llewellyn, and he was the silent alpha, there’s no denying that. But this business with Tabitha becoming a protector is the stupidest thing I ever heard him say. He never groomed her to be like a son, he just let her become her own person, and he’s the greatest dad I know of for that. But as I’ve explained, he would have caused chaos with this decision. There’s only one reason I think he wanted this after he saw her potential on her hunting trial. It’s because he didn’t have a son, and he couldn’t have any more children.”

Ren smiled, “Mmm, maybe. But he might have pushed for it because he wanted her to fulfil her potential, or maybe it’s just because he loved her.”

“You could be right, but my thoughts are clear on this matter, and whatever you think, my answer will always be no, for the good of the clan.”

“I understand where you’re coming from, so that’s the end of that matter. We’ll speak of it no more.”

Aelish intervened in the conversation. "Ren, I'll have to suture some of your wounds before I dress them."

"As you wish, Healer," Ren replied.

"So, what of Gus?" Balgair asked.

"His time in the hole will help him reflect on what he's caused. After his time there, he'll be sent back to your home village, and he'll continue his days there as a protector. He will not be part of your party, is that understood? If I'm to lead the clan my way, I must remove one of the old leaders permanently from a position of power and influence."

"I understand. You're already wiser than I thought. You'll make a fine alpha."

At that moment, Ren realised that Balgair didn't just respect him, but had now started to admire him. As Aelish sutured his wounds, his face did not even flicker with any discomfort.

"I'm glad you two can see eye to eye. I think, with you two in charge of the clan, we'll have nothing to fear," Aelish smiled.

After five minutes, Aelish had finished closing Ren's neck wounds up. "I'm done now. Keep your neck clean and try to avoid turning into wolf form or you'll rip the stitches out," Aelish advised.

"Ok, Healer, I will. Thank you for your time and care. Balgair, I'll see you tomorrow. I think I need some rest now," Ren replied.

As he exited the hut, Balgair called out. "It hurts, you know."

"What, Balgair? Your wounds?" Ren asked.

"No. Losing your title as alpha. You'll come to know what I feel in time when a new alpha rises, no matter how old you become or how ready you think you are to pass the mantle, it'll hurt like nothing else."

Balgair lowered his head so Aelish could tend to his wounds. Ren's eyes lowered for a few seconds before he exited the healers' hut. Reflecting on what Balgair had said, he knew it to be true because, at that moment, he felt quite the opposite.

Early the next day, Tabitha woke in a sweat, reliving the horror of her father's death. Gasping for air, she sat up quickly and looked around the room. Staring hard at the bottom of the bed, a tear escaped her eye. As her breathing recovered, a wild knock from the front door broke her trance from the foot of the bed. Removing her bedroll from her legs, she rolled out of bed and got dressed, hearing the loud knocking on the door again. Exiting her room, she looked around and called out, "Mam?"

When there was no reply, she knew her mother had left the hut. The door banged again, and she opened it, finding Wikki stood in the doorway. "Tabi, come with me."

"What's up?" she replied.

"Come on, I'll explain when we get there."

Tabitha frowned at Wikki as he turned and walked away. Closing the door, she followed. Wikki guided her into the forest, stopping where Llewellyn had fallen. Tabitha's chest tightened and her eyes began filling with tears. "Why have you brought me here?"

"Because you...we need this." Wikki turned back around and stared hard at the site of battle. "If we let our fears control us, then we've lost."

Tabitha walked forward as Wikki turned to face her again. "I don't get what you mean."

"You will. Now, defend yourself," Wikki spat, unsheathing his hunters' knife.

Lunging forward, he swung his knife towards her. Tabitha jumped back, dodging his attack while shouting, "What the fuck are you doing?"

Wikki took a fighting stance and replied, "Teaching you a lesson."

Advancing again while thrusting his blade forward, she sidestepped and grabbed his arm, pulling the knife from his hand, tossing it to one side. He grabbed her waist and picked her up, throwing her to the ground. As she looked up at him, he stopped his assault.

"So this is it, is it? You're just gonna give up like this, become a bitch and fall in line," Wikki spat.

"What?"

"Your dad knew you were better than this, and now you've been denied to ascend the ranks, so you're just gonna submit. That's not the Tabi I know. Now, fight back!"

Wikki dived down on Tabitha, pinning her to the ground, slapping her face twice. With gritted teeth, she grabbed his arms, brought her legs forward and wrapped them around his neck, pulling him to the ground. Pain surged through his back from his injuries as both of them scrambled to their feet. Smiling, he held his hand out, ending the scuffle. She knew he was holding back, but he had never attacked her before.

Red-faced, Tabitha screamed, "What the fuck was all that about?"

"You needed some tough love, and it was up to me to give it to you. Also, without your dad around, you need to be able to defend yourself now," Wikki replied.

"What?"

"Look, I know you have your mam, and even though I look at you like my little sister, we will start to drift apart. We won't be strangers, but I'm about to do my final trial and become a protector. That means I'll be away training a lot, so maybe I can make my dad proud one day, even if he does love Gibbi the most. I will always be there for you to some degree, but now" – Wikki looked deeper into the forest – "you must stand on your own four feet. The fight that happened here, there's something deeper behind it, I just know it. Hopefully, I'm wrong, but it could be the beginning of something darker."

Looking at her feet, she mumbled, "I think you might be right, but what can I do about it?"

"Rise up, Tabi. Your dad knew there was more to you, and so do I. If there's anything I've learned from this, it's this. Male, female, it doesn't matter because, to the evil and wicked, we are all prey to them. If you want to wallow in your self-pity, then go ahead. But I know our people will look to you for inspiration in the future, no matter what rank you are."

Wikki turned around and began walking away, only to be stopped by Tabitha's reply, "Wikki, wait..." Turning around, she continued, "...thanks."

"Come on, I'll take you home," he grinned.

Collecting his knife from the ground, they both made their way home.

Quinn walked to the edge of the town to liaise with his party as his friend walked towards him. "Hello, Balgair, how are you feeling?"

With the whistle still in his speech, Balgair replied, "I've been better, but I could be worse."

"What is wrong, are your wounds still hurting?" Quinn asked with genuine concern.

"No, not my physical wounds. I just feel broken inside. This is how Niall Greyclaw, the alpha before me, must've felt. Ren is stronger than I've ever been, and I was foolish to underestimate him."

"He is very strong, indeed, but don't think your worth has come to an end. He is very young, so he will need your wisdom and guidance more than any other alpha before him."

Balgair paused for a few seconds and gave a little smile. "Thank you for your kind words. So where will you go first?"

"I will go to Black Forest City, then on to White Castle. So I should be gone for no more than four weeks, unless the clans are not welcoming, of course. Then, I might be back a little sooner."

"Be safe, Quinn. We shall look for your safe arrival."

"Thank you, and make sure you heed to what I have said."

Quinn patted Balgair on the shoulder before he walked past him, making his way to his party. Balgair watched his friend leave before lowering his head and continuing on his way, ready to remove his belongings from the alpha's hut and place them at the pathfinder's hut, where his new home would be.

Chapter Seven

A PEACEKEEPER'S DUTIES

Approaching his party, Quinn started to brief them. "Thank you all for being patient and waiting for me. Has everyone got what they need? We won't be able to rely on the towns and villages of the other clans for aid when we leave our borders."

"Yes, we're all ready to go, Peacekeeper. So when you're ready, we'll depart for the black wolf capital," Abaigeal replied.

Abaigeal Grey-Ear was 23 years old and next in line to be the possible peacekeeper. The people from all over the Grey Wolf Clan loved and admired her. She was sweet, gentle and spoke softly. Even though she was an inertia, she had been known to stop any person or wolf in their tracks, with a calming aura that amazed all of her peers. She even calmed wolves from other clans as the rumours went.

If possible, a peacekeeper must seek out a potential person they think could take their place, and Quinn was lucky enough to find her. Hearing of the respect and love a young seventeen-year-old girl had gained, with tales of inner strength.

When she turned eighteen, he met her and started to nurture her for the position of peacekeeper, which she would likely be voted for in the future. She was excited and overjoyed, to say the least, and her family was proud of her when Quinn asked their permission to train her for this very honoured position. In time he realised that she had something else to offer; she could look at someone she had just met and instantly have a gut feeling about their personality, good or bad, fascinating Quinn with this unknown power of hers.

"Good, then let us be on our way. Abaigeal, I think when we finish at the white wolf capital, we will pass your home town of Red Thorn. So, I was thinking, maybe I can leave one of my men with you for two months, so you can see your family if you wish it," Quinn suggested.

Abaigeal smiled as it had been too long since she saw her family. "That would be great, Peacekeeper. Thank you so much."

"I am 61 years old now. Soon, I will look to step down as peacekeeper. After this journey, you may like to continue your future alongside me, or you can remain with your family until that time. I'd bet my soul that you will be voted for after my time has ended."

Abaigeal frowned. "I never thought about it, to be honest."

"After this, you will be ready for the position, so I recommend that you live your life a little before serving the clan. Start courting and make yourself a family because if and when you are peacekeeper, you will find it harder to do these things. But I will keep one of my men with you for two months, so you can decide then and inform him of your decision. The person I will leave with you will be your personal protector until that time. For now though, you must keep your mind on the task in hand. You will find that other clans do not like outsiders, even in times of peace."

"Ok, I'll think about it after this task," Abaigeal replied.

"Good. Also I thought you might want to know who has volunteered to be your protector." Abaigeal raised her eyebrows as he continued, "It is Ieuan Grey-Eye; he has taken quite a liking to you. He firmly insisted that he be your personal protector."

Abaigeal blushed and gave no reply.

Quinn smiled and called his party over for their orders. "Gather around, men. It is time for us to take our leave. We will head west to the capital of the Black Wolf Clan. We should get to their borders in two to three days. We will rest at Shrompy at the border. After that, we won't stop at any civilised place until we get to the black wolf capital. Stay alert and make sure you know your guard rotas when we stop. Ieuan, that will be your responsibility. Is that understood?"

"Yes, Peacekeeper," Ieuan replied, giving the wolves' greeting.

"Good. We leave now."

Eight long days had passed before they arrived at the edge of Black Forest. Within the dense forest, formed of the largest trees they had ever seen, stood the capital of the black wolves, Black Forest City. The grey wolves were the only clan without a city, but they had more towns and villages than any other clan.

Quinn turned to his party and gave them orders. "We are now entering Black Forest. We will not be fully welcome here, so we must abide by their laws and customs that slightly differ from our own. No one is to speak unless spoken to. We are here to tell them of our new alpha, not to fight or challenge them. Be submissive, but always be alert and ready to fight if needed."

The party members nodded, with few of them agreeing verbally.

"Peacekeeper, what if we surprise or startle them with our presence?" Abaigeal asked.

"Don't worry about that, they probably know we are here already," Quinn replied.

After two hours of wandering, they came across the city. Large pieces of lumber side by side produced high walls, towering twenty feet high, surrounding the entire city for miles to stop any outsiders from getting in. Being a very secretive clan, all the settlements of Black Forest Plain were gated communities, and if they could have achieved it, they would have walled off their country to the entire world of Xancrylor. Quinn's party arrived at the city, with four black wolf protectors stood atop a platform next to the main gates.

One of them shouted down to the strangers before them. "Who goes there? Advance and be recognised!"

Quinn walked forward by himself, addressing the protector in command. "Hello there, Protector, I am Quinn, the peacekeeper of the grey wolves. I have come to speak to your peacekeeper and alpha."

"Wait there. I'll get my peacekeeper to verify what you've said."

The black wolf protector disappeared, but another two took his place in quick succession.

Quinn looked at Abaigeal and stated, "If I manage to get you inside here, you must not speak until spoken to. They have slightly different laws and customs to us, but it's mostly the same. I'm not insulting your intelligence, but you must understand the black wolves are not to be insulted. Do you understand?"

"Yes, Peacekeeper. I understand," she replied.

Quinn addressed the rest of his party. "As for the rest of you, I'm sure you will be denied entry. Just stand down where they can see you, eat, and I will get us supplies when I get in there."

The men nodded and got their cooking supplies out.

After a short while, the gates slowly opened, but only enough for one person to get through at a time. The initial protector that spoke to them came through the gates and pointed at Quinn. "You can come in."

"Thank you, Protector. I was wondering if you would also give passage to another person from my party. She is under my guidance, and she will not leave my side at any time."

The protector looked back for a few seconds, nodded and turned back around. "Ok, but if you break your word, you'll be held responsible for her actions."

"I accept these terms, Protector. Thank you for accommodating me," Quinn replied.

Quinn and Abaigeal followed the protector through the narrowly opened gates. As they passed through the opening, the gates instantly closed behind them, revealing two black wolves behind each gate. In front of them, another two black wolves stood with the peacekeeper between them. She gave the wolves' greeting and bowed her head. "Hello, Quinn, we meet again."

Returning the wolves' greeting, he bowed his head while replying, "Hello, I remember you, Forba. Thank you for your welcome. This is Abaigeal, my apprentice. For the others around you, I am Quinn, the peacekeeper of the grey wolves."

Abaigeal gave the wolves' greeting and bowed without saying a word.

"Your apprentice? So you think she is the one to take your place in due time then?"

"Yes, I believe so. Have you found an apprentice?"

"In that case, she will be treated with the respect you carry. As for your question, the answer is no, but there are tales of a young man I have heard of, so I might have an apprentice soon enough. Now for the formalities, come forth and whisper to me the sacred word of the peacekeepers."

All the clans used a sacred word passed down from peacekeeper to peacekeeper, but no one knows how, as many have been killed in the past for this word. No one apart from them has knowledge of the word, being the closest guarded secret of all the wolves. They have been tortured in the past for this information for tactical reasons, even by their own leaders, but no one has ever given up the word. With this word, they can move from one clan to the next under the peacekeepers' law, giving them protection. If used in the wrong way, a false peacekeeper could use this word to get close to another clan's leaders, causing war and conflict. Quinn walked up to Forba, put his head next to hers and covered his mouth with his hand so no one could lip-read what he said. He stepped back and gave the wolves' greeting again as she responded in kind.

"Welcome to our capital, Grey Wolf Peacekeeper. You and your apprentice are allowed to go around our city, under the supervision of a protector, of course."

"That is very kind of you. Are we permitted to get supplies after my affairs are done with?" Quinn asked.

"Yes, you may pick up what you need for you and your party," Forba replied.

"Thank you. We have come to speak to you and your alpha."

"The alpha is out on patrol with his party. So, in the meantime, please follow me, and I can show you around so you know where to get your supplies."

"We would be honoured to be escorted by you personally," Quinn smiled.

Shown around the city under the escort of Forba and a protector, Abaigeal had never seen anything like it before. The grey wolves were the most primitive compared to the other clans, and it showed. This was the first time she had seen real steps not made of wood, let alone a hut on top of another, and she was overwhelmed by how different the black wolves were to themselves.

Forba could see the excitement in Abaigeal's eyes, so she would use this opportunity to show off the black wolves' newest invention. Even though they were secretive, they loved to show off what they had if the opportunity arose, to demonstrate that they were 'better'.

"Would you two follow me? I have something that might interest you," Forba smirked.

Led into a hut which had a very strange smell they did not recognise; they saw pots and cups filled with strange powders and plants they had not seen before.

"This is what I wanted to show you. Our alchemists have made something very interesting," Forba boasted.

Abaigeal leaned over to Quinn and whispered, "What's an alchemist?"

"What did you say, my dear?" Forba asked.

"Um, I'm sorry for interrupting, and I don't mean to be rude or sound stupid, but I was asking what an alchemist is."

"I forget, you don't have them, do you? They are people that mix things to create better things, like medicine."

Quinn intervened, "Sorry for my interruption, but I think it might be better if I explain, because this is her first time here." Forba smiled and gave a slow nod of approval, signalling him to continue. "It's hard to explain fully because we don't use much medicine, but the black wolves are the best in the known world at alchemy. We have some medicines, but we normally trade with the black wolves to get them. They can get a plant or rock or something and mix it with something else to create a new thing."

"Oh, ok, I think I get it now," Abaigeal replied.

In the centre of the hut stood a fireplace with a chimney above it, supported by four pillars. Forba picked up a cup and poured some dark grey shiny powder into her hand. "This is our latest creation."

She threw the powder into the open fire, and the small flames between the burnt logs exploded into one big flame for a split second.

"By the Great Wolf, what was that?" Abaigeal gulped.

"It is what we call fire salts. We created it about a month ago, but now we're finding a use for it."

Quinn stared hard into the fire. "That is very impressive, but it looks dangerous."

"You are correct. Three of our alchemists were killed by a large amount of this exploding in the other alchemist hut, well, what's left of it anyway."

A knock on the door interrupted the conversation, and it immediately opened. A protector walked through and declared, "Peacekeeper, I'm sorry for the intrusion. The alpha's party has returned and is aware of the grey wolf peacekeeper's presence."

Forba nodded and replied, "Ok, tell the alpha we will be outside his hut straight away." She turned to Quinn and Abaigeal and continued, "We must cut this tour short, I'm afraid. The alpha is not a man that likes to be kept waiting. You can address him and tell us your news when he addresses you, and not before."

"That is fine, please lead the way," Quinn replied.

As they approached the alpha's hut, they saw a small gazebo with only one seat in the centre, where the black wolf alpha sat.

Abaigeal raised her eyebrows and asked, "Look, they only have one seat, why is-"

Quinn cut the question before she could finish. "Abaigeal, please, this is not the time or place for questions."

Understanding her wrongdoing, she replied, "Sorry, Peacekeeper."

Giving the wolves' greeting, Forba introduced the grey wolves. "My Alpha, this is Quinn, the peacekeeper of the grey wolves, and his apprentice Abaigeal. They have news to give to us."

Quinn and Abaigeal gave the wolves' greeting and bowed.

Harri stood up from his chair and gave the wolves' greeting back. "Ah, hello, Quinn, it's been a long time. Are you here about the tenebrous menace that happened around a week ago?"

"We were attacked around the same time as well. We did not know the trouble found its way here," Quinn replied.

"Oh, I see you're not here about that, then, by the tone of your voice."

"No, we thought that had just happened to our clan. We lost good warriors that day at the Town of Niamh."

Harri sat back down. "I see. We knew of their arrival and struck them before they got too close to our capital. Why did your people not sense them?"

Quinn took in a long deep breath, thinking of a reply not to offend him. "With all due respect, we have dealt with it. It is a grey wolf matter."

"I see. We all have our secrets, I suppose. So, why're you here then, Grey Wolf Peacekeeper?"

"As tradition dictates in our clans, I have come to inform you of a new alpha that has risen in our ranks."

Leaning forward in his chair, he questioned, "So, who would have the strength to beat Balgair in single combat? They must be a strong individual. Was it Llewellyn Greyclaw?"

Even though Quinn wanted to smile, he kept a blank expression on his face, not to insult anyone in the Black Wolf Clan. "His name is Ren Greyfang, but our people call him Ren the Unbeaten. He is the youngest known alpha to rule from all the clans."

Harri sat back in his chair and raised one eyebrow as he asked, "How old?"

"He is 22 years of age."

"Hahahaha, the great Balgair beaten by a boy," Harri scoffed to his clan.

Most of the people gathered started laughing at the prospect of someone so young beating an alpha and leading a clan. Quinn raised his voice, not to offend, but to be heard. "He has never been beaten, and he is one of, if not the strongest wolf I have ever encountered."

The laughs of the crowd died down as Harri looked Quinn squarely in the face and said, "That's ludicrous; he's but a boy. How strong could he be?"

Quinn showed Abaigeal a lesson she would not forget, demonstrating what it truly meant to be a peacekeeper and the potential dangers that came with the title.

Looking back into Harri's eyes, he spoke few words, but the impact revealed his individual talents as a peacekeeper. "His strength is something you could only dream of achieving, Black Wolf Alpha."

Harri's nose scrunched up, his mouth downturned, as though the words equalled Quinn spitting in his face. Standing up, he looked at them both. "You've given your message. Now I believe our peacekeeper has agreed to let you get provisions for your party. Get what you need and leave. This meeting is at an end."

Harri departed to the alpha's hut, and the crowd that formed around them started to disperse, muttering amongst themselves.

Quinn saw the look of admiration Abaigeal gave him. "Ok, young apprentice, I know you have questions, but we are not safe to discuss what has happened here. It would be insulting, so keep your questions to yourself until we have left the city."

She acknowledged his advice with a nod, and the two of them quickly gathered what supplies they could secure, knowing the black wolves' hospitality had become limited.

Exiting the front gates, Forba asked a final question before they left. "Quinn, is it true what you said to Harri? Is Ren really that strong?"

He stopped and turned around with a grin. "What I said in there was not a ruse to keep your alpha in line. I meant what I said. He is young and very powerful. I expect great things from him."

Without a reply, Forba smiled and nodded before retiring back into the city with the gates closing behind her.

Quinn and Abaigeal liaised with the party outside the gates, and they began packing their equipment away as Quinn gave new orders. "Ok, men, it seems we have outstayed our welcome, so we will not rest here. We will immediately move onwards to White Castle."

Abaigeal looked at Quinn and asked, "When you say White Castle, do you mean an actual castle?"

"Of course, it even makes this city look primitive," Quinn smirked.

Abaigeal's eyes lit up. "I thought castles were just a story."

"As impressive as it may be, it is not as impressive as the cities of the Southern Kingdoms. There is also much in this world that even I do not know about. Some say that even magic is real. Now, come every one, we must leave immediately."

As the party exited Black Forest, Abaigeal had a burning question she wanted to ask. "Quinn, back there when you spoke to Harri, why did you risk yourself insulting him like that?"

He looked out to the horizon and replied, "Because I must keep the peace. Ren is young, so the black and white wolf alphas would see his age as a disadvantage. He is still not in his prime, so the other alphas could attack our clan through mere speculation of a 'boy' ruling, or the most likely reason is through fear. Ren is strong enough at his young age to be alpha, so how strong will he be when he reaches his prime in a few years?"

Abaigeal thought about it for a second. "So, ultimately, they won't attack us."

"No alpha would ever risk giving Ren a reason to become omega alpha. No clan wants to be ruled by another, and with Ren being so young, no one truly knows what type of alpha he will become, and that includes myself."

"So, do you worry that Ren might do bad deeds in the future?"

"I do not know, my girl, I do not know. Not all the alphas in the past have been valiant. The same could be said about the omega alphas, and in fact, only one omega alpha has been truly worthy. The first one."

"I have heard of the stories of the first two but not the last one. Is there a reason why the story is restricted?"

"Abaigeal, my dear, you have a lot left to learn, and I will teach you the true history of the wolves when you have been voted in as the peacekeeper."

"Why can't you tell me now?"

Spinning his head to one side, he glared at her. "Because it is only for a peacekeeper's ears. We use this knowledge to pass to an alpha when needed, to show them reason if they start to lose it, so don't press this matter. Now, you know the peacekeepers' duties are more than just passing messages on, we keep the peace within and beyond our clans."

Abaigeal looked down and replied, "I'm sorry, I meant no offence."

"I know, maybe I was too harsh with my response, so I apologise. Now, let's go. We have a long journey ahead of us."

White Castle stood on the furthest north-western point of the West Plains, making it a long journey to avoid the marshes, filled with artesian wells, rivers and springs, creating un-walkable terrain for any traveller. After twelve days, they finally made it to the white wolf capital. It was an epic site to behold. Over 2,000 stone houses stood at the base of the city, or the lower ring as it was called. At the rear of the lower ring, walled defences intertwined with natural defences of cliffs dropping into the sea.

Arriving at the portcullis behind the lower ring, they could see the stones were at least six feet cubed. How they got them on top of each other baffled their minds, including Quinn's, who had seen them before. The walls stood thirty feet tall to each side of the gate. The skill and craftsmanship to build these structures were great, but not the greatest in Calinthia. The portcullis opened vertically, acting as the main gate to the upper ring. The gate, made of wooden beams reinforced by crossed iron brackets, exposed what was behind. As they peered through, they saw a narrow path no more than thirty metres wide leading up to the castle and the upper ring of the city, mounted on a high peninsula surrounded by cliffs. Each side of the path initially dropped thirty feet into rocks and sea below, reaching one hundred and thirty feet at the end, and it did not matter if the fall didn't kill you, because the sea would claim you. The coast of the Xarbon Sea was wild, untamed and unforgiving. The turbulent waves crashed into the rocks, dragging any debris back a good ten to fifteen feet, before wildly rushing back to the coast and smashing white spray into the cliffs.

Quinn quickly briefed his party. "We have arrived. Now, these wolves like to live like the cat race, and if they had their way, we would be bowing to kings and queens instead of earning our place. Their peacekeeper is not all there, but he is a personal friend. So, apart from him, not even I care for these bastards, but you will remain respectful nevertheless. Is that understood?"

With everyone agreeing, Quinn went ahead. Beyond the portcullis stood two protectors deep in conversation, unknowing of the party's presence.

Quinn called out to one of the protectors, poorly guarding the gate. "Excuse me, Protector, may I talk to you?"

They both turned around and marched down to the gate, slightly agitated because they had been caught not performing their duties.

"What do you want?" one of them spat.

"Sorry to bother you, but I am here to see the peacekeeper and the alpha. I am Qui-"

The other protector looked Quinn up and down, interrupting him before he could finish his sentence. "Who do you think you are asking to see them? Do you even have an appointment?"

Caught off guard by their rudeness, he remained calm and replied, "No, I do not have an appointment, I'm afraid, I-"

Interrupting for the second time, the protector dictated, "Ha, no appointment, he thinks he can just stroll in here. Go away, old man and stay away."

The two protectors started to walk away, and Abaigeal spoke, "Excuse me, boys, can you help me, please?"

The protectors turned and saw one of the biggest cleavages they had ever seen, eyes fixated on her breasts as they asked together, "What can we help you with, sweetheart?"

"We need to get in because it's really important that we see the peacekeeper and the alpha."

Looking at each other, they smiled. "We'll open the gates now, sweetheart," one of them said.

Surprised, Quinn turned to her and frowned. "You have undone your top a little."

"You have your strengths of persuasion, and I have mine," Abaigeal replied.

Quinn smiled and turned back around.

With a curious clunking noise, the portcullis started to rise, making it appear that the gate was cut in half, as only the lower section of it moved upwards, going behind the top half. As it rose, the party walked through the entrance.

"Hey, hey, hey, who're you lot? You can come, sweetheart, but these people can't," one of the protectors protested.

The other white wolf protector grabbed Abaigeal by her arm, pulling her towards him, sneering, "Yeah, you lot better leave before you get into trouble, and we wouldn't want that, would we, sweethe-"

Before he could finish his sentence, Ieuan had his hunters' knife on the protector's throat as he demanded, "Let her go or I'll open your fucking neck, you wet mutt."

Two other party members restrained the other protector, so the one holding Abaigeal knew he was on his own. He let her go and held his hands in the air. "Hey, no trouble, I've let her go, n-now let me go."

"Wait," Quinn ordered.

The protector looked at Quinn, wondering what was happening, with wide eyes and his face turning pale.

"Now listen here, the pair of you, I am here to meet up with your peacekeeper and alpha. I am Quinn, the grey wolf peacekeeper. So, gentlemen, we can do this one of two ways, and both ways are mine. You can take us to them, and we will forget this matter ever happened, or I will let my protector here kill you and your friend because you caused me to be under threat. So, as the laws state, I can give the order with your life forfeit. So what is your decision, Protector?"

With haste, the one pinned by Ieuan replied, "Yeah, yeah, the first option is the one we choose. Yeah, we'll take you straight up to the great hall where they are, no problem, friend."

"Let them go," Quinn commanded.

As Ieuan released the white wolf protector, he instantly rubbed his neck while saying, "Follow me, I'll take you there now."

The other protector remained at his post as the party followed their escort to the great hall. The eighty-foot-tall castle was a grand sight indeed, so impressive that the entire party, including Quinn, were astounded that something like this could be built at all, let alone by their cousin clan. Large reinforced wooden doors opened, revealing the biggest room they had ever seen, and to top it off, they had coloured glass in the windows displaying pictures. Initially, the grey wolf party was confused as to why the stained glass displayed two wolves, and then it dawned on some of them, these wolves were the last two omega alphas.

Four steps led to a platform at the end of the hall, with four seats at the back. Surprisingly, all the leaders were in their respective seats already. The white wolf peacekeeper saw the party enter. He immediately smiled, advancing with open arms, welcoming his old friend. "Welcome, Grey Wolf Peacekeeper, welcome, yes, yes."

As he walked closer to the party, Quinn gave the wolves' greeting.

"My peacekeeping brother, how have you been? How were your travels? You and your party must join me at my home for food, you all look famished, yes, yes." Crey said.

Bowing his head, Quinn replied, "Thank you for your kind words and gesture, we would be honoured to join you at your table, but until that time, I have come to you with official business."

"I see. Will this business take long, because we have a very important matter to attend to shortly, yes, yes."

"As a matter of fact, no, it will not take long at all. So should we exchange the sacred word before we continue?" Quinn asked.

"The formalities, I almost forgot, my old friend. Please come and present me the word, yes, yes."

Quinn gave the sacred word, as most of his party stared at Crey with frowns and open mouths, with the knowledge of him having a few screws loose.

"Come, old friend, come. I will present you to the alpha. I will ask that you tell your men to wait outside. And, oh, who is this young lady, your apprentice, Quinn? Yes, yes."

"Yes, Crey, she is."

"Ok, she can come with you. I will hope that I find one of my own soon. Your men outside, you two with me, please. Yes, yes."

Crey escorted them both down the hall and presented them to Gwyn. "Alpha, this is the grey wolf peacekeeper, Quinn, and his apprentice, yes, yes. I forgot to ask your name, dear."

"It's Abaigeal," she replied while giving the wolves' greeting.

"Welcome to our city," Gwyn responded.

Quinn gave the wolves' greeting and announced, "I know you are currently very busy, White Wolf Alpha, so we will not waste any of your time. We have come to declare that we have a new alpha, Ren Greyfang. Or, as our people call him, Ren the Unbeaten."

A voice from behind them sounded, asking, "So, this Ren the Unbeaten, how strong is he truly, old man?"

As Quinn and Abaigeal turned, they saw a young boy in manacles.

"Hold your tongue, Alsander!" Gwyn shouted.

The boy spoke no more, but did not cower to his alpha's demand.

"Thank you for the information, but I have matters to attend to now. Please leave, because this is a white wolf matter," Gwyn said.

Quinn and Abaigeal gave the wolves' greeting and walked away.

Crey briefly joined them, apologising, "No, no. I'm sorry for the blunt and short meeting, my friend."

"It is ok, Crey."

"A dark matter indeed. So young yet on trial, but too young to be on trial. Only sixteen he is. Oh, what a shame, what a shame, yes, yes," Crey frowned.

"Are you ok?" Quinn asked.

"I'm sorry, you must leave now. It is time. This is a white wolf matter, I'm afraid. Do you still know where my house is? Yes, yes,"

"Yes, I do," Quinn replied.

"You and your party will go there, and I will meet you there. Go straight in, the door is open, make yourselves at home, yes, yes."

As Crey left, Quinn and Abaigeal noticed Alsander staring at them, with a wicked look in his eyes and a sinister smile.

Abaigeal looked at Quinn and said, "That boy. He's evil. Maybe the most evil person I've ever come across, I can see it in his eyes. He's cold."

"For once, I fully agree. Come, we must leave."

As they left the hall, Gwyn called out to the prisoner. "Alsander White-Ear, stand before me."

Chapter Eight

A COMPLICATED PAST

Eight years had passed since Ren became the alpha of the grey wolves, and peace prospered across the West Plains.

Gwyn decided to walk through the city to take advantage of the beautiful day. Age had caught up with the white wolf alpha, his hair thinning and grey, and his muscular physique barely recognisable. Walking down from the upper ring, he came across Crey approaching on the narrow, peninsular path.

"Good morning. How are you, my old friend?" Gwyn asked.

"I am good. How are you, my friend? Yes, yes," Crey replied.

Age had also found its way to Crey. His milky grey eyes blurred his vision, with dry grey hair forcing its way down his back, resembling dehydrated grass.

"I'm fine. I'm going for a wander into the market," Gwyn replied.

"There are new wares from a northern trader, brave enough to travel here, yes, yes," Crey declared.

“So I’ve heard. It’s unlike the bears to trade. Is this the boy you have told me about?” Gwyn asked, looking a young man up and down.

“My replacement, I’m sure he will be, much potential in this one, yes, yes.”

Gwyn frowned. “What do you mean?”

“Unsure of himself, but he has a good heart and untapped strength, a good peacekeeper he will be, yes, yes.”

Still looking at him, Gwyn asked, “So what’s your name, boy?”

He gave the wolves’ greeting and answered, “My name is Bleddyn, Alpha.”

His blue eyes were friendly and inviting, complemented by short, light blonde hair and a neatly trimmed beard covering the lower part of his face.

“Bleddyn. Are you of the Whitetail pack?” Gwyn questioned.

“Yes, my oldest brother is a member of your party, the leader of the protectors.”

“Ha, what a small world. Looks like you come from good stock, boy, so keep up the good work.” Gwyn smiled. “Well, Crey, Bleddyn, I bid you both a good day.”

As they continued walking up the path to the upper ring, Bleddyn said, “He’s getting old, isn’t he? Is there someone who you think will take his place?”

“He grooms another for alpha, but a darkness may get in his way, yes, yes.”

Bleddyn tilted his head and frowned. “What do you mean?”

“Complicated his past was, which puts him on the path of darkness, he might challenge, yes, yes.”

“What? I don’t know what you’re talking about? Are you talking about the guy Gwyn is training?”

Crey smiled, “No, no, not the person I talk of at all. Alsander, he was a nice child, but a hard life he had.”

Bleddyn searched his memory and said, "I don't think I remember you talking about him."

"A sad story, he did not have a chance. Not born evil, just conditioned that way, yes, yes," Crey said, as his smile faded away.

"So why has he not been banished or killed?"

"Gwyn's fault, he knew, he knew. He done nothing, but now his guilt will follow him to the Meadowlands. Alsander has broken no other laws, so there are no grounds to punish him further. He is the biggest mistake Gwyn has made, poor boy, yes, yes."

As they reached the upper ring, Crey and Bleddyn saw two men by the castle.

"They're staring again," Neil sneered.

"Let them stare because, in time, we'll be all they see," Alsander replied.

Alsander and Neil wandered off to Tristan's garden on the far northern side of the upper ring, looking out to the empty sea behind the castle. The beautiful garden was tended to with much attention to detail. Four rocks near the edge of the cliff were covered in a beautiful creeping flower, encompassing each rock with thick foliage, mimicking four large bushes.

"I think it's time we talk about the future of this clan," Alsander said.

"I agree. But I think it's time I knew the truth after years of being at your side. What is the real reason for you killing them?" Neil inquired.

Alsander's emerald green eyes stared into the vast emptiness of the sea. A gentle sea breeze blew his long white hair backwards, as he started to think back to his childhood.

Alsander had a good upbringing initially, like any other. His father hoped to climb the ranks from hunter to protector, so his parents decided to hold off having any more children until Parlan achieved his goal.

Parlan took Alsander out hunting at every opportunity, taking him out for a few weeks to the prohibited land of the Great Plain on his twelfth birthday. He had recently failed another protectors' enlistment, but Alsander still saw him as a hero. In his eyes, no one was as strong as his father, and he bragged about his strength to the other children, as proud sons do. As they arrived at what was once the capital city of the blue wolves, Alsander noticed the place filled with ruins and decay. The old huts consumed by Nature's power, as moss and ivy covered the remains of each wall.

"We're the biggest and best wolf clan in all of Xancrylor, my son. The other clans are not as good as ours, and they never will be," Parlan declared.

Alsander looked up to his father, hanging on to every word as if it were gold spewing from his mouth. "Really, Dad?"

"Yes, we proved that we're the best clan by having two omega alphas."

"Wow. So where are we?"

"Where the Blue Wolf Clan used to live."

Alsander was as inquisitive as any other child his age, investigating the ruined city. "Why don't they live here anymore?"

Parlan gave a smile, staring into the distance as he replied, "Because they were weak. They didn't deserve to live here or anywhere else. So our clan destroyed them."

Alsander peered into one of the ruined huts. "That's horrible. Why would our clan do that?"

Pain emerged in the left side of his face before he blacked out. As his eyes opened and refocused, he found himself on the floor. A sensation he had never felt before moved across his face, warm at first, until the breeze drifted past. Parlan stood over him, scowling, with his fists clenched, as his eyes burned with a furious rage. "How dare you! They didn't deserve to live in our lands. We're the only clan that deserve to live in the West Plains. Don't you ever forget that."

Alsander started to whimper, with pain creeping across his face. "I'm sorry, Dad, I didn't know."

Grabbing his shirt, Parlan lifted him off the ground. "I will not tolerate weakness in my pack, do you understand? I'll make a man out of you and remove any weakness you have. I'm raising a warrior, not a weakling."

Shoving him to the ground, Parlan mounted him and proceeded to hit him over and over again. With each hit, Alsander's face produced a fresh mark or cut. With the show of blood, he punched faster and harder as a surge of power flowed through his body. All Alsander could see were his father's fists pounding into his body and face, over and over again. His left eye almost closed from swelling, and something stirred inside that he had never felt before. Breathing faster and faster, his mouth became dry as his chest tightened, feeling the impacted areas worsen.

"Dad, stop. Please!" Alsander cried.

"Shut up, boy, I'll make a warrior of you yet," Parlan snarled.

The next minute felt like an eternity to Alsander as the onslaught continued. The pain was nothing like he had ever felt before. Parlan did not hit the centre of his body, because he lay in the foetal position, protecting himself as best he could, while his white shoulder-length hair became matted with blood.

Alsander started to scream and cry, thinking, *This is it, I'm going to die.*

Breathing heavily, Parlan broke out of his trance and calmed. After a few deep breaths, he grabbed Alsander's left arm, pulling him up from the ground as he stood. “Get up. We’ll head home now because we have a long journey ahead.” As Alsander found his footing, he continued. “Now move, boy, or you’ll have another beating.”

Walking forward with each step causing him pain, tears and mucus ran down his face, mixing with the blood. All he could do was think about what he had done to upset his father.

“I-I-I’m s-s-sorry, Dad. I-I-I didn’t mean t-t-to upset you.”

“Just keep moving, we’ll be home in four weeks, and we won’t be stopping at any place on the way either. When you get home, you will not tell anyone what happened here because this will make you stronger. Do you understand me?”

“Y-y-yes, Dad. I-I-I understand.”

Alsander lied because he didn’t understand; he just wanted to do anything for his hero—his father.

Things went back to normal until Alsander had his first transformation after his thirteenth birthday. After a day of hunting, Parlan staggered through the door late one afternoon with the smell of mead on his breath. “Can you believe it, Lara? Our son is the first of our pack to change in generations!”

“Yes, we’re blessed to have him. He could be a protector someday, don’t you think?” Lara replied.

“What did you say, you fucking bitch? I’m the first in this pack to be a protector. Come here.”

Lunging forward, he grabbed Lara by the neck. Trying to scream while being throttled by a tight grip, she felt her nose pop as his forehead smashed into her face. He changed his target, punching her in the ribs as she brought her arms up to shield her body. Her defence proved feeble as he kept punching until he noticed Alsander stood in the doorway. Stopping his attack, he gave a deathly stare at him for a few seconds. "You! You think you're better than me?"

Alsander felt a familiar wave of fear encompass his body, stepping backwards as he replied, "No, Dad."

Flinging Lara to the floor, he darted over, grabbing Alsander's right arm. Lara, powerless to do anything, began to scream. With his free hand, he clenched his fist and started to punch Alsander over and over again, shouting, "You're not better than me!"

This beating was different from the first one. This time, he aimed for his chest and abdomen, so other people would not see the bruises he would create on his son. Luckily for Alsander, he was too drunk to cause any major damage or breaks, but it hurt him nevertheless. Parlan slowed the assault, catching his breath. In between his rapid breathing, he hissed, "There, now you know your place, you little bastard."

Alsander was devastated, hearing his father, mentor, and hero say that after what he had done, the words hurt more than the physical beating. He didn't want to make his father feel bad, but he could not figure out how to stop it.

For three years, violence in the White-Ear household was normal for Alsander, always careful that no one discovered the bruises on his body. Not long after he turned sixteen, his hunting trial had come. In a changing den, the pathfinder came across him undressing, revealing new and old bruises on his chest, back and abdomen.

"What's that all over your body?" Cai asked.

"It's just some knocks I've gotten from doing some extra training," Alsander replied.

"You should be more careful, or you could cause a nasty injury."

"I'll be more careful in the future, Pathfinder."

The trial had been completed, with Alsander being top of his group. His mother was overjoyed with his progress, but his father was not so pleased. Parlan hid it well by pretending to celebrate and became very drunk during the festivities, but when they all got home, he unleashed his full anger, with Alsander being the first victim. With three quick and precise punches to the head, he knocked his son out cold.

"Parlan, don't do this, please," Lara pleaded.

Noticing an iron poker next to the fireplace, he picked it up as Lara looked on in fear.

"This is what you get for trying to be better than me," Parlan fumed.

Raising the heavy piece of iron over his head, he drove it down, hitting Alsander's body over and over again. Crunching sounds could be heard as his ribs and arm broke. Then he smiled, striking the side of Alsander's head twice, but this time Lara intervened, shielding her son's body to take the third blow meant for his head. "Fucking bitch, how dare you!"

Parlan kicked Lara in the face, turning his attention to her with the poker. After hitting her three times, he lost balance and fell to the floor. Getting up, he left the room and went to bed as if nothing happened, falling asleep instantly due to his intoxicated state.

Slowly recovering to her feet, holding her right arm, tears rolled down her face as she managed to limp over to Alsander. Kneeling down, she started to shake him gently. "Ok, ok. Alsander, can you hear me?"

Lara knew she needed help this time because, without a healer, he would die. Leaving her house as quickly as she could, she saw no one in the street to help her as she limped to the healers' establishment. With her left arm, she pounded the door as hard as she could and screamed, "Help! Help me!"

When a healer answered, she broke down and told him what had happened. He disappeared inside, emerging with another healer, running to the house and leaving Lara behind.

A little while later, Lara was sat in a room downstairs when a healer appeared, sitting next to her and held her hand.

"I'm sorry, but your son's in a coma. With what's happened, we don't know if he'll ever wake up."

Raising her left hand to her face, she broke down, uttering one word, "No."

The healer added, "We need to let you know, we'll be informing the alpha of what's happened."

She dropped her hand and looked over to the healer, pleading, "No, please, Parlan is a good man. It's just that he's frustrated with his son having a better chance of being a protector. He didn't mean for it to go this far."

The healer had seen this type of behaviour before, where the victims would make excuses for their abusers. Releasing her hand, he stood back up. "I'm sorry, but this is not your decision now."

Lara pleaded again, "Please don't. He won't do it again."

"We've already sent another healer to inform Gwyn. I'm sorry."

Lara placed her left hand back on her face as she sobbed. "By the Great Wolf, no, this can't be happening."

The healer spoke one last time. "Please come with me, so we can tend to your wounds, and then you can see your son."

Without a word, Lara followed the healer's commands.

A few hours later, woken up by a loud knock on his door, Parlan opened his eyes and started to yawn. Rolling out of bed, fully clothed and holding his head, the door banged again, so he shouted, "All right, all right, I'm coming!"

As he opened the door, two protectors burst in, slamming him to the ground. A protector placed his knee into his spine, with his right hand pushing his head into the floor. The protector put his head next to Parlan's ear and sneered, "The alpha wants to see you, so I suggest you comply, or I'll end you. You fucking weakling."

The other protector pulled out manacles from his knapsack, fitting them to Parlan.

Within the hour, he stood trial in front of the leaders at the great hall. During his judgement, he became quick with his words, blaming the mead, and claimed he was remorseful, even though deep down, he didn't care what happened to his son. Gwyn placed Parlan in the castle dungeon for two weeks as punishment, before letting him go about his normal duties and believing the matter to be resolved. Even though Gwyn and Cai were close friends, they had nearly come to blows over this matter with differing opinions involving Parlan's punishment, but as everyone knew, the alpha's words were law.

Alsander woke from his coma a month later, but something about him had changed. He became cold and detached, but the healers put this down to his injury, causing the psychological change, ignoring the fact that he had battle stress. After a further month of recovery, he was allowed to go, so Lara collected him in the morning, and they went home. She left him at the house to search for Parlan, but he returned before she did. Closing the front door, he saw Alsander sat in the darkest corner of the dining room.

"Hello, Dad."

Glancing at his son straight-faced, he replied, "You're back then."

Alsander leaned forward, dipping his head slightly, glaring directly at his father as he asked, "Yeah, that's right. So have you got anything to say?"

"No, not really."

"Just as I thought. So why did you try to kill me?"

"You needed to be taught a lesson in strength."

Alsander leaned back in his chair, folding his arms. "I see. So through true strength, there must be no remorse."

Parlan's fists began clenching. "That's right, the White Wolf Clan never back down, we're the strongest, and you'll have another lesson if you want."

Producing a sinister smile, Alsander sneered, "There's no need for any more lessons, Dad. I've learned all I need from you. Now I'll become the strong one."

Alsander leapt forward and transformed. Jumping slightly to the right, his head came down to the left, opening his mouth, and bit into the front and back of Parlan's chest. As he screamed, Alsander picked him up, swung him to the right and released him. Slamming into the dining table with a mighty crash, he caused the dining table legs to break on one side with the chairs toppling over as Alsander snarled, displaying his teeth and gums.

"Ok, you made your point, now back down, or you'll be sorry," Parlan demanded.

His words fell on deaf ears as Alsander manoeuvred forward, tipping his head to one side while clamping his jaws as tight as he could. No verbal response came from Parlan this time; only a loud snap and crunch could be heard. Alsander's mouth almost closed, and a small amount of blood spurted from around his jaws. Placing his left paw on his father's chest, he ripped his head in an upward motion. As the top half of his skull separated from the lower half, he threw it, splatting brain matter and blood across the wall. Changing back to a human, he returned to the chair in the corner of the room, and sat down naked with his father's blood around his mouth.

Five minutes later, Lara walked in, seeing the massacre before her. Closing the front door quickly, she gasped, "By the Great Wolf, what happened here?"

"I've become strong like Dad wanted me to," Alsander replied.

Eyes jittering back and forth, she took in two deep breaths and said, "Alsander, it's ok, we can get through this, but I think we need to leave."

Alsander's nose wrinkled, lowering his head as he smiled. "No, Mam. I've become strong now. You let him beat me for years, and you tried to stick up for him after he nearly killed me. Why?"

"I'm sorry, I was too afraid of him."

"I see. So Dad was right about the weak, I suppose."

Lara's arms dropped limp to her sides. "What do you mean?"

"The weak do nothing. And they don't deserve to live in my world."

Alsander jumped forward, transforming again, hitting his mother with the top of his head. Crashing into the door behind, the wood snapped outwards as she let out a loud scream. People passing by the house saw the door snap and heard the commotion inside.

Alsander looked through his mother with cold, dead eyes.

"I'm sorry, Alsander, please don't hurt me anymore," Lara pleaded.

As she reached out with her right hand, powerful jaws clamped onto her arm, dragging her into the centre of the room. Placing his right paw on her chest, he shook his head violently until her arm separated from her body. She screamed in a higher pitch as blood gushed out of her wound, causing hypovolemic shock to set in. Her complexion became pale, and her body grew cold. As Lara's voice became faint, she spoke her final words, "Alsander, please. I love you."

Ignoring her, he covered her face with his left paw and placed his right paw on her left leg, pinning her to the ground. His teeth sunk into the sides of her chest before throwing his head back and forth aggressively. Her ribs started to shatter and break apart, with her screams muffled by his paw on her face. As he felt the resistance lessen, he pulled hard, opening her chest cavity, her left lung partially sliding out. Removing his paws from her body, he lifted her high, throwing the fresh carcass onto Parlan's remains. Transforming to a human, he sat back in the corner of the room, covered in his parents' blood.

Not long after, a protector opened the broken door, immediately seeing the two corpses on top of each other, one with half a head missing and the other torn apart. Scanning the room, he saw brain segments and a pool of blood. Upon further inspection, he saw Alsander covered in blood, head lowered with a smile on his face. The protector's eyes widened as he shouted, "I need some help over here!"

Two other protectors on route to the house heard his call and picked up their pace. The three of them just stared into the house at the doorway, never seeing such carnage before, with a young boy covered in blood smiling at them.

Another protector joined them briefly, ordering, "Quick, we need all protectors. There are three tenebrous outside the city limits."

The first protector on scene gave his orders. "Ok, you two go, and you stay with me. We'll deal with this."

Still staring out to the sea, Alsander clenched his jaw with his mouth downturned, filling with a familiar rage.

"You haven't said anything for a few minutes now. So what happened?" Neil asked again.

His gaze broke, turning to Neil. "They were weak, so I disposed of them."

Neil gave a smile, tapping him on the shoulder. "There's too much weakness in our clan. We should think about disposing of that as well."

Alsander looked back over the cliff, dipped his head slightly forward and gave his sinister smile. "Yes, I think it's time."

Chapter Nine

THE WHITE WOLF ALPHA

"It's time I call out our alpha. He's old and weak," Alsander declared.

"Yes, I agree. And what of his pathfinder and prodigy?" Neil replied.

"You can do what you want to the old pathfinder, but leave his prodigy to me."

Neil looked out to the sea. "That's the best decision I've heard all day. It's been a long road, but after years of training, I think we're ready."

Unknown to the pair of them, Crey hid in the garden, listening to what was said. Turning away, he muttered to himself, "No, no, this is bad, bad news indeed, the alpha must be warned, he must be warned. But where is he, he is gone, and I don't know where he has ventured. The market, but is he still there? Dark times ahead if I do not find him." Shuffling away as fast as he could, he continued to mutter. "I must find him, yes, yes."

Alsander and Neil walked from the garden directly to the great hall as Crey rushed to the lower ring, continuously muttering to himself.

"Halt. What's your purpose here?" one of the protectors challenged.

Alsander looked the protector up and down, replying, "We're here to see the alpha. Our business is our own."

"He's not here, he's gone for a walk," the protector informed them.

"We can wait inside for his arrival then, can't we?" Neil suggested.

"Ok, but you will not go anywhere else apart from the great hall. Is that understood? The rest of the castle is out of bounds to hunters."

Alsander smiled, "Yes, we know our place, and we know hunters are not allowed anywhere else."

"That's fine, but I must inform everyone upon entry," the protector replied.

Entering the great hall, Alsander noticed the pathfinder sat in his chair.

"Ok, the pathfinder's here, so don't let him have a reason to interact with us. Just pretend to be interested in the hall until the alpha gets here. We must do this officially, or we could be banished," Alsander explained.

"No problem. Besides, I can just talk shit to him and ask about his pathetic war stories if he does interact with us," Neil snorted.

Crey wandered around the lower ring, asking random people if they had seen Gwyn, but with each failed attempt to find him, the more anxious he became. Suddenly, a face appeared in the crowd that he knew. "Conwy, my boy, trouble is afoot. We must find Gwyn, yes, yes."

Conwy, being a short man, stood tall with pride. High and tight crewcut black hair, and a clean-shaven face emphasised his crisp clothes. He was not overly fond of Crey, but he respected him nevertheless. "What trouble do you speak of, Peacekeeper?"

"Danger and darkness approach, Gwyn. We must move and find him, yes, yes."

Conwy's eyes squinted. "What do you mean, Peacekeeper?"

"Follow me, and I will explain, yes, yes."

As they began their search, Crey told Conwy about the discussion between Alsander and Neil.

At that same moment, entering the great hall, Gwyn and Alsander's eyes met.

"You've finally arrived, Alpha," Alsander sneered.

"What's my arrival to do with you, Hunter?" Gwyn asked.

"You're one of the final pieces to my plan."

"What're you talking about?"

"You should've done the right thing eight years ago. You would've avoided a lot of carnage, old man."

Remembering everything he spoke of, Gwyn replied, "What you did to your parents was your doing. I had no part in that."

Cai stood up from his chair, overhearing what Alsander said, shouting, "Stand down, Hunter, you talk out of place!"

He looked over to Neil, commanding, "Make sure he stays where he is."

Transforming into a wolf, Neil ran over to Cai, causing him to stumble backwards into his chair.

Alsander looked directly into Gwyn's eyes with a cold, unemotional expression and declared, "You shouldn't have restricted me to being a hunter. You're partially to blame for my parents' deaths, and holding me back will do you no favours. You think that I'll feed off the scraps of society forever. Would you think that I'd be happy being held down by society at the bottom of the classes? When you get branded a criminal in this clan, it's evident that there're no second chances."

Gwyn widened his eyes and replied, "You murdered your parents. What have I got to do with your crimes? I gave you a second chance to fit back in with a good rank among the clan. You were too young to understand, and clearly, you've learned nothing."

"No, Gwyn, you're wrong. You let my dad off lightly for nearly killing me, and now you're directly punishing me for retaliating. You're weak, and we're the best clan in the West Plains. You're no longer fit to rule."

Having learned where Gwyn had gone, Crey and Conwy returned to warn him of what was coming, and entered the great hall at the same time as Alsander made his declaration: "I challenge you for the position of alpha, Gwyn Whitepaw."

Crey's heart sank as he heard the challenge. He looked at Conwy and said, "No, no, we are too late, danger has arrived."

"You're but a hunter. You would be foolish to challenge me," Gwyn declared.

"Shut up and transform. It's time to purge the weakness from this clan and Calinthia."

Transforming, they charged at each other. As the two warriors collided, Alsander proved too strong, hitting Gwyn backwards into the wall behind him with a loud thud. Hurt badly from the impact, he realised he was too old at the age of sixty-five to be in combat with a young wolf. Struggling to get back to his feet, unable to succeed in time, Alsander had his jaws around his front left leg, pulling up with all of his might and flipping Gwyn onto his back. Landing hard, Alsander's jaws wrapped around his throat with his left paw pushing his head down to the ground. Surprisingly, he let his neck go, lifting his head to look at Crey, cutting the fight short.

The words felt like glass scraping his tongue as they came out of Crey's mouth, but he knew he had to say it, as it was custom and law. "The alpha has fallen. A new alpha we have. Alsander White-Ear, yes, yes."

Alsander looked at Crey and Conwy, putting more pressure on Gwyn's left leg, extending his neck. Spearing his head down, Alsander bit deep into his neck while shaking his head back and forth, tearing it open. With his might, he pulled his head upwards. A line of blood squirted onto the wall, also pooling around Gwyn's head and neck.

He changed back into a human, turned to Neil and nodded. Enveloping Cai's head in his mouth, Neil violently shook his head back and forth. Cai's body swung until his head separated from his body, and Neil tossed his headless corpse through the air before it slammed onto the steps.

Conwy's fists clenched as his adrenaline pulsed throughout his body. His neck veins bulged as he started to shake, taking a few steps forward as he thundered, "You wet mutts! How dare you! They were old and defenceless compared to you! What are you doing?"

"The old leaders are dead because they were weak. But now, you're the final part of my plan, Conwy. My glory cannot be secured by killing a weak, old man. You'll secure that for me," Alsander's eyes bore into him as he continued to provoke him. "Now, don't disappoint me, Gwyn's prodigy."

"So be it, I'll make sure you have the shortest recorded reign of any alpha. Alsander White-Ear, I challenge you!"

Although he was a small, skinny man, Conwy swung the other way after transforming, becoming the largest white wolf in the clan. But Alsander was almost equal in size. As they transformed, no time was wasted, with their battle beginning instantly. Alsander made the first strike, but Conwy outmanoeuvred his assault, being a seasoned fighter at 29 years old. When Alsander missed his mark, Conwy found his, biting into the side of his neck. Before Conwy had a firm grip, Alsander sidestepped and pushed hard, making Conwy lose his balance, forcing him to stumble sideward before he felt a sharp pain in his rear leg. Clamping his jaws together, he twisted his head in the opposite direction. Dragging Conwy's hind leg, he lifted him through the air, but Conwy proved too big and heavy to clear any good distance.

Neil transformed, cheering Alsander on, "That's it, become the strong so we can purge the weak!"

Landing hard on the stone floor, Conwy wondered how Alsander had got the better of him initially. As a hunter he should not have this kind of combat experience, but in secret, Neil and Alsander would fight all the time, making them stronger.

As Conwy Lost his temper, he hastily scrambled to his feet to meet his nemesis head-on, Alsander took the lead again, but Conwy manoeuvred out of his way and countered. Turning quickly, he sprang forward and head-butted Alsander's ribs, driving him into the floor with so much force, he rolled over. Conwy mounted him and bit down hard between the shoulder blades. As there was not much flesh to secure a good grip, Alsander recovered to his feet and darted forward, escaping his onslaught. Conwy led the next assault in the hope his enemy would be caught off guard.

Spinning around quickly, Alsander executed a risky move, diving forward while turning his body side on to the ground through the air, sweeping Conwy's legs from under him. Rotating his body back to neutral alignment and placing all four paws on the ground underneath his challenger, he pushed upward, flipping him onto his back. Conwy instantly rolled in the direction he fell, using a barrel roll technique for momentum to quickly get back to his feet.

The great hall doors opened, and Bleddyn entered, looking for Crey, noticing the two corpses in the great hall.

"Crey, what's going on?" Bleddyn inquired.

"No, no. I was too late. Alsander is alpha, and Conwy has challenged him, equal fighters they are, I don't know who the winner shall be." Crey replied.

Bleddyn turned back to watch the duel, but had no excitement for this fight due to the loss of life before him.

Conwy turned quickly and counteracted Alsander's charge, biting down hard on his snout and twisting his head. Alsander rotated in the same direction, but his muzzle bled from his opponent's fangs splitting his flesh. Stumbling to one side, he pivoted with great speed, lunged forward and hit Conwy's chest with his paws, knocking him over.

Bleddyn's eyes widened. "This is brutal. I can't believe it's come to this."

"One shall fall, and the other defines our future, light and dark battle this day, yes, yes," Crey replied.

Alsander bit down on Conwy's front right leg again. With a twist of his head, he stripped the flesh around the bone, shredding the tendons and muscles in the process. Conwy displayed his pain by letting out a high-pitched yelp. Rolling over to his feet, he was unable to put any weight on his front right leg. Bleeding profusely with each rapid heartbeat, he knew he was losing blood fast, and he had to end this now or not at all, but he did not know how with his injury. Alsander dived forward, dipping slightly to his left to use Conwy's injury against him, as his eyes widened. With an instant strike, his teeth bore deep into Conwy's neck, pushing his body up then driving it down, smashing his challenger's head hard on the stone floor. He placed one paw on his head and one on his chest, yanking his head backwards several times while growling until Conwy's neck tore open. The blood splattered over Alsander, quickly staining the floor as Conwy's soul left the mortal plane.

With tears forming, Crey declared the champion. "The challenger has fallen, and the alpha remains. Yes, yes."

Three corpses soiled the floor of the great hall. Alsander transformed, his mouth and chest covered in the blood of his opponents, his nose and back bleeding from his wounds. Standing in the great hall naked, breathing heavily, he lifted his arms out to his sides before shouting, "It's done!"

Neil started to laugh, clapping his hands.

Regaining his breath and composure, Alsander gave his orders. "Crey, I think it's time for you to prepare for your journey." His eyes moved to Bleddyn as he continued. "I believe your brother is the leader of the protectors. Tell him his new alpha summons him. We've got a lot to talk about."

Crey and Bleddyn gave the wolves' greeting and said together, "Yes, Alpha."

Neil had donned a battle robe, and now made his way outside past Crey and Bleddyn. As they turned to leave, Alsander gave Crey one last order. "Crey, while you're at it, go get me some healers to tend to my wounds and clean this mess up. After that, you're no longer required. The meeting I have with the lead protector is not of your concern."

Crey turned around and replied, "As you wish, Alpha, yes, yes."

After exiting the great hall, Crey made an unusual request of Bleddyn. "My boy, I must speak with your brother before he sees the alpha, it is of great import, yes, yes."

"I'll make sure he sees you before he sees Alsander, but why do you want to see him?"

"Dark times ahead, I fear, history repeating, very bad, very bad indeed. Yes, yes."

Bleddyn's eyebrows lowered. "What do you mean by history repeating?"

"I will tell you, but not yet. Go now and bring your brother to me quickly, yes, yes."

"As you wish," Bleddyn replied.

Carrying out his orders, Bleddyn ran as fast as he could to his eldest brother's house. As Crey made his way to the healers' building, he heard Neil declaring the new alpha of the white wolves to the people passing by the great hall. "Everyone, listen to me! Gwyn is dead! You now have a new alpha, Alsander White-Ear. Rejoice in knowing that the White Wolf Clan will claim its former glory. Tell everyone you meet!"

Crey turned back around with tears rolling down his face, knowing not only that darkness lay ahead for the White Wolf Clan, but also that he had lost two leaders that were his good friends.

Back at the Town of Niamh, Tabitha heard a wild knock on the door. When she opened it, Wikki was stood in the doorway. "Hey, Tabi. I need you to pack some things; we're going away for a little while."

"What are you talking about? Going where?" Tabitha frowned.

"Just trust me, now, hurry up. We don't have much time," Wikki replied.

Tabitha packed a few belongings into a backpack and returned to Wikki, waiting outside.

"So, where are we going?" Tabitha asked.

Wikki looked around and replied, "Keep it down. Come on, let's go."

As Wikki walked away, Tabitha followed, heading out of the town.

After walking for three hours, they stopped at a small wood, littered with oak. Wikki looked around, seeing a path of branches that had been snapped. The exposed wood underneath the bark of each broken branch had turned dark brown, displaying that they had been damaged many years ago.

"This is the place," Wikki said.

Tabitha looked around with a frown. "What's so important about this place?"

"This is where your dad fought Andrew, the colossal bear."

Her eyes scanned the damaged trees. "So this is where my dad and my family were..."

"That's right, so there's no better place for it," Wikki intervened.

"Better place for what?"

He drew in a deep breath, turning to her as he replied, "To train you."

Tabitha took a step back. "What do you mean to train me?"

"Look, you remember when we were younger, and I said that I'd train you after I became a protector, right? I'm fulfilling that promise," Wikki smiled.

"Wikki, we both know you can't. You'll be killed if you train a woman."

"That's why we're here. No one comes here anymore. And, years ago, I was watched by everyone, so I couldn't train you. Just like this place, my intentions have been forgotten."

"Well, I've become happy with my place in life, so there's no need to risk training me."

He looked at her squarely in the eyes. "I'm not training you for that. Years ago, when those stygians attacked us, they also attacked the other clans' capitals at the same time."

"So? They haven't come back, have they?"

"No, I think they will, though. Everyone's forgotten about it, but I know that it was a calculated plan. It's too convenient. Don't you think? That's why I'm going to train you. I think they're going to come back, and you need to be ready."

"Ready? For what?" Tabitha asked.

Wikki looked down. "I don't know, I could be wrong. But it's better to be prepared, and I won't let my best friend become defenceless."

"You can't expect to train me for a year; someone will notice," Tabitha stated.

He shook his head and chuckled, "Tabi, please don't take offence to this, but you ain't no tactician. I'm just going to give you the advanced fighting techniques. So, it shouldn't take more than a few months, on and off of course."

"Ok, but what about-"

"Don't worry, she knows, and she agrees with what I'm doing here, so don't worry about it," Wikki stated. "Ok, so we'll start with advanced knife fighting, then we'll move on to advanced fighting in wolf form. Now, watch me closely and listen in to what I'm going to tell you."

After Crey completed Alsander's instructions and made his way home, Bleddyn's brother arrived. Looking like an older version of Bleddyn with longer, slicked back, blonde hair reaching his shoulders. Darker blue eyes displayed the same kindness as Bleddyn's, but Kennon had a much larger frame, ripped with muscle.

Kennon gave the wolves' greeting and spoke: "Hello, Peacekeeper. You've summoned me? My brother's filled me in with what Alsander has done, and it's terrible news indeed."

Crey gave the wolves' greeting back and replied, "My boy, you are strong indeed, but not as strong as Alsander, so caution we must have. Refuse my request if you want because danger it will bring, yes, yes."

Kennon took a slow deep breath and answered, "I trust your judgement, I will not challenge him, but I'll never fear him either. What's the task you wish me to fulfil?"

"Report to me after he has council with you, plans with you and the clan I believe he has got. You must tell me the plans. I will try to save us from darkness if needed, yes, yes."

"How would you do that?" Kennon asked.

"No time to tell you. Go to him now and tell me what he says. Remember, you must be formal, yes, yes."

"I will, and I know that you said I'm no match for him, but I'll challenge him if I must as a last resort," Kennon declared, as he gave the wolves' greeting.

Crey watched him leave, and, with sadness in his voice, he muttered, "With challenge comes your death, Protector, yes, yes."

Entering the great hall, Kennon saw a human carcass thrown on top of two wolf corpses near the main door. As he looked up, streaks of blood showed where the dead bodies had been dragged from the pools of blood on the floor. His eyes continued wandering along the great hall, spotting Alsander and Neil in the alpha's and pathfinder's chairs, both wearing robes, with Alsander's wounds weeping into his.

"Kennon Whitetail, is it?" Alsander asked.

He gave the wolves' greeting and replied, "Yes, Alpha."

"I see that you're the leader of the protectors. This is Neil Whitefang. He's your pathfinder."

Gazing over to Neil, he gave him the wolves' greeting and addressed him. "Pathfinder."

"I've summoned you here because I want to know what your stance is on what I have to say next," Alsander inquired.

"As you wish, Alpha. What is it you want to know?" Kennon asked.

"What do you think of our great clan?"

His eyes rolled up to Alsander as he frowned. "Alpha?"

"The White Wolf Clan, we're the greatest of all the clans, are we not?"

Taken aback by this strange question, he didn't really know how to reply, but he knew if he did not come up with an answer quickly, he would have the two of them to deal with, and he was definitely not strong enough to take on the both of them. "Our clan's the greatest, Alpha."

Neil stood up and walked over to Kennon, looked him directly in the eyes and declared, "He could be one of us, Alsander."

Kennon still frowned as Neil turned around and walked away from him, sitting back down in his chair.

"Good. Kennon, you're strong, and I respect that. You're young to be the leader of the protectors. How old are you again?" Alsander inquired.

"I'm thirty-five."

"Ah, so not as young as I thought. And do you have a family of your own?"

"Yes, I have a son and two daughters."

"Good. Now wouldn't you want them to live in peace, in the greatest clan in the West Plains?"

Concerned where this conversation was going, he managed to keep his cool while replying, "I think that's what many people would want."

Alsander leaned forward in his chair, and their eyes met, striking Kennon with a fear he did not think he had as he replied, "We're going to make that a reality."

The conversation was interrupted as five healers entered the great hall. One of the healers gave the wolves' greeting and said, "Hello, Alpha. I've come as you've requested."

Alsander gritted his teeth, wrinkling his brow. "We're busy. Get out and wait outside the great hall until you're called upon."

All the healers gave the wolves' greeting and exited the great hall as Alsander sat back in his chair. "Now, where was I? Ah yes, the matter of our clan. You see, we're the best clan, so I think it is time to change the lives of all the clans in the West Plains."

Kennon's eyes widened. "What do you mean, Alpha?"

"We'll have a hierarchy and govern ourselves away from outdated laws and traditions. From this point, the wolves will move with the times."

"I'm unsure of that," Kennon replied.

Alsander stood up from his chair, staring off into the distance of the great hall. "Listen, I have a plan. But I must trust you before I reveal it. You're either with me or against me. You must decide now."

Filled with mixed emotions, he didn't know how to truly answer, but he did anyway. "Yes, I'm with you and the clan, Alpha."

Alsander started to laugh, sending chills down Kennon's spine. "Good. Come back tomorrow afternoon, and I'll reveal my plans. In the meantime, it's your task to find me thirty-five of your best protectors that'll not only serve me, but the good of the clan. If I deem any of their resolve opposed to mine, or weakness within them, I'll kill them, and maybe you. Do I make myself clear?"

"Yes, I understand perfectly, Alpha."

"Good. The men you choose will come here tomorrow, and I'll inspect them alongside the pathfinder here. You will not let me down. Now leave us, and on your way out, send in the healers."

Kennon gave the wolves' greeting before leaving the great hall, heading directly to Crey's house,

As soon as he arrived, Kennon told the peacekeeper everything. Crey sat in his rocking chair, staring into the flames within the fireplace. "As I thought, yes, yes."

"I'm not sure what he wants to do. Do you know what his intentions would be?" Kennon asked.

Crey lifted his arm, resting his head on his hand. "Hmmm, a task you have, and you mustn't disappoint. You must leave now. Your brother, I will see tomorrow morning. Not sooner, nor later. A dangerous task I have for him. Safe he shall be if he follows my instructions, yes, yes."

"I understand. I'll carry out my task for the alpha."

Crey stood up, reaching out to hold Kennon's shoulder, and said, "See me again, I doubt you will, Protector. Follow your heart, your brother is strong like you, you don't need to worry about him anymore, yes, yes."

Kennon knew keeping the peace might cost him his life. He gave the wolves' greeting and left Crey's home, wondering what fate would have in store for his brother.

Chapter Ten

THE TRUTH OF A DARK HISTORY

Dawn broke the next day, and Crey had not slept. Before preparing for the day ahead, he stood in his bedroom, looking out of the window down to the lower ring. Placing a piece of parchment on the table, he started to write a will addressed to Bleddyn. He signed the parchment's bottom and sealed it, stamping the peacekeeper's symbol into the wax with his signet ring, placing them both on a table in front of the fireplace. He did not have any family in the city, as his relatives that were still alive lived at Fullurdale, bordering the Great Plain, and he was never close to them. Despite his madness, he became a very wise man, but he never wanted much. He never mated as he knew if he bore children, he might pass the madness on, so, in effect, he was never interested in finding love. He was happy to be on his own to concentrate on his duties. Many would find this way of life sad, but to him, it was a happiness that only he could describe.

Crey left his home to go to the lower ring, arriving at Bleddyn's house. He knocked on the door, waking Bleddyn and his mother. Rolling out of bed, she stormed to the front door, pulling it open and seeing Crey in his finest garments. "Peacekeeper, I'm normally happy with your visits, but this is too early to be calling. Come back at a more suitable time, please," she said, shutting the door.

Feeling resistance, Crey stopped her closing it with an outstretched arm. "Your son, I must see now. Urgent it is, yes, yes."

"I'll go and see if he's up, but your business must be taken elsewhere. Me and my mate are trying to sleep," she replied.

Flinching, her eyes widened as Bleddyn emerged from behind her unannounced. "It's ok, Mam, we'll leave now, and I'll see what the peacekeeper wants."

Holding her hand on her chest, she uttered, "Don't scare me like that. Now go, the pair of you. I want my sleep, and you better not wake your dad. You know how he can be when he doesn't get enough sleep, and I ain't dealing with him bitching all day."

Ushering him out of the door, Bleddyn looked at Crey and smiled, "I don't think waking my parents up at this hour will make you popular."

"Come with me, you must. Final task I have for you, yes, yes," Crey ordered.

"What do you mean, final task?" Bleddyn asked as his smile faded.

Looking at several different places on the ground, he replied, "I will explain on the way, go now we must, yes, yes."

"Are you ok? You seem different today," Bleddyn inquired.

"Come. Come now. I will explain, yes, yes."

They walked to the upper ring as Crey told Bleddyn what his brother had told him the night before. When Crey finished telling him what Alsander's plans were, they arrived at Tristan's garden.

"That's terrible news. What are his exact plans?" Bleddyn asked.

"That is all. He will tell more to your brother today, yes, yes."

Concerned with what Crey had told him, he inquired, "What can we do about this?"

"Stop him I must, or danger the clans will be in, yes, yes."

Bleddyn's eyes widened as his voice went higher in pitch. "What? How would you even attempt that?"

Crey put both hands on Bleddyn's shoulders and said, "Trust in me and my plan, you must. If I fail, you must find a different way to stop him, yes, yes."

"I don't like where this is going. What do you mean?"

"Direct approach I will try. His reason or my death will come. You must not stop it. Expendable and old I am, the future you are, yes, yes."

With that being said, Crey leaned into Bleddyn, giving him the sacred word of the peacekeepers. Bleddyn knew he was serious, and his eyes widened. Crey gently pushed him into the thick foliage of creeping flowers covering a rock. "Stay here, you must, hidden from sight and smell. Quiet and still you must be. I will get him now and bring him here. Quiet and still, yes, yes," Crey instructed.

"What should I do if things start to look bad?"

"Quiet and still, listen you must, everything else you must not. Swear this, swear it."

With a downturned mouth and raised eyebrows, sadness grew in his eyes, but he trusted Crey and his wisdom. "I swear to you I'll do nothing apart from listen, keep still and be quiet."

"Nothing else you must do. This is very important, yes, yes."

Crey rearranged the foliage of the flowers and leaves, fully covering Bleddyn. Even though no one could see him, Bleddyn could partially see through the foliage.

Leaving the garden and entering the great hall, a protector stopped Crey and asked, "What're you doing here so early, Peacekeeper?"

"Get the alpha you must, important it is, yes, yes."

The protector frowned. "At this time? I'll not wake him."

"Wake him you must, Protector, an order I give you. Tell him I told you to, yes, yes."

The protector bowed his head and carried out his request. Crey heard his mutters as he walked away. "Damn crazy old fool's gonna get me killed."

After ten minutes, Crey could hear running footsteps coming down the spiralled stairs, and then the protector ran straight past him, exiting the great hall. Alsander came out of the same doorway straight after the protector, wide-eyed and red-faced.

"What're you waking me up for at this hour, old man?" Alsander spat.

"Alpha, Tristan's garden, you must go with me. Urgent news I have for you, yes, yes."

Alsander squinted at him, suspecting some repercussions or trap for what he had done yesterday. "Ok, I'll come. I'll meet you there in twenty minutes with Neil. If I suspect anything dodgy, I won't hesitate to kill you."

He gave the wolves' greeting and replied, "As you wish, Alpha, yes, yes."

Crey retired to the garden, waiting for Alsander and Neil. Arriving five minutes early, they started to investigate the garden, expecting someone else to be there. When they both stood in front of him, Neil walked over to the rock where Bleddyn hid, but his search was interrupted by Crey.

"Information I have about your plans and the dangers. The past, you must be told before you make a final decision, yes, yes."

Alsander's face scrunched up, shouting, "You woke me up to give me a history lesson, you stupid old fool!"

Neil turned from the flower-covered rock and said, "Let's leave, he's being crazy as usual."

As they walked away, Crey spoke to them, sparking their curiosity. "Tristan and the Blue Wolf Clan not interesting to you? Yes, yes."

They stopped, looked at each other with smiles before turning back around. "Now you have my attention, old man. Speak," Alsander smirked.

"One hundred and twenty years ago it was. Since then, change to the story there has been. Twisted with lies, but the truth I have, yes, yes."

Alsander and Neil fixated on Crey, eager to know the true story of the third omega alpha.

It all started when Tristan was 21 years old, being a protector keen to prove himself and taste battle. The continent of Calinthia was at peace, with the last war being over two hundred years previous between the cat and wolf races. He joined a hunting party for extra training, and they found themselves at the east border, next to the Great Plain where the blue wolves dwelled. This was a famous land throughout Calinthia, as the war of the Great Plain happened here around 1,500 years ago against the bears of the north, producing the first omega alpha, with tales told and songs sung of their valour to this day.

The deer evaded the hunting party, crossing the border and caused them to stop. Tristan changed back into a human and said, "What're you guys doing? They'll get away."

The hunting party turned around, and the inertia huntress mounted on one of the wolves declared, "They now belong to the blue wolves. Just leave it be. We'll have more to hunt soon. Now, if you don't mind, can you change back because I don't want to see your manhood? Thank you."

Tristan, displeased by this news, replied, "What're you afraid of, the blue wolves? We're the ones hunting, not them."

The huntress responded, "Look, you're a protector, so you outrank us, which means I won't tell you what to do. But I will say this. Yes, we do fear them, and so should you. Just leave them be, there's plenty of deer to go around."

Shocked and appalled by the huntress's attitude, Tristan shook his head. Even though she was right in being respectful and cautious, he thought of this as weakness. "I'm getting what's rightfully mine."

Tristan transformed back into a wolf and gave chase to the deer, crossing the border into the Blue Wolf Clan's territory. He ran for about three miles, coming across dead ground the deer had run into. He wasn't going to give up his hunt and training, so he kept running, clearing the banking and exposing the dead ground, seeing them for the first time in his life.

He had seen grey wolves before and one black wolf once, but these were different. The average wolf stands between six and seven feet tall, but the blue wolves were around twelve to fourteen feet tall. They had navy blue fur with small amounts of white fur markings, such as white patches or stripes. The thing that struck fear into Tristan the most was not their monstrous size, but their eyes. They were not normal eyes. They were yellow, not just the irises that they all have in human form, but the complete eyeball. As one of them saw him on top of the banking, it howled three times.

Tristan knew he made a fatal error, and now he was the hunted because they had declared a sighted enemy. He turned around to run away, but as he did, two blue wolves advanced behind him. As he ran, trying to evade the both of them, one of the blue wolves charged and head-butted him several metres back down the banking, causing him to roll several times. As he got up, he found himself surrounded by seven blue wolves and two inertia hunters mounted on their comrades. One of the inertia hunters jumped off a wolf, drawing his hunters' knife, and commanded, "You, change into human form, or we'll rip you apart."

Tristan obeyed the command and transformed, being overcome with anxiety and true fear for the first time in his life. The hunter smiled and declared to the party. "Ha, looks like their wolf form isn't the only small thing about them."

The other inertia hunter laughed at the joke referring to the size of Tristan's penis, and in his embarrassment, he covered his manhood with his hands.

"Why're you here, White Wolf?" the hunter spat.

Tristan swallowed hard and replied, "I was just hunting the deer that passed you."

The hunter raised one eyebrow, tilted his head and added, "You should know that when they pass your border into ours, you lose the hunt, and they become ours. We respect that rule for your clan, so what makes you so high and mighty to break the rules against us?"

Tristan's breathing became more rapid with each moment, and his head moved around, with his eyes rapidly looking at all of them as he thought of an answer. Behind the blue wolves on top of the banking stood ten white wolves and the inertia huntress that had advised Tristan not to continue the hunt. The huntress dismounted the wolf she rode, placing her bow over her head, and walked down the banking into the middle of the circle.

The twenty-three-year-old, plain-looking hunter showed more courage than Tristan, placing herself in a dangerous position. She gave the wolves' greeting, then spoke directly to the dismounted blue wolf hunter. "Hello there, please excuse the intrusion. I'm Lilly Whitepaw of the White Wolf Clan. Please don't be hard on this young lad. He's not a hunter like us, and he doesn't know the rules."

The blue wolf hunter walked towards Lilly, stopping a few feet in front of her. "If he's no hunter, then what is he?"

Lilly looked over at Tristan, blinking in slow-motion, and exhaled a deep breath before turning back to the blue wolf hunter. "He's a trainee. He just managed to get away from us, so we followed him here to retrieve him. I know he's old for a trainee, but he failed his final trial when he was eighteen."

Lilly showed great intellect because if she had told them his actual rank, they would have killed him, and most probably the hunting party, instantly.

"You know that when you cross into our lands, your lives are forfeit, right?" the blue wolf hunter replied.

"Yes, we're very sorry, and we mean no disrespect. In fact, we have two deer we've already hunted. Please take them as part of our sincerest apology."

The blue wolf hunter looked at the deer and grinned, "Oh, they're very nice. I see one is a twelve pointer and the other is an eight pointer. Ok, that'll be acceptable with one other condition. That trainee of yours is to walk all the way to your border, unchanged and naked."

Lilly smirked. "That's a reasonable request. He may learn something from that experience."

“Ok, drop your offerings and get out of here before I change my mind,” the blue wolf hunter ordered.

Lilly gave the wolves’ greeting and nodded her head. Turning around, she walked over to Tristan, grabbed his arm and dragged him out of the circle of blue wolves. In hushed tones, she whispered, “Now, listen to me, you will not change all the way to the border. If you endanger me or my party, I’ll open up your neck myself. Do I make myself clear?”

Amazed with what she had done, he nodded in agreement. She mounted one of the white wolves, and they all made their way back to their lands of Marsh Plain empty-handed, with the blue wolves watching.

Once they crossed the border back into their lands, Lilly dismounted from the wolf and walked over to Tristan. “I know you’re a protector, but maybe in the future, you’ll be less arrogant and listen to others’ advice. You put yourself and us in danger, without just cause.”

Tristan lowered his head and replied, “Yes, I’m sorry and thankful for what you’ve all done. I’ll inform the alpha of what has happened.”

“There’s no need to do that. What’s done is done, and that’s the end of it. We won’t howl you out,” she reassured.

Tristan raised his head with a smile. “No, you don’t understand. You all came to my aid, so you’ll get what you deserve.”

“What do you mean?” Lilly asked.

“You all showed bravery back there, so I’ll nominate each and every one of you for the selection process to be protectors, if you want it. And as for you, Lilly, I know our peacekeeper is looking for an apprentice. I think that could be you if I’m to be honest. You kept those blue wolves calm and sorted me out as well.”

“But won’t you be in trouble or get demoted?”

"I'm not worried about that. I have something else I must do, and it'll take up all of my time, so I might step down as a protector," Tristan replied.

"Why would you do that?"

Tristan looked back to the Great Plain, staring hard at the blue wolves that watched them. He dipped his head slightly, and his smile faded, clenching his jaw for a few seconds as he replied, "I have my own reasons."

"You're ok, though, right? Because I know how it must feel being overpowered and overwhelmed by the experience you just had." Lilly asked with concern.

"Yes, I'm fine, it's just opened my eyes, that's all. Let's go home."

Being true to his word, Tristan recommended all of the hunting party that helped him to the alpha, while also praising Lilly's abilities to the peacekeeper.

Not long after that day, Tristan left the protectors to pursue his own training, which was so intense, the people that knew him personally saw a change, seeing an obsession like no other which consumed him.

Six years had passed with changes in the White Wolf Clan. The capital city had moved from Fullurdale to the most north-westerly point of their country, erecting a new city that had been under construction for the last forty years. No longer would the white wolves live in clay huts, but houses made of stone, wood, and glass complemented with thatched roofs, with the construction of the castle nearing completion.

It was the peak of summer, and Tristan's personal training was done. Both in human and wolf form, he had grown to be a very large man. His muscles were defined, with bulging veins under skin, and he now sported short hair. As a wolf, he looked even more terrifying, with muscles that were not defined on any other wolf chiselled into his body. His training was like no other before his time, or since he passed on. He was beyond a warrior, becoming a fighting machine.

The clan's new alpha had reigned for the past two years, being a few years older than Tristan, a strong and reliable leader, loved and respected by the clan.

Testing his newfound abilities, Tristan hunted deer outside the old capital, where he still lived. He was a powerhouse of strength and speed, but even after years of training, he could never master the other wolves' agility, a weakness he could never overcome that was worsened by his sheer size.

He tore apart two deer with the strength of his bite, but one evaded him. As it crossed the border into the Great Plain, he decided to finish what he had started, breaking the border law again. This time, the deer only managed to flee a mile into the Great Plain before losing its life. Less than half a mile away was a party of four blue wolf hunters, two in wolf form and inertias riding them.

The blue wolves charged up to him, halting their intruder. "Hey, what're you doing here?" one of them asked.

Tristan turned into a human and replied, "I'm hunting. Now leave me be."

The other inertia hunter and blue wolf advanced. "You can't hunt here, so I'm afraid I'm going to ask you to leave and go back to Marsh Plain, White Wolf."

Lowering his head to neutral alignment, Tristan scoffed, "You can try and make me if you wish."

The first hunter who spoke to Tristan also advanced with the wolf he was on. "Now there's no need to be disrespectful, White

Wolf. You're trespassing, so if you don't remove yourself, then we'll be forced to take action," he declared.

"I haven't got all day, Blue Wolf," Tristan replied.

Transforming back into a wolf, he engaged. Being outnumbered did not slow him down; it only made him more powerful and determined to best these powerful wolves. The fight did not last long as he found the blue wolves had underestimated him.

When he ripped open his last challenger's neck, the blue wolf gave a yelp of pain, dying after a few breaths, as the blood from its arteries sprayed over Tristan and the last survivor. The inertia hunter was all alone with a broken bow next to him, with his knife trembling in hand. "S-s-stop right th-th-there."

Tristan changed back into a human and declared, "You're by far the scariest wolf breed I've ever seen, but I expected" – he walked over to the petrified hunter with a smile – "well, more. You see, your clan might have the natural strength and speed, but now I've shown you what we're capable of. You'll live today because I allow it. Now go and tell your alpha what has happened here today."

Without hesitation, the hunter sheathed his knife and ran away.

Tristan turned back into a wolf, running hard and fast over the next four days to get to the new capital, only stopping at towns and villages along the way for food and rest.

He had never been to the new capital, and he was in awe with what his clan had achieved over the years. He got through the lower ring, and there it stood, upon the high peninsula, almost complete, the white castle. He walked up to the new gate at the peninsular path, coming across a protector on guard. The protector peered through the gate and declared, "I'm sorry, but all public access is forbidden until the construction of the castle is complete."

Tristan peered back and replied, "Hey, Dai, is that you?"

Advancing closer to the gate, recognising a familiar face, the protector's eyes widened as he asked, "Tristan, is that you?"

"Yeah, it's good to see you, Dai. It's been what, five years since I last saw you?" Tristan smiled.

"About that long, yeah. Shit, you're massive. What happened to you?"

"I left the protectors because I began my own training."

"You look good, my old comrade."

"Hey, I was wondering if I could ask a favour. I need to see the alpha for a short while. Would you let an old friendly face enter to go see him, and have a little look around?" Tristan asked.

Dai rubbed his chin. "All right, but only this once, and you better not tell anyone, or it's me that'll be disciplined. I'll just lift the gate a little, so it's not obvious that I'm letting you in. Just roll under it."

"Thanks, Dai, you won't regret it."

As the gate opened slightly, he rolled under. Standing up and tapping his old comrade on the shoulder, he said, "Cheers, I'll see you when I get back down, ok?"

Dai pointed at him and ordered, "Hey, no longer than an hour, all right? I might finish my guard duty in two hours, but I want you long gone before that point."

Tristan grinned, "No problem, it shouldn't take long anyway."

He walked up the path towards the castle with only one objective in mind. To become the new alpha of the white wolves.

Chapter Eleven

DEMISE OF THE BLUE WOLF CLAN

Three weeks had passed, and Tristan became the white wolf alpha during his visit to White Castle, but he had not sent his peacekeeper to declare this information to the other clans.

"Why have you not released me, Tristan? You're stopping me from performing my duties, and I'll not tolerate it, alpha or no alpha," Lilly spat.

"I understand, but there's a valid reason. You can go within the next few days because their peacekeeper should be here soon," Tristan replied.

"What do you mean?" she frowned, shaking her head slightly.

"You'll know in due time. Now, please make your party ready for your duties, and await my orders."

After three hours, the leaders of the clan were dealing with petty matters. Suddenly, the heavy doors swung open, slamming into the walls, and the blue wolf peacekeeper barged into the great hall, demanding, "Where's your alpha?"

Lilly walked towards him and gave the wolves' greeting. "Hello there, Bran, please advance and tell me the secret word of our respected title."

Bran walked forward, giving the wolves' greeting, and whispered the word to her.

"Welcome, Blue Wolf Peacekeeper. Before we start, can you ask your party to wait outside? You're safe here," Lilly requested.

"That's fine. You lot wait outside and await only my orders."

Bran's party confirmed the order, leaving with immediate effect, except one person. "This man stays with me," Bran demanded.

Tipping her head, she replied, "That's fine. So how may we be of service?"

"Get me your alpha, Rab. We need to talk now," Bran thundered.

"I'm sorry, but we now have a new alpha. His name's Tristan, and you can talk to him. He's behind me," Lilly replied.

The man that remained with Bran pointed at Tristan and shouted, "That's him, he's the one I told you about!"

Bran's brow dropped, and he bit his lower lip as he walked past Lilly, speaking directly to Tristan. "Is this true? Are you the new alpha?"

"Yes. Rab's my pathfinder now," Tristan replied.

Bran looked at Lilly and spat, "How long has he been the alpha?"

Lilly drew a deep breath. "Three weeks."

"Why are you still here? You should be informing the other clans. It's your duty, not a leisurely activity you can do as you please."

Before Lilly could reply, Tristan interrupted, "I commanded her to wait because I've been expecting you."

"That's no excuse! You know the traditions of the clans, and your peacekeeper is well overdue to inform them. She should already be out there," Bran concluded.

"There's nothing we can do now, so why have you come to talk to me?" Tristan asked.

"You have committed atrocities that were not valid. You attacked and killed three of our hunters almost four weeks ago. How do you plead to the allegations of this hunter here that witnessed it?" Bran questioned.

"What he said is true. Now you can go back to your alpha with the same message that I'll give my peacekeeper."

"What message?" Bran hissed.

Lilly was initially confused, but she figured out that this was the reason he would not release her to complete her duties.

Tristan stood up and declared, "Lilly, you're to go to the Grey and Black Wolf Clans. Tell their alphas what I tell this blue wolf peacekeeper. In eight weeks, our clans will meet at Borders Cross."

Borders Cross was a massive field encompassed by a forest, making the field an oval shape. The grass was short, and the field slightly declined to the east. Just over the halfway point to the south of the field, the ground level dropped down with a medium-sized banking. This place was where all four borders of the wolf clans intertwined, and it was a famous battleground for one purpose.

"We will all meet there, where I openly challenge all alphas for the title of omega alpha. If any clan does not turn up, then that clan will be dishonoured throughout history."

Tristan sat back down, Rab's eyes widened in shock, and Lilly looked at him, shaking her head.

"So be it, White Wolf Alpha. You're a fool to challenge my alpha, and I'll look forward to seeing him rip you apart," Bran sniggered.

With immediate effect, Bran turned around and left the great hall with his hunter without saying another word.

"Tristan, are you mad? You cannot expect to challenge all three alphas and win," Lilly advised.

"We will see, won't we? Now you're released to perform your duties. So go and give my declaration to the other alphas."

Lilly gave the wolves' greeting and replied, "As you wish, Alpha."

Eight weeks had passed, and during that time, Tristan had been challenged twice for his position. The alphas from the other clans had also been challenged several times, with only the Black Wolf Clan gaining a new alpha, which during a challenge for omega alpha, needn't be declared to other clans.

Emerging from the treeline surrounding the field, the four clans met in full fighting force ranking from hunter upwards. With the exception of peacekeepers and a few healers, only men filled the ranks.

First to emerge was the black wolf alpha, making his way to the centre of the field, then the blue wolf alpha was next to follow, with the grey wolf alpha and Tristan being the last two to join them at the same time. Stood around three hundred metres apart, transforming into wolves, they advanced and stared each other down.

The grey wolf alpha took a few steps towards the blue wolf alpha, bowing his head low before lifting it high, howling as loud as he could. The Grey Wolf Clan followed his actions by howling and shouting, displaying that the Grey Wolf Clan had fully submitted to the blue wolves' alpha. The black wolf alpha limped forward, injured from claiming his title. He submitted to the blue wolf alpha, and so did his clan, in the same fashion as the grey wolves.

Tristan and the blue wolf alpha locked eye contact, with neither of them backing down. The challenge for omega alpha had now been met, and the strongest warriors were ready for their mortal combat. The black and grey wolf alphas both retired hastily back among their people, ready to see who would be the ruler over all four clans.

Tristan was the first to go on the offensive, and the blue wolf alpha responded immediately. They collided with so much force all of the clans' members could hear a mild thud. The blue wolf alpha, with a superior size and weight advantage, only stumbled backwards a few feet. However, Tristan bounced off the giant wolf, falling onto his back. The blue wolf alpha ran over and encompassed the back of Tristan's neck as he recovered to his feet. Due to the blue wolf's natural size and strength, he picked Tristan up as if he were a small deer, slamming him into the ground with so much force, a loud thud could be heard by everyone. Tristan cried out in pain, not just from the impact of his body being smashed into the dirt; he also received deep wounds on the back and sides of his neck. But he was strong, very strong, so he fought on.

Tristan's speed while running in a straight line was unmeasurable, but what let him down was his lack of agility. With nearly all wolves being able to turn ninety degrees at full sprinting speed, he was just about able to turn forty degrees, useless in evasion and combat. But what he lacked in agility, he made up for in guile and pure strength.

The fight was the longest anyone had ever seen. After around forty minutes of running, jumping, throwing, biting and scratching, it looked like the two alphas had come to the end of their energy reserves. The blue wolf alpha, almost black in colour, and Tristan, almost pure red with patches of pink, proved to everyone present the two of them had fought hard, covered in both each other's and their own blood.

With the loss of blood and high-intensity fighting, both alphas were breathing rapidly, with their strength leaving them. Tristan's vision started to blur, and for a split second, it blackened, causing him to stumble. As his vision returned, he used the little strength he had left to regain his balance. The blue wolf alpha made an advance, but his two front legs gave way, causing him to collapse. His muzzle smashed into the dirt with so much force, his head bounced before hitting the ground again. With his body rolling to one side, Tristan knew he had to press his last attack now, or the blue wolf might recover and gain the upper hand. Tristan could not run with the pain in his legs due to his puncture wounds. Sidestepping around his challenger while in immense pain, he aligned himself with the blue wolf alpha's neck. Using the last of his strength in his hind legs, he leapt forward with an open mouth, biting down into his challenger's flesh.

Three minutes, that's how long Tristan had to bite down on the blue wolf alpha's neck before his life extinguished. It was a long time for anyone to endure, but it had finally finished.

Tristan turned back into a human, covered in blood, cuts, and deep wounds, displaying the price he had paid through honourable combat. The third omega alpha had risen with the White Wolf Clan howling and cheering, as the blue wolves howled, submitting to their new leader.

Bran broke ranks, advancing towards Tristan. He gave the wolves' greeting and bowed before his new leader, with tears in his eyes. "Omega Alpha, congratulations on your new title. You're very strong, indeed. I come before you to ask for a favour.

Would you permit us to take the body of our beloved alpha back to the Great Plain, so we can give him a warrior's ritual?"

He could not hide the pain in his eyes as the adrenaline wore off, but he still spoke with a steady voice. "Yes, you take him back to your homeland. I'll see you when I've recovered."

"Thank you, Omega Alpha, you're very kind," Bran replied.

Tristan turned around and collapsed as his healers and protectors got to him. The healers put him onto a stretcher, carrying him away to tend to his wounds.

His physical recovery only took two and a half months, but mentally, he grew darker, becoming more withdrawn than ever. He was no longer able to transform into a wolf because of his condition, battle stress. It was not physically a permanent condition, but mentally, it could last forever as it would take him time to recover, if he could, and he would have to recover from his battle stress alone.

It was a long two years for him, but during his recovery, he snapped as darkness consumed him. Fear had taken hold of Tristan, and he became petrified of the blue wolves. Although he was able to transform again, his battle stress remained, waking from night terrors due to recurring dreams of the first time he encountered the blue wolves, and the fight he had with their alpha. During all of this time, he had not picked a blue wolf pathfinder, which the blue wolves were not happy with, but they had no say in the matter. After Tristan gave Lilly orders to summon his pathfinders, he sat in the great hall surrounded by his council. The grey and black wolf pathfinders wondered what he had summoned them for.

Tristan stood up and spoke to the council of only three clans. "I'm the omega alpha and your true leader, am I not?"

Everyone in the hall verbally agreed and nodded.

"Will you follow my every command, as is law?" Tristan inquired.

Everyone in the great hall nodded and concurred again.

"Then it's time to assemble your armies and meet me at the old white wolf capital of Fullurdale in nine weeks."

Lilly stood up from her chair and challenged his command. "Why, Omega Alpha? What's the purpose of this?"

"All will be revealed when we meet up. You have nine weeks to bring all your fighting force to the old capital."

"What of the blue wolves, Omega Alpha? Does this involve them?" Lilly quizzed again.

"It does, but that's not of your concern right now. Just trust me. I know what I'm doing," Tristan replied.

Because of law, tradition and the fact he ruled over all clans, Lilly fought against her gut feeling and thought of the only reasonable explanation, the coronation of the blue wolf pathfinder, which had been overdue.

Nine weeks later, all three armies of the Black, Grey and White Wolf Clans were together. All three pathfinders stood in front of their armies, awaiting their orders from Tristan and the reasoning of why they were there. All of Tristan's council had the same questions—was it a test to see how fast they could assemble their armies, or was this for some build-up to coronate a blue wolf pathfinder?

Stood in front of his pathfinders, Tristan declared his intentions. "I've gathered you all here today to put an end to a threat that has plagued our lands for far too long."

The black wolf pathfinder responded to his statement. "Omega Alpha, the stygians have not come back to our lands since our clans drove them out. Have they returned?"

"No, there's a new enemy within our race. The blue wolves are too powerful to be left alone. We must deal with this issue now," Tristan commanded.

Rab frowned, challenging Tristan's words. "They are very strong and powerful, Omega Alpha, but very few in number. We've been living alongside them for thousands of years. How've they become a threat now?"

Tristan glared at Rab and shouted, "Because I say they are! Do you dare question your omega alpha?"

Rab lowered his head and replied, "No, I'm sorry, I will not speak out of turn again."

"Good, now we'll divide into two forces going from village to village, town to town until we reach their capital. And you will kill every blue wolf you come across, and I mean every blue wolf. We move now."

Tristan transformed, and the armies followed his lead changing into wolves, with the inertias mounting their comrades. 8,000 warriors marched north-east with Rab and the black wolf pathfinder. The grey wolf pathfinder with 9,000 warriors followed Tristan travelling east.

The first village Tristan came across was small, making it easy work to kill all of the residents, razing each hut to the ground as they left. However, Llanor was the next town they came across, filled with people celebrating two mating ceremonies that day.

Two children playing at the edge of the town saw Tristan's half of the army advancing a mile away. The children thought that they were part of the mating ceremonies, so all they did was smile, wave and shout with joy and amazement.

When Tristan led the assault on the town, the children stopped waving, smiles faded, with joy was replaced by terror as they saw Tristan's face baring his large teeth, with thousands of wolves running behind him with the same expression. Tristan barged into one child with so much force; she flew into a hut as a blood splatter from the back of her head flicked up the wall, ending her life. Leaning his head over while running, he bit into the other child fleeing from him, skewering the boy's body with his fangs and powerful jaws. Tossing the child's corpse at the congregated crowd, everyone screamed in horror. Around fifty blue wolves managed to transform and fight back, but Tristan's manpower overwhelmed them, making them easy prey.

Most of the town's people had been killed, but one of the inertia blue wolf protectors questioned Tristan with tears in his eyes. "Why're you doing this? You're our leader, our omega alpha."

Tristan dived forward, turning his head sideways, biting into the trunk of the blue wolf protector. Engulfing the majority of his upper body, Tristan lifted the protector up, shaking his head violently. Screaming in pain, the protector's head was smashed into a wall of a hut several times, demolishing his skull and allowing blood and brain matter to escape. After the assault, Tristan noticed a woman holding her two-month-old baby with a six-year-old child behind her. He dropped the corpse while locking eyes on the mother, but suddenly his glare was interrupted.

"Stop this madness now, Tristan!" Lilly shouted, standing between him and the mother. "What you're doing here is wrong. Please call off your assault. There are too many innocents dying."

Refusing to transform to give a dignified response, he barked at her, so she continued her plea, "This is wrong, and as your peacekeeper, I'm informing you that if you continue to walk this path, you'll have to go through me. I saved your life once, and this is what you can do to repay that debt. Just leave the rest of their clan be. You've crippled them."

Tristan's muzzle wrinkled up, exposing his teeth and gums, displaying his displeasure. Lilly turned around to the mother and shouted, "Run!"

Drawing her hunters' knife with her right hand, she swung an axe with her left at Tristan. Expecting her attack, he paced back, dodging her strike. Diving forward, she swung her axe again, hitting his muzzle, splitting the skin open.

Darting his head forward with an open mouth, he engulfed her head, missing her neck as he travelled too far down her body, clamping his teeth into her shoulder blades and collarbones. Dropping her axe, she stabbed wildly into Tristan's lower jaw with the hunters' knife, but with her arm movements restricted, she did not cause enough damage to hurt him badly. Lifting her up, Tristan threw her behind him to the other wolves, and she hit the ground hard with one of her collarbones broken from the bite. He turned back into a human with his nose and chin covered in minor cuts and blood. "She's betrayed the law and has attacked her omega alpha. Rip her apart!"

Lilly had no chance of survival, suffering a horrendous death at the hands of her comrades, torn limb from limb as she screamed.

Tristan transformed again and gave chase to the mother and her small children, fleeing fifty metres away. Shoulder-barging the mother, her baby flew out of her arms, knocking her other child over as she stumbled to the ground. The infant screamed in pain as its left arm and shoulder were dislocated and broken from the impact.

The six-year-old child sat up, screaming, "Mammy!"

Pivoting, he charged at her again, clamping his jaws around the mother's right leg. Lifting her high into the air, he threw her down hard into the ground with all his strength, fracturing her skull while snapping her neck. Focusing his attention on the six-year-old child still crying, he charged forward relentlessly, biting into the boy's torso, teeth penetrating the chest wall with his right canine piercing the child's heart. Dropping the young corpse from his mouth, he stopped to look at the baby screaming on the cold hard ground.

In his hesitation, his heart filled with regret and anger towards himself. He closed his eyes and wondered if this was the correct solution to his own twisted fear. Opening his eyes, he dipped his head down and charged at the infant, scooping it up in his mouth. As his jaws closed around the baby's body, he could not feel the typical crunch of bones between his teeth; instead, he felt a soft, rubber-like feeling before the baby's head and body created a popping sensation in his mouth. The silencing of the infant's screams, followed by the sweet taste of blood, confirmed to Tristan that he had extinguished the baby's short, young life forever.

Just over 2,500 Blue Wolf Clan members had died up to this point, with Tristan's army sweeping through the towns and villages. But now their main prize stood before them, the blue wolves' capital city. Unbeknownst to the people of Drysor

Glas, a large army advanced to send thousands of souls to the Meadowlands. No one had managed to escape any of the previous towns or villages to warn the inhabitants, as every single person was killed along the way. This onslaught had been going on for two weeks, but the slaughter was just beginning. With Tristan's half of the army advancing ten miles south of Drysor Glas, he howled, commanding a slow advance.

At the south of the city, Bran was alerted by Tristan's howl to the large number of wolves approaching.

"What're they doing, Peacekeeper?" a protector asked.

"I'm not sure, but I feel it's not a welcoming party. Assemble our forces to counteract." Pointing at another protector, Bran commanded, "And you, start the evacuation of the city."

As Tristan's army covered the first four miles on their slow advance, blue wolves emerged from between the huts, ready to defend their homeland and loved ones. Bran looked at the invading force, and he knew there was only one explanation of why this was happening. His eyes scanned the entire army before him and muttered, "So this is the end of my clan. You might've fought bravely at Borders Cross, Tristan, but you've proved yourself cowardly and weak. You're not worthy of your title, and I hope the Great Wolf makes you the eternal hunted for this crime of yours."

Bran took a few deep breaths, grimaced and shouted to his men. "So be it, kill as many of those wet mutts as you can! We'll fall today, but at least we fight with honour! Onwards, my brothers, for today we join the Great Wolf defending our people!"

The blue wolves charged at Tristan's force, closing ground to go head-to-head, until the blue wolves heard screams from behind. As one of them turned around, he could see smoke emerge from the north of the city. This alerted Tristan that the other half of his army had arrived, breaching the city limits and starting their assault on innocent people. Half of the blue wolves turned around, running back to aid the people of the city, making the battle a guaranteed, easy victory to Tristan's force.

There was not much of a fight when the wolves clashed, as the defending force consisted of a mere two hundred and fifty wolves against just under 9,000 black, grey and white wolves. As strong as the blue wolves were, they were no match for the overwhelming numbers of Tristan's advance. After the short-lived battle, Tristan and his forces could hear screams and wolves yelping, so he led his force into the city, making the army complete once more while killing everyone and razing the blue wolves' capital to the ground.

After the fall of Drysor Glas, it took a total of three months to wipe out the Blue Wolf Clan. With the Great Plain being sacked, all the buildings were turned to rubble and ash, and the ground ran red with blue wolves' blood. Tristan had succeeded, and all the wolves of the west ultimately lost. Once the task was complete, the armies dispersed back to their respective clans, and everyone who took part in the slaughter was ashamed of their actions for one man's conquest, creating the darkest period in the wolves' history.

Five years later, the Blue Wolf Clan became but a bitter memory. Tristan found a mate and had two children of his own, one son and one daughter. As they grew older, he grew more depressed with the knowledge and guilt of what he had done to shatter the West Plains. Because of his fear, he devastated the balance of the world, with the wolves no longer being the strong and respected race they once were.

A few nights after his son's fourth birthday, he could not contain the guilt anymore. He went into the great hall and wrote on a piece of parchment, explaining the horrors that kept him up at night due to his actions and fears, confessing how the ethnic cleansing of the Blue Wolf Clan had solved nothing. He sealed the parchment with wax and stamped it with the alpha's signet ring, placing it on the peacekeeper's chair with the hope that he would find it first. Tristan stood on his chair, rocking it back and forth until the chair fell over, causing his legs to dangle above. With him gargling, his body fought for air as his legs kicked around and twitched for several minutes before they went limp. And just like that, the third omega alpha's reign came to an end.

A few moments later, a protector on guard duty walked into the great hall, discovering Tristan hanging off one of the metal fixtures by a small length of rope around his neck. As his house was the closest, the protector ran directly to the peacekeeper to tell him of his discovery. With the peacekeeper commanding a protector standing guard outside to join them, they all entered the great hall.

As all three of them looked at Tristan's suspended body, the peacekeeper came up with a plan. "Now, this is a complicated matter. If we utter a word of what's happened here tonight, there could be more death over the West Plains. We must keep this secret. The two of you will say you saw Tristan leave this hall, and he went to his favourite spot. You will say he was drunk, and you saw him stumble and fall."

One of the protectors frowned and asked, "Fall where?"

"Over the cliff's edge. If word gets out that he killed himself, then others involved in the Blue Wolf Clans' demise might take their lives. The West Plains has lost enough as it is," the peacekeeper turned to the other protector and ordered, "Now, cut him down, and between us, we will dispose of the body correctly. The sea will take him now."

As the protectors cut him down, the peacekeeper saw the parchment on his chair and opened it. Finding the contents disturbing, he immediately burned it on one of the torches, and then they carried the corpse out of the great hall. They swung Tristan three times before throwing his carcass over the cliff's edge, where the sea claimed his body.

The peacekeeper turned to one of the protectors and commanded, "I suggest you look startled and surprised, get in that great hall and shout for help."

The protector nodded, running to the great hall. The peacekeeper had one more task to perform for the good of all the clans, visiting Tristan's mate to perform his final task regarding this carnage, forcing her to a vow of secrecy within her own pack.

Chapter Twelve

THE FALL OF REASON

"That is the tale of the last omega alpha. One more secret I have for you, yes, yes." Alsander stared hard as he continued, "You see, his pack name is a secret. What pack name you wonder...White-Ear. He is your great, great-granddad, last of your pack to change into a wolf until you, yes, yes."

Alsander shook his head and scrunched up his face. "Don't lie to me, old man."

"The truth I speak, Alsander, if only you stop to listen. A nice child you was, and you could redeem your pack name. You and only you now have the power to change the future, yes, yes."

Alsander looked to the ground and raised his head back up, bearing his sinister smile. "You're right there. I do have the power to change the future, and I will. I'll finish what Tristan couldn't."

Alsander turned and started to walk away with Neil, but they were stopped a last time by Crey's words. "No, no, not Tristan's plan. Misunderstand the message you have. A nice boy you was, but that boy is gone, only your dad I hear now."

Turning back around red-faced, Alsander thundered, "I'm not my dad. He was weak!"

Transforming into a wolf, he charged at Crey, piercing his left shoulder with his fangs, eliciting an agonising scream while lifting him off the ground. As he shook his head violently, Crey shouted a final time, "I have failed, but you can succeed!"

As Crey fell to his death, his eyes locked with Alsander's, looking down at him from over the cliff's edge. Thudding into the rocks at the bottom, his old and frail body separated into several segments, leaving entrails on one of the rocks briefly before the sea claimed his body. Alsander changed back into a human, and he and Neil both retired back to the great hall, with Neil laughing.

Meanwhile, in the foliage of the flower-covered rock, Bleddyn stood silent and still, with tears rolling down his face. He had seen and heard everything, and it hurt him, watching his mentor and friend getting murdered like that, but there was nothing he could do. Alsander was the alpha, and that was the end of it.

A few hours later, Kennon entered the great hall with thirty-five protectors he had chosen.

"Stand in a line over there, men, and await further instruction," Kennon commanded.

The men fell in line, standing to attention while waiting for their alpha. Alsander and Neil appeared from the stairway, approaching Kennon.

"Are these your men?" Alsander asked.

“Yes, and they’re very capable warriors. In fact, ten of them are the best protectors,” Kennon boasted.

Alsander walked past them all, inspecting them one by one. “Yes, these are the type of warriors I’m looking for. Now, you tell me, what do you think of the Black and Grey Wolf Clans?”

“The Grey Wolf Clan have great warriors, and the Black Wolf Clan have great alchemists. I respect them,” the protector replied.

Drawing his hunters’ knife, Alsander slashed the protector’s neck open. Blood pumped out of his wound hard and fast, with one spurt landing on Alsander’s face. As the protector collapsed forward, his shoulder rubbed against Alsander. Glaring at the next protector in line, he questioned, “You, what do you think of our black and grey wolf cousins?”

“They’re weak, Alpha, and they should all bow to the greatest clan, our clan,” the protector answered.

Alsander smiled and addressed the rest of them. “If you don’t believe in what this protector has said, then I suggest you step forward, so my Pathfinder can ask you why you hate your clan.” None of the protectors moved an inch, so he continued, “Good, this is what’s going to happen. Firstly, we need a new peacekeeper. The crazy old man had himself...an accident. After that, we’ll go into the black wolf lands and attack one of their villages, or maybe two to draw out their alpha. Our new peacekeeper will come with us, and then we’ll do the same with the grey wolves. Because the new peacekeeper will be with us, he can give false information so we can attack the villages.”

“What about Ren of the grey wolves? He’s known to be strong, and he has never been beaten in combat before,” Kennon replied.

Alsander leered at Kennon with rage in his eyes as he responded through gritted teeth. “I know of his reputation, and I don’t care. When I bathe in his blood, I’ll seal my glory forever in history. Only the strong will survive, and the weak will be destroyed."

"As you wish, Alpha. I don't doubt your resolve or your strength," Kennon said, bowing.

"Neil, get the people to vote. They'll have until tomorrow to cast them," Alsander commanded.

"What about the other people in the clan that live beyond the city?" Neil asked.

"I don't care about them. Just get it done! In time, we'll not need peacekeepers after my plans are finished."

"As you wish, I'll get it done immediately," Neil replied as he walked off and exited the great hall.

"Now, as for you, ready yourselves because in two days, we leave for Black Forest Plain," Alsander commanded.

They all gave the wolves' greeting and left the great hall to prepare for their expedition.

Kennon asked Alsander a final question. "Alpha, what's it you're hoping to achieve in all this?"

Alsander gave his sinister smile and replied, "A new future our clan can be proud of. Now go."

Kennon gave the wolves' greeting and exited the hall, wondering what happened to Crey.

The next day, city folk came to cast their vote for a new peacekeeper, and they all voted for the same person. By early afternoon, Bleddyn Whitetail was voted as the new peacekeeper of the white wolves.

With great humility, he addressed the people before him. "Thank you all for placing your faith in me and my judgements past, present and future. I swear, from this day as your chosen peacekeeper, I'll do my best to achieve what's right for the future of this clan and all of you."

Watching and listening from the back of the crowd, Alsander gave an order. "Neil, bring our new peacekeeper to me now."

"He'll be with you momentarily," Neil replied.

Alsander retired back to the great hall as Neil barged his way through the crowd to get to Bleddyn. "You! The alpha demands your presence right now."

Bleddyn nodded and replied, "As you wish, Pathfinder."

Escorted to the great hall by Neil and presented to Alsander, Bleddyn gave the wolves' greeting and bowed. Alsander looked him up and down, and he began asking him questions. "So, your speech out there was quite impressive, but I want to know, are you really ready to do what it takes for the clan?"

Bleddyn took to one knee and spoke as if he swore the words on his very soul. "Yes, I'll do anything for the good of the clan, no matter the cost."

"Good, that's what I want to hear, because I have a task for you. You'll be coming with me to Black Forest Plain."

Bleddyn looked up and questioned, "Why would you venture to the land of the black wolves?"

"You'll understand when we're there. That's all you need to know, so get yourself ready. We move out tomorrow morning."

Bleddyn stared at Alsander for a few seconds, having a flashback of what he did to Crey.

"Is there something else?" Alsander asked.

"No, Alpha. I'll go and prepare for our journey immediately."

Bleddyn stood up and exited the great hall with Neil watching him closely. When the great hall doors shut behind him, Neil turned and advised, "For some reason, I think he knows. We should be careful around him."

"It doesn't matter. If he proves to be strong, then he can remain, but if not, you can have the pleasure of killing him yourself if you wish. Like I said yesterday, we won't be needing peacekeepers in the future. I have one more favour from you; find me someone you can trust because I have an important task."

Neil smiled and wandered out of the great hall.

Alsander sat back in his chair and muttered to himself. "See Dad, if you weren't so weak, you could've been part of this, but now I'll be the wolf king without you, and I'll be the greatest leader the white wolves have ever known by redeeming our honour."

Breathing heavily, Tabitha recovered, sheathing her knife. Wikki looked at her with amazement. "By the Great Wolf, it takes a protector in training two months to complete advanced knife fighting. It's like when we were at the forest on your eleventh birthday. I just don't know how you pick up fighting techniques so quickly."

"Well, from my experience, I found other women picked up training techniques just as quick as me. Some are better in other areas too," Tabitha smiled.

"Really? It doesn't surprise me too much," Wikki replied, "but now we'll see what you've truly learned."

Rummaging around in his backpack, he pulled out two wooden knives, throwing one to Tabitha. "What are these for?" she asked.

"To fight each other, of course. This isn't official, but I'll treat it as such. If I win, you fail; but if you win or draw, then you would have achieved a pass. Are you ready?"

Tabitha held out the wooden knife, smiling at Wikki, and as he smiled back, they ran at each other. She speared the knife forward, grazing his arm as he spun around, hitting her in the side of the neck.

"Ah, fuck! That really hurt," Tabitha complained.

"Yeah, what did you expect?" Wikki chuckled. "So that was a quick fail. Now come on, stop messing around and take it seriously, or I'll just keep hitting you until you do. I know you picked it up quickly, but don't be overconfident even if it looks like your opponent is losing. Always fight with the intention to kill because, one day, your life may depend on it."

Tabitha stopped rubbing her neck, taking up a fighting stance again, and this time neither of them was smiling. She paced forward, slashing her hand towards Wikki, but he pushed her arm up and jabbed the tip of the wooden knife into her ribs. Dropping her knife, she crumpled to the floor, holding her chest while clenching her jaw. "Fuck!"

"I warned you not to be overconfident. Are you ok to continue?" Wikki asked.

"No, not yet. Just give me a few minutes, for fuck sake," Tabitha spat.

"Yeah, ok. Look, why don't we have some food while you recover, and then we can continue? How does that sound?"

Tabitha looked up at him, red-faced. "Yeah, ok. But I want you to know I'll make you pay for that after we've eaten."

"I'm sure you'll try," Wikki smirked.

The next day, Alsander and Neil were met by their party on the city's outskirts. Bleddyn did not have his own party yet, but he had some comfort knowing his brother would be by his side. He looked at Alsander and had another flashback of what Crey had told him, devising his own plan to stop him from the possible destruction he could cause, knowing time was not on his side.

"We're all here. Are you all ready for the journey ahead?" Alsander asked.

"Yes, we're ready, Alpha," Kennon replied.

"Good, because this is the plan. First, we'll go to Ternaid, and that'll be the first test of your loyalty. We'll use our peacekeeper here to gain entry into their village as they're all gated from outsiders. When we're in, I'll lead the assault, and we'll make sure their village will burn brightly to catch the attention of their alpha."

Kennon frowned. "Alpha, why don't you just send a small party with my brother here? He can give the message directly to the black wolf alpha. I'm sure that will be enough."

Alsander dipped his head forward and spat, "Because I'm the alpha, and my word here is law. We must show that we mean business, so the challenge will be met by both alphas. Without making war, they'll not come."

Kennon gave the wolves' greeting and replied, "As you wish, we'll take out their warriors."

"Good, now don't question me again. If you do, I'll take the next interrogation as a challenge. You're either with me, or against me."

Kennon nodded, and Alsander led the party to Black Forest Plain to begin his plan. On the journey, Alsander and Neil would often speak together, away from the party of protectors. Either they did not trust them yet, or they were using caution with their plans. Either way, this caused tension within the party.

They had been travelling mostly in wolf form for a week, and they were about an hour away from their destination. At this point, they continued the last leg of the journey in human form. Bleddyn had been thinking long and hard for a plan to emerge, but his mind and lack of life experience were failing him. Now he had to try a new tactic to get the answers he sought, with a gut feeling that Alsander was hiding something.

"Kennon, may I speak with you alone?" Bleddyn asked.

"Of course, brother. What troubles you?"

"It's about Alsander. I think he's being consumed."

Kennon stopped, grabbing Bleddyn by the arm and whispered, "You had better make sure your words don't go past me, because even talk like that would be enough for him to kill you."

Alsander turned, seeing they had stopped and wanted to know what was going on between them. The party halted, looking at the two brothers.

"What're you two doing?" Alsander enquired.

"I'm sorry, Alpha. My younger brother here has never seen combat, so he was just asking my advice," Kennon replied.

"Hurry it up, and don't fall too far behind. I'll need everyone here for the glory that awaits us."

Alsander continued walking, as Neil commanded the rest of them to follow. The other party members turned and continued on their way.

"Bleddyn, continue what you were saying, but speak in hushed tones, so the others definitely don't hear."

"Alsander is twisted by his past and is indirectly doing his dad's bidding," Bleddyn replied.

"What're you talking about? You're starting to sound like Crey. You're speaking in riddles, little brother."

"We don't have much time, but it's to do with Alsander's pack."

"What about his pack?" Kennon asked.

"I can't go into too much detail to back up my words, so not just as your peacekeeper, but also as your brother, would you trust my words and not tell another soul?"

"You're my little brother; we've a good bond. So I'd have no reason not to trust you."

"Ok, then I'll tell you. Crey told me of Alsander's dad a few months ago. I was unsure what he was talking about at the time, but now I remember. His dad found out some information when he was a boy, and he became obsessed with it. His dad was so obsessed, it crushed him when he couldn't transform, so he wanted to ascend the ranks to be a protector instead."

"Ok, but I don't see what you're getting at; you're starting to confuse me again."

"Let me finish, and you'll understand. We don't have much time. The partial information Parlan found out was fully told to Alsander by Crey. Alsander is the great, great-grandson of Tristan White-Ear, the last omega alpha."

Kennon's eyes widened with an open mouth. "He's Tristan's heir?"

"Yes, and his dad has beaten and conditioned him to become a ruthless warrior, so much so that he even killed his own mam and dad eight years ago. Crey was led to believe that he killed his dad as a sign of strength, and then he turned on his mam because she was weak. But that was just his speculation, because no one truly knew his motives on that dark day."

Kennon shook his head and held his brother's shoulders. "What're you trying to say, the things Crey had told you have come to pass?"

"Yes, I believe so. I'm not sure how dark his heart has gone, but Crey used to say there was good in him as a child, and maybe there still is. With this information, I believe he wants to become omega alpha, just like Tristan. I don't know why he wants that title, but that's all I can come up with at the moment."

"It's a shame he isn't here anymore. Maybe he would know what to do," Kennon sighed.

"He already tried to reach out, and that didn't work, so he called it like he saw it. Alsander has the same lust as his dad, to become like Tristan."

"How do you know this?" Kennon exclaimed.

Bleddyn looked Kennon directly in the eyes and replied, "Because I was there, hidden away, but there nevertheless, and I heard and saw everything. Alsander didn't like what he heard with regards to his dad, so he murdered Crey and threw his body off the cliff in Tristan's garden."

Kennon inhaled a deep breath. "He told everyone he had an accident. The bastard. I'll challenge him."

"No, brother, he's too strong. I'll come up with something to try and thwart his plans, but I must do it in a different way. Please, don't challenge him."

"Fine, I won't challenge him for now. I'll play along so I can help you to get his mind away from what he wants, but like I told Crey before, I'll challenge him if the need arises."

"Thank you. I'm not sure if he can be changed. All of his young life, he has been groomed into what he thinks the world of the wolves should be. It's not his fault he ended up this way. But I do know one thing, Neil's a source of that problem, and now I can see that he's enabling this thought process, causing a further issue."

"Ok, I see what troubles you now. I'll try and help you in any way I can, but no matter what, I'll never forgive him for killing Crey," Kennon declared.

"Then, that's your choice, and I'll respect it."

Kennon looked up for a second, thinking of an idea. "Look, we won't have time now, but after we do what has to be done at

Ternaid and we defeat their warriors, I can try and get Neil away from Alsander for you to speak with him if you wish."

"Ok, that might be of some help, thank you. I feel that he's walking down a dark path, and if he keeps going in that direction, there'll be no turning back from it. Neil will also resist, so you might have to protect me from him."

"That's not a problem, I'll take him. Come on, we must go, or they might suspect we are up to something."

"Ok."

Walking towards the party at a fast pace to catch up, they liaised with them within ten minutes. At that point, they all saw it in the distance, the black wolf village of Ternaid. It was a small village surrounded by a twenty-foot-tall circular wooden wall, with spikes shaped into the black wood at the top.

Alsander stood in front of Bleddyn and said, "The time is now to prove your loyalty to me, Peacekeeper. You'll use your methods of persuasion to get them to open their gates. After that, we'll take it from there."

"And what of me?" Kennon asked.

"Follow our lead. While you were preparing your brother, I briefed the rest of the party on what they have to do. You're a skilled warrior, so just follow the others this time."

"As you wish."

Alsander looked at Bleddyn and reinforced, "Now's the time to prove your loyalty to the clan as you've said before. Get them to open their gate, and we'll take it from there."

Bleddyn knew there was something more sinister at hand with the full plan, he could feel it in his gut, but he had no choice at this stage. He would have to fully obey Alsander if he was to gain his trust to stop him, so he nodded and replied, "It'll be done, Alpha."

The party approached the entrance to the village, but unlike their capital city, it had no platforms overlooking the front gates. Instead, they had a small opening, around five and a half feet high, in the centre of the gate. This small opening was twelve inches tall and ten inches wide, and opened and closed on a hinge so a guarding protector could see who was outside the entrance of the village. Alsander, Neil and the other protectors who could transform stayed low and close to the wooden walls on either side of the gate, so they would not be seen. Taking their battle robes off and placing them by the wall, they waited for their peacekeeper to deceive the black wolves, ready to transform when the gate opened.

Bleddyn stood in front of the peephole with three inertia protectors with him. Knocking hard on the gate, the small door opened, and a face replaced the wood.

"Who're you, and what do you want?" the protector questioned.

Bleddyn bowed his head and replied, "Hello there, I'm Bleddyn of the white wolves. I'm the new peacekeeper, and I was wondering if you would accept us into your village because we have run low on supplies. We have silver to trade with you."

Looking around, only seeing four people in front of him, the protector scrunched up his face and said, "Nah, we don't like outsiders here, lad, try the next village. We ain't interested."

The protector pulled his face away, closing the miniature door, stopped by Bleddyn's next sentence. "We'd also accommodate you, of course."

The miniature door reopened, and the guard's face reappeared. "What would you accommodate me with then, lad?"

"We've got silver. I can give you ten pieces if you would help us in getting supplies," Bleddyn replied.

Bouncing his head from side to side, thinking of the offer, he replied, "Nah, lad, that's not worth it because we really don't like outsiders."

"Ok, how about this as my final offer to you, forty pieces of silver. That's the limit that I can afford because we'll need the rest for supplies."

The guard nodded and agreed, "Ok, but you'll have to get the things you need and leave straight away. You got it?"

"Of course, thank you for helping us."

The guard licked his lips and demanded, "Hand it over then, lad."

Bleddyn pulled out a small sack from his pocket and counted forty pieces of silver. They were rectangular in shape, smooth with no markings and around half a centimetre in width, two centimetres in length and only one millimetre in thickness. Gold and silver pieces were the main currency the wolves would trade with, but they still traded items for other items as well.

Bleddyn halved the pile. "I'll give you half now, and the other half after you open the gate. I think that's a fair deal."

"All right, all right, hand it over then, lad."

The guard stretched his arm through the peephole, holding his palm out flat to gain his imbursement. As Bleddyn placed twenty silver pieces into his hand, the protector made a fist around his payment, and his arm shot back through the peephole at great speed. He lowered his head to inspect each piece, ensuring they were the real deal. Looking back up, he smirked, "Hold on a minute, lad, I'll open the gates for you now."

The guard closed the peephole, and then two clunking noises were heard, followed by what sounded like a large piece of timber dragged across the gates. With one final clunk, the gates shook slightly, showing that they were unsecured.

Bleddyn moved to the centre of the gates as they opened, and Alsander nodded at Neil beyond the other side of the gate. The protectors with Bleddyn were inertias, which was why they were standing with him. The gates opened wide, but due to their position, the guard could not see the others. After the protector pushed the other half of the gate all the way open, he stood in the centre of the opening and questioned, "Now then, lad, what about the rest of them silver pieces?"

Bleddyn looked up with sadness in his eyes, and muttered, "I'm sorry."

Chapter Thirteen

SPARKS OF WAR

"What do you mean you're sorry, lad?" he frowned.

As the guarding protector saw Alsander break cover naked, he placed one leg back and drew his hunters' knife. Transforming, Alsander jumped over Bleddyn, charging at the black wolf protector.

"Enemy! Enemy! Enemy!" the protector screamed.

Alsander sprang forward, turning his head side on, opening his mouth wide. Surrounding the protector with his teeth, he snapped his jaws shut, piercing the skin and pinning the protector's arms to his sides, causing him to scream in pain. Ragging his head back and forth, tearing open the protector's flesh, he opened his jaws, throwing the protector into one of the gates. With a loud crash, the gate wobbled from impact, rendering him unconscious, before he struck the ground and went rigid from the head injury.

What have I done? Bleddyn thought to himself.

The other white wolf protectors broke cover, entering the village while transforming. Bleddyn stood central to the opening, as the three inertia protectors charged alongside the white wolves into the village on either side of him. This small village only had around thirty huts, and most of its residents were congregated in a market on the main street. Only three black wolf protectors transformed to counter the intruders, making a target of themselves. The people dispersed to the shelter of their homes as the white wolves started to spread out and hunt them.

Alsander and Neil targeted one of the transformed protectors, and the three of them engaged. Within seconds, the defending protector had Neil's teeth deep in his throat, accompanied by Alsander's mouth wrapped around his front right leg. The other white wolves charged past them to engage the others, making it a short-lived battle, with the white wolves overwhelming the black wolves' defences.

Kennon engaged the second black wolf. Being young and inexperienced, he stood his ground nevertheless. Even though Kennon was slightly smaller than his challenger, the black wolf was about to experience the power and combat knowledge of the lead white wolf protector. Leaping high into the air, Kennon transformed back into a human, unsheathed his hunters' knife and threw it. It found its way into the black wolf's left eye. Changing back into a wolf, he bit into the side of his opponent's neck, continuing to run forwards while maintaining a strong grip. The flesh tore away from his body, pulling the black wolf backwards while rotating him, as he was mounted by two other white wolves, finishing Kennon's fight while bringing the young warrior's life to an end.

Within moments, all the black wolves were but corpses, forming pools of blood on the ground. Kennon transformed and retrieved his knife, wiping the blood off on the black wolf's fur. Spotting an inertia protector drawing his hunters' knife between two huts, he transformed again and gave chase away from the main street.

The other protectors slaughtered the villagers, making everyone a target, with nowhere off-limits. They kicked open doors, dug holes through the clay walls, set huts on fire and climbed through windows to get at their newfound prey. All that could be heard from the village were screams of pain and terror.

Bleddyn stood at the entrance of the village with tears in his eyes, witnessing the tragedy before him, which he had helped create. At this point, he knew he could not change or help Alsander; all he could do was survive until he thought of a different plan to stop him.

Alsander heard someone breathing heavily under a market stall table filled with jewellery, so he dipped his head while sniffing. He could smell the adrenaline of someone hidden under the stall, so he circled around and stopped at the back. He could not see who was under there because a large piece of brown cloth covered the table, hanging all the way down to the ground. He remained cautious, as it could be a protector or hunter waiting to strike from underneath. In front of the stall, Neil signalled a plan by lowering his head.

Alsander placed his paw on top of the table, pulling it towards him so it could act as a shield, the table tilted to a forty-degree angle, and most of the jewellery slid off the cloth and hit the ground. Now, at tipping point, the cloth on top of the table exposed an outline of a person curled up underneath. Neil saw the silhouette and nodded, signalling him to pull faster to topple the table. Aside from a few stray pieces of jewellery still falling, the table banged on the floor, exposing a petrified woman underneath. Neil ran at the defenceless lady trying to scramble away, but she proved nowhere near quick enough. He bit into her leg and dragged her back into the middle of the street, causing the woman to scream loud and hard. Leaping over the table, Alsander placed his paw on the back of her head, pushing down hard to pin her to the ground, as Neil let her leg go and bounced to the side.

The woman's screams shifted from fearful to painful as Neil bit her body over and over again, puncturing her flesh with his teeth. Blood rapidly escaped her from deep wounds, and her lungs collapsed from the air filling her pleural cavity. When she became silent, Alsander knew Neil had finished her, and removed his paw from her head.

Walking off to search for others to hunt, they heard a door hinge creak, making the both of them turn around. Still standing at the entrance of the village, Bleddyn could see into the doorway of the hut, and his eyes widened.

The door fully opened, with a twelve-year-old boy emerging, rubbing his eyes before stretching and yawning as if he had been woken from a nap. His eyes adjusted to the daylight, seeing two white wolves for the first time, opposite the hut. His vision wandered to the jewellery stall that had been knocked over, seeing his mother on the ground. The boy dashed towards her and Neil lunged at him, but being small and clever, the boy rolled under him as he was mid-air. As Neil landed, the child got back to his feet and took a few more steps. He saw the blood on his mother's body, and her lifeless eyes gazing into the distance. Turning, he saw both Alsander and Neil advancing. The boy thought that she was just injured, having not seen death before. Unfortunately, this juvenile did not see the gravity of the danger he put himself in, but he proved braver than most. Standing tall, he puffed out his chest and shouted, "You stay away from my mam!"

The young adolescent transformed into a wolf, defending his mother's remains from harm. Like most that could transform at his age, he found that he was two feet smaller and very skinny in comparison to the adult wolves approaching. Jumping forward and snapping his jaws, the young boy produced a high-pitched bark as a warning to the white wolves. Alsander and Neil did not even flinch, with the both of them giving a cold stare at the young wolf as they advanced.

The juvenile wolf snapped and barked again, backing away from them until he felt his mother's corpse on his hind legs, stopping him from going any further. Staring hard at the white wolves, the young wolf cub saw Alsander dipping his head slightly. As Alsander's mouth started to quiver, his teeth slowly displayed with a growl. When Alsander darted forward, the little wolf lowered his head and closed his eyes, hoping that the imminent danger would disappear. Dipping his head down, Alsander bit into the boy's scruff.

Lifting him up, the young wolf began screaming in pain at a very high pitch, over and over. The screams empowered Alsander, and he swung the child around ferociously. Excitement brewed as Neil ran forward, biting hard into the boy's abdomen, puncturing his skin. Releasing his grip slightly, he dragged his teeth down the tender child's body and left leg, ripping the flesh apart and generating even more pain. Reaching the bottom of the child's leg, he clamped his jaws down hard to get a good grip, breaking the cub's bones in the process. Alsander released the child's scruff briefly in mid-air, biting down deeper into the top of the young wolf's neck for better grip. With Alsander and Neil in the perfect position, they started to shake their heads violently together, pulling away from each other as hard as they could whilst growling.

With the child's flesh being tender and not fully developed, his torn abdomen could not take the force of the two powerful wolves, and his skin separated. Intestines protruded through the torn skin, and the leg Neil gripped began to pull away from his body. The screams turned into whimpers as they gave one last tug, tearing the child's abdomen wide open. The young body could take no more punishment, his pupils dilated as his soul left the mortal plane. They released the young cub's lifeless body, dropping him to the ground.

Looking away during the boy's final moments, Bleddyn could not bear the child's torture or his own shame.

The onslaught of the village only lasted a mere fifteen minutes until almost everyone joined their ancestors in the Meadowlands. Most of the people were killed, and the white wolf protectors turned back into humans, setting the huts ablaze with the use of torches or furniture to feed lit fires within the huts.

Kennon walked from between two huts in human form, inspecting the scene. He looked at the dead wolf cub before him, and he could not contain his rage any longer, making a choice to break his word to his brother, even with the warnings he had against challenging Alsander. Red-faced, Kennon's teeth exposed through tightened lips. "What've you done? That was a child, you fucking evil bastards! You're not fit to lead, and I'll not let you prey on the weak! I challenge you for the position of alpha. When I'm done, you won't be given mercy, you dishonourable wet mutt! After I'm done" – he glanced over to Neil – "you're next to die!"

Kennon took three paces and transformed, charging forward, but Alsander jumped to the side just before he hit his mark. Alsander landed with his front paws skidding across the mud path, facing Kennon side on. Bringing his hind legs forward as they touched the ground, he sprang into Kennon's chest, hitting him with so much force he lost all balance and rolled on the ground.

Alsander sidestepped, pounced forward with his mouth clamping down on his muzzle. Kennon let out a small whimper, but Alsander did not let up, pulling his head back, tearing the skin. Using his legs as a pivot weight, Kennon arched his back and quickly rolled over towards him, hoping he would be too close to thwart another attack, but Alsander had already jumped back a small distance, leaving him wide open. Seeing Kennon's neck exposed, Alsander lowered his head, shuffled forward quickly and sank his teeth into his flesh. Kennon snapped his jaws frantically to hit him with his teeth in a last-ditch effort of survival, but all he hit was air. He found it harder to breathe as Alsander's grip became tighter, closing off his windpipe while lifting him off the ground. With the sensation of pain, he also felt the pressure on his neck move as Alsander shook his head back and forth. Feeling a strange sensation in his neck, he partially breathed through a wound, with the air feeling cold as it passed the nerves beneath his skin. Using his front legs to kick Alsander away, he hoped to free his neck from his jaws, but the attempts proved feeble. Suddenly, a new sensation emerged in his neck, a throbbing that double kicked. Ba bump. Ba bump.

As fast as the sensation came, he felt it become weaker and weaker, along with his body, due to one of the main arteries in his neck being severed. Feeling his own heartbeat failing him, Kennon's vision blurred and darkened. As the pain in his neck eased, the bumping sensation faded away. Unable to move his legs anymore, the last of Kennon's strength held his head up. After ten more seconds, his neck muscles relaxed, eyes filling up with tears, knowing his life was coming to an end.

His eyes flicked around the sockets as he tried to think of a plan, but unable to think straight, he gave up. By failing to stop Alsander and his conquest of darkness, he became overwhelmed with anger towards him for taking his life. Regret started to fill him, knowing he should have taken his brother's advice as his children would be left fatherless. Then shame reared its ugly head because he felt he let everyone down. But after these initial thoughts, a wave of peace drifted over him, helping him accept his fate. He thought of the good memories of his family, growing up with his brothers and sister with all the trouble and mischief they would get into. Then, he thought of the four happiest days of his life, the three days his children were born, and the day he met his mate, the one whom he loved unconditionally. After a few more seconds, his vision went black, and then a bright green light blinded him.

When his vision returned, he could see a rock face that completely surrounded him, with lush green grass under his bare feet. He turned around to see his relations that had passed on, standing on top of two sides of a cliff to welcome him. At the opening of the oval-shaped cliff leading into vast fields and gentle rolling hills stood five strange cloaked figures. One of them spoke with a smile and open arms, giving the warrior a warm welcome into the Meadowlands.

Bleddyn fell to his knees as he saw his brother's lifeless head flop down, with Alsander still holding a tight grip on his neck. His vision blurred from the build-up of tears, mourning for his brave brother. He did not speak or declare Alsander as the victor because he knew at this moment, he was truly alone in the black wolves' country, surrounded by danger from both sides, wondering if his time on this world would be short like his brother's.

Kennon's body collapsed to the ground as Alsander released it, changing back into a human as the other protectors gathered around. He glared at each protector with a downturned mouth, announcing, "If there are any more challengers for my position, then declare yourselves now!"

Unable to look him in the eyes, they all lowered their heads except one. Transforming back into a human, the brave protector walked towards him. "Alpha, I suppose now you're looking for a new leader of the protectors. Let me prove myself at the next village and become your voice to our elite fighting force."

"What's your name, Protector?" Alsander asked.

"It's Byron."

Alsander's mouth lifted into a grin. "I like you already, so I'll let you prove yourself when we fight more of these black wolf scum. Now, everyone else, burn this place to the ground and finish off any survivors you find."

After twenty minutes, all of the village's huts and most of the surrounding wall became engulfed in flame. Black smoke rose from the fires high into the cloudy white sky, able to be seen from miles around, and seen they were. The party headed east to the next village descending a small hill, until one of the protectors noticed something on the horizon to the south-west of their location.

"Alpha, I've spotted something," the protector declared.

Alsander turned around, walked back to the top of the hill and asked, "What've you seen?"

"Over there, it's a party of black wolves, I think, but they're too far away for me to count."

Examining where the protector pointed, he saw them. Turning back, Alsander looked down the hill. "Byron, you might be able to prove yourself sooner than expected. It looks like a hunter or protector party in the distance, and I'm sure they'll come and investigate."

Byron gave a wide grin. "Alpha, it would be an honour to show their warriors the true strength of the White Wolf Clan."

Alsander smiled and nodded at him, turning around to look at the black wolf party again. After mustering a plan, he gave his orders, "Listen up, all of you. We'll lie low here until they've investigated the village, and then I'll show myself on the top of this hill. I'm sure they'll attack, and when they charge at me, we'll show them true strength and kill them all."

All of the party but one started to cheer. "Shut up, or they'll hear you!" Neil snapped, being right to do so.

The black wolf party might have been around seventeen to eighteen miles away, but in wolf form, they could hear as far as fifteen miles, depending on the climate.

The men stopped cheering, and they started to eat some salted, smoked meat they had found, knowing they had around an hour before the black wolf party got to them. Alsander placed a guard position on the brow of the hill to monitor the black wolves' progress, as some of the men admired their spoils from the massacre at the village, some claimed jewellery, some took food, and two of them removed trophies from their victims that consisted of ears and teeth.

"I can't believe your progress over the past week. You're brilliant, you know that?" Wikki stated.

"Well, a student is only as good as her teacher," Tabitha replied.

"You've learned four and a half months' worth of combat training in a week. No matter who teaches you, that's beyond impressive," Wikki smiled. "But you lack in experience, which unfortunately is something no one can teach you."

Tabitha hugged him tightly. "Thank you for teaching me. I really appreciate it."

"Your training is over, so now comes the final part. Put your wooden knife in your scabbard because, now, I'm going to test everything that you've learned," Wikki said. "I won't do it the usual way because there's only one of me, but I'll tell you what you need to do when we come across one."

"Across one what?" Tabitha asked.

"Come on, you'll understand."

Tabitha frowned at him as they picked up their backpacks. Leaving the wood, Wikki began his search to test her abilities.

After an hour of searching, Wikki spotted a lone deer in a field. Scanning the surrounding area, he knew no one was around, and dropped his backpack to the ground. "Ok, are you ready for your final test?" he asked.

Tabitha dropped her backpack and nodded.

"Look, we also need to be careful that no one sees what we're doing, for obvious reasons. I can't fully test you like a true protector, but I know how to make my own test. I'll merge a final trial for potential protectors alongside the final test to become a protector. There is one downside to it though. We can't injure each other because we'll need to head home straight after this, and I know you'll be on hunting duty soon." Wikki looked back at the deer as he undressed. "This is what you must do. You must protect that deer from me. If I kill it, you fail. It will be limited to only a mile hunt, but after that, you'll have to defeat me. You got it?"

"Yeah" – Tabitha started to remove her clothes – "I got it."

Wikki transformed and charged at the deer. Caught off guard that he had begun the hunt instantly, Tabitha transformed and chased after him. The deer spotted them both and fled, with Wikki hot on its tail. Tabitha struggled to keep up with him, showing her that he had done a lot of training to improve his physical strength over the years. Almost on top of the deer, he exposed his teeth, ready to end the hunt, but she picked up her speed to get alongside him. As he lunged at the deer, she sidestepped and knocked him off balance, causing him to fall over with the deer running away.

Picking himself up off the ground, Wikki faced Tabitha for a head-on challenge. She sprinted at him, but he sidestepped and transformed, throwing his wooden knife at her. Turning back into human form, she twirled through the air and avoided his knife, as he transformed back into a wolf. Charging at her, she had little time to react, so she unsheathed her wooden knife and threw it at him, hitting his face and slowing him down a little. Changing back into a wolf, she dodged his attack. As he turned, she jumped at him with an open mouth, nipping his hind leg, while body-slamming him to the ground.

Wikki changed back into a human and held his hand out. "Stop. I think that's enough, or we'll start injuring each other. Let's go back to where we started, and I'll tell you how you did."

After they got dressed, Wikki looked at Tabitha with a smile.

"Well, how did I do?" Tabitha asked.

"I know it's not a full test, but personally, I think if it was, the results would be the same. You pass. But know that you still have a lot to learn and experience, and that's a path you must take on your own." Wikki replied.

"Thanks for doing this for me. I know that just by training me, you've risked a lot," Tabitha smiled.

"Don't mention it, and I mean that in more ways than one."

"I think we should go home now, or people may become suspicious," Tabitha suggested.

As soon as they started to walk back to the Town of Niamh, Wikki looked over to Tabitha and said, "Your dad was right, you know? You would've made a fine protector."

Tabitha looked over at him with a smile, as a tear rolled down her face, hoping deep down that Llewellyn could see what she had achieved to make him proud.

Approaching from three miles away, a protector signalled the party by a short sharp whistle, followed by waving his hand. The men took their battle robes off and lay down on the brow of the grassy hill, waiting for their prey to get into position.

Another ten minutes had passed, and there were eight black wolves transformed, and three inertia Black Wolf Clan members riding on their comrades. The inertias dismounted, gingerly removing their backpacks and getting out battle robes for the others. After donning their robes, they lined up. Alsander could not tell if they were protectors or hunters, but he didn't care as this was the first true battle that he wanted. The black wolf party members entered the smouldering village, one by one, until they were all out of sight. Alsander took his place, standing on top of the hill so he could be seen when they re-emerged.

The black wolf party entered the village filled with bodies, hut walls still lit with embers and ash filling the village's atmosphere, all looking horrified as the black wolf pathfinder entered. "Fan out and search for survivors!" Erskine ordered.

The party scattered, searching for any life within the village, but deep down, they knew their searches would be in vain. Some of the men cried, and some of them were filled with nothing but anger and hate for the people responsible for this. Erskine walked down the main street, inspecting a young woman's body on the ground.

"Bastards, this was a wolf attack. You can tell by her wounds." Looking away, he noticed black fur five metres from her position. His eyes widened as his jaw clenched a few times. "The fucking bastards killed the young as well. Whoever did this will pay dearly."

One of the protectors came up the street from the back of the village. "Pathfinder, everyone's dead, but there's our answer. See" – The protector turned around, pointing at Kennon's body – "it was the white wolves."

Erskine walked next to Kennon's corpse and said bitterly, "At least we took out one of those wet mutts. I hope he becomes the hunted in the Meadowlands."

As he finished the sentence, he spat on Kennon's face before turning around. The two protectors with him also followed their leader's actions, spitting on his body as well. "Get everyone back to the front gates. Have one of them check for a scent that we can track, and have another travel up the hill to the east to see if they can spot a white wolf party," Erskine ordered.

"Yes, Pathfinder," they replied.

At 63 years old, Erskine was still a capable warrior, even if he was not what he used to be. Spiked up like a brush head, his short grey hair appeared perfect. As his lips tightened, everyone could see his mouth was missing three teeth, but it was quite common to start losing them at his age.

His party gathered by the front gate, and one of the protectors stared at the hill, spotting something of interest. He quickly turned around and looked at Erskine with wide eyes.

Chapter Fourteen

CLASH OF BLACK AND WHITE

"What do you see?" Erskine enquired.

"Up there on the hill. There's someone there," the protector replied.

Erskine walked forward, looking in the direction where the protector nodded. He inspected the hill as best he could, but his old eyes were failing him. Too embarrassed to ask for help, he used a tactful question as cover. "How many do you see?"

The protector scanned the hill again. "Just the one, Pathfinder. But he might not be alone."

"Is he one of our clan, or can you not see that far?"

"I'm not sure, they might be from this village. No, wait. His hair, it's white. It's pure white. I'm not one hundred per cent, but I'm pretty sure his hair's white, so that must mean..."

Interrupting, Erskine came to the same conclusion. "He must be one of them white wolf bastards."

The party stood as one, staring at the hill together. Looking back at them, Alsander dropped his head slightly and gave his sinister smile. "Prepare yourselves, men, they're unsure of who I am, but I'll show them. When I give the second howl, we'll engage."

His men remained silent, not to give away their numbers. Alsander transformed, giving a long, high-pitched howl.

"It's a white wolf all right. I doubt he'll be alone, so make sure you're ready for a fight. We'll kill those wet mutts for what they've done here. Transform and prepare yourselves for battle," Erskine commanded.

The black wolf protectors disrobed and transformed, and the three inertias left their robes where they lay, mounting three wolves with their backpacks to the front. Rummaging around, all three of them removed wooden lids and threw them down.

"Pathfinder, we only have three each. Hopefully, they're ready," a protector explained.

Erskine, now in wolf form, looked back at the inertia protector and nodded, confirming what he had said. He barked four times, clearly giving an order as all the protectors in wolf form fell in a single line. He growled and sounded off again. "Grrr Arrf."

Waiting for them to gain half a mile, Alsander gave his order, howling for a second time. His men transformed, and the three inertias mounted their comrades, with bows in hand. His party broke the silhouette line of the hill and advanced, all except Bleddyn, watching from the top. Alsander gave another order, barking twice, with his party moving in an arrowhead formation as they picked up their pace towards the black wolf party.

The black wolves had a total of eleven members, outnumbered by thirty-six white wolves, but one black wolf stopped his advance when seeing them. The rest of Erskine's party matched the speed of the white wolves, charging towards each other.

When the two parties were roughly one hundred and fifty metres apart, the three inertia black wolf protectors carefully pulled out metal orbs from their backpacks, spherical in shape with strange shards protruding from the metal. The shards were different in colour, covering most of the orb, not shiny like the main body, but a dull grey. A ring mounted on the top of each orb had a long piece of rope attached to it, and for some reason, the protectors were very cautious of these strange objects they had brought into battle. Holding the rope at the furthest point from the orb, the protectors initially swung them with care, ensuring they didn't hit the wolves they were riding. When the momentum built up, they swung them faster until the orbs twirled above their heads. One protector released his orb, slinging it high into the air at the white wolves. It went off course slightly, flying towards the right flank of the white wolf party, hitting the ground approximately ten metres in front of them.

BOOM!

The orb emitted a small fire ball, turning to smoke. Two white wolves fell, covered in wounds, revealing them to be no ordinary orbs. The dull-looking metal shards protruding from the orbs were pieces of flint, and inside was the black wolves' creation, giving the weapons the name, fire-salt orbs. The other two threw their orbs, but one went way off course and exploded away from the battle. The other one directly hit a white wolf on the left flank, killing a further three white wolves and an inertia after the explosion.

Panic and confusion settled into the minds of the white wolves, never hearing loud explosions before, wondering why their comrades were falling, but two wolves were not even shaken by the loud bangs. Alsander and Neil barked at their warriors, maintaining control.

Now less than one hundred metres apart, the inertia black wolf protectors pulled out the last six orbs, one in each hand. Digging their heels in to the wolves they were mounted on for balance, they twirled the orbs, knowing that the accuracy would be compromised with this method, but at least the new weapons would be destroyed so the white wolves could not replicate them. Two of them threw their orbs, and three out of four went too high, flying straight over the oncoming white wolves. The last one hit the wolf next to Neil and, luckily for him, the other wolf took the brunt of the blast. A loud bang, followed by a cry of pain from two protectors, muffled his hearing with a constant ringing. Then, he felt a twinge in his back leg, as a piece of flint had gone through him. The wound was not great, but enough for him to feel it.

A white wolf inertia loosed an arrow, striking the last protector with the remaining two orbs in the chest, forcing him to release them prematurely. One orb flew behind the black wolf party, but the other struck the ground next to him. The blast took out a total of two black wolves, another inertia black wolf protector and himself. The jagged shards of flint tore through the four of them like a hot knife cutting through butter, and the explosion tore a massive hole through the chest wall underbelly of the wolf he rode. Even though the newly invented weapons worked well, they had backfired and reduced the numbers of the force defending themselves from the invaders, due to lack of experience and training.

Erskine figured out who the leader was from watching Alsander's every move from the top of the hill, never taking his eyes off him for a second. With the commotion happening around him, he made Alsander his only target. If he killed him, the leaderless wolves might disperse and never return. With both parties colliding, Erskine dived at Alsander, but Neil turned and jumped at the last second, hitting Erskine in mid-air while clamping his jaws into the side of his neck. Snapping at Alsander, Erskine missed, with Neil's strength, speed and weight pushing him backwards.

Taking the advantage, Alsander lowered his body, looked up at Erskine and pounced forward to secure the kill. But a black wolf protector manoeuvred sideways, pushing him off balance, missing Erskine while stumbling into one of his own protectors instead.

Bowled over with Neil landing on top of him, a searing pain pierced Erskine's front right leg. Landing hard, the bone snapped and the jagged edge tore through the skin, causing him sheer agony. Neil's grip on Erskine's neck released after he flipped over him. Landing on his back, a small rock knocked the wind from Neil's lungs, immobilising him from the fight.

Two protectors on Alsander's right flank made short work of the black wolf protector as he recovered his balance. Charging at Erskine, Alsander aimed for his face with an open mouth. Watching him advance, Erskine could not dodge the assault due to his broken leg, with Alsander biting into his face several times, sinking his fangs into his eyes, permanently blinding him. Screaming over and over, Erskine felt more teeth penetrate his body with two more white wolves joining the attack. Erskine had only one more fight left within. With great struggle, he managed to roll over onto his back, as Neil re-entered the fight and gave the killing blow to his neck.

The white wolf numbers were too great, making the intense battle short-lived. The white wolves tore the flesh off their black wolf kin, killing all who opposed them. The black wolves put up a good fight with such small numbers, even killing another two white wolves, but in the end, their fight was truly in vain.

With all but one black wolf soul ascending to the Meadowlands, Neil and Alsander gave chase to the last black wolf protector that didn't engage. With him already having a head start, they let the last black wolf flee back to his capital. Returning to the remainder of the party, they gathered at the top of the hill, transformed back into humans and donned their battle robes.

"What in the Great Wolf's name were those things they threw?" Neil asked.

Alsander looked back down at the battleground. "I don't know, but those things lowered our numbers. Bleddyn, what do you know about them?"

Bleddyn's eyes moved around as he answered, "I remember Crey talking about what the last grey wolf peacekeeper told him. About eight years ago, the black wolves invented a thing called fire rock or something. I'm sure that's what they must have been."

Alsander turned back around. "Those things took out more men than I was expecting. Looks like the black wolves have a few tricks of their own. We must be more careful from now on until we know more about them. Next time we encounter them, we won't keep a tight formation to ruin their plans."

Bleddyn looked at the battlefield. "You still wish to continue then, Alpha. You've lost ten protectors in one battle. Don't you want to return to replenish your numbers?"

"Stop being such a cub. We still have enough to take out the next village to trigger what we want."

Bleddyn gave the wolves' greeting and nodded. He might have failed to get Alsander to withdraw, but he hoped maybe the black wolves would be able to stop him with the new weapons at their disposal.

"What of that protector?" Neil asked.

"Leave him. He can tuck tail and run back to Harri. Maybe that'll draw him out of his capital."

"You know he's old now, he won't meet the challenge," Neil replied.

Alsander looked at the fleeing protector and said, "I'm counting on it."

Moving away from the party, they started whispering in secret, looking back at the party members every now and again.

"Listen up, men. I've decided to make a new lead protector. Byron, step forward." Byron took a few steps forward and kneeled down as he continued. "Me and my pathfinder have come to an agreement that you should take Kennon's place. Bleddyn, do you agree?"

At this moment, Bleddyn knew that his services were no longer needed. Cut out of the council with their decisions, he had only one reply that would keep him alive. "Yes, Alpha, he's a good choice."

Alsander gave his sinister smile. "Doesn't it bother you that he's taken your brother's position?"

Bleddyn was young, but he was the new peacekeeper for a good reason. Crey had chosen well. "Not at all, Alpha. Only the strong should remain and gain what's theirs."

Tilting his head to one side with a normal smile, Alsander replied, "It looks like you've come around, finally. You'll go far."

Alsander and Neil looked at each other and grinned, giving new orders to their men. "We'll rest here for a few hours, and then we'll move out towards the next village. We should be there before dawn tomorrow. Byron, make sure you place a stag position on top of this hill."

A roaming guard duty within the wolf race was known as a stag position, and Byron had earned Alsander's trust to enforce the party's safety.

Byron gave the wolves' greeting and bowed. "As you wish, Alpha."

Alsander thinking Bleddyn had come around had bought him time for his final and only plan he could come up with. However, he needed more information about Alsander's plan, and Bleddyn knew just how to get it directly from his own mouth. This would take time, though, and unfortunately, more sacrifice.

At the peak of night, clouds covered the light of the moons, making it hard to see, with a cold breeze blowing through the forest. The protector ran as fast as he could for hours all the way back to the capital. He arrived at the main gate of the city with great difficulty due to the darkness causing him to bump into trees on the way. The young protector changed into a human, breathing heavily, with the cold air wrapping around the thin layer of sweat over his naked body, causing him to shiver. "Let me in!" he shouted.

Another protector emerged from the top of the tower holding a lit torch. Even with the light emitting from the torch, he still could not see who stood at the bottom of the gate. "Who goes there?" the guarding protector demanded.

"I'm one of Erskine's party, and I must see the alpha at once! Erskine has fallen!" the naked protector shouted.

"Open the gate!" the guarding protector ordered.

The gate opened, and the naked protector ran through in a panicked state. "Take me to Harri quickly. Erskine has fallen."

Another protector went ahead to the alpha's hut, and the naked protector was given one of the spare battle robes from the gatehouse, before being taken to their alpha. As the protector arrived, Harri burst through the door and ran towards him. "What's this I hear about Erskine? Is he ok?"

Diverting his gaze down, he replied, "No, Alpha, I'm sorry. He was killed by a large white wolf party. They killed everyone from my party along with all the people of Ternaid."

Harri put his hands on the side of his head, sliding up and interlinking his fingers. "No, not Erskine. This cannot be, he's a strong warrior."

The protector looked up at him. "I'm sorry, but it's true. I'm the only survivor. There was thirty-six of them, but Erskine and his men took out ten of them head-on, and used the fire-salt orbs as well."

"So the orbs work. How did you survive?" Harri enquired.

The protector's brow fell as he looked to the ground again. "I'm ashamed to say that fear took hold of me, and I fled the battle. I was too afraid because there were so many."

A tear rolled down the protector's face, and Harri removed his hands from his head, placing one on the protector's shoulder. "It's ok. There's not much more you could've done. And I'll never be ready to sing the song of the fallen for my grandchild. Go inside the hut, I'll ask you everything, and then you can eat and rest." He looked at another protector and ordered, "You there, gather the remaining council members at once. After that, wake as many of the protectors as you can and bring them here."

The protector bowed and ran off to carry out his orders. Harri returned to his hut, asking his grandson about everything that happened.

Within an hour, everyone started to gather outside the alpha's hut. Harri emerged and sat in the alpha's chair, waiting for more people to arrive, and during this time, Alsander and his men had made their move to the next black wolf village under the cover of darkness. Six three-foot-tall open iron baskets circled the alpha's chair, with another in the centre of the circle in front of Harri, filled with wood that burned brightly to give light on a dark night. The cold breeze cut through the city, so most of the people had tightly wrapped robes and blankets around themselves. Most of the people were fatigued as they had been woken from a deep sleep, with a few of them yawning and muttering amongst themselves, wondering why they had been summoned at this unsociable hour.

Harri stood from his chair, addressing the council and the people that had arrived. "I'm sorry for summoning you here at this hour, but dark times have come to our lands. A band of white wolves have attacked and destroyed Ternaid. They killed everyone there, even the young. On top of that, Erskine and his party were wiped out, after fighting the white wolves responsible."

Forba stepped forward from the crowd. "What are your plans, Alpha? Are you going to counter their attack on our lands?"

The crowd began talking and muttering amongst themselves, as the tension started to build up between them. As a protector ordered silence, the noise from the crowd started to die down, with everyone looking at Harri in anticipation, wondering what his answer would be. "I'm not sure, Forba. I think that we should decide together on what to do," he replied.

Someone from the crowd shouted, "You're the alpha, so you should decide!"

Arguments brewed within the crowd; some people agreed, while most of them did not. Most of the people were happy with their lives, so they did not want to jeopardise their good lifestyles with war and death. The black wolves had become too comfortable with their standards of living, and they did not want to make any sacrifices. In other words, the Black Wolf Clan had become soft compared to the other clans.

"Silence! Hold your tongues and let the alpha speak!" Forba shouted at the crowd.

Everyone listened, and the voices disappeared once again.

Forba faced Harri and asked, "So what is your command?"

Harri sat back down in his chair, placed his hand to his chin and inhaled deeply. "I think that we should stay. They don't have the numbers they require to make any more assaults on our villages now. This issue should blow over."

A young protector emerged from the crowd, and all eyes fell on the short, portly man. His jet black, greasy hair amplified his pale complexion.

Harri looked into his brown eyes. "Do you have anything to say, Gruffin?"

"I think that's a terrible idea. We should go on the hunt for these white wolves and demonstrate our strength. You said that they don't have the numbers now, so how many are left?" he said.

"They have twenty-six warriors. So what makes you think that my plan is not a good one?" Harri replied.

Gruffin grinned, "Because your plan is as weak as you, old man. I challenge you for the position of alpha."

Gruffin had always dreamed of being in a position of real power, and now came his chance against this warrior of old. He knew he could not maintain the position for long with many protectors being stronger than him, but he had already devised a plan if he succeeded.

"Ha, you might be able to beat me, lad, but you won't rule the clan for long. You would be foolish to continue," Harri scoffed.

"That's not the point. I still challenge you. Do you accept?"

Harri stood up from his chair and smiled, transforming into a wolf, and Gruffin followed suit. Harri immediately submitted by bowing to him, followed by lifting his head high and howling. Transforming back into a human, Harri declared, "I'm too old to fight now, and unfortunately, I've not found anyone to take my place. If you want the alpha position, it's yours. Though I'm sure the other protectors would disagree and challenge you soon enough, worm."

As Gruffin changed back into a human, the people started to chuckle, so he grimaced and leered at all the people laughing with Forba announcing the new alpha of the black wolves.

"I don't like being called worm!" Gruffin thundered.

He marched up to Harri and, in a quick motion, drew his hunters' knife, jabbing it into him. Harri grabbed Gruffin's arm tightly, but he pushed the blade deeper into his neck as their eyes locked. Legs buckling under his own weight, Harri collapsed to the ground with the knife withdrawing from his neck, spraying blood over Gruffin's face and chest.

"I'm the new alpha, and this is what I say. Whoever was in Harri's party is to come with me, so we can hunt the white wolves. Once that's done, we can see who deserves to be the alpha."

Gruffin knew that this was a risky move, but if his plan worked, then he would secure his newfound position. If it failed, he knew he would probably be ripped apart by one of the protectors from Harri's party. Not giving the people time to process what happened, he transformed and made his way out of the city quickly, knowing Harri's former party would have to follow immediately.

Chapter Fifteen

BETRAYAL OF POWER

Gruffin led his party through the pitch-black forest and out into the plains. Even with the night vision the protectors had in wolf form, it was still hard to see with no natural moonlight. Running for hours until dawn broke, all of Gruffin's party halted. Hearing no footsteps of wolves behind, he stopped and turned to find everyone standing and staring at him.

One of the protectors transformed. "Gruffin, turn into human form so I can speak with you."

Gruffin transformed and walked back to the protector. He knew that they would not hurt him in any way without an official challenge, but he had still put himself in danger, knowing if he was killed by any of them, they would all band together and deny it. Luckily for him, these were honourable men, and they would not step out of line, as the title of alpha was sacred to them all.

"What do you want, Protector?" Gruffin asked.

Pushing his chest hard caused Gruffin's head to whip back, before he stumbled backwards and fell over with his naked bottom and back, landing on the cold, damp ground.

"Don't think for one second we'll follow you forever. You killed Harri in cold blood, without honour. After today, when the white wolf menace is dealt with, I'll take your title and bury you in your own blood, you fucking wet mutt. When we get back to the city, expect my challenge," the protector snarled.

Turning away, the protector transformed, re-joining his brothers in arms. None of them acknowledged what happened, and even the inertia Protector turned away with a grin. Gruffin picked himself up off the ground, wiping away the excess mud and grass on his back and buttocks. He changed back into a wolf and ignored the threat he had just received, continuing to lead them onwards.

Gruffin and his party travelled for another forty minutes, but it looked as though they were too late. In the distance, they could see a large plume of black smoke emerging as Alsander sacked the village of Sooth, razing it to the ground. Unfortunately, the party could hear the screams of the remaining villagers in the distance.

The same protector that threatened Gruffin transformed and said, "Gruffin, what's your plan? These wolves seem to be strong, and you bolted out of the city, causing us to leave with no supplies and only our hunters' knives for weapons."

Gruffin transformed and answered, "We'll find out who these white wolves are and what they want. If they are banished from their clan, then we'll kill them. If not, then we can make diplomatic enquiries with them."

The protector scrunched his face and clenched his fists, advancing towards Gruffin, but then he had a thought, *If this fool tries to talk to them, they'll kill him for us. But if not, when this is done, I'll be the next alpha and make sure he suffers for what he's done to Harri, and I'll hunt the wet mutts who killed our people. Either way, we can find out why they're attacking us.* Unclenching his fists, he sniggered, "If that's your plan, then carry on, we won't stop you."

The protector changed back into a wolf, as did Gruffin, continuing to run towards the smoke in the distance.

Approaching the village, the black wolf party could see the white wolves. To the black wolves, it appeared they had lost another wolf, but in reality, they had lost two, as Harri's grandson did not account for Bleddyn within their ranks.

Changing back into a human, Neil pointed in their direction. "Alsander, look over there. Black wolves are coming."

In the hopes it was the alpha's party, Alsander became excited. But he didn't know what Harri looked like, so he would have to wait a little longer to confirm it was him.

Three miles away on top of a gentle rolling hill, the black wolf party stopped as Gruffin changed back into a human, giving his orders. "We'll advance towards them at walking pace, so they know we're here to talk first. When" – he looked at the inertia protector – "we're a mile away, you'll give me a robe, so they can see me in a peaceful manner. We'll walk until we are five hundred metres before them, and at that point, you'll transform, put on robes and remain. I'll go alone to talk to whoever's in charge."

No one in his party cared for him; they were only loyal to one person, which was Harri. They knew he had gotten away with his plans a few hours before, but that did not matter at this point because he had manipulated them into doing his bidding. Now, his current party wanted him dead, either by the white wolves or their own hands, it made little difference to them. Gruffin's time on this world was ticking fast.

The white wolf party remained where they were, and they could see the black wolves approaching them in a non-aggressive manner. Alsander and Neil noticed a black wolf transforming into a human, donning a battle robe a mile away. Was this a trick or some dishonourable tactic they had devised? Either way, Alsander and Neil knew they outnumbered this party as well, noticing only one inertia, so alone he could not throw as many fire-salt orbs.

The black wolf party stopped approximately five hundred metres away, and Gruffin broke rank, heading towards the white wolves alone, as the others changed back into humans.

"Alpha, I think they want to talk to us. Maybe we should go and speak to him?" Bleddyn suggested.

Neil looked at a protector and demanded, "You, give us some robes now."

One of the inertia protectors scrambled in his backpack, producing two battle robes, giving them both to Neil.

"Here, put this on. Do you want me to come with you?" Neil asked.

Putting his robe on, Alsander replied, "Yes, I don't see why not. Bleddyn, you should come as well."

Though he was confused as to why he was involved all of a sudden, it was a good time to get Alsander's plan out of him, one way or another. "As you wish, Alpha," Bleddyn replied.

The three of them married up with Gruffin, and he gave the wolves' greeting. Alsander and Neil stood behind Bleddyn, so they could figure out what this black wolf wanted.

"Hello, I'm Gruffin, the new black wolf alpha. Who might you be, and what're you doing in our lands?" he asked.

Bleddyn gave the wolves' greeting back and replied, "I'm Bleddyn, the new white wolf peacekeeper, and behind me is Neil the new pathfinder, and Alsander the new alpha."

Gruffin looked at the men behind Bleddyn, and he could see flakes of dry blood still around their mouths. Smart enough to work out Alsander's intentions, he still wanted to hear it from his own mouth to confirm his thoughts. "Why've you come here and attacked our people?"

Because Bleddyn didn't know Alsander's full plans, he could not answer, so he turned around and gave him a vacant look. Grinning as he walked past Bleddyn, Alsander stopped in front of Gruffin, puffing out his chest. His eyes looked directly into Gruffin's so he could work out what type of warrior he was.

Unable to meet the challenge, Gruffin felt uneasy and looked away as he spoke again with a faint smile, knowing the answer to his question. "So, you want to be the next omega alpha?" He turned back to look at Alsander again, noticing his eyes light up. "I see. I'll be honest with you if you're honest with me."

Alsander's eyes went back to normal, speaking to Gruffin with confidence. "That's correct. Are you going to stop me?"

Gruffin cocked his head back and shook it side to side. "No, I'm not strong enough. There are stronger men behind me, and between us, they want me dead as much as you."

Alsander chuckled, folding his arms. "If you're weaker than them, how did you become the alpha?"

"Through timing and precision. He was an old man, so I would have beaten him in a challenge, but he never put up a fight, so I cut his throat," Gruffin briefly explained.

"What makes you think that I won't kill you? You're very confident coming up to us alone, with your men way back there."

A smile emerged from the corner of his mouth. "You see those men behind me, they want you all dead, and then they want me dead. But here's the thing, they're not that bright. So if we could make a deal today, I think we would both benefit and prosper in the near future."

"Ok, then let's hear what you have to say," Alsander frowned.

"Firstly, I need to know if I scratch your back, will you scratch mine?" Gruffin asked.

"Tell me what you're planning, and then we'll see if I agree or not."

"How will I know?"

Alsander dipped his head forward, giving his sinister smile and replied, "Because you'll either be alive or dead."

Gruffin's eyes widened as a shiver travelled down his spine. At this moment, he knew he was in deep water, and if he made a wrong move, he would drown. It would be all or nothing. Either way, his chances did not look in his favour. "Ok, I see. You wish to be the omega alpha, and I can help you do that. My men won't forgive you, and they're not loyal to me. They're loyal to Harri and the clan. If one of them kills me and takes my place, they'll surely challenge you."

Alsander scrunched up his face and replied bitterly, "So what?"

"Alsander, please don't be angry. You need to hear me out. If I remain alpha, I'll submit to you, so long as I can retain a good rank. Your pathfinder of the black wolves, for example."

Alsander's eyes became beady, shaking his head in disbelief from the weakness of this so-called alpha, as he hissed, "I can kill any of your men, so I don't see why I would need you."

Knowing he touched a nerve, Gruffin took a step back and held out his hands. "I can give you one good reason why you would need me for the omega alpha title. Ren the Unbeaten."

Alsander took two steps forward, grimacing as anger surged throughout his body. "What did you just say to me, you wet mutt? Do you think me weaker?"

"No, no, not at all, but this is the reality of your situation. You've come to our lands and killed our people. You might be strong enough to fight Ren the Unbeaten alone, but not a black wolf alpha as well. And who do you think these men will side with, huh? They'll all look to fight you hard, and then they would probably submit to Ren over your corpse. If you think otherwise, then you're a damn fool because with a different black wolf alpha and Ren fighting you, they'll definitely rip you apart, and that's a fact."

Alsander's fists clenched, but he calmed at the voice of the man he trusted indefinitely. "Alsander, I think he might be right on this occasion. Don't do anything rash." He turned to face Neil as he continued to explain, "Look, you're strong, and I fully believe that you can kill Ren, but not if he's aided. This could be a good opportunity that could work very well in our favour."

Alsander turned back around and snapped, "So if I let you live, you'll submit?"

"Yes, you have my word, but there's something I need to ask of you first," Gruffin nodded.

"What's it you want?" Alsander spat.

"Firstly, you must injure me today, not badly so I'll be challenged and lose, but enough for a story to tell my people when I return."

"And what story is that then, Black Wolf Alpha?" Alsander enquired.

"The story of how I fought you and became the only survivor, if you get my meaning."

"Ah, I see, so I injure you, and you claim that my men done that?"

"Not exactly, I'll tell them that we fought and I gained the upper hand, but for my survival, I let you live, and in return, your men let me live. That way, no one will challenge me before you challenge the clans for the omega alpha title."

Alsander smiled, "You're a smart one, ain't you. So be it. Neil, take our men and kill them all. No survivors."

"As you wish," Neil replied, instantly walking back to his men.

"As for you, Gruffin, wave your men over, and we'll take it from there. Bleddyn, I suggest you go and cower behind the men," Alsander ordered.

Happy his plan had worked, Gruffin turned around, waving his party to come closer, luring them to their deaths. As his party saw him waving, they assumed there had been a negotiation, so they advanced to his location in human form. He was excited to be able to remain the head of the Black Wolf Clan until the end of his days, even if it meant betraying all of his people in his quest for power.

Neil informed the men of the plan as quickly and silently as he could. "Make sure none of them survive, except the Alpha. He's not to be harmed by any of us."

The white wolf party waited until the black wolves came close enough to spring their attack. Less than twenty metres away from Gruffin, the white wolves transformed and charged at their prey. Even though they had become victims, they were not defenceless, being seasoned fighters with hatred for the white wolves and their atrocities of late. The black wolves transformed to counter the attack, but their attempts failed.

Unable to fully defend themselves from surprise and superior numbers, the fight ended in less than five minutes. In the confusion of the battle, the black wolf protector that threatened

Gruffin charged at him, knowing he was responsible for this. He almost got close enough to finish what he promised, but Alsander transformed and came to Gruffin's aid by killing him. The white wolves had won yet another battle at the cost of one protector's life. Alsander turned to Gruffin, still in wolf form, staring into his eyes.

"Now, don't injure me too badly, but make it look genuine," Gruffin reminded him.

Gruffin transformed, awaiting his injuries from Alsander. He bit down hard into the scruff of his neck, and he yelped in pain. Then, he started to nip him at different points over his body, making sure that he would not be immobile. After biting him six times, he decided it was enough to bloody his fur for his return to the black wolf capital.

Alsander turned back into a human, relaying his commands to Gruffin. "Four weeks. That's all you have. You'll bring your clan to Borders Cross, and there you'll submit to me. You will not help in any way when I fight Ren, because he's mine and mine alone."

Gruffin, still in wolf form, nodded and retreated back to his capital alone. Alsander had gained what he wanted, with his plan coming to fruition.

The white wolf protectors turned back into humans, getting dressed as best they could in their torn robes, awaiting their alpha's instructions.

Alsander donned the remains of his battle robe and addressed his party. "Well done, men, we've shown these weaklings the strength of the White Wolf Clan. With a small number of us, we have destroyed two of their villages and wiped out two parties. We're truly the strongest clan in the West Plains," the men started to cheer as he continued, "but it's now time for us to return and prepare for the final part of my plan for our clan. Byron, come forward."

Byron broke rank and stood before his alpha. "I've got a task for you because you'll get there quicker. You're to go to the Town of Niamh where you'll call out Ren the Unbeaten on my behalf. He has four weeks from this day to arrive. Tell him if he doesn't turn up, his challenge will be forfeit."

"As you wish, Alpha." Removing his torn battle robe, Byron transformed and ran to make better ground against the clock.

Bleddyn moved closer to Alsander and Neil, who had started one of their secret conversations, but they did not sense his presence.

"You chose well there. Now our plan can come to light," Neil said quietly.

"Yes, soon I'll claim the rank of omega alpha and become the first wolf king of the West Plains. Our glory is at hand, my friend." Neil grinned and nodded in agreement. "As you know, Tristan wiped out the Blue Wolf Clan, and I think it's time our clan finished what he started. That way, there'll be no more wars between us, and we can have a hierarchy, which our clan has desired for many years. With the other clans gone, we can achieve that dream. No more customs or laws we all abide by. We can have our own laws and customs instead of sharing them with the weak. After I kill that black wolf alpha and Ren, the two clans will be leaderless. The black wolves will be the ones to fight the grey wolves, and when they're both done killing each other, we'll have our clan mop up and destroy whoever's left. We'll be the only clan, and finally, the weakness and impurities of our land can be cleansed. I can-"

Hearing the information he needed, Bleddyn interrupted, "What? You can't just wipe out the other two clans. Your great, great-granddad has already destroyed the balance of our entire country. Why would you do this?"

Alsander and Neil turned around, eyes boring deep into Bleddyn's with hatred. "Yes, I can, because they're all weak.

They don't deserve to live in this country, in my country!" Alsander declared.

"If you know what's good for you, you'll shut the fuck up, Peacekeeper," Neil suggested.

"No, I've held my tongue for long enough. Crey was right, you're lost, and all that's left in you is your dad. There's no helping you now."

Alsander's eyes widened, and he spoke with a furious rage in his tone. "How do you know about that?"

"Because I was there, hidden from sight, but I saw and heard everything. Crey told me you might be lost, but now I see you're far from lost. You've turned into your dad. He was weak, and so are you, you murdering, wet mutt."

Alsander gave his sinister smile and said, "Now you're a full-blown traitor to your clan. What do you expect to do now?"

"There's nothing I can do, but I know someone who might be strong enough to destroy you, the one that you challenge. Ren the Unbeaten," Bleddyn replied.

"Ha, you're a fool. How do you expect to outrun any of us when I give the command to kill you? Do you think you can make it to Niamh Plain all by yourself?" Alsander scoffed.

"Crey once told me the difference between a good leader and a bad leader, and one of the differences is this. A good leader knows his people."

Bleddyn turned to the east and started to run, but after a few steps, he transformed into a wolf, sprinting at great speed.

Alsander raised his eyebrows and said, "I didn't know he could change, no matter." He pointed at two of his protectors and ordered, "You two, kill him."

The two protectors transformed and gave chase to their peacekeeper, beginning a new hunt.

Chapter Sixteen

A PEACEKEEPER GOES ABOVE AND BEYOND

Bleddyn had been running at high speed for thirty-six miles, still hunted by the protectors. As all peacekeepers were skilled with evasion tactics, he used the terrain to his advantage, keeping them at bay. Nearing the border of Niamh Plain, he could see the grey wolf village of Shay four miles away, which could be his salvation. However, he battled fatigue from the pace of the hunt. Still, he knew that the protectors chasing him would also be struggling.

Nearing the village, the protectors picked up their pace and powered through, sprinting hard to catch him before he reached it. Only two miles away, Bleddyn had a trick up his sleeve, using the universal signal for enemies sighted by howling three times. Five grey wolf protectors heard the howls, exposing themselves at the edge of the village to investigate, discovering three white wolves advancing. Without hesitation, four of them transformed, and the inertia protector quickly mounted one of the wolves, with his bow and arrows at the ready. Charging towards the white wolves, they became confused, unable to see a grey wolf that might have sounded the alert.

Less than a quarter of a mile away, the grey wolves noticed Bleddyn was one hundred metres in front of the other two. Thinking quickly to get the grey wolves on his side, Bleddyn turned around and charged at his own kin.

Confused, the grey wolves second-guessed their intent as the white wolves turned on each other. The inertia protector could clearly see he was missing something deeper to this encounter.

Bleddyn pounced forward, biting into a protector's scruff, pulling him downwards. The other protector saw through his attack and jumped over his comrade, knocking him away by using a body slam. Fatigue caught up to Bleddyn, his muscles burning with lactic acid, lungs tightening. His chest pounded from the run and adrenaline as fear seeped into his soul, desperate to survive for the greater good of all the clans. Picking himself up off the ground, he mustered one last call, howling twice. This specific howl was used only when a peacekeeper was in distress, obliging all protectors from every clan to intervene and aid them. Now, he had to fight his own kin until the grey wolves arrived, being his salvation or destruction. Bleddyn squared up to the protector that body-slammed him as the other rose to his feet. As they charged at each other, the inertia grey wolf protector loosed an arrow into the air, flying in a straight line directly at his target, finding its way into the head of the charging white wolf protector. Bleddyn stopped as the protector screamed out in pain, turning to see how far away they were.

When the white wolf protector turned to fight the oncoming threat, two of the grey wolf protectors had already started their attack. One speared forward and hit the white wolf protector's nose with the top of his head, the other flanked him and aimed low, biting the white wolf's hind leg while clamping his jaws shut. With momentum and body weight aiding his attack, he dragged the white wolf backwards, dislocating the leg. The white wolf cried over and over again in immense pain.

The inertia protector loosed another arrow, hitting the other white wolf protector in the side of his chest as he stood up. The last grey wolf protector used this as an advantage, biting the white wolf's tail, still running at full speed in a similar fashion to that used by his comrade with the other's leg. Unlike a leg covered in muscle and supported by strong bones, the tail ripped open and nearly tore off, dragging the white wolf backwards. He howled in pain as the grey wolf with the inertia protector on him found his mark, biting down hard into his shoulder.

Throwing down his bow, the inertia unsheathed his hunters' knife, leapt off the wolf, spinning through the air and drove his knife deep into the side of the white wolf's chest. Using his momentum and body weight, he dragged the knife down through the intercostal muscle, causing the white wolf to collapse. Climbing onto its back and running across his body, he plunged his knife into the side of the white wolf's neck. Twisting the knife, he jumped to the side and ran the blade through the flesh, lacerating the wolf's neck open. The blood streamed out with each heartbeat, killing the white wolf in mere seconds.

The last white wolf protector had no chance of survival. Crippled and outnumbered, he could not fight nor flee, and panic settled in as he knew the grey wolves were not reputable for their mercy. He did not want to be ripped apart by the four of them, so he held his head high, hoping they would give him a clean, quick death. As they surrounded him, he did not move an inch, accepting his fate. "I'll do it," the inertia protector said.

Walking around the corpse he had made, he approached the last white wolf protector, placed his knife on his neck and declared, "You've shown bravery, White Wolf. Now be with the Great Wolf in the Meadowlands."

The inertia protector made a small opening on the side of his neck, cutting the carotid artery. Blood gushed from his wound with each rapid heartbeat, the blood volume and pressure lessened with the distance of spraying blood. The white wolf collapsed with his soul leaving his body.

The grey wolves turned from the two white wolf remains, gazes fixed onto Bleddyn. He immediately changed into a human, instantly giving the wolves' greeting and holding his other hand out to show his submission. At this point, he hoped that the grey wolves would listen. Struggling to breathe, he found it hard to speak in a full sentence. "Please don't...attack until you've...heard what I...have to say...I'm...the new...white wolf peacekeeper."

"Hold up," the inertia protector commanded.

The four grey wolves stopped and let Bleddyn explain why he was in their land.

"Make it quick, so-called Peacekeeper. You used the call of distress, so if you're fooling us, then we'll kill you as well because you're trespassing."

Bleddyn put his hands together and bowed his head, buying a short amount of time for his breathing rate to recover. After taking a few deep breaths with his hands on top of his head, he replied, "Thank you. I was hunted by these two on the command of my new alpha, whom has just laid waste to two black wolf villages. He's also killed the protectors of the black wolf alpha's party."

"That's a good story. So what else have you got because you missed the black wolves' alpha in that?"

“That’s because he made a deal with my alpha. Please, I must speak to your alpha post haste. Your peacekeeper will confirm who I am.”

The inertia protector looked off to the sky, scratching his head. “Thing is, there’s another white wolf that came here not too long ago, demanding that he saw our alpha. Is this a plan to attack our village as well?”

“No. Please, I tried to help my alpha, and he’ll watch you all burn. I need to see Ren, and I’ll not waste any more time bouncing this conversation back and forth with you. Either kill me or do as I say,” Bleddyn demanded.

“Look, I suggest you talk to us with a bit more respect. We just fucking saved your life, you wet mutt.”

One of the grey wolf protectors changed back into a human and said, “He might be telling the truth. Those white wolves back there didn’t engage us, they were after him. I can take him to the alpha alone because if he tries anything, I’ll end him. That way, if he’s lying, our village has you four and the other two sleeping at the protectors’ hut to guard this place.”

Nodding with agreement, the inertia turned to one of the other wolves and gave his orders. “You, go and wake the other protectors that’re doing the shadow guard. I believe the night’s watch are in their homes, so wake them as well. That way, we’ll have three more protectors to defend if needed.” He turned to the wolf that would travel with Bleddyn. “As soon as you take him to our capital, come straight back with the others, and take care.” Looking directly at Bleddyn, he declared, “And if you try anything, this protector here is a fine warrior, and he’ll kill you. It’ll take you no more than two days if you both transform and run hard. It’ll also mean that you can catch your friend that passed through here not too long ago, who was also in a rush.”

Both the grey wolf and Bleddyn transformed, running towards the grey wolf capital, but they would not get there until the late evening the next day. Bleddyn had no choice, racing against Byron to get information to Ren, meaning little rest and more running.

Midday the next day, the sun shone brightly at the Town of Niamh. Everyone seemed happy with their lives as the town's people were getting ready for a final trial the next day.

"Really, is there any point in us going out to hunt? There'll be nothing left if that hunting party continues," a hunter exclaimed.

Returning to the town, all twelve wolves had a deer in their mouths. This amount of food would normally take the biggest part of any day to gather, but this party had proved extremely efficient, collecting this number of deer in a space of just over two hours. Two inertia hunters riding on the backs of two wolves grinned at the other party, as one of them shouted down to them. "She took out all twelve of them by herself within five miles. Good luck trying to beat that."

The hunter that initially complained, replied, "Yeah, if it wasn't for her, you wouldn't be so smug, so shut your face."

Tabitha dropped one of her kills outside the butcher's hut and made her way to the changing den, transforming back into a human. She put her clothes on that were neatly folded in the corner. As she finished dressing, she turned around, greeted by her closest female friend. "Hey, it looks like the hunt went really well for you again," Abaigeal said.

"Yeah, not a bad day today, but with final trials coming up, I think another hunt later should make sure there's plenty of food for everyone," Tabitha replied.

"Oh, ok, are you free at the moment? I would like to have a word with you if that's ok?"

"Yeah, I'm free. What's up?"

"I just need to ask you something, but it's not very important."

Exiting the changing den, they made their way to the market.

"Hey, good hunt today, Tabitha. Maybe you can teach me a thing or two, you know, just the two of us," one of the male hunters said, winking.

Tabitha tutted, rolling her eyes at him as the two girls carried on about their business.

"You're still getting a lot of attention from the guys, I see," Abaigeal grinned.

"Yeah, they won't take no for an answer. I don't mean to be bitchy, but when I tell them no, they just press their advances," Tabitha replied.

"Yeah, the guys at the capital can be a bit forward, but do you blame them? I mean, come on, you're one of a kind."

"Well, from the outside, it looks nice, but it's really a pain to be honest."

"I can see that. So, what I wanted to talk to you about, well, ask you actually, is would you like to join me, Ieuan and Ren for a meal at my home later this evening?"

Tabitha's face scrunched up. "I'll be busy tonight. I've already made plans with Wikki and his mate Arwyn. Apparently, they have something to tell me."

"You're so full of it. Come on, Ren is going all out to get your affection."

"Yeah, I know, but I'm not lying. They really do want to see me tonight, so I promised them first. Maybe another time with just us two, you know, a girls' night."

Shaking her head, Abaigeal grinned. "All right. I like our girly nights anyway."

Abaigeal's smile faded, and she looked off to the distance. She could hide things well, but Tabitha knew when there was something on her mind. "Is there something else you want to ask me? Are you ok?" Tabitha asked.

Abaigeal looked up at Tabitha. "Maybe, I'm not sure. I'm seeing the healers later. You can come around my place after your second hunt today if you want, before you go to Wikki's."

"Yeah, that's fine. I can come over before I go there." Tabitha turned, looked into the market place as they arrived, and sighed, "Oh, here we go."

Just as they entered the market, Isolde spotted the pair of them, walking in a direct line to Tabitha. "Why've you got a look of dread on your face, missy?" Isolde inquired.

"Mam, please. Not this talk again. I told you last night I'm not interested in talking about it," Tabitha replied, rolling her eyes.

"Interested or not, you must talk about it because I want to know the next steps in your life. Look, you'll always be my daughter, so I'm just looking out for you," Isolde replied.

Abaigeal felt a bit uncomfortable; fortunately, she had somewhere else to be. "Umm, Tabitha, I've gotta go to the healers' hut because they want to see me. I'll see you later, yeah? Isolde, it was really nice seeing you again."

She did not wait for a reply, disappearing into the crowd at the market place.

"Now that your friend's gone, we can have that talk because I know you're free before your next hunt."

Tabitha slouched forward and sighed loudly, displaying her disapproval and annoyance.

"Word around town is that Ren has taken a liking to you. Apparently, he's liked you for some time," Isolde stated.

"Mam, I'm not interested in him. Can you just leave it, please?"

"You had better hurry up and choose a man, because I want grandchildren."

"It's not your decision when I have children," Tabitha protested.

"So what's wrong with Ren or all the other men that are falling over themselves to be your mate, huh?"

"Stop going on about it. By the Great Wolf, it's my decision. I ain't blessed like you to find someone like Dad at a young age. All they want is a trophy mate, either because of my looks or my hunting skills. None of them take the time to get to know me."

"It's always a bonus to have all this male attention, because it won't last forever. I don't want to see you put on 'the shelf' because you let all these opportunities pass you by. I know I was lucky with your dad, but sometimes when you're courting, you'll get to know each other that way. You just gotta give someone a chance," Isolde explained.

"Well, when a guy's interested in the real me, I'll give him a shot. But until that time, they can all piss off," Tabitha spat.

"Ok, ok, no need to get uppity with me. I'm just concerned that even with all this attention, you might just be a little shy. All your friends have a mate, that's all I'm saying."

Tabitha shook her head. "That's not an excuse to just be with someone. I'm glad my friends are happy with their mates, but I just haven't clicked with anyone. I'll know when I know, you know."

Isolde frowned. "What? That made no sense."

"Well, I know what I mean, and that's all that matters for now. So, in other words, just drop it."

"All right, all right, there's no need to bite my head off."

Tabitha looked past her mother's head, noticing Ren peering at her from halfway down the market place. "Mam, I've gotta go now. I'll see you after I've been to Wikki's, ok?"

"Why're you going there?" Isolde asked.

Ren started advancing to Tabitha's location.

"I'll tell you later. Bye, Mam."

Tabitha kissed her mother on the cheek and darted away, disappearing among the crowd. As Ren approached, he realised she had gone. Looking around, he asked, "Isolde, where's your daughter gone? I just saw her here."

"Why? What's her whereabouts got to do with you?" Isolde said bluntly.

Lowering his head, Ren retreated quickly with Balgair behind him, laughing loudly.

"What're you laughing at, Balgair?"

"Nothing, nothing at all." Through his chuckles, Balgair continued the conversation they had before Ren got distracted. "Look, I think it's time. You need to find someone else now."

Ren exhaled heavily. "I haven't got a clue who I'd even choose. The only person that would've been a strong candidate would be Ieuan, but when I asked him to come away from Abaigeal's party to mine, he challenged me."

"Yeah, that's right, I remember, and he put up a good fight too, but you can't separate them, I'm afraid. They love each other's company, and he'll always be Abaigeal's personal protector."

"The thing is, after our fight, we've become close, and he's the only person I truly trust, but he'll never leave Abaigeal's side. I just don't know who to choose."

"Look, it's nice if you manage to find a strong pathfinder, but it's not always the best option. You're strong enough to fill both positions. Pick someone else that you can trust without question. I'll give you a month, but after that, I'll be stepping down because it's a young man's game. I'm an old man now, and I miss Gus."

Ren gave a little smile as he nodded. "No, you're right. I'm just being selfish. You've been a great pathfinder, and you've served me well. I think it's time you enjoy your retirement and live out your days back in your hometown. I'll ensure that you'll have the best hut in the village."

"That's very kind of you, Ren. Thank you."

Tabitha returned to her hut and had a few hours rest before the next hunt, thinking of what her mother had said. Over the years, she had come to enjoy her life, and the fire inside her to become something more than a hunter was but a distant memory, even though Wikki had secretly trained her. She had a good life and was content, but from time to time, she would miss her father dearly and always remembered fond thoughts of him. Sometimes, she would dream of him. He would not speak in the dreams, but it was as if he watched over her. After time with her thoughts, she gathered her party members together to hunt one last time that day.

A few hours later, completing their second hunt in the late afternoon, ten more deer were added to the next day's celebrations. Tabitha went home quickly to wash the deer's blood from her body, making herself presentable and changing into her best clothes. Leaving her hut, she bumped into Wikki and Arwyn as they walked past.

"Hey, Tabi, how's the hunt?" Wikki asked.

"Well, it's a good day today. We managed to get twenty-two of them," Tabitha replied.

"I'm guessing you mean the royal we, like the cats?" Wikki joked.

Tabitha frowned. "What do you mean?"

"Word around the town is you hunted them all by yourself, and the cats' royal we means I, it's a joke," Wikki chuckled.

Tabitha and Arwyn looked at him and shook their heads. "Wikki, that's terrible," Tabitha snorted.

"Ahhh, you two don't know funny anyways. Now we have you here, me and Arwyn wanted to tell you something very important, and it won't take long. If that's ok?"

"Um, ok, no problem. I was on my way to Abaigeal's before I was coming to you, and I really want to go there sooner rather than later because of...reasons," Tabitha replied.

"Yeah, no problem, it's just an announcement, really. I'll let you tell her if you want."

Arwyn smiled and held her stomach before she gleefully said, "Ok. Tabitha, we're having our first child."

"By the Great Wolf, that's amazing!" Tabitha exclaimed.

She threw her arms around Arwyn, hugging her tightly. Then she released one arm from her, pulling Wikki into a group hug. Tabitha took a step back and looked at both of them, grinning from ear to ear. "I'm so happy for both you guys. Wikki, I can't believe you're gonna be a dad!"

"To be honest, I can't believe it either. The healers said our firstborn will be due in four months."

"Well, you have the old man jokes down to perfection," Tabitha smiled.

As Arwyn and Tabitha laughed, Wikki folded his arms and cocked his head back, scrunching his face. "Pfftt, like I said, you guys don't know funny."

They stopped laughing, and Tabitha cut the meeting short. "Guys, I don't mean to be rude, but I promised Abaigeal that I would be over soon. Can we just postpone this for now? I can still come over after I've seen her."

"Yeah. Besides, we can celebrate, just us three before we tell other people. We gotta have Auntie Tabi with us," Arwyn replied.

Tabitha gave a big smile, displaying teeth white as fresh snow. Giving them both a quick hug with a kiss on the cheek, she made her way to Abaigeal's hut.

Chapter Seventeen

AN UNEXPECTED CHALLENGE

Tabitha knocked on the door, and Abaigeal answered with red, puffy eyes.

"Hi, sorry I'm late, but I bumped into Wikki on my way over here," Tabitha explained.

"Hello, I'm glad you came. Please come in."

Abaigeal moved towards the door, pushing it wider. As Tabitha entered, eyes fixed on Abaigeal, she asked, "Are you ok?"

Closing the door, Abaigeal turned, immediately hugging her while beginning to sob. "I'm sorry, Tabitha. I don't want to burden you, but I don't know who to turn to."

Tabitha frowned. "You don't have to be sorry. Just tell me what's wrong?"

Letting go of her, she wiped the tears away. "You know I told you a month ago that I was carrying a child?"

"Yeah, is everything ok with the baby?"

"That's just it, there is no baby," Abaigeal said.

"What? Did you miscarry?"

"There was never a baby. I went to the healers' hut after I saw you because they wanted to see me, to check up on the baby and stuff. They checked and felt my breasts to see if I was 'preparing', but they had not grown in size."

"So, what does that mean?" Tabitha asked.

Abaigeal started to tear up again. "They didn't grow because there is no need for any milk. I can't bear any children because I've gone through menopause early."

Tabitha held her hand up to her mouth, unable to think of anything to comfort her, becoming teary-eyed as she felt empathy for her friend.

Abaigeal couldn't hold back the tears anymore. "I have let everyone down, and now I have let Ieuan down too. He would have been a great dad, and now he won't be able to have any children because of me."

Tabitha moved forward, holding her tightly. "Don't be stupid, this isn't your fault. Have you told Ieuan yet?"

"No, I don't know how to tell him. Maybe it would be better if he left me and found another mate he could have children with."

"No, I'm sure that he will still love you unconditionally, no matter what."

Abaigeal's voice broke as she replied, "But everything is different now. I can't even give him one child, and I know he wants to be a dad so much."

"Well, I know I said that I'd leave, but how about I stay and help you prepare the food for your meal? I'll even stay and eat with you. Wikki will understand." Abaigeal looked up, nodding with approval. "You'll have to tell him, though. He needs to know," Tabitha suggested.

"I know. I will tell him when the time is right."

"Well, you'll know when the time is right, and you know I'm always around if you need me, right?"

"Thank you, you're a great friend," Abaigeal replied, wiping her eyes and face.

No more words were spoken between them as they prepared the food in silence. The ingredients were scattered on the table, a deer's leg that had been skinned next to some unpeeled potatoes, fresh carrots covered in a dusting of mud, onions still with their skin on, one large swede, mushrooms and some florets of broccoli and cauliflower. Tabitha placed the venison leg on a metal grate above the hot embers in the fireplace, as Abaigeal started to clean and peel the vegetables. Tabitha grabbed a large cauldron, taking it outside to the closest well, filling it two thirds with water. When she got back, Abaigeal had already started to cut up the vegetables. Tabitha removed the leg of venison after cooking it on both sides for forty minutes, replacing it with the cauldron of water, stacking fresh blocks of wood on the embers to add heat from fresh flame.

When Abaigeal placed the cut vegetables in the water, she sprinkled in some salt and crushed peppercorns to the makings of a stew. Tabitha pulled apart the venison with two forks, placing the pulled venison on a plate so it could be added to the broth when ready. The scent of stew encompassed the entire hut, smelling gorgeous and inviting. Unsurprisingly, Tabitha's mouth watered, and her belly rumbled from the smell. Keeping each other company in silence, the stew had cooked. Even though the pair did not speak to each other, Abaigeal was grateful for Tabitha's help and calming presence.

"I was wondering if I could ask you one last favour tonight." In her gut, Tabitha knew what was going to be asked, dreading the question. "Would you stay here when I tell Ieuan what has happened?"

Tabitha's heart sank, thinking this issue should be conducted in a private manner, not with a witness. A loud knock on the door saved her from the awkward conversation for a few minutes. Answering the door to reject anyone going to bother Abaigeal with their petty matters gave her a little time to come up with a tactful answer. She opened the door, revealing a protector behind it. "Hello, Tabitha, is Abaigeal there, please?" he asked.

"Yes, but she's not seeing anyone today, so please leave," Tabitha demanded.

As she closed the door, the protector intervened by holding his hand out, stopping it, while he explained, "I'm not here for myself. The alpha has demanded her presence. A white wolf has come to see him. He said that she must be there because it's official business,"

"Ok, I'll bring her. Tell the alpha she won't be long," Tabitha replied.

The protector gave the wolves' greeting and left to inform Ren that she was coming. Tabitha turned around, but Abaigeal had already heard the conversation. "I know, I'll get my robe, and we can go."

"Are you ok to do this?" Tabitha asked.

"Yes, it is my duty to the clan, so I must go if the alpha needs me."

She observed Abaigeal for a few seconds, admiring her strength and courage to continue with her duties first. Opening a wardrobe, rummaging around for a few seconds, she found what she was looking for. Pulling out a beautiful robe she used for official duties similar to the ceremonial robes, she draped it over her clothes, keeping the hood down. Leaving the hut, they made their way to the alpha's pavilion, where the town's people gathered. Just off to one side of the alpha's pavilion, tables and benches were out in preparation for the following day when the final trials were being held, and some of the town's people were sitting on them already. As they got closer, Tabitha could see her mother sat on one of the benches. "I'll sit with my mam, ok? Come find me after this."

Abaigeal nodded, making her way to the peacekeeper's seat next to Ren. Giving both Balgair and Gethin already sat in their respective chairs the wolves' greeting, she ascended the steps and sat on her chair.

In front of the alpha's pavilion, four protectors stood guard, so the white wolf could be stopped if needed. He waited for the alpha he had heard so much about, roughly one hundred metres away. Still in wolf form, dried blood and charcoal marks stained his fur, with a faint smell of smoke around him from the burned black wolf villages.

One of the grey wolf protectors walked over to him with a battle robe. "Hey, you, I suggest you turn into human form and put this on, or the six protectors around you will rip you apart. Ren is a fair man, but you'll do well not to test him."

Byron transformed into a human. Long brown hair, thinning on top, fell down each side of his face. His naked skinny body had charcoal stains and dried blood on it, but there was no fear in his brown eyes.

Grabbing the battle robe from the protector, Byron was unimpressed. The basic material felt rough, unlike the elegant style of white wolves' battle robes. When putting it on, his skin, clearly not used to this basic fabric, started to itch, causing him to scratch every now and then. He thought to himself about his first experience with the Grey Wolf Clan. *What a primitive bunch this clan is, even their clothes are ancient in design. Alsander would do well to rid us of these backwards people.*

"You there, why've you brought this white wolf here? Who is he?" Ieuan asked.

"Sorry, Ieuan, he approached our village unarmed and alone. He claimed he's bearing a message from his new alpha or something."

Unimpressed by the protector's answer, he snapped, "What do you mean or something? You'd better not waste Ren's time with any nonsense, or it'll be you who'll get the blame."

Byron intervened, answering Ieuan's question. "I've come here to-"

Ieuan's eyes opened wide at Byron, interrupting him. "Shut up! If I want you to speak, I'll tell you to speak. If I tell you to jump, you'll fucking jump. You hold no rank here, White Wolf."

Becoming slightly anxious, Byron thought he might be in over his head. Being set aback by Ieuan's attitude, he did not reply to acknowledge his command. Ieuan walked up to him to give him a string of interrogating questions, interrupted by the declaration from his mate. "The alpha has arrived. Bring forth the white wolf messenger," Abaigeal ordered.

Byron walked down the main street, being the longest one hundred metre walk he had ever done. Running down both sides of the street were hunters and protectors, either in wolf form or with inertias armed with combat weapons, and there were at least one hundred of them. None of them was aggressive, but they didn't need to be as he could feel all of their eyes on him, staring in silence. Personally, he would have preferred them to bark, snarl or shout, but the deafening silence put him on edge even more. Ieuan grabbed him by the shoulder ten metres away and stopped him in position.

"Stay here and speak when you're asked to speak, answer the alpha's questions when he asks them to you, and behave," Ieuan commanded.

Ieuan left his side, wandering past the four guarding protectors in front of the pavilion, stopping at the bottom of the steps. During Byron's walk to the pavilion, he didn't notice that Ren had already arrived, sitting in his chair.

Staring hard at the white wolf, Ren noticed the blood stains and charcoal around his face and neck. Everyone waited thirty seconds so Ren could compose his questions in his head and also test Byron's attitude, before asking, "Who're you?"

"I'm Byron White-Mane. I'm the lead protector of the white wolves."

"Who sent you?"

"My alpha, Alsander White-Ear."

"I've never heard of any new alpha. Why has your peacekeeper not come to tell us, as is tradition?"

Byron bit his lower lip. "He could not come. He is busy on another errand."

Ren sat forward in his chair and glared at him. "If you lie to me one more time, pal, I'll order my men to rip you limb from limb. Now, I'll ask you again, why has your peacekeeper not come to inform us of a new alpha?"

Byron had no choice but to tell him the truth. "He's also new, he became the new peacekeeper after our new alpha took his place."

Leaning back in his seat, Ren looked over to Abaigeal, speaking softly so Byron could not hear him. "You've met Crey, is there any reason you could think that he would step down? Because from what Quinn has told me about him, he was going to die with that title."

Abaigeal took a few seconds to think with the only logical explanation she had and replied, "Maybe he stood down because the white wolf council are his closest friends. I think that could be the only explanation. But I can go to Quinn's hut and ask more because he's a friend of Crey's, despite him being a white wolf."

"Ok, thank you for that, I might not need you to ask about it, but I'll keep that in mind," Ren said.

Abaigeal nodded in silence to acknowledge his kind words.

Turning his attention back to Byron, Ren asked him more questions. "What happened to Crey, your old peacekeeper?"

"He's disappeared. I don't know where he is. He was just gone, so we voted for a new one."

Ren gazed over at Abaigeal quickly, and she shook her head.

"Where's your new peacekeeper? Why've they not come to us with this message from your alpha?" Ren inquired.

"He's with my alpha. He's busy on a mission."

"I can read people well, and my peacekeeper here also has concerns. You might've stopped lying, but you're withholding information. As alpha of this clan, I now declare you my prisoner until you either give me the information I want, or until we investigate what you've said."

"What! That's not any of your concern. That's a white wolf matter, and you do not have the right to confine me," Byron protested.

Ren stood up and made his position firmly clear. "You're not a peacekeeper, so you have no protection in our lands. I'm the alpha in these lands, so I can do what I damn please with you, pal."

The tension of the conversation was interrupted by a grey wolf protector, shouting, "My Alpha, I have a white wolf that needs to speak to you!"

Everyone, including Byron, looked behind at the grey wolf protector. Still standing, annoyance and confusion overcame Ren. "What do you mean? There's already a white wolf here!"

The protector stepped to one side, held his hand up and presented Bleddyn, lowering his hood to reveal his face from a battle robe he borrowed at the entrance of the town. Byron's view was obstructed by the grey wolf protectors behind him, bobbing his head back and forth to gain a clear view of this white wolf. Managing to find a gap between the protectors, he saw who it was. With a downturned mouth, he muttered, "Bleddyn."

His mutter was not as quiet as he thought as Ren heard him. "Do you know this white wolf?"

He turned around and replied, "Yes."

A few seconds of silence past before Gethin stood up from his seat. "The alpha asked you a question, so answer it fully if you value your life."

Bleddyn walked down the one-hundred-metre stretch, littered with grey wolf warriors, stopping five metres to Byron's left. Presenting himself with the wolves' greeting, he bowed, showing his respect. Being the peacekeeper, he already knew when to talk, waiting for Ren to ask him who he was. Impatient with Byron's clear disrespect and insolence, Ren turned his attentions to Bleddyn. "Who're you?"

"Hello there, Grey Wolf Alpha. I'm Bleddyn White-Tail, the white wolf peacekeeper."

Sitting back down, Ren asked Abaigeal to perform her duty. "Check him out. If he isn't who he says he is, don't mention it until you're safely back here."

Abaigeal nodded, initiating her task immediately. As she walked down the steps of the pavilion towards him, she was immediately escorted by Ieuan. This time, he had withdrawn his hunters' knife to protect his world at any cost, without hesitation.

She stopped five metres from Bleddyn and turned to face Ieuan. "Wait here. You know what I must do."

Making sure that Bleddyn could hear him, he replied loud and clear, "As you wish, Peacekeeper, but if he even twitches a muscle, I'll kill him."

Abaigeal put her right hand on Ieuan's chest, soothing his nerves. Bleddyn became so nervous he did not even give the customary wolves' greeting, through fear of what Ieuan would do, not moving a muscle.

Spinning around, she gave the wolves' greeting. "Hello, Bleddyn. If you are who you say you are, you will have my word that my mate here will cause you no harm. Speak to me the word of the peacekeepers, and you can rest easy."

She walked up to Bleddyn, held her hand next to her ear, making sure she covered his mouth so his lips could not be read. As he whispered the sacred word, she stepped back with a smile and bowed. "Welcome to the Town of Niamh, White Wolf Peacekeeper."

Bleddyn could see that Ieuan had sheathed his knife, placing him at ease, so he gave the wolves' greeting and bowed to return the compliment. "Thank you for your warm welcome, Grey Wolf Peacekeeper."

"Please call me Abaigeal. You are welcome here, so maybe you can help us. This white wolf protector of yours is insulant and rude. He thinks he is safe, but his life is in the balance."

"I'm here to help you beyond what you know. Please go back to your seat up there and don't take your eyes off him. He's not to be trusted," Bleddyn replied.

Abaigeal glanced over at him, but Ieuan heard what Bleddyn had said, so under a second, he cleared the five-metre gap, with his knife on Byron's throat. "Abaigeal, do as that white wolf says," Ieuan demanded.

Even though Abaigeal outranked her mate, she listened to his command, rushing back to Ren's side.

"Why're you here, Bleddyn?" Byron asked.

"Hold your fucking tongue, or I'll pull it from your throat, you wet mutt," Ieuan spat.

Ren, confused by Abaigeal's and Ieuan's actions, regained control of the situation. "Ieuan, sheath your knife. Abaigeal, why're you two acting strange?"

"The white wolf peacekeeper said we should not trust the other white wolf," Abaigeal replied.

"You. Bleddyn, is it? Come forward so you can address me better," Ren commanded.

The night started to draw in as two hunters walked around with torches, igniting small pyramids of wood dotted around the town and pavilion. Bleddyn walked forward, with the fire lit next to the pavilion partially blinding him for a few seconds. As his eyes adjusted, he looked up at Ren, ready for his questions.

"Why's that other white wolf here?" Ren asked.

"Has he not told you? The white wolf alpha extends a challenge to you, for the title of omega alpha at Borders Cross, in under four weeks' time."

Ren stood back up with a faint smile on his face, muttering to himself, "Finally, I can become the omega alpha."

"Grey Wolf Alpha, please don't underestimate Alsander. He's possibly as strong as you, but twice as ruthless. He'll not hesitate to kill all of you if he wins," Bleddyn warned.

"Please excuse my interruption, Alpha. But what did you mean, Bleddyn, if you don't mind me asking?" Abaigeal frowned, tilting her head slightly.

"If Alsander wins, he'll destroy both the Black and Grey Wolf Clans," Bleddyn replied.

Byron looked over at Bleddyn and spat, "So this is why you're here then. Fucking traitor! When Alsander wins, he'll make sure you'll suffer for what you're doing here if I don't do it first. As for the rest of you, your time's fading fast. But" – he looked at Abaigeal with lust in his eyes – "before we destroy you, we'll make sure we have some fun with your women."

Scowling at Byron, Ren's accommodation for his attitude had finally run out. But before any order was given, Ieuan unsheathed his knife again and, in one swift motion, drove the blade hard and deep into Byron's abdominal area, piercing his liver. Known to be noble within the clan, he could be very ruthless when it came to protecting his mate in any way. He knew that, with this injury, Byron would have a slow and painful death. Gripping onto Ieuan's arm with both hands, the blade twisted and withdrew quickly, cutting Byron's left hand as the blade passed.

"Protectors, rip him apart!" Ren ordered.

The grey wolves around Byron did not hesitate, biting into his left arm, legs, and right shoulder as he screamed out in a low pitch. Growling and shaking their heads, the grey wolves separated his limbs. His left arm and leg tore from his body, the right leg partially severed, and his right shoulder was torn, crushed and dislocated. The wolves let the trunk of his body hit the ground. Ieuan turned around and looked at Ren, who gave him unspoken permission with a nod to finish what he had started.

Abaigeal did not like violence, so she had already turned away before the wolves began their method of punishment, as not to see the massacre in her presence.

Ieuan made sure he suffered with his last breaths as Byron somehow survived the assault. Flicking his knife around, he stood over the remainder of his body and brought himself closer to his target with a wild look in his eyes. Raising his arm high, he drove the knife down using all his might. The blade cut through the right side of his torso, breaking the ribs apart. Repeating the process over and over, he turned his right chest wall into pulp, with Ieuan becoming red-faced as he screamed with rage. His eyes burned with hate for this man for making such a comment towards his mate, with each blow eliciting involuntary noises from Byron, and sounds of each rib snapping. When he struck the eleventh blow, Byron remained silent. Life had left his body, and Ieuan's rage for this man died with him.

"Dispose of this wet mutt, so our peacekeeper doesn't have to see it," Ieuan demanded.

Still in wolf form, they picked up the biggest remains of his body, taking them away, as two inertia hunters gathered the rest of his body parts. Ieuan's breathing rate recovered as Bleddyn stared at him, wondering if he was next.

Abaigeal turned around gingerly, not to see any of the decimated carcass that had been removed. "Bleddyn, what was he talking about with our time running out?" she asked.

"He's right. If Alsander wins, his first command will be to pit the Black Wolf Clan against yours, then whatever clan survives, my clan will destroy. I'm sorry I have to give this information to you, but the black wolves don't know of this plan, and the new black wolf alpha has already struck a deal with mine," Bleddyn replied.

"No, how can this be? Has your clan learned nothing from the past?" Abaigeal stated.

"It's deeper than you all know. My alpha, Alsander is the great, great-grandson of Tristan White-Ear, and he wishes to finish what he started."

Most of the people in the crowd began muttering amongst themselves, not knowing the true history of the Blue Wolf Clan.

"Is there any way to stop him without the threat of all-out war?" Abaigeal asked.

"There's only one way now. Ren, you must kill him. We've tried to stop him, but Alsander killed Crey, had me hunted, and he's wiped out two black wolf villages already, killing everyone. He's lost beyond help because of his dad's actions," Bleddyn replied.

"Can his dad stop him?" Abaigeal inquired.

"No. Alsander killed him and his mam when he was 16 years old, about eight years ago."

Abaigeal thought for a second, and then it clicked. The boy she had met in manacles in the great hall of White Castle was the same person. Now she knew there was no way to stop him without killing him.

"Ren, you must meet his challenge. I'm sure you're the only one that can stop him. You must kill him," Bleddyn pleaded.

Ren held out his arms to his sides, addressing everyone present. "Don't despair, my people. I'll kill this white wolf alpha, and we'll have the first grey wolf omega alpha...Me!" His people started shouting and cheering. "With recent and past events the white wolves have created, there's only one solution to save our people. When I become the omega alpha, I'll make the black wolves fight with us and not against us, and together we'll end the White Wolf Clan...Permanently!"

The crowd cheered more loudly as Abaigeal opened her mouth, shocked by Ren's response.

"I'm so sorry, Dad, but I must," Tabitha muttered to herself.

Tabitha stood up from the bench, presenting herself twenty metres in front of the pavilion. She looked across to Bleddyn, hunched over, looking at the ground with tears falling from his cheeks. Feeling the despair from Bleddyn, her jaw tightened as her fists clenched, shouting at the top of her voice, "No!"

The crowd stopped their cheers, and the people became silent, with all eyes on Tabitha.

Isolde stood up, trying to control her daughter. "Tabitha, what're you doing?"

"Enough, Mam, this is beyond you and me now." She looked at Ren squarely in the eyes, continuing her protest. "You can't do this. The white wolves have done terrible things in the past and of late, but there's good within their clan!"

"Are you kidding me, Tabitha?" Ren replied smugly.

"No, I'm not. The white wolf peacekeeper is trying to stop him in his own way. Even though he'll be surrounded by enemies from outside his clan as well as within, he came here to warn us anyway. That's evidence enough with a show of courage and honour. What about their women and children? Are they part of this ethnic cleansing you're planning?" she spat.

"Tabitha, I know that I've been trying to gain your affections, but I'm the alpha, and this ain't a matter for females to attend to."

Tabitha's red face scrunched up as an old familiar rage started to build up inside her. "How dare you! This is concerning everyone, not just men. It's always men causing devastation for their so-called glory. Killing innocent people is not the answer."

Ren turned around to sit in his chair.

"Don't you turn your fucking back to me, you wet mutt!" Tabitha shouted.

Pivoting around quickly, Ren's face became red with both rage and embarrassment. "I'm your alpha, woman. If that's my decision when I become omega alpha, then there'll be nothing you or anyone else can do to prevent it, as it's law. Now don't confuse my affections towards you being the top of my priorities now. I have what I truly want at my fingertips."

Looking back at Bleddyn again, Tabitha shook her head before gazing over to her mother, with Wikki and Arwyn standing behind. She looked up to the clear starry sky, with all three moons high above her, thinking of what her father might say, *He is the alpha, you need to stay in your place. This is not a game, Tabitha.* Then she glared at the ground, thought back to her childhood and her father's words to her, the night she had her first transformation: *You are the best of us all.*

One tear fell from her left eye as she muttered to herself. "Now I know what you mean, Dad. I'm sorry if I disappoint you, but I must do what I think's right."

"What did you say?" Ren asked.

"Well, it looks like there's only one way to stop you and your plan," Tabitha spat.

Raising his arms, he boasted, "I'm sure we'd all like to know what that is."

Tabitha took in a slow deep breath and declared, "I challenge you for the position of alpha."

The crowd laughed as Gethin stood up from his seat, shouting, "You stupid girl, no female has ever been a protector, let alone been stupid enough to challenge for the title of alpha!"

Holding his hand out, Ren shouted to the crowd, "Enough!"

The laughter died down as Gethin sat back down.

Staring at Tabitha, Ren declared, "If this is what you want, I'll grant it for the memory of your dad. If you lose though, I'll have no choice but to banish you to the Eastern Wastes. Is that what you want?"

Tabitha looked to Isolde, Wikki and Arwyn, all with despair in their eyes, stating to all three of them. "I'm sorry, I'm not doing this for glory. I must do what is right for all of our people."

She transformed into a wolf, stood tall, with her eyes burrowing deep into Ren.

Removing his shirt while descending the pavilion steps, Ren professed, "It's a damn shame that it has to end this way, Tabitha. I could've made you a happy woman."

He transformed into a wolf and walked to one side of the pavilion. As Tabitha growled loudly, he barked at her, and the people dispersed from the newfound battleground. Both of their muzzles wrinkled, exposing their fangs, with intense growls emitting from every breath. Their eyes locked with intensity, initiating the fight as they both charged at each other at full speed.

Chapter Eighteen

THE BACKUP PLAN

The white wolf party returned from their expedition just over a week after Bleddyn evaded them, surprised to see over half of the white wolf army camped at the capital, preparing for war.

"What's going on, Alpha?" one of the protectors asked.

Alsander gave his sinister smile, watching the army ranks grow before his eyes. "I had someone that Neil trusted to get my army ready for the challenge at Borders Cross. When I claim the omega alpha title, I'll pit the Black and Grey Wolf Clans against each other. When one clan falls, I'll have the white wolf army destroy the victors. From there, we'll cleanse our lands of weakness, wiping the weaker clans off the face of Xancrylor, making our clan the greatest again."

Already planning the formation of his army, he knew the other clans could not muster their armies at full strength with the time he gave them, giving the white wolves a great advantage over their future enemies. Having over two weeks ahead of any clan to strengthen his ranks, and within the two weeks left to prepare, he would have neared his full fighting force with the knowledge of the grey and black wolves having half the manpower at best.

"Come, Alsander, you must get some rest. When we're at full strength, we can inform the army of their duties and what you expect from them," Neil advised.

"Yes, I agree. All of you, go home and rest. You've done the clan a great service. Return to the ranks in two weeks before we leave," Alsander commanded.

Giving the wolves' greeting, the party dispersed and waited for time to pass with their loved ones as the army numbers continued to increase.

Over at Black Forest Plain, Gruffin had organised his army as a display of power to present to Alsander if he won the challenge against Ren. He stood with his only friend on top of a tower at the front gates, and they watched the army gather.

"Jock, this'll work in our favour in the next three weeks," Gruffin said.

"How? You can't beat Ren and Alsander if they both turn on you, and even if you did beat Alsander, Ren would kill you," Jock stated.

"I lied about the fight against the white wolf alpha, and I've struck a deal with him," Gruffin replied.

"What deal are you talking about?" Jock inquired.

Watching hundreds of black wolves pour into the city, he smiled, "You see, I'm going to submit to Alsander. I've heard of the grey wolf alpha's reputation, but I've seen the white wolf alpha in action. He could win this fight."

Jock shook his head. "But why the white wolf? Why would you submit to that wet mutt after what he's done?"

Slapping his hand on Jock's back, Gruffin explained his plan. "You're not looking at the bigger picture, my friend. I submit to him, he wins, and I become his pathfinder. My title will then die with the new omega alpha, and no one can challenge me for the pathfinder rank. That way, I can rule this clan for most of my life without ever looking over my shoulder." He grabbed Jock's shoulder and continued, "You've always stood by me, so I'll make you the leader of the protectors, but only if you want it. I'll always look out for you, but the rest of these bastards can burn for all I care. I know I betrayed the clan, but I don't care for them. What do you say, my friend? Do you want to be at my side as the leader of the protectors, ruling over these simple-minded fools?"

Jock's eyes opened wide with excitement, grinning as he nodded. "Yeah, I'd like some power for myself, this clan might have shunned us in the past, but now they'll bow to us."

"That's the spirit, my friend. Look out for number one, and climb over anyone to get what you want no matter what. This clan is now ours," Gruffin chuckled.

"Do you think anyone would challenge you before then?" Jock asked.

"No, they're all stupid. They actually believed my story about the 'battle' with the white wolves. And Forba believed my lies as well, even if she is growing suspicious. Some of these wet mutts now fear me a little with that information. No one in any clan would be stupid enough to challenge their alphas at this time. The deed is done, and the players are set. This game is nearly over, and we're going to be some of the top players," Gruffin replied.

Jock picked up two wooden tankards and a bota off the floor, pouring wine from the bota into the tankards. This alcoholic drink was very rare in the West Plains, because only the people of the Southern Kingdoms had the skill to produce this exquisite drink. The strong, fruity smell escaped the bota and tankards into Gruffin's nose.

"Is that wine?" Gruffin asked as his sight fixated on the tankards.

"Yeah, that's right. It was my dad's. He said he traded it for a hunters' knife many years ago with a cat. A red cheetah nomad, if I'm correct. He was travelling, and he went past my dad's home town of Thansware."

"I'm impressed. Most around here have never tasted wine. Many of the people have never even heard of the stuff. You should have saved it for a celebration," Gruffin remarked.

"No, I think now's the time to celebrate. We're about to be the rulers of the Black Wolf Clan. Together, we'll have what we want, power, respect and women," Jock said with a large grin.

Gruffin grabbed Jock by the arm, expressing his pleasure by shaking him a little while laughing. They both picked up the wine-filled tankards, clinking them together to toast Gruffin's successful plan. Raising the tankards to their mouths, they tasted wine for the first time. The smell of alcoholic fruit hit their noses with great potency, and after the first taste, the wine slightly dried their mouths as they swallowed.

"Wow, that's really good," Gruffin said.

"You're not wrong, my friend. To our bright future."

With both of them smiling, they clunked their tankards together again, drinking more wine while watching their clan's warriors pass through the city gates.

Two weeks later, the white wolf army mustered outside the lower ring, with improvements being made to the city limits. A stone wall would be erected with an estimated time of a year to build it, alongside two gates and gate houses. Alsander raised another leader of the protectors from his ranks, with the assumption that Byron was dead as he had not returned from his task, and as for Bleddyn's position, he did not care to fill it.

Walking to the city limits alongside Neil and his new council, his eyes scanned across his 7,000 white wolf warriors. Even though his army was not fully assembled, he was delighted with the outcome. Ready to address his clan as best he could, Neil ensured certain protectors throughout the ranks acted as messengers, so everyone would know what their alpha had said. Four protectors erected a four feet high soapbox, so most of the warriors could see him. Aided up onto the soapbox, Alsander addressed his army, giving details of what he expected from them, shouting so his people could hear him. "My people, listen to my words! We're the greatest of all the clans! We move out today to Borders Cross where I'll claim the title of omega alpha, burying Ren the Unbeaten in his own blood!" The army shouted and cheered for a minute, and then their cries of pride died down. "In just over a week when we arrive there, we'll secure our rightful place in this world as the greatest clan of Calinthia, by becoming the only wolf clan in Xancrylor! The grey and black wolves will fight each other on my orders after I win! After one has defeated the other, we'll then destroy the surviving clan's warriors! It will be an easy fight because I've assembled you before I issued the challenge! They should only be at half of their strength with the short time I've given them! After we kill their warriors, we'll wipe out the rest of their filthy, weak races, starting with the grey wolves!"

After thirty seconds of the message being passed through the ranks, the warriors cheered and shouted again. Alsander dipped his head forward and gave his sinister smile, pleased with the happiness of his people willing to carry out his sick and twisted plans. "No longer will our children have to fight for the scraps of society, and neither will they suffer from others failure! After I win, we will have a hierarchy just like the cats of the south, with me being your first king! We move out now! In a week, we can look to rid ourselves of outdated customs and laws to make our own! Follow me where a brighter future awaits us all!"

As Alsander got down from the soapbox, his army cheered with high morale, following their alpha to Borders Cross.

At that same moment, Gruffin addressed his army of around 2,500 men. Standing within the wall limits, the army trailed through the streets of Black Forest City. Having the same method of relay speakers so everyone could hear, he stood on the gate tower, giving his speech. "Today, we leave for Borders Cross! There, we'll show our strength and might! I have injured the white wolves' alpha, so I'll help Ren the Unbeaten take down the wet mutt that attacked our lands! We'll get revenge for our fallen!"

The army cheered loudly, showing their admiration for their leader. Only Jock knew this to be a lie, but Gruffin manipulated the weak minded, bending them to his lust and will. "Let's go forth and make history together and show the other clans what the black wolves can do! For honour and revenge!"

The crowd shouted, and some of the men transformed to howl. As Gruffin got down from the tower, a hunter stood at the bottom waiting for him.

Squinting briefly at the hunter, he asked, "What are you doing here?"

The hunter gave the wolves' greeting and bowed. "Alpha, I know it's not traditional for anyone under the age of eighteen to go to Borders Cross, but he's only two months away from doing his final trial. I was wondering, with your permission, if I could take my eldest son with me. He would be under my constant supervision."

Still looking at the hunter, Gruffin noticed a young boy stood behind him. He didn't care about tradition, because he had been breaking it himself his entire life. "Step forward, boy," he commanded.

The young man walked forward a few steps, presenting himself with the wolves' greeting.

"What's your name?" Gruffin asked.

"I'm Torry Blackpaw, Alpha," he replied.

"You wish to come to Borders Cross. Why?" Gruffin questioned.

"I'm hoping that, after my final trial, I'll become a protector. My dad said I could learn a lot from this experience."

Torry's father stood tall, puffing out his chest and pulling back his shoulders. Smiling with wide eyes, he nodded at Gruffin to gain his approval.

Gruffin squinted again, looking back at Torry's father. "So be it, your son can come."

Bowing low, Torry's father grabbed his hand, blessing his new alpha for the opportunity. "Thank you, Alpha, you're very kind."

Gruffin frowned, pulling his hand away as the hunter stood erect again with the wolves' greeting. Turning around, he tapped his son on the shoulder, and Torry gave the wolves' greeting, joining the ranks.

Having the least amount of time to get their army ready for Borders Cross, the Grey Wolf Clan did well, gathering over half of their fighting force. Making the last of their preparations for the journey, one final task took place to ensure the survival of the grey wolves if their alpha failed to succeed. Gethin organised the protectors, Balgair briefed the hunters, and Ren hand-selected protectors for his plan.

"You five go to every town and village and make sure everyone gathers at Wolf's Fang. We can ensure the clan's survival if the women and children are ready to evacuate if they need to. As for the people that have gathered here, I can send two protectors if we fail. They'll be able to gain two days travelling over any army to ensure our race survives, so get it done," Ren ordered.

The five protectors transformed, running out of the capital in different directions, beginning the preparation for the mass evacuation of the Grey Wolf Clan.

The collected hunters and protectors were together, all 3,500 of them waiting another two hours before leaving for Borders Cross, just in case any more men could join the ranks. After that time had elapsed, they would have no choice but to leave and witness the event that would decide the future of all the wolves of the west.

"Ren, we don't have enough fighters for Borders Cross. This could be bad if we lose," Gethin reported.

"We won't lose, so don't worry about it," Ren replied.

"You're very confident then?"

"Of course I'm confident. This plan is just in case we fail. The escapees will have the last of the hunters and protectors to look after them if we do. Now, we'll depart in two hours. Make sure the protectors are ready, and see if Balgair has the hunters ready as well."

Gethin gave the wolves' greeting and nodded, leaving to carry out his task. As Gethin turned around, he saw his son. "Wikki, come here."

Hearing the call, he saw his father waving at him to be at his side. Stopping what he was doing, he went over to his father. "What is it, Dad, what do you need?"

"You know what to do when we get to Borders Cross?"

"Yes, Dad, stop going on about it," Wikki snapped.

"Hey, I'm just making sure. I suggest you say your goodbyes to your mate. You might not get another opportunity," Gethin advised.

"I'll finish what I have to over there first, then I'll say my farewells, not my goodbyes. Unlike you, I have faith in my alpha, even if you don't," Wikki spat.

"I'm on your side, Wikki, even if you think I'm not. I want what you want, our survival, but I'm looking at the reality of the matter, because we might fail. So make sure to tie up your loose ends if you have any," Gethin replied as he walked off, carrying out his orders while watching over the last minute preparations.

Wikki quickly finished the task at hand, making his way back into the town. Going directly to his hut, he burst through the front door, and Arwyn jumped a mile. "By the Great Wolf, what do you think you're doing bursting in here like that?"

"I'm sorry, I'm just nervous, that's all," Wikki replied.

"Don't lie to me, I know when you're lying," Arwyn said, folding her arms.

Wikki gazed at her growing belly with his child within, then he looked up, and their eyes met. "I'm sorry. I'm scared that I'll be leaving you here and I won't be returning. I'm afraid that I'll leave you alone and our child without a dad, possibly in a strange country, with a hostile race."

Arwyn took a few steps forward, reaching out to grab his hands, placing one of them on her growing belly. "Listen to me, great warrior. You'll be coming back to us both, I just know it. I have faith in our alpha, and so should you. I know nothing is set in stone right now, but we must fight and survive, so we don't become lost or, even worse, extinct like the blue wolves."

"It's all down to our alpha now because, if the alpha fails, then both the Black and Grey Wolf Clans will fall," Wikki replied.

Arwyn let go of Wikki's hands, throwing her arms around him. "I know you would have liked to get Tabitha's advice, but everything has changed now. This is where you must stand on your own four feet and trust your instincts and knowledge. Have faith in yourself, as I do. You're stronger than you know."

Wikki looked down to Arwyn as a tear rolled down his cheek. "I know."

Arwyn was another beauty of the Grey Wolf Clan. Long fiery, ginger hair formed perfect spirals down to her hips. Her light brown eyes gazed into Wikki's, calming the storm within him. Pushing herself up on her tiptoes, she kissed Wikki with her rose-red lips, before saying, "I'm so proud of you. Now go make your name within the clan."

Wikki smiled, giving her another kiss before leaving to re-join the army. As he turned around to look back at the hut, Arwyn waved him off, and he gave one last smile before walking away, looking down to a lock of her hair in the palm of his hand.

The time had come to depart from the Town of Niamh and Ren was examining the army stood before him, when Abaigeal greeted him from behind. "Are you ready, Ren?"

"It doesn't matter now. Ready or not, we leave. We're all fated to what the Great Wolf has in store for us."

"That's true. But I have faith that we will persevere," Abaigeal said.

"And what of you? I hear your mate is not impressed that you are going to Borders Cross," Ren replied.

"I outrank my mate, so he has no say in the matter."

"Rank or not, I do have a say," Ieuan replied from behind them.

Feeling the instant tension rise, Ren left to lead the army.

"Ieuan, please don't be mad that I am coming. It is my duty to be there. I am this clan's peacekeeper, it's tradition," Abaigeal pleaded.

"I don't care; if we fail you'll be in a place of danger. I want you and our child to be safe," Ieuan replied.

Abaigeal took in a slow, deep breath. "I need to talk to you before we get to Borders Cross if possible, or when we get there at the latest. It's important."

"What's wrong, my love? Can't you tell me now?"

"I would, but Ren is leading us there now. We must go there with the others and not delay."

Ieuan saw the army leaving, so he had no choice but to agree. "Ok, I'll take my place in the ranks, and we'll meet up at the first encampment. We've just under a week to get there."

"We might not meet up until Borders Cross, my love. I will have to see to the welfare of the clan, and you will have your duties. I promise we will talk at Borders Cross at the latest, before the alphas engage."

Ieuan nodded, removed his battle robe and handed it to the inertia protector behind him. Transforming, he fell into rank within the army, leaving Abaigeal for the first time since they had been mated. As Abaigeal watched him fall in, a tear rolled down her cheek. Wiping her face, she mounted a protector, as they all headed to Borders Cross.

Chapter Nineteen

MEETING OF THE CLANS

The air whisked a warm south-westerly breeze between the tall pine trees at Borders Cross, encircling the large field covered in dry green and yellow grass. White and grey clouds cast over the sky, blocking the sun and making the perfect conditions for an even battle.

Arriving first, the White Wolf Clan emerged through the treeline from the north-west. The army broke ranks, spreading out so they could all see the future battle before them. The therianthropes of the clan were already in wolf form, minus Alsander and Neil.

The inertias of the White Wolf Clan were armed with axes, knives and spears, wearing beautiful armour to protect their bodies from transformed wolves. The armour consisted of multiple layers of deer leather and steel plates. The helmets mimicked the head of a wolf, with no faceguard covering the wearer. Steel wolf ears sat atop the helmet with long metal plates riveted into the leather, protecting the skull. Resembling the top of a wolf's muzzle, peaking forward four inches in length across the forehead, steel teeth accompanied by two steel canine fangs blocked part of the wearer's peripheral vision. This helped in large battles, narrowing their vision, as the wearer could concentrate on the enemy before them and not either side. Two generic wolf eyes were carved into the steel just above the muzzle of the helmets, mimicking a complete wolf's head. It was clear the White Wolf Clan were dressed, armed and ready for war, not to witness a fight for the omega alpha title.

At the front of the army waiting for the other two clans to arrive, Alsander and Neil grew impatient, with Alsander pacing back and forth with excitement brewing. During the journey, Alsander changed his image, cutting off his long hair and giving himself a buzz cut.

"Are you ready for the fight?" Neil asked.

Alsander smiled, dipped his head and leered into the empty field. "Yes. In fact, I'm quite looking forward to fighting this Ren. He may be from a weak clan, but he'll give me the challenge that I've desired for many years. And with that, my eternal glory with his death."

"Don't be overconfident. Fight Ren with everything you've got and don't hold back. After this day, we'll rule supreme over these lands without any challenges," Neil advised.

"Oh, don't worry about that. They'll receive no mercy from me. None of them."

Neil looked over to him and grinned, "Good. Soon, it will be time. Why don't you rest a little? I'll call you when they come."

Alsander nodded, turned and tapped Neil on the shoulder. "For the glory of the clan."

Retiring behind the first rank of his army, he sat down on the grass and started to eat venison jerky.

Two hours later, the Black Wolf Clan emerged from the treeline to the south-west, with the wolves transforming back to humans. The inertias were not fitted for battle, with everyone only carrying hunters' knives for protection. Just over 2,500 warriors of the clan came to witness this rare event, but fear shrouded the men as they looked over at the white wolf army. All kinds of thoughts entered their heads, but there was one that came to most of their minds. Why did they look ready for war? Not only were the White Wolf Clan inertias fully clad in armour, but their army was almost at full strength, causing more concern within the ranks, because they all knew that they had planned something.

"Keep calm, my people. We'll be safe! They initiated the challenge, so that's why they have full ranks!" Gruffin stated.

The anxious members talked amongst themselves, and Gruffin knew he was losing control, because he was no leader.

"Everyone, listen! The Grey Wolf Clan will be here soon! Be patient and try to calm yourselves!"

Relaying what he said through the ranks, they started to calm with the information Gruffin gave them, if only by a little.

A medium-sized banking lowered the terrain of the field where they stood, so the clan members moved northward of the field, claiming a better view of the sacred battleground.

Waiting patiently for another hour, the Grey Wolf Clan showed themselves from the treeline to the south-east. Because of the banking and the lower tier of the field, they moved northward for a better view. The black wolves looked at the force of

3,500 men and wolves, noticing that they had turned up in the same fashion as the White Wolf Clan, suited up for war in armour, carrying weapons, and grey wolves remaining in wolf form. The Black Wolf Clan clearly knew they were missing something here, feeling something ominous about to happen on the horizon, and they were not prepared for whatever was to come. Outnumbered and outmatched in every way by the other two clans, the feeling of dread filled their hearts.

Forba broke ranks, marching up to Gruffin. "What information have you kept from us?"

"I've told you about the challenge, Peacekeeper. Don't despair, they're probably just trying to scare us," he replied.

"No, Gruffin, you have been deceived. Something is going on that we do not know about, and you have kept something from us. It is not traditional to come to this place ready for war. The clan's presence is purely to witness the rise of an omega alpha, not a display of power. You are a fool."

"You won't be saying that after today, Forba. And, for that comment, I'll make sure you're punished for your insolence," Gruffin promised.

Forba smiled, giving the wolves' greeting. "As you wish, Alpha. I think as we are all here, the peacekeepers are to convene to see when the alphas are to challenge."

Walking away, Forba ignored Gruffin's threat, glaring at her as she passed him. She now knew he kept something from the clan, but at this point, there was nothing she could do. Advancing to the centre of the field, she waited for the other peacekeepers.

Abaigeal managed to find her mate in the ranks. "Ieuan, I must speak to you now."

He turned back into a human, and an inertia protector gave him a battle robe. "What is it, my love?"

"Can we talk in private behind the ranks, please?" Abaigeal asked.

"Of course."

Passing through the ranks in silence, Abaigeal led the way into the forest for some privacy. Stopping, she turned around to face him and confessed, "Ieuan, I know that this is not the best time to tell you, but I must tell you before whatever happens here today happens. I am not carrying your child." Ieuan frowned as she continued, "I'm sorry I've kept this from you for so long, but you must know. I have gone through the 'change' early. I cannot bear any children. I'm so sorry that I have let you down. I'm a failure, and it's all my fault. You would have been a great dad, and I have stopped you from becoming one."

Ieuan tightened his lips and asked, "How long have you known this for?"

Tears rolled down her cheeks as she replied, "About three weeks, the same day the white wolves arrived at our town. I'm so sorry, I'll understand if you want to leave me and find someone else. I'm no longer a woman because I cannot give you what you want."

Ieuan grimaced, clenching his jaw hard as he sprung forward, wrapping his arms around her tightly. "How dare you. You don't get to decide for me. You've done nothing wrong. I love you so much."

Abaigeal looked up at him as he wiped away her tears from her eyes and cheeks with his thumbs.

"I thought you would be mad at me or hate me."

"Oh, I'm angry at you, but not for you going through the 'change'. I'm angry at you because you should've told me sooner. You shouldn't carry this burden by yourself. I'm here to carry any burden or problem you have. I would never leave you. You're my life. I love you so much, and together we'll get through this," Ieuan said, as tears rolled down his face.

Feeling emotionally safe, Abaigeal put her head into his chest and sobbed as she apologised again. "I'm sorry about everything."

"No, I'm sorry for not being there when you needed me the most. But I'm here now and always. You're mine, and I'm yours, and that's that," Ieuan replied.

Removing her head from his chest, their eyes interlocked. Ieuan leaned his head down, giving her a passionate kiss. When he pulled away, he looked at her and wiped her tears off her face again as she smiled.

"There's my Abaigeal, just don't bottle anything up like this again. You can tell me anything. I love you."

"Ok, I will. I love you too."

This beautiful moment together was interrupted as a protector came looking for Abaigeal. He saw the two of them together and felt awkward being in their presence, but he had to be there. "I'm sorry to disturb you, Peacekeeper, but the black wolf peacekeeper is waiting at the centre of the field for you."

"Then let her wait!" Ieuan spat.

Abaigeal stroked her hand through Ieuan's hair, calming him. "It's ok, my love, this is my duty," – moving her head slightly, she looked at the protector – "I will be there shortly. Thank you for informing me."

Giving the wolves' greeting, the protector quickly retreated back through the trees. Abaigeal wiped her eyes to prepare for the meeting of the peacekeepers. She took a few deep breaths and wiped her eyes one last time.

"Come, I must go now," Abaigeal said as she grabbed Ieuan by his hand, escorting him back to his rank.

Abaigeal turned around and kissed her mate again. She let go of his hand and made her way to the centre of the field.

"I'll be right here when you get back," Ieuan declared.

Spinning around, she walked backwards, gave him a smile and turned back to continue on her way.

"I believe you should leave, Bleddyn. You should be at the centre of the field. You're not to return here after your meeting. Go to your clan," Ren ordered.

"As you wish. Don't forget what I've told you. If your clan fails, he'll kill you all," Bleddyn replied.

Balgair appeared and stood next to Ren on his right-hand side. "Are you still here, White Wolf?"

"I am about to take my leave. I wish your clan all the best today, for all of our sakes," Bleddyn said.

He gave the wolves' greeting and left to join Forba in the centre of the field, nine hundred metres away.

As Bleddyn and Abaigeal advanced to the centre of the field, he was spotted by his own clan, stopping them nominating a messenger.

"Look, there he is, the fucking traitor," Neil sneered.

Alsander glared at him, raising his upper lip. "When I kill Ren, you can kill that wet mutt if you wish. We won't be needing him anymore."

Neil smiled, "I can't wait."

Forba greeted the two peacekeepers with the wolves' greeting as they arrived.

"Hello, Abaigeal of the grey wolves." Turning to Bleddyn she asked, "Who might you be?"

Bleddyn and Abaigeal gave the wolves' greeting back as Bleddyn spoke first to answer her question. "I'm Bleddyn, the new peacekeeper of the White Wolf Clan. It's a pleasure to meet you, Forba. Crey told me much about you."

Forba frowned and looked over to Abaigeal. "Can you confirm this information?"

"Yes, he is the white wolves' peacekeeper. I have confirmed this with the sacred word of the peacekeepers order," Abaigeal replied.

"If you have confirmed it, I will trust you. Now, it's down to business. A challenge has been issued, bringing us here to this sacred place. We must agree on a time for the alphas of each clan to meet. The rules that will be witnessed by all the clans are complete submission of your respective alpha, or a fight to the death. No weapons are to be used, and this must be fought in wolf form, the same as the challenge for the alpha position. If your alphas transform halfway through the battle, then the fight proceeds as normal. Do you all understand and agree to this?"

"Yes," Abaigeal replied.

"Of course," Bleddyn said.

"Bleddyn, your alpha has issued the challenge for the omega alpha title, and my alpha accepts. What about your alpha, Abaigeal?"

She nodded. "My alpha has answered the challenge also."

Forba declared, "Good. Today, there will be the rise of the fourth omega alpha, so we speak the sacred laws of this customary challenge. Whoever rises as the omega alpha will never be challenged, even after their last breath has passed. No person from any of our clans will challenge or attack the omega alpha, through punishment of death or banishment, but if the omega alpha wishes another form of punishment, then their word is law. If the omega alpha wishes a new law to be passed, then it will be done, and they will be restricted to only making a maximum of three new laws. They will have full control and power over all the clans. The omega alpha can call upon any or all clans as they see fit, for the purposes of war, and their command will never be challenged. If the omega alpha is in unwarranted danger, then it is every wolf's duty to protect them. But in times of war, that will not always be possible. Nevertheless, every clan member must still do their best to uphold this law. If there is anything I have missed or you wish to add, please speak now."

"Yes, I have something to add," Abaigeal said, "The omega alpha will have powers to declare each clan a pathfinder, and only the omega alpha can make them or dismiss them. These chosen people will be the omega alpha's right hands, and they are under the protection of the omega alpha's ancient law. Upon the omega alpha's death, the pathfinders will become the alphas of their respected clans, so only at that point can they be challenged for their position. There is also the title of the protective father. He will be the leader of all protectors under the omega alpha's reign. When the omega alpha has joined the Great Wolf, then their title is instantly removed. The protective father will be chosen by the protectors of all the clans in a voting process, similar to our titles. I believe that is all I have to add. Has anyone anything else to add to the laws?"

The three peacekeepers thought hard to ensure they knew all the laws of old to declare to their clans.

"I believe that is all there is to the omega alpha laws. Now we'll need time to get to our clans and declare the laws to our people. Now, for the last thing, we need to discuss timings. We'll need time, and then our alphas will need time to prepare. How long will we agree to?" Bleddyn said.

"I think twenty minutes will be enough," Forba replied.

"I disagree; I think thirty minutes will be a more respectable time," Abaigeal stated.

"I agree with the grey wolf peacekeeper," Bleddyn answered.

"Then, it is settled. After thirty minutes, the alphas of the clans can enter the field from their ranks, alone and unarmed," Forba said, giving the wolves' greeting.

Abaigeal and Bleddyn gave the wolves' greeting back to Forba, and then each other.

"Farewell, White and Black Wolf Peacekeepers. Good luck, and may the Great Wolf watch over you both," Abaigeal said, turning around to re-join her clan.

"Forba, do you have time to listen to me quickly?" Bleddyn asked.

"I am afraid not. I must leave and inform my clan of the laws. You would do well to do the same, White Wolf Peacekeeper," Forba replied.

Bleddyn nodded his head, and they parted ways to re-join their respective clans.

Approaching his clan, Bleddyn was met by Alsander, wrinkling his nose as he spat, "How long have you all agreed on?"

"Thirty minutes, My Alpha," Bleddyn said.

"Your alpha? Don't make me laugh. You're a dead wolf, traitor. When I rise, you'll fall. Neil will make sure of that. Declare the laws and wait for your death," Alsander hissed, giving him his sinister smile.

Bowing low, Bleddyn rose with a large grin on his face. "I wouldn't worry so much about my death, Alsander. The day's not won yet."

Scowling, Alsander spat on the ground by Bleddyn's feet, ending the conversation. "Wet mutt."

He walked over to Neil and ordered, "Make sure you make that bastard suffer. I want to hear him scream."

"It would be my pleasure...my absolute pleasure," Neil said, glaring at Bleddyn with a grin.

Forba and Abaigeal had already started to recite the laws of the omega alpha title to their clan members. Bleddyn recited the laws to his clan, and there were protectors that would project what they all said, ensuring the clans heard the laws.

Twenty-five minutes had passed, and the clans stood in silence, waiting for the challenge to take place for them all to answer to one leader. Ren walked forward, ready to witness the outcome between the black and white wolf alphas. Folding his arms, he looked down to his bandaged arm before gazing out to the field.

Balgair walked up behind him, placing his hand on his shoulder, and said, "Remember what I said to you all those years ago about it hurting when you lose. Just imagine that for the entire clan. It could be us or them today. Either way, many people will feel the pain."

He tapped his shoulder twice before taking a few steps backwards. Wikki walked forward and stood to the left of Ren, and gave him an update. "The two protectors are behind me, ready to order the evacuation if we need them to."

Ren turned around, only replying with a nod before turning back, looking out to the field once more.

The thirty minutes of preparation had come to an end, marking a historical day.

"It's time!" Forba shouted to her clan.

The Black Wolf Clan members knew he would never be omega alpha, but they were happy that their alpha would avenge their fallen from the two villages, so they cheered him on.

"The time has come!" Bleddyn yelled.

The white wolf army shouted at the top of their voices with the wolves howling, giving support to their alpha.

"This is it!" Abaigeal called.

The grey wolves, also shouting and screaming, encouraged their alpha to fight hard for the future of their race.

Chapter Twenty

THE DEADLY CHALLENGE

Removing his battle robe, Alsander became the first to transform. The white wolf army continued to praise their alpha.

"Go on, Alsander, you can do this. Kill them all!" Neil bellowed.

As Alsander advanced into the field, Jock broke rank, and he walked towards Gruffin. "Do what you need to do and return to us as our future leader."

Gruffin smiled, "Don't worry, Jock. I'll do what I have to, so I can secure our future in this clan."

Transforming, he walked up the banking north of the field, turned right and slowly advanced towards the Grey Wolf Clan, stopping halfway down. The men of the Black Wolf Clan watched hard, wondering why he stopped.

Forba had a feeling Jock knew his plans, so she went over to him for an interrogation. "You there, what did Gruffin mean, and why has he stopped? He said he was going to team up with Ren the Unbeaten."

"You'll find out soon enough. Our future will be secure for a lifetime. We're fed up of your judgements and putting us down. Even though he was a protector, you all looked down on him and called him a worm. He should've had respect from you bastards, but now he'll get his respect, or you'll pay for your insolence. He's secured a deal and our claim to power within the clan," Jock declared.

Forba spat, "You stupid fools, you and Gruffin have secured your own fates."

Alsander progressed towards Gruffin until they were face to face. Gruffin bowed low, showing his complete submission towards him and his clan.

From the ranks of the black wolves, a hunter shouted, "You traitorous wet mutt, you've dishonoured our clan! That bastard killed our people, have you no honour?"

Torry broke rank and turned to his father. "Dad, what does this mean?"

His father sighed, answering his son. "It means that it's over. We've submitted to the white wolf alpha."

Gruffin raised his head high and howled, as was tradition in submitting to another alpha. Alsander watched him for a second before he lunged forwards, biting hard and deep into his neck. His howl turned into a gurgling sound as his neck ripped open. With Alsander shaking his head back and forth with great ferocity, Gruffin did not know what to do or how to react, knowing he had been beaten at his own game by a better player. Alsander pulled back and twisted his head, pulling him to the ground, and shook his head violently again. He had Gruffin in a good position, unable to counter, and now aware of the strength that Alsander possessed. *I don't want to die!* Gruffin thought to himself as he felt his body become weaker. Alsander pushed his front paws onto his chest and shoulder, and with a mighty pull, he removed Gruffin's trachea from his body. Blood sprayed over his face and the right side of his neck as Gruffin's body went limp and lifeless, with his soul leaving the mortal plain.

The Black Wolf Clan wolves howled, acknowledging Gruffin's submission and Alsander's victory over their clan, with Jock falling to his knees with tears in his eyes.

"Don't you worry about Gruffin now. He is gone. I would worry about yourself from now on," Forba declared.

As she nodded, two inertia protectors grabbed Jock by his arms, pulling him to the rear of the clans' ranks.

Alsander turned to look at Ren, standing in front of the Grey Wolf Clan with Balgair to his right and Wikki to his left. Alsander turned back into a human, marching down the gentle gradient towards them, having no shame as he walked down the field naked and covered in blood. Smearing the excess blood from his face, he stopped fifty metres away from Ren, noticing someone moving behind Wikki.

Opening his arms wide, Alsander dipped his head and leered at Ren with his sinister smile. "Finally, I meet you face to face, Ren the Unbeaten! I have waited eight years to meet you since that old man from your clan declared you alpha to my clan's previous alpha."

Ren scrunched his face, clenched his fists and shouted, "What do you want from me, White Wolf?"

"Isn't it obvious? Your clan has acknowledged my challenge. Now, I want to see how strong you really are! Come on, I'll be the one to remove your title of being the unbeaten!" Alsander shouted with more excitement.

Ren looked him up and down, sizing him up for a fight, and then he smiled, "Yes, the grey wolves accept your challenge, White Wolf."

"Yes! Now I'll secure my own legend by burying you in your own blood. When I destroy you, I'll then destroy your entire clan! What do you think about that?" Alsander declared.

"We already know of your plans. It's no surprise, pal," Ren replied.

"I don't care if you know or not. I just want this fight! Now, prepare and defend yourself, Grey Wolf Alpha!" Alsander shouted for the last time.

Transforming back into a wolf, his tail wagged back and forth, growling and baring his teeth at Ren.

Folding his arms, he looked directly into Alsander's eyes, as Isolde immerged from behind Wikki standing next to him. "I'm the pathfinder," Ren declared.

Alsander's eyes widened with this new information, thinking, *Who's strong enough to defeat him?*

At the halfway point of the grey wolf army, Tabitha broke rank, removed her battle robe and transformed into a wolf. The grey wolf army shouted and cheered on the first-ever female alpha of any clan.

Alsander looked over to the centre of the grey wolf army, seeing a female wolf standing alone. *What? A female alpha? This is a trick,* he thought to himself.

Standing five hundred metres away from him, they could see each other clearly, as their eyes locked in a deathly stare. At this point, he knew this was no trick or joke; this female was the grey wolves' new alpha.

Alsander snarled and growled at Tabitha, with their battle about to begin. One of these great warriors was about to become the next omega alpha, and the other would be in the Meadow Lands. Tabitha made the first move, charging directly at him at phenomenal speed, so much so she could be the fastest sprinter throughout the entire history of the wolves. Becoming infuriated with the fact that a female thought she could defeat him, Alsander wanted to make her suffer slowly. Responding to her challenge, he charged right back at her. As the two warriors closed ground towards each other at great speed, Tabitha would use this opportunity to test his strength.

As they clashed, she bounced off him, displaying to her that he was at least double her strength, if not more, but she had strengths of her own. Rolling on the ground, she displayed her superior agility by flipping herself straight back onto her feet. Alsander continued his charge, expecting another head-on challenge, but she sidestepped and darted straight past him at such a speed, she almost resembled a blur to him. He slowed down to turn, but as he did so, she was already charging at him, throwing him off guard. With hardly any time to recover, he realised her speed was her strength.

Leaping forward with an open mouth, hoping to feel flesh between his teeth, he watched her come directly at him. However, she turned right, then left and left again at ninety-degree angles, jumping forward at the last turn. This manoeuvre was executed so fast, her own people were amazed by her speed, even though some of the hunters had seen her do this before.

Alsander tried to recover, but being in mid-air from his jump, all he could do was watch her bite into his left flank around the abdominal area. Her upper teeth scraped through his flesh as her lower jaw pierced into his underbelly, forcing him to produce a high-pitched yelp, igniting a greater rage within him. The grey wolf army cheered, with some of them making snide comments about Alsander's poor fighting style.

"She could actually win this," Balgair said.

"Of course she can. She beat me, didn't she?" Ren replied.

Curling his body inwards, Alsander managed to bite down hard into her rear leg. The bite, being so powerful and painful, made her release the grip on his flank. With all of his might, he pulled on her leg, and her body followed. Tabitha found herself being dragged backwards as he rotated his head to cause more damage, but she went with the direction of his head twist, falling to the ground and reducing the injury. After he released her leg to get up quicker, they scrambled to their feet.

She knew if she fought in the way Alsander wanted, he would be too strong, so she made sure that she would lead the fight. Tabitha had to regain the upper hand, so she baited him to follow her. A risky move, but if executed, she could snare him into her trap. Darting forward and sidestepping again, caused him to involuntarily bite down hard into nothing. Slowing down slightly, she saw him take the bait, so she picked up her speed again. She wasn't running at her full pace for two reasons. The first reason was for him to think that he had injured her rear leg badly, and secondly to test his agility.

Alsander could see her rear end, more arched as was every female wolf's anatomy. Her tail wagged slightly, displaying her excitement; now knowing he was being baited infuriated him even more. But even though he knew, he went along with it in the hope she would be cocky and make a fatal mistake. Chasing her across the field, she headed up the gradient towards the White Wolf Clan.

Alsander began breathing heavier from the pain in his side and underbelly, quickly inspecting the source while running, seeing his white fur stained with blood. He looked back up at Tabitha, closing in on her. His muzzle wrinkled with his nose pointing up, exposing his gums and displaying his anger to everyone. Tabitha sped up slightly, turning northbound, ninety degrees to her right. He tried to follow, but when he turned, he saw her pelvic area and tail as she had already turned back to the left, running west. She was proving too agile for him; he barely managed to keep up using the maximum potential of his agility.

Running towards the white wolf army, Tabitha spotted Neil and Bleddyn standing twenty metres apart in front of the clan. She knew Neil was the pathfinder because Bleddyn had given her a description a few days earlier. Black, bowl cut hair sat upon his head, accompanied by a large scar running down his right cheek into his defined goatee. As she got closer with Alsander close on her tail, he grimaced with his remaining black and yellow teeth. "What's this shit?" he mumbled to himself.

Approaching within two metres of Neil, before turning ninety degrees to her right, caused him to become so anxious of her running line, he stumbled backwards. As Alsander turned to follow, he knocked him over.

"What the fuck! How's that bitch doing advanced fighting manoeuvres? Only protectors have advanced fighting knowledge!" Neil shouted, to no one in particular.

Noticing Bleddyn smile at him, he snapped, "Enjoy your moment, traitor, because she can't keep doing this all day. She'll have to fight Alsander head-on at some point, and that bitch will no longer be here for you to sniff around."

Alsander was trying to keep up by following her every move, but she turned right again, running back from where they came. Slowing down with him slightly behind, she started turning left and right repeatedly, at ten to twenty-degree angles. Having trouble predicting her movements, he felt his more muscular body lose balance as he began to do the same.

Tabitha sped up, and with a final jump, she landed, turning ninety degrees to her right. Alsander tried to replicate her but failed, losing his footing and falling over, rolling twice across the ground. Hearing his body strike the ground, she skidded to a halt, spun around and sprinted forward as he got back to his feet. Body-slamming him side on forced Alsander to crash to the ground again; quickly recovering and jumping forward, she bit down hard into his scruff, slamming her two front paws into the side of his neck.

Pushing her paws out as hard as she could while pulling her head backwards, Tabitha's teeth tore the flesh open on Alsander's scruff, and the pain sent him into a 'red' rage. Losing control of his full consciousness, his animalistic instincts kicked in, using his superior strength to get to his feet. As her teeth had already ripped through Alsander's flesh, she had no anchor point to recover her balance as he sidestepped, falling backwards. Twisting his hind legs, he darted downwards, using his front paws to push her body down and pin her to the ground with his strength and weight. As she landed, her back legs scrambled, claws scratching deep into his abdomen, over and over. The skin around a wolf's abdomen was thin and weak, not designed for that type of punishment, but Alsander continued his attack, powering through the pain. Biting into her chest with no excess flesh to grab, he looked for another mark.

His hind legs inched forward as he hitched up her body to get a better vantage point, but her back legs were not giving up the fight. Moving up her body enough so he could try and bite her face, he shot his head down, but she managed to twist her upper body and make him miss. Counteracting, she bit into the side of his muzzle as her hind legs broke the skin, causing his abdomen to bleed. Unable to withstand the pain any longer, he jumped off her, fleeing a few steps away.

Rolling over quickly, Tabitha recovered to her feet, knowing she had to bait him once more. This time, she would go all out with her agility, showing all the clans what she could truly achieve. The Grey Wolf Clan cheered again as Tabitha recovered because, from the angle and distance of where they fought, it looked like Alsander was about to win the fight.

"Llewellyn was right about her, and I was a fool to doubt him," Balgair said.

Isolde, Wikki and Ren looked at him after he made the comment.

"What did he tell you?" Ren asked.

"After her hunting trial, Llewellyn came directly to me and told me of her superior agility and speed. He told me she was the best of us all, and she could become a protector. I laughed in his face, and I swear I thought he was going to kill me that day. I just thought he was blinded by his love for his daughter. I was wrong, and he was right," Balgair replied.

Isolde smiled, looking back at her daughter's fight. "My mate was the wisest person I've ever known, and he had a kind heart. Sometimes, he would stick up for our daughter when she was in the wrong. But you're right, he did see things in people that others couldn't."

Tabitha knew she could not bait him in the same manner again, so she tried a new tactic, unconventional and very dangerous on her part. Transforming back to a human, she mocked, "What's wrong, wet mutt? Are you losing to a girl?"

Still in his 'red' rage, he lunged at Tabitha to finish her, but from a crouched position, she transformed with each step and broke into a sprint.

"What's she doing, the stupid girl?" Ren said, through clenched teeth.

Turning left twice with Alsander behind her with every move. Becoming more dangerous, he adapted to her fighting style. As she would manoeuvre, he would slow down slightly, mirror the manoeuvre and pick up his speed again. His hackles stood up on end with his muzzle permanently wrinkled, baring his teeth and gums. Not even Neil had ever seen him so angry. As she picked up her speed, Alsander continued adapting to her every move. Turning slightly right, he slowed down, turning in the same direction. Then Tabitha turned left, performing a two hundred and twenty-degree turn in the air as her legs tucked close into her body. Her paws hit the ground, sliding back a mere half a metre before bolting off in the opposite direction. He tried overcorrecting his turn, but no male could ever achieve this great feat at that speed. The male wolves' bone density, muscle mass and body shape made it impossible to be as agile as a female. Even so, this move excelled beyond any other female before her time, making Tabitha a prodigy.

"What the fuck was that?" Neil said to himself.

"I knew she had great potential," Isolde beamed.

"Wow, she's surpassed everyone," Wikki exclaimed.

Snapping his jaws to catch any part of her anatomy as he flew through the air, he crashed into the ground, tumbling over three times with two loud thuds, as Tabitha ran down the ranks of the white wolf army.

Neil's face became so red, his veins displayed around his temples and neck, shaking with ultimate rage as he shouted, "Stand and fight, you fucking bitch!"

As Tabitha ran past Neil, she snapped her jaws at him, sounding a high-pitched bark, sending him stumbling back onto his arse again through fear. Bleddyn found this very amusing and he started to chuckle.

Running towards the Black Wolf Clan southward of her position, Alsander got back up, feeling the pain in his body. The fur on the back of his neck and left flank was becoming matted from his own blood, his abdomen so scratched up, it stung from the open air and his white muzzle became pink.

Formulating another plan, she slowed down so Alsander could gain more ground, but not too much this time. *One hundred and fifty metres should do the trick,* she thought to herself.

Some of the Black Wolf Clan warriors cheered as she ran past them, disappearing from Alsander's sight, down the banking to the south. Pivoting one hundred and eighty degrees, she lay at the bottom of the banking, waiting. Using years of hunting experience, she listened to Alsander's heavy footsteps approach the banking. Tabitha's hearing, so fine-tuned, predicted his running line. Shuffling to her left slightly, she listened again, hearing his footsteps getting louder. Moving a bit more to her left, she fabricated the kill zone. Slightly lifting her body off the ground as his paws pounded loud enough to calculate his distance, she set off. Alsander jumped over her, exposing his abdomen as she ran up the banking. Vaulting upwards, her teeth sank deep into his stomach, tearing the delicate flesh of his underbelly. The force was so great she dragged him backwards in mid-air, twisting her head and body at an awkward angle, flipping him underneath her.

Tabitha landed on top of him as he slammed into the dirt. Rolling off him, she recovered to her feet instantly and faced her challenger. Having a full view of Alsander's abdominal injuries, she saw several wounds with his intestines protruding through the holes in his flesh, surrounded by many scratches. Appearing to struggle to his feet, he limped forward as his back legs started to buckle. Even with Tabitha claiming dominance of the fight, he snarled, transitioning into several deep growls with each breath in and out, so she bared her teeth and growled back.

"Don't do it, you stupid girl, he's baiting you. Don't do it," Ren muttered, pacing back and forth.

At this exact point, Tabitha became confident that she had ensured the claim to the omega alpha title, with only one solution to end this once and for all, a head-on fight. Their eyes locked, saliva spitting from their mouths, building with ultimate hate for each other.

"You stupid girl, he's not weakened yet, don't do it," Ren muttered again.

Hearing what he said, Wikki watched Alsander move towards Tabitha, seeing what Ren saw. Wikki ran forward a few steps, shaking from the adrenaline building up in his body, with a heavy heart filled with dread, shouting as loud as he could, "Tabitha! Nooo!"

Chapter Twenty-One

THE FOURTH OMEGA ALPHA RISES

It was evident that Tabitha was a hunter unmatched by anyone, but she was not a true warrior yet. Clearly, her advanced combat training became obvious to everyone present, but her combat experience came next to nothing. Alsander, about to exploit that weakness, set his own trap, drawing her in. Becoming so focused on him, she did not hear Wikki's cry, and lowered her head to finally end this.

Ensuring she could not dodge him, Alsander waited until she got close enough to meet his challenge. As they clashed, he used the strength in his back legs, pushing Tabitha upwards, unable to counter his attack. With both of them balancing on their hind legs, he moved his left leg inwards, pushing out with his front right paw on her chest, forcing her to lose balance. Now he had her right where he wanted, his mouth opened, swiping down in a diagonal motion to his left.

His right canine tooth found its target, sinking into Tabitha's left eye socket. The tooth plunged deep into her eye, popping the eyeball as clear liquid and blood squirted onto his tooth. His left canine tore open her muzzle, and his lower jaw clamped shut, scooping underneath her upper lip. Tabitha fell with Alsander rolling over her, clenching his jaw tight with all his lower teeth under her cheek, ripping her face open.

"Arrgghh! Arrgghh! Arrgghh!"

Over and over, her screams could be heard by all. The pain was so intense the vision in her remaining eye darkened. Rolling back to his feet, enjoying the screams while becoming empowered, Alsander's senses heightened, vision narrowed, and adrenaline surged with excitement. Lowering his head while shuffling forward quickly, he opened his mouth and sank his teeth into her head. His fangs scraped along her skull, clumping the scalp with her left ear in his grip, while wagging his tail high the entire time.

Most of the people's hearts sank with the distressing noise emitting from her. Most wolves didn't fear death, but this was something else, even causing some of the warriors from all clans to look away. Dragging her body ten metres down the hill towards the Grey Wolf Clan, Alsander shook his head violently, tormenting his challenger turned victim. Tabitha's screams became more and more frequent, powering Alsander's blood lust.

Neil ran forward a few metres, shouting in the direction of the Grey Wolf Clan with his arms out to his sides. "Listen to your alpha scream!"

Bleddyn placed his hands atop his head in despair, not for himself, but for the future of the wolf race.

Tugging her another five metres across the field, Alsander shook his head ferociously again, separating Tabitha's scalp and left ear away from her head.

Eyes opening wide, forehead frowning and tears building, Isolde screamed, "Tabitha!"

Running to her side, Ren grabbed her right arm, throwing her to the ground. His mouth downturned, eyes burrowing into Isolde's face as he fumed, "Enough! This is the law of our clans. There's nothing you can do for Tabitha now. This is the reality of a woman fighting in a man's world."

"She's my daughter!" Isolde pleaded.

Ren looked away from her. "That doesn't matter now."

Unable to contain the tears in his eyes, Wikki's hands hit the ground as he collapsed to his knees. "No, not you, Tabi. Not like this."

"Balgair, bring me the two protectors that I've nominated, now! We've lost this fight. Gethin, prepare the clan for a fight with the black wolves," Ren ordered, turning around as he muttered, "Only the Great Wolf can save us now."

Spitting Tabitha's ear out as she continued to scream, Alsander bounced in excitement to his left, searching for his next target on her body.

Two protectors came to Ren's side. "When the final blow is struck, you must run and evacuate the rest of the clan. Don't stop, because the white wolves will probably target our clan first. They know we know their plan."

The two protectors gave the wolves' greeting, watching the fight end.

Alsander found his next mark, seeing Tabitha's neck wide open to attack. Lowering his head again, he shuffled forward to make the killing blow. Lying injured side down, she watched his quick advance with her remaining eye. As he widened his mouth and lunged forward, Tabitha rolled over to her right, using her left leg as a shield. Clamping down into the lower part of her leg, he started to shake his head, raging as she defended herself. Screaming loudly again, she tried to recover to get away from his onslaught. He moved to his left, aligning his body with hers, hopping slightly before pushing his legs into her chest, pinning her to the ground once again. Clenching his jaws even tighter, they both heard a crunch from her leg bone snapping.

Isolde tried to run to Tabitha's aid again, but this time Ren snared her by wrapping his arms around her body.

"Get the fuck off me!" Isolde demanded, thrashing her legs wildly.

Ren did not reply, he just continued to watch the fight while holding her.

Tabitha started kicking her back legs out, and the first two strikes hit nothing but air. Rolling her pelvis towards Alsander, she kicked out a third time, scraping his abdomen. Shaking his head, he tried to remove her leg, as tears rolled down her face. At this point, Tabitha had a feeling of dread, convinced she was about to die.

She placed her rear paws together on her fourth kick, and both paws found their way into Alsander's abdominal wounds. With all the strength left in her body, she pushed her rear legs outwards, tearing the stomach wall open. Alsander's intestines escaped his body, landing on her abdomen. His kidney and a part of his liver dangled from his body by connective tissue. His rear legs buckled from the release of pressure and pain, and then his jaw relaxed with his front legs slipping to both sides off her chest. Lifting his head, his vision fixed on Neil and his clan.

This is it, Tabitha thought.

Even though she was in extreme pain, she stopped whining for a moment, jolting her head upwards and twisting it side on to Alsander's neck. Clenching her jaws as tight as she could, she could feel his body getting heavier.

Witnessing the final blow, Neil shouted, "Nooo!"

Unable to breathe, Alsander's eyes opened wide, with a tear rolling down his face as he had one last thought, *Dad, I've failed. Mam, I'm sorry.* After a few seconds, his pupils dilated as his body went limp, ending the fight.

Tabitha had finally done it, rising to become the fourth omega alpha of all the giant wolves of the west.

As Alsander's lifeless body collapsed, she could feel his entire weight on top of her. With the last of her strength, she moved him over to her left side as far as she could, opening her mouth as his carcass crumpled to the ground with a mild thud.

Transforming back to a human, Tabitha recovered to her feet, nearly falling over in the process. She looked down at her left arm, seeing the skin torn apart. As she inspected her mangled arm, she could see that the muscles, tendons, and fatty tissue bulged from within. Raising her right hand to the left side of her face, the tips of her fingers touched the wound on her cheek, torn open so badly it folded downwards in several places, exposing her back teeth. With further exploration, her hand travelled higher, feeling the destruction to her left eye. All that remained was an excessively large eyelid, drooping down so much it exposed the sensitive, bright pink flesh underneath, along with blood and clear liquid running down her left cheek. With the blood pouring from her face and head, she could not decipher the origin of the blood covering her mangled arm.

Her right hand wandered further around her head, creeping underneath her long hair, matted with blood. The scalp hung off her head, exposing her skull, which felt like soft, damp rubber. Then she noticed one more thing; her left ear was missing. Her right hand went back down to support her left arm, discovering more open wounds.

Hobbling forward, her adrenaline levels depleted. With the pain intensifying once more, she had forgotten what her eye felt like. Releasing her left arm, she had another gentle feel, placing the flat of the fingers over it, sensing its complete obliteration. Staggering forward a few more steps, she stumbled sideways before collapsing to her knees. With her adrenaline reserves totally depleted, the pain became unbearable.

Her speech was impaired, but she still managed to scream out at the top of her voice. "M-m...M-m-m-m...Maaammm!"

In shock at what he had just witnessed; Ren did not realise that he was still restraining Isolde, until she shouted her daughter's name. He released her, and she ran to Tabitha's aid. Screaming her last scream, Tabitha passed out from the pain, falling forward and landing face-first on the ground. Being closer to the Black Wolf Clan than any other, Isolde had further to run than she desired.

Wikki wiped the tears from his eyes, standing back up in disbelief at what they had all witnessed.

The white wolves howled, acknowledging Tabitha's victory, and the grey wolves followed suit.

"Shut up! Shut the fuck up! We don't submit to a bitch, not now, not ever!" Neil shouted to his clan.

Two protectors walked up to him, knowing that Neil was still a dangerous warrior, fearing him just as much as Alsander.

"That's not your decision to make, Neil," Bleddyn stated.

Neil looked over at Tabitha and looked back at his clan, with rage alive in his eyes, bellowing, "Is this what you all want" – he turned back around, staring hard at Tabitha's limp body with his arms shaking – "to be ruled by a bitch? I won't be ruled by a fucking bitch."

Neil transformed, instantly sprinting at Tabitha, as two protectors also followed his lead. Ren and Wikki looked over at the three white wolves running to Tabitha's location. All of a sudden, Bleddyn transformed and gave chase. He knew he could not stop Neil in time, but he could show the other clans his intentions. Catching up to the rear protector, he dived on top of him. With this action, everyone knew what they were doing, but the reaction was not as it should have been. Transforming, Wikki and Ren sprinted hard to Tabitha's aid, but even with their speed, Neil would win the race.

At this point, the men argued amongst themselves about having a female leader. The arguments turned from words to violence, creating chaos and death within the ranks of the Black and White Wolf Clans.

"I'm sorry, Dad. But I must do this for the good of our people," Torry said.

"No, you're not ready," his father replied.

Torry transformed, dashing towards Tabitha as well.

With panic rising, Wikki knew there were two wolves that would definitely reach Tabitha first. *I won't let Tabi die,* Wikki thought to himself. Even though their attempt was likely to prove feeble, Ren and Wikki ran past Isolde at great speed.

With his muzzle wrinkled and an open mouth, Neil's eyes fixed on his kill five metres away as he jumped forward. Leaping hard and fast, Torry clashed with the white wolf. As he sank his teeth into the side of Neil's neck, they both fell over, tumbling on the ground with one going over the other.

Ren being the first to engage was unfortunate for the white wolf protector behind Neil. Manoeuvring underneath the white wolf protector, his teeth sank into the protector's neck. With superior speed and strength, Ren pushed the white wolf upwards, instantly breaking his neck before slamming his body into the dirt.

Wikki turned his attentions towards Neil fighting Torry, but in the corner of his eye, he saw a grey wolf charging towards Tabitha. Spinning, he dashed forward and blocked the path, standing firm and growling at the oncoming grey wolf, protecting his best friend.

Gibbi transformed back into a human and said, "Wikki, join me. Together, we can rid our clan of this bitch, and Ren can be back in charge. That way, everything can go back to normal."

Advancing slowly, Wikki's mouth quivered, displaying his teeth and gums whilst growling.

"Blood is thicker than water, you fucking runt. No wonder our dad's disappointed in you. You're a runt, and that's all you'll ever fucking be," Gibbi spat.

Hearing enough, Wikki bounded forward as his brother transformed. Seeing the clash of brothers, Ren knew there was more to this fight than just Tabitha, so he decided to help Torry, being overpowered and pinned down by Neil.

A group of grey wolf protectors ran to Tabitha's aid, immediately circling her with a defensive formation in all directions.

Isolde ran through the grey wolves surrounding her. She looked down at her daughter's mangled body, screaming out, "By the Great Wolf. Tabitha, no!"

Kneeling down next to her, she tried her hardest to roll Tabitha onto her back. But because she was unconscious and practically dead weight, Isolde's attempts failed no matter how hard she tried.

More help came, consisting of Aelish riding on a protector with another healer and Abaigeal behind them riding on the back of Ieuan.

Fighting strongly against Ren and Torry, three grey wolf protectors turned up, and Neil knew he was outmatched. He transformed back into a human, lowered himself down to the ground, and began laughing. Bleddyn had got the other white wolf protector to submit, forcing him to transform as he stood over him.

The black and white wolves fighting within the ranks could see Tabitha secured and safe from further danger, so the violence dissolved and order naturally restored amongst them.

No one interfered with one of the fights, knowing this battle of honour could only be resolved between them, as they were almost upon each other, drawing an audience. As they clashed, Wikki shoulder-barged his brother backwards, displaying dominance of strength as Gibbi crashed to the ground. Wikki did not let up, biting down hard into his rear leg, jumping forward and spinning him around, tearing the flesh open as he was dragged over. Before he fully rolled to his side, Wikki struck again, biting into his muzzle. Pulling back hard and fast, he created multiple lacerations as Gibbi yelped from the pain. Wikki jumped over him, turned quickly and lowered his head with an open mouth, rushing at his scruff. Biting down hard and lifting him up, Wikki turned his head, slamming his brother back into the ground with a loud thud.

With Wikki stood over him, Gibbi turned back into a human, screaming, "I submit! I submit!"

Looking around, Wikki found himself surrounded by a few grey wolf protectors staring at him, including their father mounted on one of them. Gibbi was a fool to think of his brother as the runt of the litter because, over the years, Wikki had become a strong and seasoned fighter. Growing up and being the disappointment of the pack his entire life, Wikki was always overshadowed, with Gibbi being the untouchable 'blue-eyed boy'. Now he had proven his strength, Wikki thought his father would finally be proud of him, but that was not the case. After Gethin dismounted, all Wikki could see was the pain in his father's eyes as he looked at them both. With a down-turned mouth and frowning, Gethin lowered his head and turned away, barging through the protectors while leaving Wikki with the decision of Gibbi's life or death.

Gibbi lay on the ground, looking up at Wikki; blood ran from his nose onto his cheeks and lower eyelids, and his leg was cut and bleeding badly. Wikki snarled and bared his teeth at him and, for the first time in his life, Gibbi was petrified of his little brother. When Wikki moved closer to his brother's face while opening his mouth slightly, Gibbi turned his head away, closing his eyes in fear of his brother's ability to take his life. With one bark, he snapped his jaws shut right next to his face, and a whimper slipped out of Gibbi's mouth as he squirmed.

As Wikki backed off, two inertia protectors ran over, placing Gibbi in manacles. As he turned back into a human, another inertia protector handed him a battle robe, and as one warrior to another, the protector nodded at him.

Four inertia protectors at Ren's location shackled Neil. As they placed the manacles on him, Ren turned to Torry, nodding his head out of respect for what he had done. Torry burst with pride from being revered by the reputable grey wolf.

Aelish and the other healer arrived at Tabitha's side, along with two female healers from the Black Wolf Clan. "We're here to aid you," a black wolf healer said.

"Come, we must move quickly if she's to survive. Help me turn her over," Aelish ordered.

Grateful for the extra help, they all got down on their knees next to Tabitha.

Aelish picked up Isolde, still at her side by her shoulders, and said, "I'm sorry, but you must let me heal her."

Isolde stood up and paced backwards, eyes fixed on her daughter. As the healers log-rolled Tabitha over, the devastation of her wounds could be seen clearly. So shocked at what she saw, Isolde's right hand covered her mouth as she fell to her knees with tears streaming down her face.

"Quickly, use this on her," a black wolf healer said.

Pulling out a pouch of fire salts, she poured the explosive powder on the wounds to her arm. "I'm glad she's unconscious for this. Everyone, stay back," the black wolf healer suggested. Removing flint and a small piece of jagged steel from her pocket, the healer struck the flint near the fire salts on her arm, creating a flash of fire. Letting it burn for a few seconds, she dabbed a damp cloth over the burning salts.

"This'll slow the bleeding for now, but we must get her to a healers' hut because this is only temporary," the black wolf healer stated.

"Red Thorn is not too far from here, we can go there," Abaigeal suggested, as she came to the scene catching the end of the conversation.

Ieuan transformed and ordered, "Protectors, bring me a stretcher now!"

Aelish dressed the wounds on Tabitha's head, arm and leg quickly, stopping any more foreign bodies entering the wounds. The protectors came with a stretcher and everyone helped lift Tabitha onto it as Wikki advanced through the wall of protectors, seeing her bandaged up. Unable to see the severity of her wounds, he still knew it to be bad. "I'll carry her, strap the stretcher onto my back," he offered.

As they strapped Tabitha to the stretcher, Wikki removed his robe, transformed and lowered himself as they fastened the stretcher onto him.

"Let's go now! We've no time to lose," Aelish demanded.

With Red Thorn thirty miles away from Borders Cross, time moved against them as blood seeped through the bandages on her face and body. Wikki began to run as fast as he could, being careful at the same time to ensure Tabitha would not fall. He was followed by the healers, protectors and Ren, and they gave meaning to the word haste because, at this critical stage, Tabitha's life was in the balance.

Chapter Twenty-Two

A NEW TITLE OF HONOUR

After travelling at speed, the group had arrived at Red Thorn, and the healers had already started their work on Tabitha. Outside the healers' hut, Isolde stood still, intensely staring at the door as Wikki paced back and forth.

"It must be done. Either hold her down or leave. I won't have you gawping at her," Aelish commanded.

Ren started shaking and became pale. After seeing the healers at work, he became in so much awe of them, it was beyond words, showing a form of strength far beyond his. "Where do you want me to hold her?" he asked.

"Hold her head and keep it still. We've finished with her arm for now, but we must remove the dead eye," Aelish ordered.

He held her head in position with a firm grip, though the blood made it difficult to secure it, along with the remainder of her scalp moving around.

"Ren, her head doesn't move, do you understand?" Aelish urged.

Nodding, he gripped her head as best he could with the aid of another healer. Picking up metal plyers and a small, sharp knife, Aelish lifted Tabitha's upper eyelid. She placed open pliers into her eye socket, closed them, and pulled what was left of her eyeball out. Ren looked away as Aelish used the small knife to remove the destroyed eyeball, by cutting the optic nerve.

As Tabitha regained consciousness, her arms and legs began twitching and flailed around, so four healers held them down. Aelish placed her instruments down on a table next to the bed. Looking around at everyone, she gave another order, "Keep holding her still."

Aelish picked up a small curved needle with thread attached to it, with her hands already covered in blood from suturing her arm back together. "I'll stitch the eye together, so help Ren hold her down. She will not like this one bit," she informed everyone.

Pinching her upper eyelid towards her, she looked around, nodding at everyone to brace themselves. She pushed the needle through the skin, just above the eyelashes, as Tabitha's body went rigid and shook violently.

"Hold her!" Aelish shouted.

Ren tightened his grip, with the healers also holding her down, as Aelish continued suturing.

"Maagghh. Aarrgghh!" Tabitha stirred.

Becoming fully conscious with the second suture, Tabitha screamed long and hard with every stitch Aelish forced into her eye. Hearing the screams outside, Wikki and Isolde felt powerless and anxious over what was happening with her, feeling pain with every scream emitting from the hut.

The screams sounded on and off for the next four hours, but the most nerve-racking part was the deafening silence, lasting for five minutes. The door of the hut opened as Ren emerged first, his complexion pale, and with tired eyes, followed by the rest of the healers.

The last to exit, Aelish approached Isolde. "I've done all I can. I've not dressed her wounds yet because I need to monitor them for infection. The fire salts should have helped with that."

"Can-can I see her?" Isolde asked as a tear rolled down her cheek

Aelish turned next to her, rubbing her hand between Isolde's shoulder blades and replied, "Yes, come on in."

Entering the hut, Aelish turned around and held her hand against Wikki's chest. "Not you. I'm sorry, but only her mam can enter, she'll need her rest. Feel free to guard the hut, but you're not to enter. Is that understood?"

Feeling anger build up inside, he watched Isolde entering the hut. Exhaling deeply, he replied, "I understand. I'll guard this hut with my life."

"You can see her soon enough, but this is not the best time. Thank you for being so understanding. You sure have grown up to be a fine man," Aelish stated, re-entering the hut and closing the door.

As Wikki stood guard by the door, he saw Ren leaving. "Where are you going?"

"I'm going to get those white wolf bastards and that wet mutt brother of yours. Until Tabitha gets well enough, they'll go in the hole. She can pass judgement on them for what they did," he replied.

Ren walked off, and Wikki, true to his word, didn't leave the door of the hut for a solid day.

Two months later, Tabitha was still recovering from her wounds, her face covered in bandages that were changed daily. Sat in the alpha's chair within the pavilion alongside Ren and Abaigeal, the town's people inquired about their daily problems. Abaigeal deflected the questions away from her, answering them all individually. She had changed since her fight, and everyone close to her could tell. Tabitha was no longer the fun, strong woman they remembered, just an empty shadow of herself.

Tabitha stood up and turned to Ren. "Gather Abaigeal's party together. It's time we bring the other clan leaders here. If any other people from the clans wish to come here as well, tell them they can come. It's time to sentence the traitors and punish them."

"As you wish, Omega Alpha. I'll sort it," Ren replied.

After Ren left, Abaigeal ushered the crowd away with their petty problems so she could talk to Tabitha in private. "Are you ok? That was a strange request."

"You have your task, I need to see Neil and find out why," Tabitha said.

"Why what?"

Without replying, Tabitha stood up and wandered off into her hut. Since the battle against Alsander, she spent most of her time closed away from the world, and when she did venture outside, it would be for very short periods of time. During the nights, the people living close or passing her hut could hear her screaming, sometimes into the early hours of the morning. Only the healers and Abaigeal understood why, but they all knew it was not a good sign.

The next day, Abaigeal prepared for her journey to each of the clans, but first, she had a personal task of her own, which was much more important in her eyes. Knocking on Isolde's hut door, she awaited a reply and after a few seconds, it opened.

"Oh, hello, Abaigeal. Ain't you supposed to be travelling?"

"Yes, I am leaving very soon, but before I go, I must talk with you," Abaigeal replied.

"You had best come in then."

Isolde opened the door further as Abaigeal entered.

"What did you want to talk to me about?" Isolde inquired.

"It's about Tabitha. She's not recovering well, and I'm concerned about her. I think she's suffering from battle stress."

"I knew something was wrong. She's been through so much over the years. First, she lost her dad, and now this."

"Yes, I know, and we must be there for her now more than ever. I don't want to lose her," Abaigeal said.

"But what can I do? I know I'm her mam, but she's become distant, and I don't even recognise my own daughter anymore. You know she was so full of life and confidence, but now it's all been taken away by that evil bastard she fought," Isolde snapped, as she started to well up.

"It's ok, she will come back to us. But I had a word with Aelish last night. We must be there for her because this is the point at which we could lose her," Abaigeal explained.

"What do you mean by lose her? Could she be like this forever?" Isolde asked.

"As you know, Aelish is a great healer, but she is as blunt as they come. In short, she could permanently be like this. But she also explained that people that suffer from battle stress have also taken their own lives."

"No, Tabitha would never-"

Abaigeal held her hands. "Isolde, please, I wouldn't say this if I did not think she would do it. She's had a traumatic experience, and battle stress can make people do things they normally wouldn't even dream of. She shuts herself away, and I have seen her being treated differently by the men of this town. She's lost, but we must help her find her way again. One thing is for certain, though. She will never be the same person we once knew. She has changed, and we must guide her."

Isolde burst into tears while hugging Abaigeal, mumbling, "I don't know how to help her. I'm just as lost as she is."

"That's why we must work together to help her through this," Abaigeal said.

"But you're leaving, so I'll be alone to do this."

Abaigeal pulled back and looked Isolde squarely in the eyes. "Listen to me now. We are not alone. We have Aelish, Ren, Arwyn and Wikki. Together, we can help her and keep an eye on her, making sure she doesn't do anything stupid. I must go now, but you must speak with the others in my absence. I am giving the clans four weeks to gather here, and then we can see what Tabitha is planning. Don't forget, we can do this together." Nodding as she stepped back. Isolde opened the door, wiping tears from her face, as Abaigeal continued, "I'll probably be coming back here with the White Wolf Clan members. Tabitha will probably make the new pathfinders of the other clans and then sentence the traitors. She did say something strange yesterday about that white wolf Neil. I don't know what she's planning, but we will soon find out."

Rubbing Isolde's arm, she left the hut and began her new task at hand. During her absence, the others kept a close eye on Tabitha.

After a month, the Black Wolf Clan members arrived first at the Town of Niamh. So as not to show intimidation, they limited their numbers to three hundred, consisting of people from all walks of life. They were greeted and welcomed to the Town of Niamh with open arms. Ren led the greeting party, looking for one black wolf in particular as he scanned the ranks, and soon he saw him. Hair as black as coal curled around his face, ending below his chin in a perfect parting, his big brown eyes with scars running down his nose made him recognisable from the wounds he received.

"Hey, pal. You're the black wolf that saved Tabitha, right?" Ren asked.

A man walked forward, puffed out his chest and smiled, "Yes, he is."

"And you are?" Ren questioned.

"I'm this boy's dad, my name's Osheen Blackpaw. You're the warrior Ren, ain't you?"

"Yes, I'm Ren Greyfang. You must be proud of your son for standing up to a powerful wolf that day."

Osheen grabbed his son's shoulder, shook him slightly, and slapped him on his back several times. "Haha, my boy's a true warrior. People all over our clan know of his bravery at Borders Cross. I'm very proud of him."

"Dad, please. I just done what's right," Torry blushed.

"Are you here with a mate?" Ren asked.

"No, his mam's at home, tending the crops," Osheen replied.

"That's fine. I respect powerful and brave warriors, so you two can stay at my hut as honoured guests if you want."

Before Osheen could answer, Torry butted in with his excitement. "What? Really? We'd be honoured to stay with you. You're like one of the greatest wolves of the West Plains."

Ren smiled, nodding at his new young friend. "Then come, we'll dine at my hut. You must be hungry. I've a cook preparing our food right now."

Without hesitation, the two black wolves followed Ren, honoured by the personal invite.

A few hours later, Abaigeal and her party turned up with two hundred members of the White Wolf Clan. They were welcomed, but not as warm or openly as their black wolf kin. All the people from each clan waited for their omega alpha to arrive at the alpha's pavilion. Ren, Abaigeal and Gethin were sat in their respective seats, the alpha's hut door opened, and Tabitha emerged. Everyone went silent as she walked to the pavilion.

Tabitha sat down, scanning the crowd to see three clans together. She had ordered her clan not to bring their children, but some people from the other clans had brought theirs. She did not feel this was the time or place for the young, but nothing could be done about it now, so she pressed on with the matters at hand. Her left arm was still bandaged up, but even with the coverings, it did not hide the deformation, and the entire left side of her head was also covered in bandages.

Abaigeal stood up, addressing everyone present as best she could. Fortunately, there were message relays amongst the public so everything could be heard. "Hello and welcome to the Town of Niamh. On behalf of the omega alpha, I welcome you all here. There are several matters that we will be sorting out today, so if you have any questions or queries, please keep them all until the end. Thank you."

As she sat back down, Tabitha stood up, taking a few deep breaths before speaking. "Forba Black-Nose of the Black Wolf Clan, please come forward."

From the front of the crowd, Forba advanced a few steps to be recognised. She gave Tabitha the wolves' greeting, before taking to one knee while bowing her head. As she stood up, she replied, "You have summoned me, Omega Alpha?"

"Yes, you're a good peacekeeper from what I've heard from Abaigeal. I don't know anyone from your clan, so I ask for your judgement," Tabitha said.

"Yes, of course, Omega Alpha. I will do everything in my power to assist you," Forba declared.

"Well, you know your people best, and I need a trustworthy pathfinder. Would you be able to nominate one for me?"

"Yes, there is one black wolf worthy of being your right hand for our clan. Of course, if you think differently, then it is your right to refuse, or you can change the pathfinder at a later date. Geraint Black-Mane, come forward and present yourself!"

Geraint walked through the crowd, taking to one knee while giving the wolves' greeting. His appearance didn't scream leader, scruffy blonde hair and a long scraggly beard took emphasis from the dark circles around his green eyes.

"I present to you Geraint Black-Mane. He is a very strong warrior, and our people have admiration and respect for him. He is honourable, patient, kind, and he would serve you well if given the chance. But the decision will fall onto you, Omega Alpha."

Glancing at Geraint and then back to Forba, Tabitha grinned, "Well, if this is who you want to choose to be your leader, then I'll trust your judgement. Geraint Black-Mane, you are my black wolf pathfinder."

The people of the Black Wolf Clan cheered for their new leader as Geraint stood up and bowed. "Thank you for choosing me, Omega Alpha. I'll dedicate my life to serve you to the best of my abilities."

As Tabitha nodded in approval, Geraint retired back into the crowd as people from the Black Wolf Clan slapped his shoulder and shook his hand, congratulating him.

"Bleddyn White-Tail of the White Wolf Clan, please come forward," Tabitha commanded.

Bleddyn walked from the midpoint of the crowd, taking longer to present himself, giving the wolves' greeting and taking to one knee, holding a sword. "Yes, Omega Alpha, how can I be of service?"

"When I met you when you first came to this town, you were unsure of yourself. You took a great risk, and I suppose because of your actions, you'll have enemies within your own clan. You'll retain your rank of peacekeeper. But in light of recent events and past atrocities to the wolf race, I, Tabitha Greyclaw, your omega alpha, hereby strip all other members of the White Wolf Clan of rank. Your protectors and your hunters are hereby disbanded from this day. Your clan will be able to reclaim their ranks after they've proven themselves worthy, regaining the honour their ranks obtain," Tabitha commanded.

"What? That's a load of shit, you can't do that!" a stranger from the crowd shouted.

"Well, I think you'll find I can! I'm the omega alpha, and my word is law! Or do you challenge me?" Tabitha waited ten seconds for a reply, but the entire crowd remained silent. "This is not a personal attack on your clan because of my fight with your late alpha. This is because your clan failed to protect the innocent. Your clan's responsible for the destruction of the Blue Wolf Clan, and in recent events, your clan destroyed two black wolf villages, killing their people, including the children and babies. Be thankful that I'm not executing each and every one of you!"

Bleddyn bowed again. "Thank you for giving us the justice we deserve. We'll try our best to redeem ourselves and our clan's reputation."

Some of the white wolves were not happy, even thinking they had been victimised. But even so, most of them understood and agreed with Tabitha's decision.

Bleddyn looked up and held out a sword with both hands. "Omega Alpha, before you continue, I would like to present you with this sword."

"Why a sword?" Tabitha asked.

"This is the sword of the omega alphas. Only the omega alphas before you wielded this sword. Until another omega alpha rises, this is now your sword, and it'll remain here with the Grey Wolf Clan," Bleddyn explained.

Descending the steps, she took the sword from Bleddyn. With one strap made from the rare shrompy weed connected to the newly made scabbard, she unsheathed the twenty-five-inch sword, revealing the blade almost looking freshly forged. But this sword was forged during the first omega alpha's reign, 1,500 years ago, showing it had been well cared for after all this time.

The pommel of the handle, rectangular in shape, bore the letters OA engraved in the silver. The handle, wrapped in fresh brown leather, sat underneath the eight-inch guard. Starting with a width of three inches, the blade stretched out an inch and a half before returning on itself by an inch like an arrowhead, widening the blade to five inches. The two points narrowed back to the width of three inches, continuing to the halfway point. The rest of the blade spanned out to five inches at the widest point, narrowing to the tip, finishing the blade in an oval shape. A fuller ran up the centre of the blade, stopping two inches from the point to form the central ridge to the tip. Sheathing the sword, Tabitha bowed to Bleddyn before returning to the pavilion and commanded, "Now bring forward the prisoners!"

From a hut near the pavilion, the door opened as two grey wolf protectors emerged, followed by Gibbi, a white wolf protector, and Neil, confined in manacles. The prisoners looked rough as they had been in the hole for three months. As they exited, another five protectors followed them out, leading the three prisoners to the front of the crowd by the pavilion. Ren stood up, walked down the pavilion steps and called them forward one at a time, while Tabitha began placing her new sword on her left leg.

"Gibbi Greyleg, step forward," Ren demanded.

Gibbi limped forward, presented by two grey wolf protectors on each side of him.

"Gibbi, you broke the sacred law and tried to take the omega alpha's life. How do you plead?" Ren said.

"Guilty, Pathfinder," Gibbi declared.

Tabitha finished placing her sword on her leg and looked over to the right of the pavilion, nodding at Wikki. Turning back, she gave his sentence. "Gibbi, you've dishonoured your pack name and you were stopped by your own brother. Wikki spared your life through love for you, and through my love for him, I'll do the same. You're banished to the Eastern Wastes. If you return during your lifetime, you'll be put to death instantly, by any protector that you encounter."

As he cried, Gibbi was immediately taken away by two protectors, escorting him to the border leading to the Neutral Land. Watching his son leave the West Plains forever, Gethin shed a tear, knowing he would never see his son again.

"Neil White-Pelt of the white wolves, step forward," Ren ordered.

Because he didn't respond, two grey wolf protectors pushed him forward, causing him to fall over. As Neil got back to his feet, he had a smirk on his face.

"Neil, you led the attack on your omega alpha and broke the sacred law. How do you plead?" Ren asked.

"Go fuck yourself. That bitch will never be my omega alpha. Alsander is my leader," Neil spat.

Descending the pavilion steps, Tabitha engaged with Neil as she walked towards him. "What? The leader I killed?"

"That was luck. You've got no real strength, woman," he replied.

Ignoring the insult, she got straight to the point to get the answers she wanted. "You were a pathfinder. It's your duty to see that your alpha stays on the right path, not to enable his evil plan. That's what a pathfinder is supposed to do, so why didn't you do your duty?"

As he started to laugh, he glanced back to his clan, and then back to Tabitha, puffing out his chest as he cheered, "You stupid fucking bitch. You'll never understand because you're a woman...well, what's left of a woman. You might've killed Alsander, but he's destroyed you. You're weak, and now you're ugly as fuck, you freak. I hope you end up killing yourself, you deformed bitch. Because no one will want you as a mate now."

As she turned away, wiping a tear from her eye, her jaw clenched and her face turned red. Her lips peeled back, exposing her teeth as her body shook with rage. Unsheathing her sword with her right hand, she spun around, striking Neil's upper left arm. As he fell to the ground with an open wound, his smile turned to a grimace of pain.

Raising the sword as high as she could, Tabitha drove it down with all her strength into the side of Neil's head. The blade landed at the wrong angle when striking, creating a hollow sound mimicking an axe hitting a dead tree. Over and over, she kept hitting him, grunting in a high-pitch with every strike as he felt every blow. His skin opened wide as the cold hard steel chipped away at his skull. On the seventh hit, she landed a perfect stroke directing the sword halfway through his head, finally killing him. As she pulled the sword backwards at a slight angle, the blade wedged itself within Neil's skull, tugging his head over slightly. Grunting as she yanked again, the sword remained imbedded, so she leaned backwards to gain leverage from her bodyweight. With a third and final pull, the sword flung out of his head, causing her to stumble over onto her side. Rolling over, she got to her feet, looking at the crowd. Breathing heavily, her jaw clenched tight again with a red face.

Wikki, Arwyn and Isolde were in tears from Tabitha's uncharacteristic reaction, breaking their hearts. Never had they seen her in a rage like this before, and it looked like it wasn't over. Raising her right arm up, pointing the sword at the last prisoner. "Fucking step forward, traitor!"

"Dad, no!" a child from the crowd shouted.

The white wolf protector turned around, looked at his ten-year-old son with a smile and said, "It's ok, son, this is how it must be. She's the omega alpha, and I've dishonoured our pack name. Look after your mam now because you're the man of the pack."

The protector turned, walked forward, afraid but accepting of his fate. "Omega Alpha, please make it clean, so my son doesn't suffer," he pleaded.

Lining up the sword to the side of his neck, she pulled her hand back, ready to strike. Then she looked over at the child, crying into his mother's belly. As their eyes met, his mate diverted her gaze, mouth downturned and tears streaming down her face.

Closing her eye slowly, Tabitha lowered her sword with tears rolling down her face, dropping it to the ground. Wiping her cheek, she turned red-faced to the prisoner again. "You're stripped of all rank forever, and you'll spend two years in the hole for your crimes! Take him away."

Two grey wolf protectors removed him instantly, as Tabitha stared at the young boy with her bloodshot eye. Her gaze broke, looking at her feet for a second before turning around to take her place back at the pavilion. As Tabitha pulled herself together, Ren picked up her sword, and he ordered four hunters to dispose of Neil's body.

Giving Tabitha ten minutes for her to compose herself, Abaigeal and her mother stood by her side.

"Are you ok to continue? We can arrange this for another time if you want," Isolde asked.

"I'm ok. I need to continue for the greater good of our people. I'm their leader now, so I have my duties," Tabitha replied.

The people anxiously looked at the pavilion, wondering what else Tabitha had to announce. Rubbing her eye, she turned around to her people. "I'm sorry you all had to witness that, but we must continue with other matters. I'm going to tell you about my first law."

Eagerly, the crowd looked on and waited as she took a long, deep breath, telling her people what they must abide by forever. "This is my law, by the powers granted to me from the title I've earned. I'll start with the simplest part, making a new honorary title to enforce my law. The lunar warriors."

Chapter Twenty-Three

TABITHA'S LAW AND THE CHOICE OF PATHS

As the people talked amongst themselves about what Tabitha had declared, Ren became impatient and shouted, "Silence!"

The people became quiet, so Tabitha continued. "My lunar warriors will be the future, being the first elite, female-only fighting force that will have the same powers and respect as the protectors. But they'll have one more purpose, upholding my law. For too long, our people have suffered horrible atrocities from power-hungry men."

She explained her law to everyone present, and instructed them to spread the word after they returned home. From this point in time, no child under the age of sixteen would be harmed in any way, ensuring the survival of any clan from future conflict. Further protection would also be given to pregnant women and mothers caring for children under the age of sixteen, but they were not to attack anyone, only defend. If a woman broke this rule and tried to abuse the powers of this law, then her rights would be immediately forfeit.

Governing this new law, the lunar warriors could use any force necessary to stop the offenders. No rank would be exempt from this law, granting the lunar warriors power to kill any ranking wolf, including any future omega alphas. If any parents abused their children, they would immediately be imprisoned for one year, followed by rehabilitation. But if rehabilitation failed, they would be banished or put to death. Finally, as there would be a protective father under an omega alpha's reign, Tabitha thought it befitting that a lunar mother would be voted into position by the lunar warriors in time.

She had been thinking long and hard about this law since Bleddyn told her the known story of Alsander's life, with this being the only solution she could think of, preventing the destruction of any more clans and to protect children from the experiences Alsander had had to endure.

"So I hope you now all understand my law," Tabitha said.

A woman pushed through the white wolf ranks. Her hair like a waterfall of snow trailing down her back, grey eyes looked up to Tabitha as she stood firm. "I'll uphold your law, Omega Alpha."

"What's your name, White Wolf?" Tabitha asked.

"Rhianna White-Muzzle," she replied, giving the wolves' greeting, and bending the knee.

"I've stripped your clan of all ranks, with the exception of your peacekeeper until you redeem yourselves." Rhianna looked down to the ground, ready to be rejected as she continued, "but you're the first of your clan to prove yourself worthy, so I'll make you my first lunar warrior."

For the first time since the gathering, the White Wolf Clan had something to cheer about, and cheer they did. After Rhianna's volunteering for the position, many more women from all the clans started to come forward.

"Please, please stop. I love your enthusiasm for the new title of honour, but just like the protectors, there'll be lunar warrior trials. Because this is all new, the lead protector from each clan will have temporary control of who enters the trial until the lunar warriors can choose for themselves," Tabitha explained.

As she finished her sentence, a protector barged past some of the people. "Omega Alpha! I'm so sorry to interrupt, but you have visitors."

"Who thinks they can interrupt the omega alpha?" Ren thundered.

"The cats, Pathfinder," the protector replied.

Ren frowned, processing the information he just heard.

"What do you mean, cats?" Tabitha asked.

"Cats from the Southern Kingdoms, Omega Alpha. I think they might be important cats, but I don't know. And I think they're here on peaceful terms," the protector answered.

Having only heard stories of the cat races from her father, excitement and anxiety rose within her.

"Turn them away and tell them to come back another time," Ren ordered.

"No, wait! I want to meet these people," Tabitha said.

The protector bowed, running off to collect them. After five minutes of waiting, the grey wolf protector came back with nine cats from the Southern Kingdoms. As the crowd parted,

Tabitha's eyes widened, surprised by their appearance. When the cats were fifteen metres from the pavilion, Ren and the protectors stopped them.

Inspecting them in their fine attire, never having seen anything like it before, every cat had black hair on their heads and Tabitha was fascinated by their skin colours, which differed from each other, being brown, black and a golden-brown. Apart from the odd nomad travelling around Calinthia, the cats had never set foot in the West Plains since the battle of Niamh Plain, during the war of the Silver Kingdom hundreds of years ago.

Tabitha's mouth went dry as she spoke to them. "Welcome to Niamh Plain. Who're you?"

A man from the small group presented himself. His brown complexion matched his brown eyes, and he was clean-shaven with a perfect hairstyle. His fancy armour made of steel, silver and bronze sported an orange cape attached to the shoulder plates. However, this armour looked too big for him. He had bare feet, displaying he was therianthrope. Two of the others had fully fitted armour, proving they were the only inertias within the group.

"Hello there, thine lady. I am the grand general of the Golden Kingdom. It is a pleasure to make thy acquaintance. May I presume thou art the omega alpha?" he asked.

"Yeah, that's right. Why do you ask?" Tabitha frowned.

The man clicked his heels together, gave the cats' greeting and bowed his head slightly. "Very good. I ask because thou art the one we haft been seeking. It wouldst be thine pleasure to introduce thineself, alongside the group I haft been travelling with further?"

Turning her head slightly, she replied, "Umm yeah, ok, I don't see a problem with that."

"I am very much obliged. I shalt start with thineself as not to confuse anyone here, with the greatest of respect. I am Kushad, a member of the Bastet pride. Thine pride name hath been revered as one of the high-born prides of the Golde-"

Hearing enough, Ren interrupted. "Come on, pal. We haven't got all day. Our omega alpha was in the middle of addressing her people before you lot butted in."

Kushad looked squarely at Ren, with one raised eyebrow and replied, "If that is thy wish, Western Wolf. I wouldst like to add, it is very rude to interrupt a guest, as it is not good etiquette."

A woman from their group stepped forward, her face covered with scars, and scowled at Ren. Her armour, scratched and dented unlike her companions', proved she was battle-hardened. Her short black hair, slicked over to one side, exposed her undercut. Cold, fearless light brown eyes bored into each and every wolf in front of her.

"This is a piss take. Did you expect anything else from these wet mutts, Grand General? Their race is primitive, and so are their attitudes. The smell here is offending my sinuses," the female cat spat.

Eyes widening, Ren puffed his chest out as he sneered, "Who're you calling primitive?"

The female cat looked at him with a grin. "Your species. You still bark and snarl in your animal form. And look at you, when was the last time you had a wash, filth?"

Dropping his brow and clenching his fists, he approached the female cat. "The way I see it, you're in our country. So you should show more respect, you milk drinker."

Tilting her head forward, her eyebrows fell, lips tightened and her jaw clenched. With tightened fists, she transformed into a lioness. The armour that was too big now fitted her perfectly, as golden blonde fur covered her entire body. Unlike the wolves, when the cats transformed they kept their bipedal form; their hands, a cross between human hands and cat paws, aided them to wield weapons if they wished it. With every breath, she growled in a very deep, bass stricken tone. Also transforming, Ren displayed his teeth and snarled back at the lioness stood before him.

"I can defeat you barehanded!" the lioness boasted.

"That is quite enough, Field-Marshal Mau," a young man said, walking between them both.

"I agree. Ren, stand down," Tabitha ordered.

The lioness smiled at Ren, transforming back into a human, before declaring, "Maybe this was a waste of time. There are no warriors here."

"Pihu, I am forbidding thee to make any more outbursts. We art here as allies, not enemies. Come back, immediately," another female cat commanded.

As if this other woman had some magical power over the lioness, Pihu did not even hesitate slightly to this woman's order, immediately turning around and walking back to the group.

"Ren, it's over. I command you to stand down," Tabitha instructed again.

Without transforming, he slowly walked back to the pavilion as requested, keeping eye contact with Pihu.

The young man that had intervened turned around, gave the cats' greeting and bowed. "Greetings, Omega Alpha. We apologise for the actions of our kin. One's name is Ankur Sekhmet, the prince of the Golden Kingdom. Mayst we continue with the introductions?" Tabitha nodded to his request. "Splendid. The first of our group to address thee is Kushad Bastet, one's grand general. Next to him is our aura, Galal Annipi. We believe thou call his trade 'healer' in these lands. The two ladies at the rear of the group, art the two field-marshals of the Tri-Kingdom Guardians, dubbed throughout our kingdoms as the Black Veil Sisters, Pihu Mau along with Issar Thoth. This lady to one's left is the princess of the Silver Kingdom, Mudiwa Hasina, alongside her regal general, Raoul Dalila. To conclude the introductions, there is the prince of the Bronze Kingdom, Rami Menhit, alongside his high general, Saba Kepi. We apologise for our bluntness with the short introductions, as we art not here for good reasons. We haft cometh to ask for thy aid, Omega Alpha, if thou wouldst be kind enough to grant it."

Tabitha frowned. "Do you mean our help?"

"Indeed, our lands haft been invaded by stygians."

"I've heard you're good warriors. Why don't you fight them?" Tabitha asked.

"This time, they art organised, fighting in large numbers. War is afoot, so we must prepare together, or all is truly lost. Wouldst thou not gather thy armies to fight alongside us, against our plight?" Ankur pleaded.

Abaigeal stood up, interrupting the conversation, "Cats of the south, please understand, our omega alpha has recently had a large and traumatising battle. We must have time to talk about this. Isolde, Wikki, Bleddyn, Forba, Geraint, Aelish and Ren, follow me and the omega alpha. Everyone else, please wait here. T hank you."

"We can talk in my hut," Tabitha replied.

Ren changed back into a human, donning a battle robe, and all the people that were summoned followed Tabitha into her hut for a discussion on what they should do.

As they entered and the door closed, Isolde was the first to speak. "I don't think we should fight their war. We've got our own problems here."

Bleddyn folded his arms. "I agree. We're in no place for a war. My clan has been stripped of their ranks, and if the omega alpha gives the ranks straight back, then what will that accomplish?"

"We need to help you, and going to war right now is not going to help," Wikki said.

"Tabitha, you will struggle to lead our people in your condition," Aelish declared.

"The Black Wolf Clan will have to rebuild its ranks, thanks to the devastation Gruffin has caused us," Forba confided.

Unable to keep up with their conversation, Tabitha felt disorientated and confused by everyone talking at the same time about the issues Alsander had caused.

"Enough. I think everyone should leave. I'll talk to Tabitha alone," Ren suggested.

"She's my daughter, and I'll stay here, you wet mutt," Isolde spat.

"Mam, please. Everyone, just stop," Tabitha ordered, taking in a deep breath. "I'll speak with Ren, but I want Wikki here with me."

Pacing forward, Isolde raised her eyebrows as she pleaded, "But, Tabitha, I'm your mam."

"Mam, I know you want what's best for me, but what's best for me isn't what's best for our people. I'd appreciate it if everyone else left. I'll not make a decision right now, but I'll listen to what Ren has to say with Wikki."

Isolde lowered her head and left the hut with the others, following Tabitha's request. As the door closed, Ren folded his arms, leaning against the wall while looking around his old home.

"I see you haven't changed much in here yet." Tabitha frowned slightly as Ren continued, "I know you've got battle stress, and I know you can't transform, which brings us a big issue. You can't lead the army if you can't change. I know it's a grey area, but have you known any alpha that has led any of the armies without transforming? No, neither have I. See what their plans are, because if they are asking us, I'm sure they'll travel north to ask the bears as well, if they haven't already."

"What's that got to do with anything?" Wikki asked.

"I suggest that if the cats are journeying north, then you should go and join them. Maybe time away from here will help to sort your head out. You need to be able to transform again, Tabitha, or all the good you've done here will all fade away if the people know you can't transform."

"Why're you helping her now? I know you don't like being below the rank of alpha, and you've only done your basic duty for her, you haven't helped before," Wikki questioned.

"It's simple. Tabitha, go and sort your head out so you can transform again, because I want a rematch," Ren requested.

"A rematch? You can't claim the omega alpha title," Wikki spat.

"I don't want the title anymore. It won't be a fight to the death, but I want to see if I'm stronger than you, or if you was just lucky with me and Alsander. It'll just be between us three, and no one except us will know the outcome. Call it a friendly rematch," Ren smiled.

Before Wikki could say anything else, Tabitha replied, "I'll do it. I'll give you a rematch. If I can't transform by the time I get back, would you take charge of our armies? People from all the clans respect you, so they would listen to you." Ren nodded his head in agreement. "Ok, then it's settled. I'll listen to what the cats have to say, and then I'll make a decision. Wikki, can you help translate as I'm having trouble understanding them."

"I'll give it a go," Wikki replied.

As they were all about to leave, Ren spoke one last time. "You make sure you get yourself sorted because I want that rematch. You promised me now, and I'll hold you to that promise."

Back at the pavilion, Tabitha started her questions with Wikki at her side. "Ok, so why should we help you cats?"

"The stygians art in their thousands, with their army growing stronger each day. Furthermore, they haft already invaded. One hath seen it first-hand. Therefore, our scouts from all three kingdoms art observing them as best they canst," Ankur replied.

"So what do you plan on doing next?" Tabitha inquired.

"We shalt travel north, in the hope of the northern bears also assisting us in this hour of need. We know this is our war. However, despite our peace being unbalanced with thy people, we haft concluded that together we couldst be victorious. If thy people dost not help us, then in time, this war shalt be upon thy lands also. Only together canst we defeat them," Ankur explained.

Tabitha sat down in her chair, looking at them all, reading their body language. She could tell they were not lying, but she needed more information, and time to recover her ability to transform once more. "Ok then, I'll travel north with you. Until I know more about this, I won't send my armies anywhere apart from White Castle to create a defensive position. Ren, gather all the people from all the clans and make your way to White Castle."

"Those art acceptable terms, for now. We just hope in time, thou shalt trust what we art saying, as well as sending thy army to aid us in these dark times. There is another matter relating to thee travelling alongside us. If thou shalt aid us on our quest, then a small group wouldst be advised, as this shalt make it harder for the enemy to sense our location," Ankur replied, bowing his head.

Abaigeal turned to Tabitha. "Omega Alpha, you will need a party."

"If Tabi needs a party, then I'm going with her," Wikki declared.

"What about your firstborn child? You'll miss its birth."

Arwyn's voice appeared from the side of the pavilion. "It's ok, Omega Alpha. I understand, and you'll need him more than me at the moment. He's a strong warrior, and he'll serve you well."

"There you have it, Tabi. I'm going with you," Wikki demanded.

Shaking her head, Tabitha smiled, "If you're sure, then I'll be happy to have you at my side." She turned to face the crowd. "I'll also need a peacekeeper. Bleddyn, I think you should be in my party for several reasons. One, it'll give your clan members time to cool off, as I'm sure you've been blamed for their wrongdoings, and secondly, I need someone I can trust, and I trust you."

Bleddyn bowed. "It would be an honour, Omega Alpha."

"What of my son, Omega Alpha? He'll serve you well!" Osheen shouted.

Ren turned to Tabitha and said, "That's the dad of the black wolf that saved your life from Neil, but his son's young, maybe too young."

Tabitha stood up. "Show me your son."

Spinning around quickly, Osheen darted back into the crowd, grabbing Torry's arm, and presented him to Tabitha with the wolves' greeting.

Squinting at him for a second, Tabitha asked, "What's your name?"

He gave the wolves' greeting and bowed. "I'm Torry Blackpaw, Omega Alpha."

"So, you're the one that took on the white wolf pathfinder on your own to protect me. How old are you?" Tabitha asked.

"I'm eighteen, Omega Alpha," Torry replied.

"Have you completed your final trial?"

"Yeah, I'm now a protector in training."

"Well, that's a title you've earned from your actions, no doubt. I've got one problem; if I took you with me, how would you complete your training as a protector?" Tabitha inquired.

Another black wolf stepped forward and gave Tabitha the wolves' greeting. "I can train him, Omega Alpha."

Tall and muscular, this young man stood with pride. Slick brown hair fell down each side of his face, parted at the centre. A leather strap around his chest showed he normally wielded some form of large weapon, but all personal weapons had been removed from all outsiders of the clan.

"And who're you?" Tabitha asked.

"I'm Lornell Blackclaw, Omega Alpha. I'm a protector and a close friend of Torry's, despite our age difference."

"And can you change into a wolf also?" Tabitha questioned.

Looking at her with dark blue eyes, he replied, "No, I'm an inertia, but I'm very skilled in spear fighting from learning the techniques of the bears' combat style, and I've taught other protectors as well."

"How old are you, Lornell?"

"I'm twenty-five, Omega Alpha."

"Well, I might make you members of my party, but without a wolf that can change to teach Torry combat techniques, I'll have to decline. So I'll leave that up to the person who taught me advanced combat. Wikki, what do you think?"

Descending the pavilion, Wikki stood in front of them. "You saved my best friend's life, so I'll always respect you for that, Torry. I can teach him, but only the lessons in wolf form. Lornell, you'll be responsible for his learning and normal combat lessons. I think that's a fair compromise."

"It would be an honour to help teach this young protector, alongside the reputable Wikki Greyleg," Lornell replied.

Wikki tilted his head and frowned at Lornell, surprised that someone from another clan had heard of him and knew his full name. For the first time in his life, he felt something stir inside him, the feeling of pride.

As the Black Wolf Clan cheered, Osheen burst with so much pride he could not contain his feelings. Marching towards his son, he grabbed his left wrist and raised it high into the air. "My son! A member of the omega alpha's party! My son!"

Osheen turned, pulling Torry close, and wrapped his arms around him, displaying his delight.

From the White Wolf Clan, Rhianna walked out and took to one knee. "Omega Alpha, can I join you and get the same lessons as Torry? There's no protectors to train me in my clan now. I know I'm asking a lot, but I wouldn't only learn the skills to be a lunar warrior, I would also protect and serve you with my life."

Tabitha looked at her with a smile. "Wikki, Lornell, would you be willing to take two students?"

"Ai, I'll be willing. It'll make for easier training," Wikki replied.

"Yes, Omega Alpha, I'll do my best," Lornell said.

The White Wolf Clan members began to cheer, knowing that one of their members was honoured by the omega alpha.

Scanning the crowd, Tabitha saw the next person she would choose. "Aelish, would you be part of my party and aid me in this quest? You're the best healer in the West Plains, and I would feel more at ease if you came with me."

Aelish took in a long, deep breath and replied, "I know you're asking out of respect, but I've got no choice anyway. You're the omega alpha, and your word is law. So I'll make it sound like my choice, and I'll say yes."

"Thank you, Aelish. I think you'll put my mam's mind at ease by coming with me."

Needing one last person, she turned to Ren and said, "I know I gave you orders to gather the clans and take them to White Castle, but I think I'll need you with us. I will need at least one of my pathfinders, but with the Black Wolf Clan needing to restructure, I think it's a good time to test Geraint's leadership. Will you come with me?"

Scratching his head, he looked over to the group of cats and replied, "Ok, I'll come with you. But if that milk-drinking bitch gives me any shit, I'll fuck her up."

"Well, hopefully, it won't come to that, but thanks for joining me." Turning to the crowd, she gave her final order. "Geraint, step forward." Marching a few paces, he halted as she continued, "Ren will no longer be taking the clans to White Castle. You'll do it. It will give you a great opportunity to show your leadership skills and protect the clans. Do you think you're up for it?"

Geraint gave the wolves' greeting and replied, "I'll do my best to serve you, Omega Alpha."

Tabitha addressed the crowd one last time. "Well, it's decided. It's late now, so we'll rest here. Our guests will be placed into huts until the morning. We'll leave at first light. Everyone else, thank you for turning up. You're welcome to stay here overnight or go back home."

The crowd cheered, celebrating their clan members' participation with their omega alpha.

"Thine prince, I hope thou knowst what thou art doing. The wolves couldst jeopardise us in our quest," Kushad said.

"It wilt work for everyone if they cometh with us, one just knows it. This is how bonds art made, art they not, Kushad?" Ankur explained.

Kushad nodded his head and smiled, "Very good. Thy father wouldst be proud of thee, Thine Prince. If this is thy will, then it shalt be done."

Tabitha left the pavilion, presenting herself to the cats. "I'll make sure your stay for the night will be as comfortable as possible. I've had one of my protectors get four of my people's huts ready for you, and before you ask, it's no trouble, it's just for a night. We'll leave in the morning."

"Very good. We all extend our gratitude for thy humble generosity. I think it best that we retire to our accommodation for the night. We art already prepared for our journey, so some needed rest shalt be in order," Kushad replied.

"Well, if that's what you want, that's fine. If some of you want to have a look around our town, then you're free to go around. Also, I'll have our people bring you food," Tabitha said.

All nine cats bowed, retiring to the huts.

Tabitha delegated protectors to ensure that her party had what they needed for the journey, giving them maximum rest before departing alongside the cats.

The next day, Isolde, Tabitha and her party were the first to wait at the outskirts of the town. Abaigeal approached her party with a familiar face, her arm interlocked with his, as Quinn shuffled towards them.

"What're those two doing here?" Wikki asked.

"I don't know, but I'll find out," Tabitha replied.

Shortening Quinn's journey by walking towards them both, she asked, "What're you guys doing here? We'll be leaving shortly."

"Still rushing around, I see, and blunt as always. I have some advice to give you. Whether you take the advice or not, that is up to you, Omega Alpha," Quinn said.

Tabitha exhaled deeply, folding her arms.

"Tabitha, I would take this advice. It might help you. He is wise, after all," Abaigeal suggested.

"Ok, so what's this advice, Quinn?" Tabitha asked.

"The blue wolves were not naturally born with the great power they had. They acquired it from the Great Wolf himself. When you go to the bear's country, I highly recommend you go to the ruined city of Drysor Glas. You might find answers for questions you have not asked. Also, you can travel east from the old capital, where there is a hidden path to enter the bear's country with a day's journey if you get there by paw. Use that instead of the Neutral Land. It is much safer."

Tabitha frowned. "What could I learn from a ruined city? There's nothing there except broken old buildings."

"I've been there, surprisingly, with your dad, years ago. There is more in that decayed city than you know. Just have a think about it. I think it's time I go home now. Will you help me there, Peacekeeper?" Quinn said.

"Of course I will, Quinn. Tabitha, have a safe journey. I'll see you soon," Abaigeal said.

"Yeah, I will. Make sure that our people are safe and well while I'm away. I'll see you soon, guys," Tabitha replied.

"Oh, you will see the peacekeeper again, but I won't be here when you return. Age has shrouded me now. I hope you find what you need on your journey, young wolf, because you have the world on your shoulders. But I assure you this, your journey will make you stronger, or it will destroy you. Farewell, Omega Al pha."

As Abaigeal and Quinn returned to the town, the group of cats walked straight past them and joined Tabitha. "Good morning, Omega Alpha. Art we all ready for our departure to the Northern Peaks?" Kushad questioned.

Still coming to grips with how the cats spoke, she replied, "Almost, but we'll be ready very soon."

"Very good. Then we wilt await thy command, Omega Alpha."

Tabitha walked back over to her party as everyone said their goodbyes.

Aelish kissed her mate and gave him a hug, turning to her nine-year-old son and six-year-old daughter. "You two, be good for your dad now, you hear? I will miss you all lots and lots."

Tears were shed between them, as Aelish had always been around, so her children became upset with the idea of her going away.

"I'm so proud of you, my son. You're my greatest achievement in life. Lornell, I'll tell your folks what you're doing as well. I know they will be as proud as I am," Osheen said.

"Thanks, Dad. When you see me next, I should be a fully-fledged protector," Torry replied.

Osheen slapped Torry and Lornell on the back, smiling at everyone else present.

"Now it's time. Be the great warrior I know you to be. I love you so much," Arwyn said.

Wikki held her in his arms and gave her a passionate kiss. "I'll come back to the both of you after I help Tabi."

Isolde handed Tabitha an eye patch made from shrompy weed. "Here, take this."

"Thanks, Mam. I'll see you when I get back."

Isolde grabbed Tabitha, hugging her tightly. "Take care and come back to me, you hear? I'll always be there for you, no matter how far away you are."

As Isolde let go of Tabitha, she smiled at her daughter, wondering if she would get any better on her journey.

Tabitha smiled, turned to her party and declared, "It's time for us to leave."

The party of wolves and cats began their expedition together, walking northward from the town, as everyone waved goodbye to the people they left behind.

After an hour of walking, Tabitha looked at Ankur. "So what happened for you guys to come here? I heard tales that you're great warriors, so why do you also need us?"

Ankur looked into the distance, eyes filling with emotion as he replied, "We wilt tell thee our story. Maybe thou wilt then fully understand why we haft cometh seeking thy aid."

"I only need you to tell me, why would everyone else get involved?" Tabitha replied.

Overhearing the conversation, Wikki explained, "Tabi, he means he'll tell you. Their royal families don't say words like I. Remember that joke I told you, you know, the afternoon before you became the alpha?"

Tabitha looked back at Ankur and apologised, "I'm sorry, I didn't know. This is all new to me."

"We understand. One finds thy speech to be difficult at times also. However, in due course, we shalt hopefully understand one another," Ankur smiled.

The party stopped on a small hill, looking out to the vast plains before them.

"Which direction shall we take to get to the Neutral Land?" Pihu asked.

"There's a better way. We'll go north, past Drysor Glas, the old blue wolf capital. Not far from there is a secret path to the Northern Peaks," Tabitha replied.

"Very good, Omega Alpha. Thou shouldst know these lands better than us outlanders. Therefore, we wilt humbly accept thy advice. Let us go north, via this blue wolf capital thou speak of," Kushad said.

An unlikely alliance had been forged as the wolves and cats worked as one. Only time could tell if it would last, and none of them knew what lay before them on their path. Tabitha looked back out to the steppe, thinking about what Quinn had told her, and out of everything he said, she knew deep down he was right about one thing. This journey would either make her, or break her.

About Author

You can follow the author on the following for future updates and news:
BlaiddGwyn.com
Twitter: @BlaiddG
Reddit: u/BlaiddGwynNovels
Instagram: BlaiddGwynNovels
TikTok: @blaidd_gwyn_novels
Facebook: Blaidd Gwyn Publications

If possible, please leave a review as these help all authors and readers.